FALL BACK AND FIND ME

By Sarah hanks

Praise for
Fall Back and Find Me

It was a joy to watch Amber, Lily, and Willow develop as women of God throughout this dual timeline women's fiction story. As a former Missourian, I was intrigued to learn about places I used to live and how they were impacted so harshly by the Civil War. Having formerly served in vocational ministry and as a bi-vocational pastor's wife, my heart ached in sympathy with Amber's need to do all the things and please all the people. Hanks weaves together the threads of three hurting hearts and how through physical brokenness they are able to find freedom and healing for their souls. To all who have ever struggled with their value and worth in a performance-driven culture, I recommend this highly engaging journey into understanding the Father's love for His daughters.

Jennifer Q. Hunt, author of the *Sorrow & Song* Trilogy
and the *Wisteria House* Trilogy

A heart-felt and inspiring story of overcoming physical and mental struggles to find joy in the plan God graciously laid out. Sarah is gifted at telling echoing storylines that tug at your expectations.

Kristine Delano, Suspense Writer and 2023 Dual Genesis Semi-Finalist and 2022 Crown and Genesis Finalist

Fall Back and Find Me is a dual time-line novel with stories intersecting in shared roots and similar health conditions. Amber is a modern-day pastor's wife who finds her purpose in church outreach. Willow is a young woman who strives for her father's approval, but when faced with being shut inside for her own protection, leaves home, and joins the Union army with her brother. When faced with a debilitating disease, both women come to grips with who they are and more importantly, whose they are. Authentic, poignant, and hopeful.

Pamela Baker, writer and book reviewer

Fall Back and Find Me is a raw and engrossing tale of three women in separate circumstances trying to make their way when life feels unfair and out of control. With a lively cast of supporting characters and storytelling that sings, Hanks applies gospel truth to the kinds of fears and trials that are as difficult to untangle as they are relatable. Hanks continues to be an author that I strongly applaud and highly recommend.

Heather Wood, author of The Finding Home series.

I love how Sarah Hanks weaves a contemporary story with one from the Civil War to give the reader a double dose of enjoyment and education. A big serving of relatable characters, absorbing themes, and crisp prose enable this story's thought-provoking messages to linger long after you've savored the satisfying ending. Clear your calendar before you begin reading it—you won't want to put it down!

Chris Posti, author of *Falling Apart, Falling for You*

History comes alive at the tip of Sarah Hanks's pen. In the historical line of *Fall Back and Find Me*, she immerses us in the blood-torn world of Civil War Missouri where the fighting boils down to neighbor against neighbor. She takes us into the heart of Willow, a young woman who fears she'll never be good enough to earn her father's love. We cheer for Willow as she fights against bushwhackers and the weakness of her own body. But her greatest battle is within her own soul. Sherry Shindelar

Award-winning Historical Romance Author
Texas Forsaken coming May 2024

SonFlower Books

Chapter 1

Modern Day
Ozark, Missouri

My two-inch heels crunch across the gravel as I meander from the bounce houses to the bustling game booths at Ascend Community Church's Labor Day carnival. The scent of grilled hot dogs and popcorn wafts on a light breeze as children's laughter tumbles through the packed parking lot. I take in radiant, smiling faces all around me, and my toes curl with the pleasure of a job well done.

And I can't wait to get home.

"Mrs. Preachit! Mrs. Preachit!" Little Gracie runs to me, blonde pigtails flying as she waves a twisted pink balloon toward the sky. "Do you like my unicorn?"

I grin. "It's beautiful! And you can call me Miss Amber."

Gracie shakes her head, and her sticky cheeks—courtesy of cotton candy, no doubt—trap several strands of hair like glue. "Mama says I gotsta call grownups by their last names."

I reach out and free the captive strands. "Well then, it's Mrs. Prichard, not Preachit, though I understand the confusion." I wink. "I don't think Pastor Mark will mind if you call him Mr. Preach-it, though."

"Okay." Her grin shows off an adorable gap in her teeth. "I love this picnic!"

Technically, it's a carnival. A picnic involves food only, perhaps a game of cornhole. Not rides, games, raffle prizes, a petting zoo, a bake sale, *and* food. *This* is magic. And all proceeds go to help foster care children in the community. But what's in a name?

I laugh as she skips off.

I've only taken a few more steps when Jordan nearly collides with me. I step back to maintain balance.

"Mommy!"

I could never chide my daughter over such a blunder, not as long as the girl still calls me Mommy at eleven years old, something her twin brother wouldn't be caught dead doing. "Can we go home yet?"

Jordan squints, face lit by the brilliant sun. Too bad I don't have a brush with me. The wind has wreaked havoc with the girl's hair.

"No, sweetie. Daddy will take you home in a couple of hours, but I'll stay until everything's cleaned up."

My daughter groans. "We've been here forever."

My cheeks warm, and I look to see who's in earshot. No one, thankfully. "I know it feels that way. Mommy's the one who set all of this up, so I have to be here to make sure everything goes as planned."

Her lip protrudes. "That's what you always say."

I attempt to run my fingers through my daughter's hair but give up when I reach an impenetrable tangle not two inches from her scalp. "I know." The price of being a preacher's kid. "Looks like you haven't gotten your face painted yet. Maybe try that."

"The line's too long."

"You've got time."

Jordan's shoulders slump as she mopes in the direction of the face painting table. A quick survey of the area shows Victor playing soccer in the field with several friends. My son always seems to entertain himself without complaint.

I continue weaving my way through crowds of mostly smiling people. I wave to Delaney as I pass her photo booth. I'd stop to chat with my best friend, but the line snakes around the corner and a hyper child just knocked half her props off the table.

What's that sound? Through the din of happy chatter, a child's muffled cries float to my ears. I scan the area for the source and find a preschool-aged boy hunkering behind a myrtle bush, face in his hands. My heart lurches toward him, and my feet follow. I'd sprint if I weren't wearing heels and a pencil skirt. Maybe it wasn't such a bright idea to schedule staff pictures this morning after all. The disheveled mop of black curls rings with familiarity. He's part of the new family who visited Ascend Community last week. I checked them in at the welcome desk. What's his name? Jimmy? Johnny?

But, man, he reminds me so much of Tim, I have to remind myself to breathe. My fingers instinctively graze the cardinal pendant at the base of my throat.

I draw near and squat to eye level, placing a gentle hand on his back. "Hey, buddy. What's the matter?" His reddened, splotched face jerks up to meet my gaze. Jerry. That's his name.

"I can't find Mommy and Daddy." He sniffles. "They left me." Tears flow freely down his cheeks, leaving dirty tracks. Oh, the sweet boy.

I envelop him in a hug. "You're Jerry, right?"

He nods, wiping snot onto my silky blouse.

"It's a scary feeling being left, I know. But we're going to find your mommy and daddy, don't worry. I'm sure they're looking for you." I rub slow circles on his back. He clings to me with chubby fists.

Whatever happened to Tim? Where is he now? His face from my childhood is one of several that haunt me. That propel me forward. Everything I'm doing today is for them, for children like them.

Jerry's panicked breaths slow and hiccups ensue as I stand with him in my arms. He's heavier than he looks, and my muscles protest at the surprising weight. I don't have to search long before I see his frantic parents circling a bounce house, peering in through each mesh window. I walk toward them. The dad's name fails to materialize in my mind, but I'm pretty sure the mom's name is Ivy, so I call for her.

She turns in my direction, and a wave of relief washes over her features. She jogs our way, the dad following on her heels.

"Jerry! Oh my gosh. We were so worried." She takes him from my arms and peppers his face with kisses.

"He's fine. He was over there." I point toward the bush. I ruffle Jerry's beautiful hair. "Stay close to Mom and Dad, okay, bud? Don't let it happen again." I wink, ignoring the burning in my throat.

The parents thank me profusely, and I assure them it was nothing before I continue on my rounds. *It's a scary feeling being left. Don't let it happen again.* I try to shoo the pesky phrases from my mind, but they persist like a mantra. I clench my jaw. I don't have time for this intrusion. I have a carnival to run.

There's a stitch in my side by the time I approach Kelly Loren at the bake sale tent.

"Hi, Amber!" Kelly grins. "You're going to win the Golden Servant Award this year, no question."

I wave her comment off as if that honor means nothing to me. It shouldn't. I don't serve in order to get an award. What

Christian would? Yet, I may have rehearsed my acceptance speech in the mirror a time or two, just in case.

Kelly's brow creases with concern. "Are *you* okay?" Her gray ringlets spring around small ears. "Need some water? It's shaping up to be a scorcher. And here I thought fall was just around the corner."

Dark circles hang under Kelly's eyes. Probably from late nights with her father. I step toward her. "How's your dad doing?"

Kelly's lip trembles. "Not good. He didn't even recognize me yesterday."

My heart twists as I imagine her sitting next to the man who once saw her as his world and now treats her as a stranger. "He's on my rotation for tomorrow. I'll visit around ten in the morning." That I can do nothing but stand by and watch, offering a friendly face that will fade from memory as soon as I leave the room, eats at my gut.

Nothing I can say will make this better, so I rub her shoulder for a minute before Rhonda McMillion huffs over. "You're out of cherry pies."

From the sparse tables, it looks like we're out of nearly everything. I'd grin at a successful fundraiser if Rhonda's glower didn't skewer me.

Kelly nods. "We ran out an hour ago."

"I purchase a cherry pie at this carnival every year. How could you not make enough?" She flings an arm in front of her. "This is a disgrace."

I blink back at her and clamp my mouth shut to keep the words in my brain from tumbling out. A disgrace? Is the woman blind to the smiling faces around her? Deaf to the children's laughter? Three months of planning and organizing have brought us to this day of *nearly* flawless execution. I inhale deeply through my nose. Exhale through my mouth. Force a smile. "Actually, I prepared for such an instance. I have a couple dozen pies in coolers in my trunk, and at least two of them are cherry.”

“Oh, God bless you!” Kelly presses her hands together as if in prayer. “You are an angel.” She turns to Rhonda. “Isn’t she amazing? There’s nothing this woman can’t do. She baked two dozen pies in addition to coordinating this carnival.”

My smile freezes in place. I didn’t say I made them. I bought them from Fisher’s Bakery yesterday. Excellent quality, but certainly not from my oven.

Rhonda shifts her weight. She exhales, and the tension that lines her face softens. “Well, as long as they’re homemade.”

A strained giggle scrambles out of my mouth. “I’ll go get them.”

“Thank you.” Kelly beams as if I’ve achieved sainthood.

“It’s the least I can do.” But why does my car have to be on the other side of the lot? I grimace at the blister forming on my heel but square my shoulders. I’ve walked this lot at least twenty times already today. What’s another couple of trips? *All for the foster children. It’s all for the foster children.*

Lord, please give me strength. And if it’s not too much to ask, maybe time for a bubble bath? Though I fully believe in the power of prayer, I blow that request off with a chuckle. What is it Mark says? God always answers prayers. Sometimes He says yes, sometimes no, and sometimes wait. I’d wager the Lord will answer my request for relaxation time with the latter, since after I clean up from the carnival, the kids will need help with homework.

What exactly am I waiting for? The kids to grow up? No. I’d freeze time if I could. The church to hire more staff? Now there’s a request I can add to my prayer list. But for now, I’ll stick with strength to make it through this delightfully grueling day.

A couple more steps and a piece of gravel lodges in my shoe. I bend over and shove it out with my finger.

I stand up, and my head feels like it's floating. For a few seconds, I'm disconnected from my body. I stand still for a moment, and it self-corrects. Maybe I should have taken Kelly up on that water. I'll grab some when I get back.

I nearly shout "Hallelujah" when I near Delaney's photo booth. The line has dwindled to only a couple of people, and she's got a teenager there to help her now. The girl with the Piglet tattoo on her forearm can spare my friend for a few without mass chaos breaking out.

"Delaney." I wave to catch her eye. "Can you help me with something?"

She drops the oversized clown nose onto the prop table and jogs over. "What do you need?"

I hook my arm through hers and steer her toward my car. "Pie emergency."

She spurts out a laugh. "Excuse me?"

"I need help carrying pies over to the bake sale tent."

"Yeah. Okay." A strand of her long blonde hair tickles my arm as the breeze dances. She peers over at me. "You doing all right?"

"Of course. Why?"

"You're leaning on me a little."

Am I? "It's been a long day."

"I bet." The concern in her gaze fails to dissipate.

I brighten my smile to reassure her.

We near the car, and I come to a dilemma. The trunk faces the crowd. "Let's move the coolers to the backseat." I pop the trunk and open the back door. The one that angles away from any curious stares.

"Why?"

I drop my voice, even though there's no one in earshot. "I have to take the stickers off the pie lids."

"Because?"

"Rhonda and Kelly think they're homemade." I heft a cooler around to the backseat, open it, and dig at an embossed seal with my nail.

"You can't be serious."

"Help, will you?"

"I did not sign up for this." But she goes to work scraping the sticker from an apple pie.

Shoot. The sticky residue isn't coming off easily. The heat built up in the car already has sweat percolating on my temples. My lower back aches as my fingernail tackles the stubborn glue. I stifle a groan. This is ridiculous. After months of work, I'm huddled in the backseat of a car because one woman demanded a cherry pie. Why couldn't she simply drive to the town bakery herself if she wanted one so badly? Or pick something else like any normal person. Why did it have to be me fixing it? Me, stuck with it. Me, solving everyone's problems and complaints. "Why do I have to do everything myself? What's the saying? Ten percent of the congregation does ninety percent of the work. I'd fall on my knees and thank God for a whole ten percent."

"Whoa." Delaney puts a hand on my arm and stoops to meet my eye. "Look around. There are a ton of people helping today, including me. Who, I'll remind you, doesn't even go to this church."

I wipe beads of sweat from my brow and sigh. "You're right. That was unfair." But frustration still gnaws at me. Maybe it's exhaustion. Pulled in too many directions. Or how easily one person can make me feel like a failure.

"Only two more to go. Then what? I help you carry them over there and pass them off as your own? I'm not the best liar, you know." She pauses to whip her waist-length hair into a quick braid.

I huff. "I didn't lie. I just didn't correct them."

"Oh, yes. I see how that's far better." Humor dots her sarcasm.

"And there's a whole other cooler."

"Joy."

I go to lift the second cooler, but my muscles protest the weight, and it slams back into the trunk. Sweat dribbles between my shoulder blades. A headache creeps around the edges of my temples. Okay, then. I'll just carry an armload of pies instead of the entire cooler. I balance five in my arms, holding them fast with my chin.

My legs shake. The screams of a child echo like a freight train in my ears. I'm nearly to the backseat when the ground tilts and sways. My heart thunders. Blood rushes in my ears. Pies fall from my arms. Delaney gasps. And then I am weightless, floating through time and space. A dozen images flash through my mind. Mark at the pulpit. Rhonda's impatient stance. Jordan dancing on stage. And the back of my father's head as he walked out of my life forever.

I open my eyes to the blinding sun. I squint and turn my head. Gravel pricks my skull. Wait. My back, my hips, and my legs too. Gravel? Delaney's worry-lined face comes into focus above me. What's going on? For a second, everything is muted as if I'm underwater. Then a bubble pops and sound blares at me. Birds. Chatter. Laughter. "The Church Clap" radiates through speakers. It all rushes at me.

"Amber!" Delaney's hand clasps mine. "Are you okay? Are you hurt?"

I crane my neck around. I'm on the ground by my car. On the ground? My breath hitches. "I fainted?"

"Are you okay?" she repeats.

Using her hand as leverage, I sit up and shake my head to clear the fog. I … fainted. It can't be.

"Here." She thrusts a half-empty bottled water into my hand. "Drink this. It's all I could find in your car. I can get more."

Water. Of course. I'm merely dehydrated. "No, this is good." I swig it down. "I'm fine. It's hot outside."

"Yeah, but—"

"Really, I'm fine." I scramble to my feet. I brace a hand on the car to make sure, but the light-headedness has passed. I peek over the vehicle. No eyes look my way. Thank God. No one noticed.

But then I go to finger a necklace that's no longer there. I suck in another breath as my hands fly across my throat. "Where is it? Where's my mom's pendant?"

Before I can scan the pavement for red and cream, there it is, cradled in Delaney's hands. "It caught on my watch when I tried to catch you."

"Did it break?" My voice comes out hoarse.

"The end of the chain broke off, but you can still fasten it farther down." She drapes it around my throat and clasps it.

Thank You, Lord. I sniff to keep all emotion in check. As I do, a hint of cherry wafts to my nose, and dread spreads through my limbs. No. "The pies."

Delaney groans. "Forget the stupid pies."

Wincing, I look down to see four pies freed from their protective lids, lying in the dust. Cherry filling oozes onto pebbles. How am I going to explain this? *Sorry, I know you think I walk on water, but apparently, I can't even carry pies from my cooler.*

"Should I take you to the hospital? Urgent care? Something?"

"No." My voice sounds sharper than I intended. I soften it with a smile. "I'll get more water and take a break, I promise. Don't tell anyone, please."

She raises her brows. "Don't tell anyone?"

"It's embarrassing."

"You passed out in the parking lot, and you want me to keep it a secret? Is this some kind of residual trauma from your mom? I mean, you are wearing her necklace today."

I huff. "No. It's just not a big deal."

She gapes at me with wide eyes. "Amber! Mark's got to know."

"I'll tell Mark. Just no one else."

It would change the way they see me, the way they relate to me.

No one else can know.

~

Lily Ware wavered in the hallway; the brochure clasped in trembling hands. There would never be a perfect time for her to bring this up with Mom. Now was as good a moment as any. She plunged forward.

Mom sat at the dining room table surrounded by three of her seven kids. A textbook sat in front of her, and various worksheets littered the surface..

Lily took a step closer, fiddling with the booklet. She bit her lip. Now or never.

Mom stopped reading about the earth's rotation around the sun. "Lily, there you are. I was hoping you could help Harvy with math. Do you have time before your class?" Her little brother sat to Mom's right, like always.

Lily checked her watch while trying to ignore Jamie, who streaked by in his underwear. "I've got about forty minutes before I need to leave, but—"

"Perfect. We're about done here. Could you get clothes on Jamie? Pants, at least."

"Actually, I"—she winced—"wanted to talk to you about something?" It sounded like a question. Great job being assertive.

"Sure thing, hon. Let me get Davy started on his history packet, then I'll be able to give you my full attention."

Lily held back a scoff. Mom's full attention? When was the last time she had that? It had to be before Harvy was born with Down syndrome fourteen years ago. Harvy had enlightened Mom to her mission in life to foster and adopt children with special needs. At twenty-two, Lily was the oldest of seven children, and the only one the world would consider typical. Harvy, the second oldest, and Davy, the eight-year-old, both had Down syndrome. Jana, who bounced on an exercise ball while filling out a packet, naked Jamie, and Blake, who wore noise-canceling headphones and rocked back and forth, mumbling to himself as he completed math problems, had various developmental delays. Oliver, her newest foster brother, was born with fetal alcohol syndrome and pretty much needed to be carried twenty-four seven. ADD. Sensory issues. Intellectual disability. Speech delays. It was all part of the mix with their crew. And since they were each adopted from either an orphanage overseas or a foster home in the States, their stories included trauma as well.

"Okay." She folded the brochure and stuck it in her back pocket.

"You'll get Jamie dressed?"

"Yep." Of course, she would. She always did. She'd do anything for her family. This odd mix of beautiful human beings that her heart was irretrievably tied to. She found Jamie's Spider-Man pajamas on the living room floor. The hunt was on. She peeked around corners and behind furniture for spikey blonde hair.

"Jay Jay. I'm gonna get you."

There it was. His laugh that could bring sunshine into the bleakest day. It skittered around the back of the recliner. She lunged, caught him, and attacked him with kisses. He was the only one who let her do that. She nuzzled his neck, relishing the smell of the berry shampoo and body wash he used. She'd miss the scent when she left.

"Spider-Man is cold without you." Lily snatched the footie pajamas and slid them over his toes.

"Is not."

"Is too. He needs you to warm him with your body heat."

He giggled. "Mom said I had to wear clothes. That means pants. I don't want to wear pants. The buttons hurt." They'd gotten rid of his button-fastening pants in favor of elastic ones, but there was no use arguing.

"I know. You can wear pajamas. She doesn't care. You're not going anywhere today." Or any day. When had Mom last ventured out in public with this crew?

"Can I watch TV?"

She squinted at the ceiling as if thinking. "Hmm. Is it the weekend?"

His mouth puckered into a frown. "No."

"Then no. But you can do your schoolwork."

"You're just like Mom."

She touched her nose to his and laughed. He raced off, fully clothed. Assignment one checked off the list.

If only she *was* just like Mom. But this wasn't her mission. Raising a family with special needs wasn't her God-given purpose. Lily had been shoved into the role by proximity. Her siblings were beautiful and smart and funny. Quirky but precious. She loved them. So why did she feel like she'd explode without a break from them? From all of this? She needed space.

She pulled the brochure from her back pocket again. Her finger traced the words, "Valley Creek Bible College" in Kalamazoo, MI. Four hundred and fifty miles away from here. Away from *them*.

"Lily? Can you help Harvy with math now?"

She was a horrible person. How could she even think of abandoning Mom to run this shipwreck on her own? She rolled the brochure. Shoved it back. It was stupid, really. There were hundreds of Bible colleges. She could get a degree in biblical studies anywhere. Valley Creek held no special appeal, other than its location. Cold. Foreign. Away.

"Coming." Lily rounded the corner and took the pages from Mom's waiting hand.

Though her mother barely looked up from helping Davy, the bags under her eyes made an impression. How much sleep had she gotten last night? Or this month? Oliver's adoption four months ago had taken its toll on her. Or were Jana's night terrors more to blame?

"Is Dad on call tonight?"

"Yes." Mom's reply held no bitterness at Dad's long hours as an ER doctor. And sure, they needed the money with all of the medical bills and private therapies. But couldn't Dad see Mom needed a break now and then?

"Come on, Harvy. Follow me to the kitchen."

Her brother complied, bringing a toy train with him. He made chugging noises as he followed close enough to clip her heels.

"Harv, remember, we talked about this. Personal space." Lily put her hands on his shoulders and prodded him to take a couple of steps backward. "That was too close. You have to give people room."

"Oh, yeah. Sorry."

"It's okay, but try to remember."

He squinted at the ceiling. His mouth contorted. She could nearly see his brain piecing together words.

"T-T-T …"

She dipped her head to encourage him to continue. Maybe the whole personal space thing was finally beginning to make sense to him. Having a question or comment about it was good. It meant progress. Finally.

"T-T-T …"

She zipped her lips together in a smile, shutting out the temptation to finish his sentence for him. She could wait. She could be patient like Mom.

"T-T-Thomas is a train."

She blinked back at his innocent face. "What does that have to do with anything?"

"I don't know."

A deep exhale. Twenty-five minutes. She'd be free in twenty-five minutes. "Yes, Thomas is a train. Now, let's do your math." She pulled out a chair and thumbed through the packet Mom had given her. On the top were written *Which Bowl Has More?* and *Which Clown Has More Balloons?* She closed her eyes. Still. Her fourteen-year-old brother was *still* on the same math concept he'd been attempting to master for two years straight. What made Mom think he'd understand this time?

He pushed the train across the table, puffing out his cheeks.

"Okay, buddy, which bowl has more cherries in it?"

He barely looked at the sheet before pointing to the empty bowl on problem three.

"This problem, Harv. Let's count the cherries. One. Two …" She pointed, and he counted along. He could do fine counting with her. It was counting on his own that gave him trouble. "Good. Seven cherries in the blue bowl. Let's count the cherries in the red bowl." They counted the three cherries. "Great counting. So which bowl has more?"

His finger poked the red bowl. "That one."

"No." She pressed her palm onto her forehead. "The blue bowl has seven. Seven is more than three. Look. Can't you tell the red bowl has more?" Even as her frustrated words came flying out, she cringed. If only she could yank them back. Her face flamed. What kind of sister was she? How could she lose her cool with this sweet boy? It wasn't his fault. She ran a hand through her hair, half expecting to feel she'd sprouted horns.

Harvy stared blankly ahead for a moment before his face fell. "You think I'm stupid." He crumpled into himself, folding his arms around his stomach, chin sagging to his chest.

She looped an arm around his shoulder. "No. No, buddy. I'm sorry." She kissed the top of his fuzzy head. "You're smart and funny and kind. It's me. I'm not good at … this."

"At math?"

One sister plus six siblings equaled failure. She knew that much. "At your math."

He frowned at his paper.

"Circle this one." She handed him a thick pencil and tapped the blue bowl. "It has more."

He did so, his jagged, lopsided scrawl encircling those seven cherries like their house enclosed the seven of them. His pencil continued to go around and around, the shape growing darker as he drew line upon line. Trapped. Suffocated. The fruit had no way out, nowhere to go. She put a firm hand on his to halt the movement. "That's enough."

She had to get out of here. Make a life for herself. Break free.

"That's enough."

Chapter 2

THE BELIEF THAT A MAN CAN RAISE HIMSELF TO THE
CEILING BY TAKING HOLD OF THE SEAT OF HIS
BREECHES—THIS IS THE *REAL BASIS* OF
EMANCIPATION STRENGTH. IT IS BY THIS NOTION
THAT THE LITTLE BAND OF YANKEE ABOLITIONISTS
& GERMAN RADICALS HAVE GOTTEN POSSESSION OF
ILLINOIS & HAVE MADE THAT PLACE AS
THOROUGHLY HOSTILE TO SLAVERY AS CHICAGO.
FROM ST. LOUIS THE IDEA HAS CREPT UP & DOWN THE
RIVERS—HAS FOUND LOCATION IN THE RIVER TOWNS—
AND GRADUALLY & SLOWLY PERVADED TO A SLIGHT
EXTENT INTO THE COUNTRY ... *HARD TIMES* WILL, I
THINK, CURE THIS DISEASE—AND WE MAY SAFELY
RELY, THAT THE REMEDY IS NEAR AT HAND.
WILLIAM P. NAPTON TO CLAIBORNE F. JACKSON,
OCTOBER 3, 1857

September 1, 1860
Ozark, Missouri

The sound of a gunshot sent Willow Forrester
scrambling out of her chair and to the front door
nearly as fast as her older brother, Milo. He'd been shoveling
scrambled eggs into his mouth in his spot at the table closest
to the exit. Of course, he'd get there first. Didn't mean he was
the fastest. She elbowed past him and spilled onto the front

porch to find their German neighbor Walter Schmidt toe to toe with Pa, spitting threats.

Willow's fingers flew to the cardinal pendant at the base of her neck. "Is he going to shoot Pa?"

Milo stepped beside her and eyed her as if she'd lost her faculties. "Don't be ridiculous. He shot at the hogs."

Out of the corner of her eye, two hogs snagged her attention. They squealed and snorted as they hustled into the woods.

"Keep them penned up, or I swear I'll butcher the lot of them." Walter spun around and marched toward his property.

Pa called out toward his retreating form, "We've never penned our hogs, and we've gotten along fine until you Dutch invaded. Them hogs are happy feeding on acorns in the brush, and no one 'round these parts has ever had a problem before you foreigners came."

Walter's form faded in the distance.

Pa spit on the ground. "Cursed Dutch."

"Deutsch," Milo whispered. "It's not that hard to say."

"Did Greta teach you?" Willow teased.

Milo nudged her. "Oh, shush."

Pa's gaze narrowed when it found hers. "Go back inside. This is none of your business."

As soon as he looked away, she stuck out her tongue. If he was going to treat her as if she were eight and not eighteen, she might as well act the part. She opened the front door and headed for the kitchen. Milo tugged her braid as he trailed her. She swatted his hand away. At the kitchen sink, Ma scraped off the pan as if nothing were amiss.

"Did you not even flinch at the sound of the gun, Ma?" Willow asked before returning to her seat and taking a bite of cold eggs.

Ma made a tsking sound. "Same old ruckus as always. Curse the day the Dutch decided to settle here."

Milo leaned back in his chair. "They're resourceful people."

Willow hid a snicker behind her napkin. Of course, he'd say so when a pretty German girl batted her lashes at him each day.

Ma turned and wiped her hands on her apron. "Haughty, if you ask me, with absurd abolitionist ideas. If we go to war, it will be because of them."

War. A wave of apprehension rolled through Willow's stomach. What would war mean for her? For their family?

Pa barreled through the front door. "You talking about impending war?"

Milo took his plate to the sink. "If Lincoln gets elected, I can't see a way around it."

Pa grabbed a mug and filled it with water. "He won't win Missouri's vote." He gulped his drink.

"That hardly matters." Milo's frown did little to settle her nerves.

Pa slammed down his mug. "It matters. Missouri stays out of it. Out of succession. Out of the war. Leave us the devil alone and let us live in peace." He narrowed his eyes at Willow. "Don't you have something better to do than stare at me? This is men talk. It doesn't concern you."

Milo cast her a sympathetic glance. Those he gave in abundance. Standing up for her with action? Few and far between.

Willow stuffed the last bite of eggs into her mouth and took her plate to the sink.

"She's helping me in the garden this morning." Ma refilled Pa's mug and handed it to him.

"Good. That should keep her out of trouble." He took one last, long drink, then gave Ma a peck on the cheek before turning to Milo. "Ready, son? I've hired out three slaves from the Hildebrink's farm to help with the harvest starting next week."

A muscle in Milo's jaw twitched, but he nodded. "We'll need the help."

The two men filed out the back door toward the fields.

Willow sighed. "Does Pa think I'm a child or incompetent?"

Ma chuckled and kissed the top of her head. "He thinks you're female, dear. No use trying to change the way things are. That man is set in his ways."

She crossed her arms over her chest. "I can do nearly anything Milo can do. Run as fast. Haul nearly as much. I'm as good of a shot, if not better."

"That's what your Pa calls trouble." Ma handed her a basket. "Now, we've got quite a lot of sweet potatoes ready for harvesting. Come make yourself useful."

Useful. Right. She didn't mind working side by side with Ma. Her mother was like a gentle breeze, soothing in all the places her father chafed. But Willow didn't quite fit into the soft curves her mother carved out for her. Too many rough edges. She could save Pa from having to hire one of those slaves if he'd let her work out in the field, but in his estimation, she was good for nothing more than plucking measly vegetables. If only she could show him how capable she was. Catch his eye. Make him proud.

But no. He'd always see her as an annoying appendage to the family. Not a vital, useful part of it. Like Ma said, no use trying to change the way things were.

~

As soon as she could sneak away from chores, Willow melted into the brush behind her home, rifle in hand. Nothing like squirrel hunting to restore her confidence. She knew every tree, rock, and crevice back here—the rocky brook that only trickled to life after a hearty rain, the softness of the moss that grew on the tree trunks where foliage blocked out all but pinpoints of light. The earthy smell of this world wrapped her in comfort. The rustle of small animals, birds, and wind whipping through the trees sang the music of her heart. Here, her soul was at peace. This was her place in the world.

Even more so with a rifle in hand and a target in sight.

Her fingers grazed the small journal she'd secured under a band of fabric across her waist. Pa's journal. Good. It was still there. She'd taken extra care to ensure it wouldn't fall out like last time. She hadn't realized it was missing until later, and she'd found it in the creek bed. Water had marred most of the entries, rendering them illegible, but the one that haunted her remained. She always kept it with her now. He hadn't noticed it missing yet, but when he did, it'd be better to let him think he'd misplaced it or some thieving Dutch took off with it than to know she had pilfered it from his desk. If he saw the water damage, he'd know it was her. Who else lived and breathed the creek bed as she did?

Why she kept the blasted journal close instead of flinging it off a cliff was anyone's guess. She surely didn't need it as a reminder that she wasn't enough for Pa. She saw as much anytime she was in the man's presence. Perhaps she held out hope that somewhere in the waterlogged, illegible script, there was something redeemable. Something that proved he loved her, even if he hadn't wanted her to begin with.

If only she could escape the impossible desire to please this man who couldn't care less.

She'd taken down two squirrels and was after a third when low voices alerted her to the fact she must be near Mr. Schmidt's property. Why couldn't her family get along with their German neighbors? Why did they have to disagree about every blasted thing? *Immigrants*, Pa would say, as if the word was bile in his mouth. But weren't all Missourians immigrants of some sort? Why fight with those who were the most recent? It didn't make sense.

The familiarity of the voices gave her pause. She crept toward the source. The late afternoon sun silhouetted two figures, facing each other, hands grasped together tenderly. She strained to hear the words that danced between them. She couldn't. But her mouth dropped at the realization that one of the voices belonged to her brother. And the other had an accent.

Greta?

She'd seen Milo's wistful gaze directed at the girl, and took great delight in teasing him about it, but had never guessed the two were … involved. The silhouettes neared each other, then merged into one another. An embrace. Then a kiss.

Willow gasped.

Pa would have Milo's hide for this. Their German neighbors. The enemy.

She swallowed.

Milo. How could he?

They were anti-Southern and abolitionist. Jayhawkers, for all she knew. They stood against everything her family believed in: states' rights, independence, and freedom.

She stepped back, muscles tensing, ready to race for home. If she wanted Pa's attention, she could have it now. Relaying this tantalizing bit of information would surely earn her esteem in her father's eyes.

The silhouettes pulled back from each other, hands stretching out as if they ached to be reunited even though they'd only been separated a parcel of a moment. The gap between the two widened, and finally, three coherent words found Willow's ears.

"I love you." Milo's voice dripped thick with emotion.

Willow's heart twisted at the declaration. He loved her? Blood thudded in her ears.

Milo loved Greta.

If she told, what would happen to her brother's heart?

No, she couldn't do that to him. He was far too dear to her to rat out for a scrap of admiration from her father. After all, she might not have endured these years of Pa's disdain if not for her brother's kindness and wit.

She bit her lip, then hoisted the sack of two squirrels back over her shoulder. If only she could impress Pa with this meager offering of meat instead, but he'd made it clear it annoyed him when *she* brought him such. Was there anything else she could do to earn his favor? Pa's journal felt stiff and uncomfortable against her hip. No. She couldn't conjure a thing.

Could she learn to live with his contempt?

She puffed out a hot breath.

Never.

Chapter 3

THE STORIES WE TELL ABOUT ILLNESS USUALLY
HAVE STARTLING BEGINNINGS—THE FALL AT THE
SUPERMARKET, THE LUMP DISCOVERED IN THE
ABDOMEN DURING A ROUTINE EXAM, THE DOCTOR'S
CALL.
FROM *THE INVISIBLE KINGDOM: REIMAGINING
CHRONIC ILLNESS*

BY MEGHAN O'ROURKE

Modern Day

Standing in the backyard, I force my face into a stern expression. "Sit," I repeat.

The dog grins at me, tail wagging. He doesn't sit. Why does he have to be so stinkin' cute as he disobeys?

Next to me, Jordan shoves her hands onto her hips and lifts her chin. "Sit."

Chipper pays as much attention to her as he does to me. He laps at the air, asking permission to come close and give us a kiss. At least he has some manners. Sometimes.

I draw near and push his bottom to the ground. "Sit."

He licks my arm but remains seated.

Jordan's voice transforms. It oozes praise. "Good dog."

His ears perk.

When Jordan suggested we train Chipper for a dog show, I tried to remain positive. The dog's unruly, but he is a beaut. Obedience lessons would do him good, and quality time with my daughter would benefit us both. How much more of that will I get? She's on the edge of teenagerhood. Will she even like me two years from now?

I issue a firm command and fight to keep the edges of my mouth from turning upward. He will not beguile me with his charms. "Stay."

Jordan and I take five steps back. Jordan holds the treat out. The command *Come* hangs on my lips. Elation bubbles inside me. This is the first time our corgi has remained stationary for more than a few seconds. Perhaps he isn't impossible to train after all.

Jordan whispers out of the side of her mouth, "He's doing it."

I mimic her. "I know!"

A squirrel dashes across the yard and bounds up the old oak tree. Chipper is off, his adorable little paws kicking up dust. He yaps and jumps at the tree as if he's a rocket without enough fuel.

"Shoot." Jordan twists the toe of her boot in the dirt. "He was so close."

I brush a strand of hair behind her shoulder. "He'll get it next time."

My phone vibrates in my back pocket, and I check the caller, then the time. Cole Miller, one of the elders, is calling during their weekly leadership meeting. Uneasiness fizzes inside. Did he find out? No, there's no way. Only Delaney and Mark know. No one else saw.

I scrunch my nose. "I've got to take this. Watch Chipper, will you?" That sneak would love nothing more than an unsupervised moment to dig under the fence.

Her answer comes on the back of a sigh. "Sure." Is she disappointed to be tasked as dog sitter or because the phone call cut our time short?

"Hello?"

"Hey, Amber. It's Cole. Do you have a minute?"

I'm a detective analyzing his voice for clues, but I find nothing definitive. Perhaps he's calling to chat about the Golden Servant Award ceremony, now only a few months away. Would it be a conflict of interest for a nominee to assist in preparations? They haven't announced the nominees yet, but I'm bound to be one of them. The most likely to win this year, thank God. We can sure use the award money. But if they think I'm incompetent because of health issues, will they disqualify me?

"Sure." I enter through the back door and sit at the kitchen table.

"We've been meaning to connect with you regarding the Outreach branch at the church. How has it been going?"

"Oh." My shoulders relax. He's only asking for an update. Or he could even be stacking up evidence for my Golden Servant win. I slide Victor's math notebook toward me, pick up a pen, and doodle on an empty page. "The Backpack Blessings outreach for underprivileged school children was an outstanding success." I draw a couple of daisies, then halt my pen. Wrong season. I draw a pumpkin instead. "We've also added ten new families to our monthly food basket disbursement and two new parishioners to our weekly nursing home visit schedule. Our next major outreach will be Blankets for the Homeless in November. I've already started creating signage and social media graphics for it. And, of course, our biggest event of the year is the Christmas gala for foster and adoptive families. Months of prep go into it, so I need to get started in a few weeks."

Silence fills the phone line. A glance at my watch shows I have twenty minutes before I need to leave to drop Jordan off at dance and catch my aerobics class. I click the pen top once, twice, three times.

It sounds like he covers the phone with his hand and murmurs back and forth with a male voice in the background.

Can't be Mark, since he's at the dentist. One of the other elders? "What is it?"

"We'd like to address what happened at the Labor Day carnival."

Every muscle in my body tenses like a taut rubber band. *We*. The elders? But they can't possibly know—Mark promised he wouldn't say a word.

I swallow. Bring the pen to the paper again, this time to draw hard, thick lines. Perhaps too hard. I tear a hole through the paper. "Of course. The Labor Day carnival raised over four thousand dollars for foster and adoptive families in our area. We're splitting that amount between two organizations, the—"

"We mean your fainting spell, Amber." His voice radiates pity.

Shame coats me like pond scum. Nausea rises.

Mark betrayed me.

I blink at the dark *Xs* I've drawn. They're menacing and overshadow the flowers and gourds. After a beat of silence, I push words through gritted teeth. "Not much to talk about there. Got a tad overheated is all. I'm perfectly fine, I assure you." And if they could never mention the incident again, perhaps I'll one day get over the mortification.

"Did you see a doctor?"

A bitter film spreads through my mouth. Surely Mark told them I don't see doctors. They never helped my mom. *You're sick, Ros, and you'll never get better. There's not a pill in the universe that will cure you.* Why waste my time with a doctor?

"There's no need for that. I'm young and strong. I haven't had so much as a moment of light-headedness since. Nothing to make a big deal out of. It's a reminder for me to stay hydrated." My gaze drifts to my nearly empty half-gallon jug sporting motivational time markers. Mark bought it for me last week. Seemed sweet in the moment. Glints a bit controlling now. "I'm drinking plenty of water. Don't worry about me."

His voice dips low. Is he frowning on his end of the phone? "Amber, it's not just the fainting. You haven't been yourself lately. The dark circles under your eyes … You seem worn out. Stressed. We were thinking perhaps you're doing too much. We discussed the possibility of canceling the Blankets for the Homeless this year, perhaps moving the nursing home visits to every other month."

My mouth falls open. "You discussed this? Without me?" A suspicion that my husband is included in the *we* sinks inside me like lead.

"It came up, yes. We know you've been asking for volunteers to help without much success. Canceling seems to be the best option."

"Last year we provided over a hundred and fifty blankets for the homeless. You'd have them suffer in the cold?" Tears threaten to burst through my words, but I hold them back.

"We can't do everything."

Heat rises in my chest. "Believe me, I know. If I could, I'd add a dozen more outreaches to our yearly calendar. Sure, we can't do everything, but we can do something. We can give someone who's down on their luck a blanket to keep them warm on a cold winter's night. We can do that. *I* can do that." Fire burns my tongue. Why do I have to defend myself, my mission? I'm the lone defendant here, and my own husband stands on the side of the prosecution. Why couldn't he bring these concerns to me himself? How cowardly. He'd do just about anything to avoid confrontation. Apparently, that includes making an elder break the bad news to his wife.

"Okay," Cole says, but it's not in acquiescence. It's patronizing and condescending. "Let's table this for now. We won't need to advertise it until next month. Let's take time to pray for the Lord's will."

I nearly laugh. Pray? To see if Jesus wants us to help the less fortunate? Seems like a no-brainer to me, but then again, I'm only the pastor's wife.

My watch buzzes. I check it to see a reminder of this evening's PTO meeting and the glaring time of 4:20 p.m. "If that's all, I need to go. I have an aerobics class to get to. Which I'm still taking, by the way, because I feel fine." I rip the page from the notebook, snap it closed, and stand.

"We mean no offense." Cole has the audacity to sound contrite. "We care about your family. We don't want you to overwork yourself. Pricilla has offered to put together a meal train. Would that be helpful?"

I cough. Gulp water. Choke on the water. Sputter out my response. "A meal train?"

"It's where—"

"I know what a meal train is. I don't understand why you'd think I need one." I pound my chest, willing this burning to cease.

"To ease the burden. We care about you and your family." He says this again, as if it's the most reasonable thing in the world. A meal train. For the woman who coordinates the weekly food baskets.

"I know, and I appreciate you looking out for me, but I'm fine." Right? Yeah, I'm fine. A bit more tired than usual, but who isn't with the changing seasons and shortening daylight hours? *Lord, help!* I *have* to be fine. Otherwise, I'll fall apart.

"Pray about the blanket outreach."

"I will. Bye." I grip my phone with white knuckles as I hang up and inhale a shaky breath. It will be okay. All is not lost. They didn't say anything about canceling the Christmas gala, and they won't. Surely, they won't. They know how much the event means to me. They know *why* my heart beats and bleeds for it.

I fiddle with my cardinal pendant. I haven't taken it off since I found Jerry, looking so much like Tim, cowering alone and afraid by the bushes at the carnival. *It's a scary feeling being left. Don't let it happen again.*

Oh yeah, I'll pray.

"Please, God, let them see the error of their ways."

~

I shift the car into park, then roll my neck side to side, willing the tension in my muscles to ease.

My mother repositions on the passenger's seat beside me and zips her fur coat as high as it will go, as if it's the middle of January and not the beginning of September. "Are we late? We're late, aren't we?"

"No, Mom. We're five minutes early, actually."

"By the time we walk into the salon, we'll be late. What if Gretchen won't take me? I'll have to reschedule. I don't want to reschedule." The pale woman grips her purse—which looks more like an old-fashioned physician's bag—with white knuckles.

"We've never had a problem with your weekly appointment. No need to worry now."

I step out of the car, then bend to see why my mom didn't follow.

Silver strands glimmer in the sunlight as Mom bobs her head and chews on her lip, but she refuses to dye her hair. Something about how hair dye contains chemicals that will rot her brain and cause dementia.

"Mom?"

She shudders. "Suckers."

"Excuse me?"

"The salon gives out suckers for children. I just remembered."

"Yes. And?"

"Do you know CPR?"

I give a curt nod. "I took a class last year. Got a certificate."

Mom's frantic eyes seek mine. "If a child chokes on a sucker, you'll do CPR? I can't go in there and watch a baby die."

"I'll save anyone who needs saving. Please, let's go before we really are late."

"Late!" Mom's holler makes my ears ring.

In a flash, she is out of the car and joins me on the sidewalk, enormous purse draped over her arm.

This is as good a time to bring it up as any. I take a deep breath before plunging in. "Now, Mom, I'm going to ask you something, and I want you to at least consider it before you say no."

Mom uses her thumb to slide her wedding ring up and down her ring finger. A nervous habit she continues to perform twenty-five years after the divorce. Dad discarded his ring long before the dissolution of their marriage finalized, but Mom? She wasn't the one to walk away, and she won't take off that ring.

I pat Mom's hand to still the skittish movement. "Come to Jordan's dance recital. It's her first since she moved up a level, and it would mean a lot to her to have you there."

Mom's head shake begins before I finish my plea. "Too many people."

"Yes, it'll be a full house, but we'll have seats near the front. We can get there early and wait until most people have left before we exit."

Her lip trembles. "So many germs."

"Mom, please." I meet her wide gaze. "Can you at least try? For Jordan." Once upon a time, she tried. For *me*. Back when Dad's calming presence was there to pacify. I do *not* have the same effect.

Again with the ring. "I'll think about it."

More like overthink about it. Bad idea. "How about we play a game? Sometimes Gretchen calls you by your first name, and sometimes she calls you Ms. McNeil. If we walk in there and she greets you by Rosalin, you'll go to the recital. If she greets you with your last name, you'll stay at home."

Mom shuffles forward without so much as a grunt. At least she doesn't disagree. A chime sounds as they enter the salon. Gretchen, young and hip with a streak of teal in her jet-black hair and tattoos peeking from beneath both sleeves, steps toward us with a smile. "Rosalin, so nice to see you today."

I gently prod my mother's side. "Yay," I whisper near Mom's ear. "Jordan will be ecstatic."

Mom shuffles from foot to foot. "When is it?"

"Thursday evening."

Gretchen gestures to the open salon chair. "Whenever you're ready."

Mom remains cemented in place. "Oh no. I watch *Law and Order* on Thursdays."

I put a hand on the small of Mom's back and guide her forward. "You can record it."

"But I always—"

My nudge toward the waiting chair might have been a tad harder than necessary, but it does the trick. Mom refocuses and sits, placing her purse in her lap.

Gretchen spreads an apron over her, then pumps the chair higher. "How's my favorite customer?"

With my mother occupied for the next hour, I excuse myself and stroll to the coffee shop two doors farther down the strip mall. I'll indulge in a blonde espresso while catching up on church emails.

So many emails. My mind reels as I make a mental to-do list on the short walk. Answer questions about the monthly food distribution, the nursing home visits, the welcome desk, and the church nursery volunteer schedule. I rub my tight shoulder muscles. Okay, yeah, I can do this in an hour. At least the overflowing inbox indicates I've found my niche and I'm valued at Ascend Community.

Thank You, Lord, for the opportunity to make a difference. Thank You that I have the privilege of being Your hands and feet.

It's what I want most of all, to contribute. For my work to mean something, for my life to matter. I'm living the dream, right?

Could You add a few extra hours to each day, Lord? The backs of my eyes sting as I add, *And could You please not yank this dream away from me?*

My hand is on the coffee shop door when my phone buzzes in my pocket. Shoot. The kids' school. I wince as I answer.

"Mrs. Prichard? We have Judson here in the nurse's office. He's not feeling well and has a temperature of 101.2. He needs to be picked up."

My shoulders droop as I let all hopes of strong coffee and an hour to myself die. I turn and walk back to the car. "Tell Victor I'm on my way."

Judson Victor Prichard. Apparently, the nurse missed the memo that we call our son by his middle name, not his first. I'll swing by and get him, return to pick Mom up from her appointment, take her home, and get Victor home to bed.

My mind's spinning so fast, I nearly forget to turn off the radio before I pull into the school's parking lot. What would they think if they heard *that* rock music coming from the pastor's wife's car? The secretary and several of the twins' classmates attend Ascend Community. My cheeks warm.

My boy looks miserable, ashen with circles under his eyes. He says he feels nauseous, so the nurse gives him a paper bag for the ride. If he uses it while my mom is in the car, she'll jump out of her skin.

"Relax, sweetie. I'll get you home as soon as I can." I offer him a bottle of water from the trunk, but he refuses. "Except we have to get Grandma and take her home first."

He groans.

"I know, but we'll make it quick."

Only a minute after merging onto the highway, brake lights shine as far as the eye can see. "Oh no. We're going to be late."

Victor whimpers from the back. I feel like crying myself. I imagine Mom pacing the salon waiting area mumbling incoherently. She'd scare the other customers away and drive the stylists to day drink.

"Mom? I'm going to be sick."

I cringe. "Use the bag."

He does, thankfully, but brown paper can't contain the stench. I roll all four windows down and pray traffic moves again. I should probably pray that whoever was in the accident ahead will be okay. I do so quickly, then pray for peace for my mother, healing for Victor, and strength to make it through the day. So much strength. I never got that coffee.

I finally pull up in front of the salon twenty-two minutes late. I've fielded five calls from my mother, yet my phone buzzes again as I exit the car and make a beeline for the trash bin to dispose of the barf bag. "I'm here, Mom. Let me go in and pay, then I'll take you home."

"Home? We haven't gone by the pet store to see the rabbits yet. We always see the rabbits on Friday."

I hang up as I step inside, the door chiming my arrival. Mom flocks to me like an oasis in the desert. I thank Gretchen, pay, and lead my mother out the door.

"I know we normally see the rabbits on Friday, but I have to get Victor to bed, so I need to get you home."

She stops in her tracks. "Who's Victor?"

I point to her eleven-year-old grandson.

"Oh, Judson. He looks just like you when you were little."

I blow out a breath. "We haven't called him Judson since the twins were three."

"Jordan and Judson, my grandchildren."

"Yes. But we call him Victor now."

Mom continues as if I haven't spoken a word, "Judson's sick. You said he was sick."

"Yes. That's why I need to take him home." I thread my arm through my mother's and lead her down the sidewalk.

"He's sick. He has germs. I shouldn't be around someone who's sick."

I slam my eyes shut and inhale deeply through my nose. I speak slowly on my exhale. "I didn't have time to take him home before picking you up." I open my eyes to see Mom shaking her head emphatically.

"Can't do it. Can't get in the car. Don't want to get sick. Judson is sick."

I pinch the bridge of my nose. "You have to get in the car. How else are you going to get home?"

"Can't do it. Too many germs. Kids have a lot of germs."

"Mom! Get in the car." My voice sounds sharp and shrill. Far too impatient for a pastor's wife. Far too irritated for any Christian. Heat creeps up my neck as I scan the area. Who overheard me? Please, God, nobody from Ascend Community. I cannot reflect badly on the church, on my husband.

A sheepish glance at Mom reveals a watery sheen in her eyes. Great. I made my mom cry. All in a day's work. How can someone I love so much get under my skin so thoroughly? And yet, the entire time I was in foster care, I craved her most. She represented everything stable in my world. My crazy mother.

Now Mom slides into the passenger's seat without another word. We ride to Sheltering Oak Retirement Community in silence, guilt and fear and shame swirling in the air between us.

And germs. A lot of germs.

~

I've never seen such an abundance of tulle. I sit back and try to enjoy the younger dancers as I wait for Jordan to make her appearance. It won't be until after intermission. I study the program and my daughter's name under the soloist section and am filled with excitement. All her hard work. My baby. My pride and joy. She's accomplished so much, and tonight she gets to show it off. I double-check my purse to ensure I brought tissues. I'll need them.

Victor sits next to me, trying to hide the fact he's playing Roblox on his phone. How hilarious that he thinks I can't see it tucked under his suit jacket. I'm letting it slide because I don't have the energy to fight another battle. I had to gather all my strength to make it here tonight. I've been tired and achy. Perhaps I caught the virus Victor had. But no fever or cough. I've powered through. I couldn't breathe a word of complaint or Mom would have heard, and I never would have been able to get her into this building.

She's sitting beside Mark, who's sitting next to Victor. I appreciate this buffer more than I can express with a gesture of prayer hands and a mouthed, *Thank you*, to Mark. God bless this man who didn't run the other way when he met his future in-laws. He's as smooth as a sateen sheet with the patience of a saint. If only he had the confidence to confront me directly instead of making the board do it. But now isn't the time to reflect on that indiscretion. This is a happy moment, and not just for me. Not only is Mark keeping my mother from rushing out of the auditorium in terror, but he has also made her smile at least twice in one night. A record.

The dim lighting and soft music do little to bolster my energy. I cover a yawn with the program. It wouldn't do to appear bored at my daughter's recital, and certainly, that's not the case. Perhaps age is catching up with me. I'm not in my twenties anymore.

A little girl with feathery bangs long enough to nearly curtain her wide eyes pirouettes onstage. Oh my goodness, she's almost a carbon copy of Kelsey at that age. I can't rip my gaze away from this girl who reminds me of Kelsey and Tim and the others who became my family after Child Protective Services ripped everything from me. My cardinal pendant feels cold and weighty against my clavicle.

The girl stumbles and falls, and suddenly I forget my fatigue. Her mouth drops open as the shock of the mishap radiates across her face. I lurch forward. The poor girl's face reddens as she stares at the gawking crowd. Everything in me leaps toward her, aching to protect her. I must block the stares toward her frozen form, shield her ears from the taunts that are surely coming. She's obviously holding back tears, and when she gasps in a breath, I do as well. She's a dam ready to burst. I move to stand, to run to her and whisk her off the stage before tears breach her defenses. I'll hold her, rock her, tell her everything will be okay.

"Kelsey," I whisper.

"Mom, what are you doing?" Victor tugs at my sleeve.

I'm halfway to my feet. What am I doing?

I blink. The girl isn't Kelsey. I'm not her mother, not her foster mother, or even her foster sister. I can't be the one to comfort her. Tears sting the edges of my eyes as I scoot back into my seat. "Nothing," I mumble and turn my head away from him.

This odd stirring of emotion is ridiculous. And look at the girl. She's recovered. She now dances in line with the others, fully in control, as if nothing had happened. Maybe nothing had. I could be hallucinating. Perhaps I'm as crazy as my mother.

My throat feels raw as I swallow back tears. My head throbs in my ears. It's nearly time for intermission, and then Jordan will take the stage. She's worked tirelessly for this moment. It's taken her years of practice to get a coveted solo. Whatever's going on with me needs to stop, for her sake.

Applause rings out, and girls in tight buns and pink tutus bow with poise and grace. House lights brighten. Voices and shuffling begin as a murmur and gradually swell until I'm reminded of the headache that pestered me earlier today. A quick glance at the program shows me intermission is ten minutes long. Enough time to grab a bottle of water and wash down a couple of ibuprofen.

Victor shoves his phone into his pocket, then stretches his arms high above his head and yawns. "They got any food here?"

Mom's head cranes around, brows knit in concentration. It's like I can see her mind tallying every possibility of contact with bacteria. Someone sneezes from across the auditorium, and she shudders. She worries her lip, but to her credit, doesn't bolt.

"Mom." Victor sounds more like a teenager than a child. It's too soon for this tone in his voice. He's only eleven. "Food?"

"I think there are concessions in the foyer. I'm going to grab water. You want to come with me and see what they have?"

He nods. I stand, and as I do, the room sways. The floor in front of me tilts ever so slightly, and I step forward to keep my footing. The feeling is too familiar, only this time, it's not hot and I have eaten. I grit my teeth. *God, not again.* Water. Hydration will help. A second later the room is back to normal. My shoulders relax. I'm fine.

Mark has distracted Mom with conversation. She's focused on him now instead of the crowd milling around her. I hear the word *hydrangea* and stifle a laugh. He knows not of what he speaks. He couldn't pick out a hydrangea from a lineup of flowers if his life depended on it. This makes his effort to appease Mom even more endearing.

I put a hand on Mark's shoulder to interrupt. "Want anything to eat or drink?"

My gaze includes them both. Mark says he's fine.

Mom's eyes flash horror. "Don't get ice. Ice is dirty. Contaminated."

"You want a drink without ice? A bottled water?"

"What brand? I only drink—"

"Dasani. I know, Mom. I'll see if they have any."

Mark stands to let Victor and me pass. I scrunch by Mom's knees and break through into the freedom of the center aisle. People swarm around me. A group of teens brush past. The light contact of a jacket sleeve to my arm causes me to teeter off balance. Victor puts a hand on my arm to steady me. As I walk toward the auditorium's back doors, the floor seems to shift underneath me. Laughter and chatter from my right resounds loudly in my ear, then the mumble of voices from the left. I can distinguish nothing. It's all noise. Loud, deafening noise. My temples throb.

Water. I must get to water. The foyer is mere steps away now. I strain to focus as my legs begin to wobble. The tilting turns to spinning. I try to blink it away, but when I open my eyes, I can't see anything clearly. The world is a blur. My head's full of air, and I'm floating as I fall into a cloud of nothingness.

Chapter 4

September 25, 1861
Ozark, Missouri

Change hung in the air like an autumn rain cloud, heavy with fat drops it could barely contain. A shift in Willow's world seemed certain as Milo ascended the porch steps, hat in hand. Something in the set of his jaw told her so. The stiffness of his shoulders. She shuddered and tightened her shawl around her shoulders before continuing to sweep leaves.

He scratched the back of his neck. "Pa inside?"

"Yep. Finishing supper." She squinted at him in the fading light but failed to uncover what secrets he harbored.

He released a long sigh before opening the door. "Come in," he said over his shoulder. "You'll want to hear this."

As if he had to say as much. Her shoe nearly nipped his heel as she stepped inside.

Milo stood ramrod straight as he spoke. "I have news."

Ma lowered her fork. The clank of it hitting the plate sounded overloud in the silence and sent a twinge of nervousness up Willow's spine. Pa sat back, crossed his arms, and raised his chin. An invitation to speak.

Milo widened his stance. "I know you wish to remain neutral in this war."

A grunt—or was it a growl?—escaped Pa's lips.

Milo ignored it. "But seeing as the Missouri State Guard won a great victory in the Battle of Lexington, I plan to go there and enlist. Help our boys defend our state."

Pa's stern expression melted into a grin. "That's my son."

Willow looked between the two men, confusion swamping her. "You're signing with the Confederacy?" Pa had railed about the rebellion. Didn't that mean their loyalty belonged to the Union? Greta's family was certainly on the Union's side.

Pa scoffed. "This is why females should stick to knitting. Their brains are stuffed with hay." Pa laughed, but his laughter transformed into a cough.

Milo met her gaze with sympathy. "The Missouri State Guard isn't part of the Confederacy."

"Union, then?"

He shook his head. "They were put together to protect Missouri from Federal invasion. They're not concerned with the larger scope of the war, only with protecting our state."

"States' rights," Pa spit out between coughs. He cleared his throat. "That's what I've been saying all along. Leave us the devil alone. Let us live in peace."

She hesitated to speak again lest Pa berate her ignorance, but confusion hung like a curtain in her mind, blocking out the light. *States' rights*. Yes, she'd heard as much from Pa's lips many times before. It made sense that Missourians would only concern themselves with what happened in Missouri, but *Federal invasion*? Did that mean …? "If they're not fighting for the Confederacy or for the Union, who are they fighting against?"

When no one so much as acknowledged her question, hot frustration bubbled within her.

Pa stood and came around to clap Milo on the back. "I'm proud of you, son. You're strong and brave. Go and show them blasted abolitionists they best not come over here trying to impose their un-American ideals."

Abolitionists. Yankees. So, he might not be joining the Confederate army, but he'd be fighting the Yankees just the same. What would Greta think about that?

As the glow of Pa's pride radiated onto her brother, Willow took a step closer. What would it be like to bask in her father's approval? Envy twisted in her gut. Milo was brave and strong, and she was stupid. She knew nothing of the complexities of this war, but how could she when the men rarely spoke of such things around her, assuming she was too ignorant to understand?

"When do you head out?" Ma spoke through pursed lips, clearly repressing the emotion evident in the watery sheen of her eyes.

"Tomorrow morning."

"Well then." She nodded, as solemn as Pa was radiant. "God be with you."

"And God save Missouri," Pa added with a slap to his thigh.

This war was about to change everything.

God save them all.

~

This time, Willow didn't accidentally stumble onto Mr. Schmidt's property. She crept there on purpose, following Milo from a safe distance. Surely, he was going to say goodbye.

Goodbye.

How could Willow stand to see him go?

Heart twisting, she hunkered behind an oak and watched as Greta rushed down her front porch steps and into the yard to meet Milo. She was too far to hear their words, but emotion lined their faces. They didn't touch, likely due to the curious stares of Greta's siblings who watched from the windows.

Willow needed to get closer. Curiosity itched at her like a mosquito bite. What were they saying? Did Greta know he would be fighting against the cause her German family held dear?

A plan materialized. Willow needed only to dash to the maple a few feet away, then to the rose bush at the side of the yard. From there, she could climb onto Greta's porch and duck behind the rocker. She should be able to hear the pair far better from there.

Milo's and Greta's brows furrowed as if they were deep in serious conversation. Best to run while they were distracted. Willow did so. At each stop, she checked to ensure they hadn't noticed her, but they remained focused on one another. As she hoisted her leg over the porch railing, her foot knocked into a potted plant, sending it tumbling from the ledge with a thunk and a crack. She cringed. Ducked. Held her breath. But Milo and Greta didn't so much as cast a glance in her direction. She tiptoed closer.

Greta's German accent lilted. "I can't bear to see you go. How will I survive without you?"

Though tempted to roll her eyes at the dramatics, Willow could ask the same. How would she survive without her brother?

"I'll return to you as soon as I'm able." He took her hand and kissed her fingers as a proper gentleman would. Nothing like their passionate display in private.

"But when will that be?" Greta faced away from Willow, but her raspy voice proved there were tears in her eyes.

"No one knows how long this war will last. It may take several months. But when I return, I'll ask for your hand."

Her hand? As in marriage? Pa would never abide it. Did Greta's parents feel the same? Willow bit her lip. And Pa said *her* head was stuffed with hay. What was Milo thinking?

"If only I had the courage to come with you, to watch over you and ensure your safety. I could be a cook or a laundress. Or even one of those female soldiers in disguise like in the papers." She shivered "But I can't abide the sights and sounds of suffering. I'm afraid I wouldn't last long near a battlefield."

Milo stroked the back of Greta's hand with his thumb. "Oh, my tender love. I wish to shelter you from all that would offend your delicate nature. I would—"

Heavy footsteps sounded from within the house.

"It's Vater."

Milo kissed her hand once more, then took a step backward. "I'll take my leave."

"Stay safe, my love," Greta whispered.

Milo slipped into the woods and disappeared just as Walter banged open the front door, rifle in hand. Willow crouched into a tight ball, holding as still as possible. "What in the blazes is going on out here?"

"Nothing, Papa." Greta ascended the steps, her skirt swishing around her ankles, her gaze low. So low it stumbled upon Willow crouched behind the rocker.

Greta startled. Walter looked down and red crept up his neck and onto his face.

"You!" he spat. "You're the filthy neighbor's girl, aren't ya?" He pointed his rifle to the sky, cocked it, and shot.

Willow jumped back, falling on her behind.

"Papa!" Greta pleaded. "Let her be. Please."

He paid her no mind. He slung his gun over his shoulder, then stomped to Willow and yanked her braid until she yelped and scrambled to her feet. Holding fast to her hair, he pulled her along, marching down the dirt path straight to her front door. He pounded his fist until it felt like the entire house rattled.

"What the devil?" Pa threw open the door.

Walter nudged her inside. "You need to pen up your girl as much as you need to pen your hogs. I caught her meddling on my property, on my very porch!"

Willow massaged the base of her skull as her mother wrapped an arm around her.

Walter's glance toward her dripped with loathing. "That one is trouble, and if you don't keep an eye on her, she'll end up shot dead by guerrillas."

Pa's ears burned bright red. "Kindly keep your hands off my women."

Walter stomped on the doorstep. "Kindly keep your women off my property."

Pa slammed the door in Walter's face. His breath came out quick and raspy. "Willow," he said with a growl.

She crossed her arms around herself. What could she say in her defense? Once again, she could divert his attention by informing him of Milo's intentions to marry Greta, but she'd have to live with her betrayal. She dropped her head and studied her boots.

Ma's soft voice contrasted with the tones the men had vocalized. "He's right, you know. You might love the woods, but they're growing far too dangerous for you to roam free in. The entire countryside is. Guerrillas are running rampant."

There Ma went, taking Pa's side again. Willow's pendant felt as if it might choke her.

Pa stroked his beard. "And Jayhawkers."

Ma tilted her head quizzically. "I thought Jayhawkers were only at Missouri's western border."

Pa scoffed. "We don't know that. Abolitionists are everywhere, and they're dangerous." He turned his attention to Willow. "You are to stay inside the house at all times, except for when you're gardening with your mother."

Her eyes widened. No. Goodness, no. "In-inside?" Away from her precious woods? The creek, the trees, the birdsong? The walls were closing in on her.

He stared at her, hard and cold. "You are not to leave this house unless you are at your mother's side. Is that clear?"

Her throat burned. "You *are* penning me, then. The hogs have more freedom than me."

He stood as impenetrable as a mountain. Unmoving. Unfeeling. "So be it."

She turned and grasped her mother's hands. "Ma. Please! Don't let him do this!"

Ma smiled sadly. "It's not so bad spending time with me, is it, dear?" She extricated her hand and patted Willow's shoulder. "We'll have plenty to chat about."

Willow's heart thrashed in her chest as hot tears threatened. With a groan, she ran to her room and slammed the door.

He'd gone too far this time.

~

Willow had always been a mite impulsive. Pa called her reckless. Trouble. But it wasn't until she hunkered in the corner of the dank barn, scissors trembling in her hand, that she stopped to think through what she was doing and realized he might be right.

But there was no going back now.

Who did she think she was? Joan of Arc herself? She'd read the woman's story cover to cover too many times to count, and now it seemed she was stepping into a similar narrative.

She angled the shard of mirror toward the candlelight. The smell of hay and manure surrounded her. The comforting smell of home. A home she would leave in mere hours.

What was she doing? How could she leave the only home she'd ever known?

She took a deep breath and set her jaw. Greta might not have the courage to face the battlefield, but Willow did, and she could watch after her brother. What she lacked in delicate nature, she made up for in bravado. She had to go through with this task. What else was left for her now?

Milo—her meager buffer against their father's cruel words—was leaving. She couldn't be left alone with a man who didn't want her, who never had, and a mother who loved him despite the fact he didn't love Willow. And she wouldn't be caged like an animal, her only solace of the outdoors stripped from her.

No. She couldn't bear up under Pa's disapproval without her brother, especially if she couldn't escape to the woods that were dearer to her than any friend. She'd follow her brother into the army. Other women had accomplished it. She'd first gleaned the idea from reading about a female soldier in the paper. One who faced battle bravely. Only, unlike that woman, she wouldn't get caught. She could shoot as good as a man. Run nearly as fast. She'd make a good soldier.

She'd be a far better soldier than she was a daughter.

Hand still shaking, she clenched her jaw and snipped. A lock of her hair fell to the hay.

No going back now.

~

Darkness clung around the edges of the dirt road as Willow followed the shadowy figure of Milo on his horse, Gallant, over a knoll. She urged Rustic, her black stallion, forward. She'd kept to the woods and stayed as far back as she dared without losing sight of Milo for the past two miles.

Now the tree line thinned, making cover more difficult. She should reveal herself soon anyway. Perhaps in another mile or so, once she was safely far enough from home that he wouldn't send her back.

"Go home, little sister."

She huffed. What? He hadn't even tossed a glance over his shoulder. "How'd you know I was here?" She prodded Rustic to catch up until she and Milo rode side by side.

"Aren't many animals in this brush that would make such a racket."

"I wasn't makin' a racket."

His smile flashed before he sobered. "Where are you goin'?"

She straightened her shoulders. "With you."

"Stop being foolish. Go home. Help Ma. Stay safe."

"With guerrillas trampling through the countryside, it's more dangerous at home than at war."

He had nothing to say to that. The rhythmic sway of their bodies and the soft clomp of hooves filled the silence between them. What thoughts whirled in his head?

Finally, he whispered, "Go home." It came as a plea, nearly strangled with emotion. It would move her if she let it. She could not let it.

She lifted her chin. "'One life is all we have, and we live it as we believe in living it. But to sacrifice what you are and to live without belief, that is a fate more terrible than dying.'"

Milo threw his head back and growled. "This is no time to be quoting Joan of Arc. This isn't some imaginary battle you reenact in the creek bed behind our home. Our country is at war."

Indignation flamed in her belly. "I know. And I will fight."

"You?" He scoffed. "You'd never make it. You wouldn't shoot a man." He shook his head and turned his attention to the path ahead.

The uppity fool. She pulled out her rifle, aimed, and shot an inch past his foot. Gallant reared back, nearly toppling Milo to the ground.

"Are you crazy? What'd you do that for? You could have shot my horse!"

"I'm a better shot than that. Call me crazy again, and I'll put a bullet through your ankle."

"Willow!" He flashed her a glare, then leaned forward and spoke in low soothing tones to his horse, petting his mane.

She took off her hunting cap to reveal shorn hair. "Call me Will."

His eyes widened. He ran a hand through his hair. "Blast it, Willow. What have you done?"

"I've made myself a soldier." She pressed her lips into a hard line.

"You look like a barbarian. However did you manage that cut?"

A barbarian? How dare he. She'd had to sneak the scissors to the barn with only a candle and a broken shard of a mirror to cut by, but it couldn't be that bad. "There wasn't much light."

He shook his head, mumbling incoherently.

"What's that? I can't make out your speech. You sound like a barbarian."

"I said I'll have to fix it when we break for a meal."

"We?"

"You don't think I'm going to let you go home looking like that, do you? Pa would pitch a fit."

"So, you don't mind? If I soldier with you?"

"Oh, I mind. This might be the most harebrained scheme you've ever concocted, and there's been a fair number of schemes." He shifted his jaw. "But if there's one thing I know about you, it's that I'd have better luck wrestling a cub from a mama bear than getting you to change your plans."

She could hug his neck, and she would when they dismounted. As long as they were out of public view. It wouldn't look proper for her to show such affection to her brother in front of others, not if she were posing as a man. She'd have to get that into her head. She'd played around boys most of her life. Surely, she'd picked up on how to walk, talk, and act like the lot of them. But the squeal she emitted at his pronouncement left a smidgen of doubt.

Milo eyed her. "What are you wearing, by the way?"

"Your old trousers." And how glorious. So much easier to ride astride in trousers than in a dress. Probably easier to do a great many things.

He made a low sound in his throat.

The sun began to crest the horizon, and with it came the promise of new adventure. That promise hummed in Willow's veins. Something other than pulling vegetables from the ground. Something more than cleaning, chopping, sowing, and canning. She might burst with the excitement of it. No one saying she was too stupid to understand. No one relegating her to menial tasks. No one speaking the word *female* as if it was a curse, as if God used up His best materials in fashioning Adam as the pinnacle of creation and threw Eve together using leftover scraps.

She inhaled the fresh morning air. She was free.

Milo's voice held none of the enthusiasm she felt. "What will Ma and Pa say when they find out you're gone?"

She sighed. "Pa probably won't even notice." She wasn't important enough to garner his attention.

"He'll notice."

"Well, he won't care. He'll probably thank God he's rid of me."

Milo shook his head at her. "Don't be ridiculous."

She glowered at him, then dug into her pocket for Pa's journal. "I'm not being ridiculous. I have proof." She held the journal up.

"What's that? It looks like—"

"It is. I snuck it from his desk and took it to the woods to read it. I intended to return it that night, but it fell into the creek, and the water ruined it. Most of it is unreadable, but there's enough"—she swallowed—"to know he doesn't want me around."

The problem was, she couldn't figure out why. The reasons had washed away, sinking to the bottom of the creek bed. Was it because she was female? He seemed to appreciate Ma's femininity.

He reached for the journal. "Let me see."

She sidled up next to him and opened to the only page that mattered, pointing to the lines that had haunted her since she'd first read them.

> *I prayed earnestly for another boy, and instead, I got Willow. Why'd the Good Lord give me a girl? Why'd He give me this girl? I don't want ...*

The words smudged and faded after *want*, leaving her to form her own conclusions.

"Willow, this doesn't mean anything." Milo shut the journal and handed it back.

"What are you talking about? Yes, it does. It means he doesn't want me."

"You don't know that." He continued forward, and she followed.

"I know."

"What does it matter anyway? Why do you care what he thinks?" His voice sounded a million miles away.

Her shoulders sagged with the weight of his question. "I don't know."

It would be easier for her not to care. But how could she? He was her father.

"Maybe it *is* good for you to get away. Ma will worry, though."

That much was true, and a swirl of guilt rose that she hadn't thought of such before. She touched the slight lump at the base of her neck where she wore her cardinal pendant underneath the male garb. A gift from her mother on her sixteenth birthday, she had yet to take it off. It was proof—wasn't it?—that she was loved by someone. Valued in some small way. And yet Ma's love lacked the strength to stand up against Pa's disdain. It was as weak as watered-down wine. Not enough. Not nearly enough to sustain her heart. But it was something, and she couldn't seem to take the necklace off, not even when she'd donned her brother's shirt and trousers.

"I might write after a bit."

Milo only grunted in reply.

They fell into silence again, only the road, their horses, and worlds of unspoken thought between them.

Fall Back and Find me

Chapter 5

Modern Day

"Amber?"

A steady beeping sound interrupts my dream of prima ballerinas prancing through hydrangea gardens. Cool air swirls around my face and shoulders. I'm lying on my back. Strange. The bed underneath me is stiff. Unfamiliar. And that smell. Antiseptic? My eyes flutter open to a white ceiling. I turn my head and confusion falls away and resurges all at once.

I'm in the hospital. An IV is taped to my left arm, and what looks to be saline drips slowly from the hanging bag above. A blood pressure cuff is attached to my right bicep. An oxygen monitor adorns my right pointer finger. Mark looks at me with concern.

I fainted. At Jordan's recital. My stomach sours at the memory. How did I get here? By ambulance, no doubt. What a scene that must have caused. Paramedics rushing into the auditorium and whisking a woman away on a stretcher. Did Jordan get to do her solo? Did anyone stay to watch? Bile rises in my throat. I search for a basin. Something. After finding nothing, I lean over and retch onto the floor.

Mark stands. "Are you okay?"

I nod and wave him off while he rushes to my side with a paper towel. "What happened?" Tears coat my words as I wipe my mouth.

"You passed out—"

"I know. I mean, what happened with Jordan. Did she perform? Did you get to see her solo?"

His frown deepens. "Everything was chaotic. We were concerned. I rode in the ambulance with you. Linda Ganset took Victor and Jordan to her house. Mr. Hundle took your mother home."

"So, no? She didn't dance?"

He shakes his head. I deflate.

"There's always next time."

Tears trek my cheeks. How dare my body betray me like this. Betray my family. My little girl.

"I'm glad you're all right." He reaches to take my hand. There's a piece of gauze taped there. He brushes his finger over it. He must notice me looking at it. "That's from the first IV the paramedics did in the ambulance. Guess it wasn't good enough 'cause they stuck you again as soon as you got in here."

How could I be oblivious to all of this? Now the big question looms. I don't want to ask it, so I focus on the board above Mark. My nurse's name is Lynn. My room number is 407. What hospital am I even in?

A nurse bustles in, getting hand sanitizer from the dispenser near the door before coming to me with a bright smile. "Ah, she's awake." Blue-streaked blonde hair and bright red cat's-eye glasses shout eccentricity.

"You must be Lynn." I try for a smile. It's got to be a pathetic excuse for one.

"You read up on me, I see."

I point to the vomit on the floor. "Sorry. I didn't see a basin."

Lynn waves me off and pages for cleanup. She steps around the other side and whips her stethoscope off her neck with the ease of a cowboy using a lasso. She slips the cold metal onto my chest under my gown and instructs me to take deep breaths, then moves it to my back. After taking my pulse and temperature, she tells me the doctor will be in to see us this morning. "Do you want breakfast, dear? I wouldn't recommend anything but the fruit and yogurt, but you're welcome to whatever you'd like." She sticks out her tongue, making a silly face.

It reminds me of Victor, which reminds me of Jordan, and guilt rolls up my spine. I shake my head.

"Can't say I blame you. Let me know if you change your mind. You can order until nine o'clock."

A janitor enters and cleans the mess on the floor as Lynn types away at the computer.

Mark stands. "Did her blood tests come back?"

Blood tests? What blood tests?

I might be reading too much into things, but her smile seems to fade slightly. She nods. "The doctor will discuss the results." Her smile seems forced now. "Use your call button if you need anything."

She's gone, and in her place is a niggling worry. What's wrong with me? I can't voice the question, but I must. It now looms so large around us I can't see past it.

My voice comes out in a timid whisper. "Have they said anything? About what this might be?"

I swallow. Do I want to hear the answer?

Mark's voice is as quiet as a breeze through dwindling autumn leaves. "No."

All the fears and worst-case scenarios I've been shoving deep down for months, since fatigue first began to encroach, come rushing to the surface.

It's cancer. It has to be. I know it in my bones. Mark and I have sat with numerous victims of the awful disease throughout the years, watching it zap the life right out of them. Some have battled through and emerged victorious. Many haven't. The monster leeched their energy and vitality. That's what it feels like now. My muscles are sore as if I've lifted weights. If I needed to itch my nose right now, could I put forth the effort? Doubtful. Exhaustion weighs me down like lead. I could sleep a year and still want a nap.

I have cancer. The doctor will come in and tell us this devastating news. Mark will try not to cry, but he's never been able to hold such emotions in when it's only the two of us. We'll weep together and then be strong for the children. I must be strong for the children. I'll do chemo, of course. I'll do whatever it takes to fight to be here for my family. I won't leave them. I clench my jaw. I *won't* leave them. I've got grit, and I'll muster it now. We'll get through this. The Lord is on our side.

I adjust the pillow behind my head. Might as well get comfortable. I'll be here awhile.

"Where's my phone?" I ask Mark. He's still standing, staring out the window overlooking the parking lot.

"I have it. Why?"

"I need to make a list of what I'll need you to bring me while I'm here." Toothbrush. Book. Sleep mask. Earbuds.

"Slow down. You don't even know how long you'll be here."

"Did you see the look on her face? I'm not leaving anytime soon."

"We don't know that. Let's take things one step at a time."

"That's the problem. Apparently, I can't *step* without fainting." He doesn't deserve the bitter bite in my words. No wonder I'm not hungry. I'm full of shame.

Mark runs his hands through his hair. "I know you're worried. That was a scary thing for you to go through. For all of us to go through."

A sob catches in my throat. Mark is by my side in an instant. He rubs my back and tucks a stray hair behind my ear.

"I'm sorry." It's all I can say, though I want to express more. This horrible disease isn't only affecting me. It's affecting everyone around me. Jordan, Victor, Mark, Mom. Oh my goodness, Mom. Is she rocking back and forth in her faded blue recliner at this very moment in fear that I might contract the bird flu in the hospital?

"You have nothing to be sorry about." Mark's voice is soft. He's used it to soothe a thousand weary parishioners. Yet, to me, it sounds shallow. His words aren't true. If I could have held myself together, none of this would have happened. If I could have kept from making a scene, Jordan would have gone on to perform her solo, then I could have gone to the doctor the next day. Figured all of this out. If only I would have held it together.

Another thought occurs to me, and I sit straight up. "Chipper. Who's taking care of Chipper?" That dog is like a third child. An adorable baby of the family. Also, the one most likely to cause my hair to gray prematurely.

Mark clicks his tongue against his teeth in the way that reminds me of a chipmunk. The way he does when he's thinking. This means it's a new thought for him. He forgot about the dog. Panic surges as I picture yellow puddles dotting every room of our home. And worse. The twins named him Chipper because the corgi always looks as if he's smiling.

Now, I imagine his lonely whine and pathetic frown as he faces an empty food and water bowl.

"Mark?"

"I'll text Mrs. Donahue. Ask her to let him out."

I rub the center of my forehead. "This is Chipper we're talking about. She can't just let him out. He's like Houdini. He finds a way out of the back fence no matter what we try. If she can't take him out on a leash, she'll have to keep an eye on him."

"I'll tell her." Mark's fingers fly across his phone keys.

"Seriously. The last thing we need is him getting loose and a truck running him over." I shudder. First cancer. Then a dead dog.

Maybe I'm being paranoid. My eyes widen. Is my worst fear coming to pass? Because there's one thing scarier than cancer, and that's turning into my clingy, needy, crazy mother.

Chipper.

Victor.

Jordan.

Mom.

Cancer. Cancer. Cancer.

These swirl in my head until it swims. I press cold fingers to my temples.

"Honey, are you okay?" Mark's voice balances precariously between pastor and husband.

No. I'm most definitely not okay. My heart thumps with this panicked realization that all is not well. Will it ever be well again?

A muscle in my cheek twitches as I say, "I'm fine."

It's not the first lie I've told.

I fear it won't be the last.

God, forgive me.

~

An hour later, the doctor enters, medical chart in hand. I grip the metal railings of my bed, bracing for the news that will change my life forever.

Mark stands and shoves his hands in his pockets.

"Good morning. I'm Dr. Grady."

A blue surgical mask covers his expression. In fact, he's covered in blue from head to toe, from the paper cap on his head to the booties on his feet. This precaution can't be for me, but my stomach wobbles. It's like a premonition of things to come.

Mark steps forward and extends a hand, but then, as if realizing the doctor wears blue latex gloves, he drops it and nods his greeting instead.

"So, what's wrong with me?" I try to keep my tone light, but the ringing in my ears makes it impossible to tell if I succeed.

"I have my suspicions. Let's get orthostatics on you." The corners of his eyes almost crinkle as if he's working to smile but can't manage it.

"What?"

"I'm going to take your pulse and blood pressure when you're lying down, when you're sitting, and again when you're standing."

"Okay." I've never heard of this being done for cancer patients, but then again, the silly procedure is hardly worth mentioning.

He loosens the machine-operated cuff already attached to my arm and slides on an old-fashioned one. "Call me a dinosaur, but I prefer to use this one," he says while he inserts the cold metal of the stethoscope head under the cuff and squeezes the bulb.

As it tightens around my bicep, I watch his face. Rather, his eyes because they're all I can see. I search them for a sign that he's about to tell me I'm dying, but I see only curiosity. Like he's trying to solve a puzzle. But he's a doctor. He hands out bad news on a regular basis. He's likely perfected his poker face.

"Now, I'd like you to sit up and swing your legs over the side." He lowers the bed rail to allow me to do so and offers a hand to help me upright.

I wait for him to pump the bulb again, but he doesn't. Not yet.

"Tell me about what happened right before the syncope."

The what?

He must read my question because he says, "The fainting."

My mind whirls as I try to recall. The dance recital. Kelsey fell. No, not Kelsey. A random girl. Victor stopped me from making a fool of myself. Intermission. I wanted water. He wanted food. We left for the concession stand. I suck in a breath. "Victor was with me."

"Excuse me?"

I ignore the doctor and whip my head around to look at my husband. "He was, wasn't he? He was right next to me when I passed out." The grim line of Mark's mouth tells me all I need to know. I drop my head in my hands. "Oh my goodness, that had to have been horrible for him. To see his mom collapse right in front of his face. Poor guy."

The doctor gives me a beat to process before asking, "Can you tell me more about what you felt like before the incident? Would you describe it as light-headedness or dizziness? Did the room spin?"

I shake my head. "I don't know. I don't remember. It moved. The room moved around me. I'm not sure if it spun."

He squeezes the bulb now, and the cuff tightens again. If only I could wrap Victor in a hug. Was he the one who called for help? Did he watch paramedics haul me off on a stretcher?

That experience is frightening enough as an adult, let alone as a child.

During a nursing home visit, Mr. Mires collapsed from a heart attack right in front of me. Even now, the image of his fall is branded into my brain. Watching someone plummet to the ground is a helpless feeling when there's nothing you can do to stop it. It only took me seconds to pull the emergency cord, but Mr. Mires didn't make it. That's a memory that would surface in therapy if I ever went. But pastors' wives don't go to therapy.

The pressure on my arm releases. My attention drifts to the bright yellow hospital socks I'm wearing. Stylish. I'd been wearing black strappy sandals. Now look at me.

The doctor once again lends his hand. "Let's have you stand now."

I do and the room lurches forward. I stumble a step.

Dr. Grady steadies me. "You okay?"

I press my eyes closed. Rock back onto my heels. Find my balance. Open my eyes. Everything is normal. "Yeah."

"Have you experienced any other symptoms besides the singular episode of syncope?"

What does that word mean again? I tilt my head.

"Fainting. Look straight at me." He shines a light in my eyes, flashes it away, then shines it back again before pocketing it. "Any symptoms like fatigue, heart palpitation, chest pains, headaches, shortness of breath, brain fog—"

I put out my hand. "Yes. All of it."

Mark's hand brushes my shoulder. "All of it?"

"Well, especially the headaches and fatigue. But a few times, I've had chest pains and felt like my heart was beating erratically. I thought I'd been working out too much or maybe not enough. Like I was out of shape. Climbing the stairs at church the other day knocked the air out of me. It never used to be that way."

He takes my blood pressure, but his eyes are steady now. No longer searching.

When he finishes, he says, "Aha."

"What?" both Mark and I say together.

"How long have these symptoms been going on?"

I wince because Mark isn't going to like my answer. "A few months. Maybe six months or so."

"Months?" Mark's voice explodes overloud in my right ear.

My shoulders curve forward. Defensive. "I've been pushing through them. Toughing it out." In retrospect, probably a bad idea. Cancer is always easier to treat the earlier you catch it.

"I see." Dr. Grady rubs his hands together as if excited by his discovery. "Your MRI showed nothing amiss, but I'm pretty sure I know what we're dealing with here. It's what's known as dysautonomia."

I've never heard of this kind of cancer. I shoot Mark a glance. His scrunched brows show him to be as confused as I am.

"You most likely have postural orthostatic tachycardia syndrome, or POTS. I'll refer you to a specialist who will order a tilt table test to confirm the diagnosis. It's characterized by an abnormal increase in heart rate upon standing, thirty beats per minute or above, and can cause syncope along with a host of other issues."

I plop back onto the bed. Dysautonomia. POTS. My brain is like a decrepit abandoned house I'm trying to make my way through. I can't see past the cobwebs.

"What is it, exactly? A virus?" This from Mark. His arms are crossed over his chest. He looks ready to tackle this problem, whatever it is.

"No, not a virus. A syndrome. There can be multiple causes or no known cause. It often causes abnormal symptoms in many parts of the body. Digestion can be affected. Temperature regulation—"

I put out a hand to stop him. "How do we treat it?"

He sobers. "There's no cure. But there are medications and different things to help people manage the symptoms."

"What kinds of things?"

"Fluid intake, mainly. And salt is actually a good thing for people with POTS. Also, compression socks."

"And it won't kill me?"

"No."

"But it won't go away."

"Correct."

"So, if I drink a lot of water, eat salty food, and wear ugly socks forever, I might not pass out as often?" Great news.

He nods. "Many people go years without getting a proper diagnosis. My sister-in-law recently got diagnosed, which is why I knew what to look for."

"Sounds like providence." Mark smiles. Actually smiles.

A lump forms in my throat. Providence? God's sovereign hand? In this? It could have been cancer. I should be happy that this condition won't leave my children without a mother. Thankfully, I won't have to plan my own funeral, but this thing is its own kind of ugly. Cancer is a horrific monster, but one I have battle plans for. You come at cancer with poison. Sometimes you win, sometimes you lose, but everyone understands the fight.

What is this is that I'm facing? What shape or form will it take? How do I fight it, and what it will cost me? It's a dark, foreboding presence hovering over me, and I'm without defenses. But, hey. I'll drink more water and hope for the best.

Dr. Grady's voice sounds not too much different from Mark's pastor's voice when he says, "It sounds like you've tried to pretend all is well and normal, but your body is telling a different story. It's in distress, and it's not going to be silent about it any longer." His gaze latches onto mine. "You aren't going to be able to wish this away, Amber. You're going to have to face it."

Those chest pains he talked about? They strike now. I press my hand to my heart and wince. "It hurts."

He nods. "I know. The good news is the tests we did indicate your heart is in excellent shape. While uncomfortable, the pain doesn't indicate a myocardial infarction—a heart attack—or any cardiac distress."

So, I *feel* like I'm dying, but I'm not. More good news.

"Are you sure? Perhaps it's something else. Something like …" I can't say *cancer*. "What about another MRI. Or a CAT scan?" Maybe they will find something else that will prove Dr. Grady wrong. Something solid and sure that I can eliminate with a pill or injection.

"It's not medically necessary at this point." He flips the chart closed as if that's the end of this conversation. I could beg, but what good would it do? Perhaps there will be another point later when I can request more scans.

Something's wrong with me that I'm even thinking this way. Who wishes terrible diseases on themselves?

I'm a mess. My body surely knows it.

My body knew it first.

Chapter 6

Near Columbia, Missouri
September 29, 1861

Willow ran her fingers through her fresh haircut, then stretched. "Isn't it 'bout time to stop for the night?" After all, the sun had sunk low on the horizon, and her stomach protested loud enough for Rustic to perk his ears at the sound.

"I want to make it another mile or so."

Another mile? What was his hurry? It wasn't like the war would end without them getting in on the action. She yawned. They'd been journeying for three days straight. This adventure had proved to be more monotonous than thrilling thus far. "Yes, sir. Corporal, sir. Or Sergeant? Lieutenant?"

Milo chuckled. "Private, I'm sure."

"Well, if you're a private, I'm going to advance to corporal." She smirked at him, holding her head high.

"And if I'm a corporal?"

"I'll be a sergeant, naturally."

"So, your goal is simply to outrank me." His cheek dimpled with his smile.

She gave a decisive nod.

"We shall see who outranks whom."

Oh, that sounded like a challenge, and she loved a good challenge, especially when it meant friendly competition against her brother. What if she could advance in rank? That would prove she was more than an unwanted waif. Her father may wish she'd never been born, or that she'd been born male, but she could prove herself valuable here. She could do anything a male could do, couldn't she? Perhaps, she could even do it better.

They came to a fork in the road with a sign for Lexington pointing to the left and a sign for Hannibal pointing to the right. Willow veered Rustic to the left, but Milo turned right.

"Where are you going? Lexington is this way."

"We're not going to Lexington."

She turned Rustic to catch up with her brother, confusion swarming her. "What are you talking about? Of course, we're going to Lexington. It's where the Missouri State Guard is stationed."

"We're headed to Warsaw, Illinois." The infuriating scamp spoke as if this was evident.

"Warsaw? What's in Warsaw?"

"The Union army. That's where the training camp is for new recruits."

"The Union?" she spit the name out.

He nodded matter-of-factly.

"But they've invaded our state."

"My allegiance is with the Union."

Her mouth dropped. No wonder. "It's because of Greta, isn't it? Your girl is German, that's why."

A glint of surprise flitted in his eyes. "It's the side of justice."

She angled closer to him. "I saw you two together."

"It doesn't matter."

She threw her head back with a laugh. "Oh, but it does. It will matter immensely to Pa. I wondered how you could fight against her family. It didn't make a lick of sense to me. Now I see. You're not fighting against Greta. You're fighting against"—the thought sucked the air from her lungs—"our family."

His jaw clenched. "I am not. Ma and Pa are neutral."

What a convenient time to spout that line. "They don't want Union troops invading our state." She ran her tongue over her teeth. "Fighting for the Union. I can't believe this." Another thought occurred to her, and she heaved in a breath. "Are you a-a Jayhawker?" Those blasted Kansans rode onto Missouri farms, stole slaves, looted, and burned and destroyed property. Likely, they were the reason for the War between the States.

He rolled his eyes. "No, I'm no Jayhawker."

Her shoulders relaxed a fraction. Still … "Do you think slavery is a blight on our nation? An intrinsic evil?"

Gallant whinnied as if in reply.

"I do," Milo answered.

She shifted in the saddle. "Them Germans have gotten into your head."

"Would you stop it? You sound like Pa."

She bristled, but the truth of his statement reverberated in her hollowed-out chest. Of course, she'd sound like Pa. Who else would she sound like? His were the only opinions she'd ever heard touted. What he said ruled in their household. "Is that a bad thing?"

"Yes!" His answer came like a slap to her face. "He's a prejudiced, bitter old man. Is that who you want to be like?"

Her stomach dropped. Was there another way? Another way of thinking? Another way of living? "It's all I know."

His voice gentled. "Then follow me."

~

October 2, 1861

Willow's stomach clenched as they neared the training base. This was it. No turning back now.

As if Milo could sense her growing apprehension, he said, "Remember everything I told you, and you'll be fine."

Oh, sure. He'd done nothing but lecture her about every minute detail she must keep in mind these past three hundred miles. How to walk and talk, what to say and not say, elements of the war Pa had kept her ignorant of, what to expect … She'd have to have a brain the size of Little Dixie to keep it straight.

Her face flamed, but she had to ask, "What about when I have to use the necessary?"

"From what I heard, camp latrines are filthy. No one will blame you for excusing yourself to the woods. I'll say you're a private chap." He chuckled.

The thought would be humorous if she wasn't so nervous. "What happens if I make a blunder? What if they discover I'm a woman?" The cool oval of her pendant pressed against her neck.

He turned to her, face somber. "They've jailed women for such an offense. Other regiments simply send them home. I assume it depends on the regiment." He rubbed the center of his forehead. "I can't believe I went along with this. Please don't get caught."

She nodded. Sure, she'd try. She wouldn't want to disgrace herself or her brother. Still, a thrill shot through her at the adventure of it all. What would Pa say if he could see her now?

She smirked. "You've made me practice talking like a man, but you haven't practiced addressing me as one. Let me hear you call me Will."

He shot her a mock glare. "Let's go, Willy. Almost there."

She picked up a pebble and tossed it at his back. "Willy?" "Stop playing around, little *brother*."

They crossed a deep gully and approached the encampment. Soldiers drilled on an open raised plain. Lines of tents surrounded the plain on all sides. Soon that'd be her. Drilling with those men. Sleeping in one of those tents. With men? She swallowed. Reality was descending like a heavy blanket. Why hadn't these concerns come up before now? Truth be told, she had rushed into this. She wiped sweaty palms on her trousers.

A couple of hours later, she stood before Colonel Bishop as he administered the oath to muster into his Black Hawk Cavalry.

"I, Will Forrester, do solemnly swear that I will bear true allegiance to the United States of America." The words came out with a croak, but she continued, "I will serve them honestly and faithfully against their Enemies or opposers, whomsoever." *Whomsoever?* Even her family? "I will obey the orders of the president of the United States and the orders of the officers appointed over me, according to the rules and articles for the Government of the Armies of the United States during the war. So help me God."

What had she agreed to? Why had she agreed to it? She and Milo had concocted foolhardy schemes before, but the time they'd put a dead lizard under Sally Montgomery's pillow or convinced Robert McClain a black bear was charging after him had been nothing compared to this. They'd deceived their folks and signed up to fight for an army their family detested.

Their parents believed Missouri should have the right to govern itself. They wanted to remain in the Union but continue slavery. Milo believed slavery was inherently evil and that the Union must be preserved. What did she believe? How could she shoulder a gun when she didn't know?

A horse whinnied in the distance. Maybe she didn't have to know right now. She'd been detailed to feed and water horses. She knew horses. Knew how to care for them. She could focus on the horses.

"Imagine that." Milo nudged her. The colonel had left, dismissing them to their tents. "Eighteen dollars a month, plus a one-hundred-dollar bounty upon discharge. What will you do with all that money?"

She tilted her head. "I haven't thought that far ahead."

He scoffed. "You never do."

She slapped him in the chest.

He ignored the slight and lowered his voice. "Four to a tent and we're not together. Be careful."

She bit her lip. Why'd they have to separate?

Milo pinched her upper arm. "Stop that."

"What?"

"The lip. No man does that."

She huffed.

"Stop that too."

Ugh. Infuriating know-it-all. She spun around and marched off, counting down the row to the sixteenth tent on the north side.

She took a deep breath, squared her shoulders, and ducked through the flap. "Hiya, fellas. I'm Will."

~

Two weeks in Warsaw and Willow had settled into army life like she'd been born into it. The routine soothed where the constant drilling grated. Rise at five, roll call at six, stable call at six twenty, breakfast at seven, water call at seven thirty, drill from nine thirty until eleven, then again from one thirty until three. Then dress parade, water call, stable call, roll call, and finally, lights extinguished at nine thirty.

The fullness of the day occupied her mind, pushing pesky questions such as what she was doing here in the first place far from her. Forward movement kept her focused on the next task in front of her, and the challenge of pulling it off while disguised as a man. No yanking up vegetables here. Her mind remained engaged from morning until night, even as she performed mundane tasks. She had to watch what she said, how she said it, and how she carried herself. It was a thrilling game she was trying to best. Better not to dwell on the consequences if she were to fumble.

Her time with the horses was the highlight of each day. She got to ride, water, and feed them. Uncle Sam's horses weren't in the best of shape. They needed extra loving attention, and she'd give it in abundance.

She also enjoyed the duty many others loathed: night guard duty. Winston and Ralph hired her to stand guard in their place and paid her fifty cents to do so. Staying awake and alert from eleven at night until six in the morning was a chore to some, but she relished it. The night sang to her. The crickets' and cicadas' songs vibrated in her body. This is where she felt fully alive.

In this camp, surrounded by Yankees, new thoughts swirled. She'd been raised hearing of "those blasted abolitionists." Pa's ranting had led her to believe that antislavery was synonymous with Jayhawking and that every Yankee was as violent as the Red Legs' leader James Lane. Here, though, she learned Jayhawkers and Red Legs—called such due to the red leggings they wore as they wreaked havoc across Missouri's countryside—used the war as an excuse to plunder and murder and didn't represent the vast majority of Federal soldiers.

Some Yankees she fought with hated slavery, but they believed in orderly warfare, not the type of guerrilla fighting that earned the term Bleeding Kansas. Other Federal soldiers cared about holding the country together and nothing more. To them, if the United States fractured, then everything our forefathers fought for was in jeopardy.

She'd been raised to believe *freedom and justice for all* meant *freedom and justice for her*. For her family. For the hardworking native Missouri farmers who lived by the sweat of their brows, and the help of a handful of slaves. This war put their freedom at risk. Abolitionist ideals sought to slice away at their hard-earned liberty. The battle cry for states' rights was a cry to fight to preserve their way of life from anything that encroached.

But to many here, *freedom and justice for all* had a different meaning, a broader one. It encompassed people with dark skin as well as Germans. The latter got under her skin more than the former. She'd had far more negative experiences with their menacing neighbor than she had with any slave.

Milo had no such trouble. He had Greta. What would it be like to experience such love and acceptance? Rejection hollowed her out like an empty cavern. Would she ever know?

One afternoon she awoke to her tentmates' loud chatter as they filed in. She'd slept through drills due to being on guard duty the night before. She rubbed her eyes and yawned.

"Doesn't that beat all? Milo. Son of a gun." Ralph made no effort to keep his voice down.

She propped up on one elbow. "What about my brother?"

He scoffed. "Captain promoted him to corporal."

"What?" She sat up. "You serious?"

"Yep. We're dividing into squads for drilling, and he's sixth corporal for Sergeant Kinsloe's squad."

Her cheeks flamed. He'd advanced so soon. Far sooner than she'd expected. Jealousy smarted. She'd done everything asked of her with precision. Hadn't she been a model soldier? When would she rank? She pictured him teasing her over her boast that she'd outrank him. For some reason, this stung more than their typical friendly rivalries.

She loved her brother. He was her only true ally in the world. But his success here made her failure gape large and obvious. Her hackles rose, and she strove for humor to cover them. A good-natured prank would get this frustration out of her system and earn a few laughs at the same time.

~

Willow sat back a good distance and watched as Milo added the last log to the stack of firewood. It took all her self-control not to smirk, but she managed to will her lips into a straight line. She scratched the back of her neck. Any minute now.

Milo lit the match.

An explosion burst forth. He stumbled back, eyes wide. A laugh tumbled from her. She couldn't help it. The look on his face. Her laughter unleashed a cascade of chuckles and guffaws from the others.

"Very funny. Who put gunpowder in the firewood?" Milo scanned each face.

She averted her eyes.

"Willow-Will." His voice hardened.

She startled at the sound of her real name. Her gaze met his steely one. She narrowed her eyes in challenge.

"You'll be digging up stumps for this."

Her mouth parted. "For a prank?"

"Dangerous actions against your superior."

"My—" She scoffed. The rapscallion.

His gaze bore into hers. She dared not blink. Why was he being like this? Lording his new position over her? She'd not let him get away with it.

When they asked for volunteers for a bayonet fight after routine drills the next day, she lifted her chin toward Milo and raised her hand. He accepted the challenge. The two of them pitted against each other reminded her of when they'd used splintered boards to sword fight in the barn as children.

Their bayonets crashed and clanked against each other as they swung and thrust. She blocked, ducked, and twisted out of the way. Her agility came in handy. The men around them cheered—some for Milo, some for Will. Her blood pumped in rhythm. She smiled at the thrill of it.

Milo's face, however, bore a grim, stern expression. Did he not enjoy the sport of this? A muscle in his jaw twitched, and his eyes clouded.

It reminded her of when he'd caught a six-inch bass, and she'd caught a ten-inch one. Or the time he'd shot a doe, and she'd killed a buck. Of course, Pa had paid her no mind, even though she'd accomplished more than Milo. He always won Pa's praises. He merely had to breathe, and Pa showered him with affection.

Heat burned in her chest. No matter how hard she worked, it was never enough. She slicked her bayonet with more force. Even after all she'd accomplished, she could never earn her father's affections.

With a grunt, she thrust forward.

Milo sucked in a breath as her blade contacted his cheek. Crimson sprung forth. His eyes flashed. "What's wrong with you? It's only a drill."

She threw her bayonet to the ground, spun around, and marched off toward the woods.

No surprise when Milo's boots crunched beside her.

"I have to use the necessary."

"Don't give me that excuse. What's going on with you?"

She rubbed her palms over her eyes. Good question. Happiness had eluded her here, despite living out a grand adventure like her heroine Joan of Arc. Why couldn't she seem to find her place?

His sigh came out sharp and filled with frustration. "I thought this experience would grow you up, but you're still walking around with something to prove. I expected more from you."

Milo's disappointment pierced her. She welcomed his anger. She'd never run from a good fight. But disappointment? That didn't sit well with her. Pa had always been disappointed in her, but never Milo. She must find success. She couldn't stand this burning failure.

She opened her mouth to defend herself but couldn't find any words. She picked up her pace instead.

"Maybe you need a change."

"A change?" She eyed him.

"Yeah. Perhaps you need to be on your own for a bit. Find out what you're made of."

She stopped, put her hand on her hip, then promptly dropped it when he raised his eyebrow in warning. "What do you have in mind?"

Chapter 7

Modern Day

Mark seems to agree with Dr. Grady's proclamation of "good news" and sings praise songs the entire ride home from the hospital while I stare out the car window. The leaves are beginning to change color, so most of the landscape is green with mere dots of yellow, orange, and red. There's a chill to the air now that most definitely wasn't present at the Labor Day carnival. It looks like it might rain, but maybe not. The sky has not yet made up its mind. It doesn't know how it feels, and neither do I. We're both on the edge of something, but not quite there. Unlike the seasons, I can't predict my new horizon. What does this life with POTS look like?

"You hungry? Want to stop and get burgers? Celebrate with a shake?" Mark grins at me.

"Celebrate what?"

"You getting out of the hospital. You don't have anything life-threatening, sweetheart. That's a reason for celebration if you ask me."

I turn back toward the window. The clouds may not be releasing their rain, but I cannot hold mine in any longer. Tears slide down my cheeks and drip onto my folded hands. My throat is too swollen to speak.

Mark taps my shoulder. "You're not hungry?"

I shake my head.

"Another time, then."

Perceptive, he is not—and never has been—but if he knew I was upset, he'd empathize. Best that he doesn't know. What's the use of us both being miserable? Especially when we're on our way to pick up the twins. They need us to be strong. Or to pretend to be. Mark has never been good at pretending.

I focus on my children as I dry my tears. My heart blooms as their faces materialize in my mind. Victor hasn't seemed to need me for years, but it has to be a ruse.

He walked a solid two months before Jordan, and that wasn't the first milestone he crushed. From the beginning, he let us know, twin or not, he was his own person. We switched from calling him Judson to calling him Victor as a way of acknowledging that.

Jordan's face emerges in the forefront of my mind, the way she looked the last time I saw her—hair in a tight bun with glitter spread throughout and light makeup accentuating her natural beauty. If there's a perceptive one in the family, it's her. She sees things, sees people. Overhears everything. You can't keep a secret from her. She's the best eavesdropper on the planet, and the one in the family who cares most about the family. She hugs trees and flowers. She loves everyone and everything. Her heart is just that big.

Unless I shattered it.

I'm suddenly warm and turn the temperature dial to crank on the AC. Mark raises an eyebrow, but to his credit, doesn't say anything.

I need a distraction. "Let's call my mom."

Mark raises a brow but presses the button, and soon her voice greets us on the car's speaker.

"Hey, Mom. Just checking to make sure you're okay."

"You have the fainting disease."

I look to Mark. Did he call Mom and tell her my diagnosis? He shrugs and mouths, *Wasn't me.* "Fainting disease? Who told you that?"

"Runs in the family, that fainting disease. All the way back to that woman with the tree name. The one in the war."

Woman with the tree name? My crazy mother. "What are you talking about?"

"I knew it. I had it too when I was young. They told me to eat bananas. Did they give you a banana?"

"No." I press a hand to my mouth to hold back a giggle.

"Eat a banana every day. That's the way to cure the fainting disease."

Mark's shoulders shake with silent laughter.

"Okay, Mom." Makes as much sense as the doctor's prescription of more salt and water. "I'll do that. You're okay?"

"Sure. Haven't fainted in thirty-five years."

"Okay. Call me if you need anything."

I disconnect the call, and we both erupt. When we settle, Mark says, "Remarkable. An entire conversation without her freaking out about something."

True.

If she's the paranoid one, why was I the one to think I had cancer? An unsettled wave rolls through me. That might not have been her usual freak-out session, but it was far stranger. Fainting disease? Passed through the family?

The trauma I've caused my children surges to the forefront again. After all I've done to be the best mother I could possibly be, the mother I wish I'd had when I was younger, I could shatter them if I don't overcome this diagnosis. If I haven't already.

We're turning into the Gansets' subdivision when Mark tells me, in his gentle pastor's voice, to calm down.

"Hmm?" I ask, but he must be talking about my breathing. My breaths come fast and shallow. My chest heaves.

"What are you afraid of?" Again with the voice that could convince bees to donate their honeycombs.

"What if I've broken them?"

"Who?"

"The children." Who else?

His pat to my knee feels patronizing. "You worry too much. They'll be fine."

This offers no comfort, but the sight of Victor bouncing a soccer ball on his knees in the Gansets' front yard slows my breathing and my pulse. He's wearing shorts. My legs break out in goose pimples at the sight. He's rolled the sleeves of his long-sleeved shirt up, and his tanned arms are exposed. The normalness of this view placates me. There's my son doing what he's always done as if his life hasn't been irrevocably shattered by my inability to hold mine together. Perhaps I haven't ruined him after all. Though I haven't figured out how to tell them about something I haven't come to grips with myself.

He jogs to the car and waves as we pull into the driveway.

I roll down the window. "Hi, hon."

"Hey, Mom. Feeling better?" His eyebrows and voice both lift. The hope in them stings.

What can I say to that? My emotions are wrung out. My body feels trampled. My mind is a fog. However, the last time he saw me, I was unconscious on the floor, so comparatively, I'm not lying when I reply, "Yes."

His shoulders relax, and a smile spreads. "Good."

Now I've started something I must finish, so I force a smile. My heart cracks in the process. Will this be my life now? Pretending I'm okay when I'm not? Forever. This will never go away. I will forever be an actress.

"I'll get Jordy." He holds the ball under one arm and runs inside, forgetting to wipe his feet on the mat.

"I'll go thank the Gansets. Be right back." Mark follows him inside.

I'm left with a swelling ache of loneliness. Silence leaves room for insecurities to chant my name. How will I perform my duties at Ascend Community if I might pass out at any moment? Will we be able to continue with the blanket outreach? Can I still work the welcome desk on Sunday mornings? What about the nursery? Is it even safe for me to hold babies?

I picture the elders sitting around the boardroom table frowning at me. "Too much," they say. "You do too much."

But if I wasn't doing it, who would? My attempts to recruit volunteers have fallen woefully short. Cole's suggestion that it's because I set up too many outreaches niggles at me. He advised us to pare down and focus our efforts so we could recruit more effectively. But every single outreach is needed. I couldn't possibly abandon any of them. My throat tightens. Especially the gala. I am needed at Ascend Community. Indispensable. I have to be.

A voice in the back of my head asks, *Who is Amber Prichard without all of that?* I try to push it away, but it persists. *Who would you be if it was all taken away?*

No. I *am* needed, and I must push through this. Surely, the specialist will put me on medication that will enable me to continue to function. To keep doing what I've always done. I nearly snort at how my attitude toward doctors has shifted. I've gone from all-out avoidance to complete reliance. How fickle I turned out to be.

Mark reemerges with a casserole dish in hand. Cameron Ganset claps him on the back, then tosses a look of pity in my direction. I duck my head to dodge it, but it lodges in my ribs. Victor waves goodbye, then hustles to the car, soccer ball in tow.

Jordan slinks behind her brother, head bowed. Her hair is a wavy mess from being in the tight bun the day before. All remnants of poise are gone. Her shoulders slump forward as she opens the car door and slides in.

I keep my voice upbeat. "Hi, princess."

"Hi." Her gaze remains on her tennis shoes.

Oh no. She's not okay. I search my mind for something to say to make everything better as Mark places the casserole in the trunk. I come up short. The best I can do is, "I'm sorry we missed your solo, sweetie. We'll make it up to you. We'll be there next time."

Empty words. Not because they aren't true but because they're not enough. Her silence says as much.

"Hey, good news." Mark slides in, either oblivious to Jordan's somber mood or purposefully acting the polar opposite. "Priscilla set up a meal train. The Gansets were the first to sign up. Looks like our meals are covered for at least the next week."

A meal train. The one I stubbornly refused. I'd laugh if I had the strength. Instead, I say what's expected. "That's nice of her."

"Sure is. Now, let's get this show on the road." He taps the steering wheel in an eager beat. "Who's up for ice cream?"

"Me!" Victor shouts.

I scoff at Mark. "You've got dessert on the brain."

He shrugs. "Pumpkin pie concretes are back at Teddy's. Sounds good, right?"

"Heck, yeah." Victor pumps his fist.

Jordan hasn't moved, hasn't spoken, hasn't lifted her head. My heart sinks as I study her. To ask her if she's okay would be futile. She's obviously not. Why would she be? Her mother ruined her recital.

"Want a pumpkin concrete, pumpkin?" Mark asks her.

"I'm not hungry." Her voice is soft and small—like when she was a toddler and feared monsters camping out in her closet. Only now it's me. I'm the monster.

My stomach lurches. I'm not hungry either.

~

The next day, Delaney visits while Mark takes the twins shopping. Victor grew out of his "new" cleats already and needs another pair. Maybe I should get a job—a real one this time that pays in more than stress and betrayal—but of course, this isn't a new thought. As the twins grow, so do the expenses. Mark's pastor salary is stretching thin. I clench my jaw when it hits me. I've been going through a list of job possibilities that would have suited me fine before my body quit on me. Who am I kidding? There will be no job in my near future.

Delaney breezes in with four cloth grocery bags hanging from her arms and proceeds to unload their contents into my fridge while I sit like a lump of Play-Doh on the kitchen chair. This is not right. She's a guest in my home. Where's my hospitality?

I shift my weight to stand. "Do you want anything to drink?"

Her brows lift as though I'm a lunatic. "Sit, Amber. I'll grab you a snack."

I huff but return to my rear end. "You don't have to take care of me, you know."

She closes the fridge and turns to lean against it. "Yeah, I kinda do."

"I'm not an invalid."

Her head tilt begs to differ. "You're trending in that direction if you keep pushing yourself mercilessly."

I scowl at her and swat her words out of my mind. I don't want to consider if they're true or not. "I don't remember inviting you."

"Har har." She glides across the kitchen, grabs two glasses, and fills them with ice water. She sets them pointedly on the table as she sits across from me as if to say, *See? I'm perfectly capable of getting my own drink.*

I push what I hope is a reassuring smile to the surface. "Seriously, I might need to tone down my activity a bit, but I'm not helpless or … needy." I spit that last word out as if it's moldy.

Delaney sits back and points both fingers at me. "Ding, ding, ding! There it is, folks. Amber Prichard's trigger word. God forbid anyone thinks Mrs. Do-it-all is needy."

I glower at her.

"I keep telling you there are therapists for this kind of thing."

"And I keep telling you, pastors' wives don't go to therapy."

She takes a drink, then spits an ice cube back into her glass. "First of all, that's a filtered Instagram picture you're projecting there, not reality. Secondly, what were the last words your father spoke to your mom before he walked out?"

I close my eyes as I reply, feeling each moment of that memory as solidly as if it had happened this morning. "Make sure Amber doesn't end up a trainwreck like you."

"Yeah, see? That'd put me in therapy."

At the touch of Delaney's hand on mine, my eyes flutter open to see her eyes full of compassion.

I swallow past a sudden lump in my throat. "I'm not my mother."

"Clearly," she says without a hint of hesitation. "So, you can let someone take care of you for a little while as your body recuperates, right? You don't have to be Superwoman. Taking a break while you wait for the specialist to develop a treatment plan isn't transforming into a leech. It's being responsible so you can continue functioning long-term."

Okay, she has a point. Fizzling out doesn't do me any good. My goal is to be a contributing member of the body of Christ for as long as I live. And she seems confident I'll recover with treatment. A pinprick of hope breaks through my clouded heart. "See, I don't need a therapist. I have you."

She rolls her eyes. "All right. Lie back on the couch, and let's talk about those six months you spent in foster care while your mom was in the looney bin."

I cringe. "I'd rather not. And a real therapist would call it a mental institution."

She shrugs. "Tomayto, tomahto."

I stand slowly and twist my back to loosen taut muscles. "I'm going to go relax on the couch, but I'll forgo spilling my guts about the past for another time."

She grins. "Hey, progress! I'll take what I can get."

"Celery sticks and hummus, please. For my snack."

The happy lilt in her voice is a familiar song I will never tire of. "You got it."

~

Two weeks later, I'm folding clothes from a seated position on the couch when my phone rings. I've got worship music blasting, and I reach for the remote to turn it down. Praise plays constantly throughout our home now. I must fight to keep my mind off the physical pain, and as my muscles scream with the simple movement of folding pants and shirts, I figured the extra volume might be helpful. It's a toss-up as to whether this idea is working or not. Regardless, the music will remain on because I must cling to the Lord if I am to make it through this completely ordinary day.

Mark has prayed for my healing every night, and I've gotten worse, not better. He reads the children accounts of healings from the gospels and Acts every night before encouraging them to pray for me as well. Bolstering their faith, I guess. The disappointment in their eyes after each unanswered prayer shrinks my heart. The fault for this must lie within me somewhere.

Now Mark talks more about how sometimes God uses doctors to heal us and how it's still His goodness when He does so. It feels like his backup plan, but no matter. If there's a pill that will fix this, I'll gladly take it. My follow-up appointment with the specialist is next week. One more week until I can hopefully get on with my daily tasks. The last watermelon of the season sits on the kitchen counter, mocking me, waiting for me to cut it, but I haven't been able to summon the energy. Pathetic.

With the music low now, I answer my phone right before it goes to voicemail.

"Mrs. Prichard, it's Ms. Beale, the school counselor. Do you have a few moments to talk about your daughter?" She sounds serious, and I bring my hand to my pendant. I soon drop it. It hurts to hold my arm up.

"Yes. Of course." Jordan's been sulking around the house since her recital—or lack thereof—but I'd assumed she perked up around her friends. After all, her issue is with me and no one else. Surely, apart from my presence, she's the vivacious, bright child she's always been.

"Thank you for your time. We have concerns." She continues to speak about how Jordan's grades have dropped dramatically in the past couple of weeks and how she's been withdrawn. "She refused to participate in a class project yesterday. When Ms. Adams told her the assignment was mandatory, she said she didn't care and that she wouldn't do it. Ms. Adams issued her a detention."

I gasp. I can't help it. My baby in detention? My sweet, compliant, straight A, exemplary daughter in detention? It's unthinkable.

"I'm going through health issues. She must be having a hard time processing everything." I cringe as I hear myself say these words. Now I'm *that* parent. The one making excuses for my child's misbehavior. I'm worthy of a social media eye roll, but I can't seem to stop the words from tumbling out. "I fainted at her dance recital and was rushed to the hospital. It was rather dramatic. I have dysautonomia. At least, the doctor at the hospital thinks I do. It's a lifelong condition with no cure." Oh. My. Word. Someone make my mouth stop. "We're all … adjusting. It's complicated."

Ms. Beale jumps in and puts me out of my misery. "I understand. That's a lot to take in. We'd like to put in a referral for an in-school therapist for Jordan. Would that be okay?"

"A therapist?" I choke on the word.

"Yes. A licensed therapist would come to the school to do weekly sessions with your daughter. We only need a signature for the referral. I can email the form today."

A therapist. I've put my daughter in therapy at eleven years old. I hesitate. We're a pastor's family. We shouldn't need therapy. Mark is the one counseling others. His own children shouldn't need to be counseled. But my heart squeezes. If this is what my baby girl needs, I can't deny her. "Okay." My voice sags.

"Would you like us to refer Victor too?"

Heavens, no. Not both of my children. I can't have ruined them both. "He's fine, I think. I mean … isn't he okay?"

A smile comes through in her response. "We have no present concerns."

Thank God. "Good."

"If you change your mind, give me a call."

I pray to God the only call I will make to Ms. Beale will be to let her know Jordan is fine and no longer needs therapy. I'll be able to call her as soon as I visit the doctor and get put on medication. When I'm back to normal, surely, she will be too. We'll move on from this nightmare. Her next recital is around Christmastime, and I will be there. Cheering. Standing.

~

Lily was about to throw an eggshell in the kitchen trash when she saw it. A crumpled blue flier in the trash can. She craned her neck to read the bold print but could only make out *Join Us*. She tucked the shell in the corner where it wouldn't contaminate the page, quickly washed her hands, and rushed back to retrieve the paper.

She glanced over her shoulder. Good. Mom whisked the pancake batter with her back to Lily.

Join Us This Sunday. A flier for a local church. Did someone put it on their door? A twinge of disappointment rippled through her chest. If only. But Mom had pitched it for a reason. Lily searched through her memory, before Harvy and Jana and Davy. When it was just her and Mom and maybe Dad if he happened to have a Sunday off. Lily had never wanted to go to children's church, so Mom let her nestle close to her side as the pastor spoke about heaven and goodness and kindness.

Only snatches of memories remained. How her feet didn't touch the floor but swung back and forth, back and forth, until Mom would put a hand on her knee to still them. Of how sometimes the drama team would do a skit onstage and Mom would hold her if she couldn't see. She would pretend not to be able to see the stage so she could be held. How the greeters would remark each Sunday that she was a "pretty little thing" and she "looked exactly like her mama.'

Church.

She had always felt safe in church. Always wanted. Like she belonged.

Until the others came along.

No wonder Mom threw the flier in the trash.

She went to do the same, but her hand hovered over the lid. Something in her resisted. A pull from that little girl with swinging legs perhaps.

"Lily, did you butter the skillet?" Mom glanced over her shoulder.

"I will. Sorry." She folded the blue paper into fourths and slid it into her pocket.

She grabbed butter from the fridge, cut two slices, and slid them into the skillet.

"I didn't get a turn to stir," Jana whined.

Lily turned to her, resisting the urge to mimic her pout. "But you put the oil in. Everyone got a turn to do something."

"I want to stir!" Her shrieks pierced the air and sent pain shooting through Lily's forehead. Jana plopped down and jiggled her legs like a jellyfish.

Lily bent and attempted to make eye contact. "Everyone got a turn. Did you have fun putting the oil in?"

"Let. Me. Stir!" She threw herself on the floor with such force, a sickening thud resounded as her head banged against the tile. Her screams escalated, but they weren't ones of pain. They were ones of rage.

Mom sighed. "Let her stir, Lily. This is not the hill to die on."

Lily's jaw clenched. "If we always let her get her way, she'll continue to throw these fits. Then we'll never be able to go anywhere."

Mom chuckled. She spoke over Jana's shouts. "Where do you want to go?"

"Church, maybe?"

Mom sobered and turned her full attention to Lily, drying her hands on the sunflower apron around her waist. "We've tried going to church, firefly."

Lily softened at the use of the pet name. "I know."

"What's the use of going if I'll never be able to sit through a service? If we both have to stay with the children or keep coming to assist? It's not fair to the church workers. It's not fair to them." She nodded at Jana, then at Davy. "I want church to be a place they enjoy. Not somewhere they feel like they're always in trouble."

"I know." Lily scrunched her nose at the scent of burnt butter.

"Besides," Mom said in a brighter tone, "you'd miss Sunday morning pancakes."

Jana's cries had puttered into whimpers. She now twisted around on the floor in circles. Harvy pushed his toy train through spilled flour while Davy licked drops of milk from the countertop. Blake remained glued to his video game.

Yes. She'd skip this for church in a heartbeat. Call her a terrible sister, but fellowship with people who could carry on a two-way conversation about something other than trains and dinosaurs sounded like paradise.

"It's too quiet. Where's Jamie?" Mom asked.

Lily stilled, listening with senses on high alert. Shoot. Mom was right. This couldn't be good. Last time this happened, he'd been hunkered in the bathroom closet, covered head to toe in peanut butter. "I'll find him."

She'd find him, they'd eat breakfast, and then maybe, if she couldn't gather the courage to talk to Mom about Bible college in Michigan, she could summon the gumption to ask for a Sunday off from pancake duty. If the whole family couldn't make it to church, perhaps she still could. Alone. As an entity separate from her family.

She set off to scour the house, peeking in every closet first. "Jay Jay, where are you?"

A trail of dirt marked a clue. It led to Mom and Dad's room. Lily followed it until she found Jamie standing in a pile of dirt on top of their parent's bed, wearing only his Spider-Man underwear. Wait. What was that smell? She stooped to touch the brown crumbs. No, not dirt. She sniffed her fingers. Coffee grounds.

"You dumped out an entire canister of coffee grounds?"

"I like the smell." He bounded up and down on the springy mattress. "I ate some too."

She rolled her eyes. "Wonderful."

"You want to eat some? You can." He jumped down and thrust a handful of grounds toward her face.

"That's okay. I prefer mine brewed."

"Brewed rhymes with stewed, rhymes with food, rhymes with mooed …"

Were Sunday mornings away from this craziness too much to ask? Mom's weary face flashed in her mind's eye. Perhaps it was, but she had to ask anyway. She was twenty-two years old. She didn't have to ask. She could *tell* her mother she'd be gone each Sunday. She pushed her shoulders back. Tilted her head up. She could. She was an adult. Perfectly capable of making her own decisions. But Mom. How would she manage without Lily's help?

That wasn't her problem.

Was it?

Chapter 8

IN THE FIRST PLACE, THEN, PEACE, IN MY OPINION, SHOULD BE MAINTAINED IN OUR STATE; AND I FULLY BELIEVE WILL BE MAINTAINED ... THESE DAYS OF TERROR AND OF FOLLY WILL PASS BY—AND SHORTLY, TOO—AND TRANQUILITY AND WISDOM WILL AGAIN MARK OUR SOCIAL AND POLITICAL CONDITION ...

NATHANIEL PASCHALL, ESQ.

EDITOR OF THE *MISSOURI REPUBLICAN*, MAY 16, 1861

November 4, 1861

Camp Defiance, Missouri

Willow stretched and stepped out of the barn and into the morning sunshine. She picked bits of hay from her trousers, then surveyed the area. Hubert and Conrad hunched around the fire, already preparing breakfast. Wasn't it her luck to be saddled with horse duty with a bunch of Germans?

At least she was free from rigid rules and drills. Here at Camp Defiance, her primary job was to guard the horses. Three hundred of them, to be exact. They were but a mile away from the training camp, but it might as well have been a hundred miles. The fourteen of them stationed for horse duty were disconnected from the rest of the unit. And war? She could nearly forget there was such a thing out here.

"You got any more apples?" She walked to the fire and warmed her hands. The air boasted of snow, but none came. Only chill. Too bad they didn't have overcoats yet. Rumor was they'd get some soon. Then again, they still hadn't gotten any pay.

Conrad looked from where he poured coffee and nodded. "Got three more left. Plan to go into town again tomorrow and get more."

"I'll take one, if you don't mind. Got to head down and relieve Charles."

Conrad tossed her an apple.

She took a bite and juice dripped down her chin. "Much obliged." She meandered to the pasture, soaking in the warmth of the sun on the back of her neck. The sweetness of the fruit. Birdsong in the distance. She shuddered when she thought of what her life would have been like if she'd stayed at home. Confined within four walls day and night? She'd have suffocated by now. She far preferred this reality, even if it often bored her.

The peacefulness of the moment collapsed when she spied Charles running toward her waving his arms above his head. What now?

She jogged ahead. "What's wrong?"

"The horses, they—" He hunched over with his hands on his knees and heaved in a breath. "They broke down the fence. Twenty of them got out. Perhaps thirty."

"Twenty or thirty? When? How'd this happen?"

He gripped the back of his neck as his face reddened. "I fell asleep."

She closed her eyes and pressed her lips together. This was the second time Charles had fallen asleep during night guard duty. More proof Germans couldn't be trusted.

"Alert the others. Grab two other men to help track down the strays and have others repair the fence. We'll likely need a few days of provisions."

His brows rose at her directness, but he nodded and ran off toward the men. She threw her apple core to the ground and headed straight for the pasture.

The break in the fence gaped wide. Several horses must have worked together to forge such an escape. It was a wonder they'd only lost up to thirty. The horses moved in restless circles, sometimes pawing at the ground, their agitation evident in their whinnies and sighs. She stood in the gap and spoke in a firm but gentle voice to the animals. "Why would you want to run away? You have a good life here. We take fine care of you. You have the distinction of being Uncle Sam's horses. Do you know what an honor that is?" Ears perked. Tails swished. It was almost as if they understood, as if her speech bolstered their spirits. "You get to fight for the unity of our nation, for the freedom of all mankind."

The words spouted among many of the men here flowed through her mouth as if she'd always believed them. *Unity. Freedom.* These were the ideals the North claimed to fight for, and she was inclined to believe them. No one spoke of oppressing the Southern people and taking away their rights. Why would she put such weight behind Pa's claims? He wasn't the kind of man she could trust.

Words from the camp preacher's sermon flitted through her mind. She'd been attending services at camp since she arrived, same as she'd always attended church back home. But the preacher here was nothing like solemn Pastor Blackstone. The pastor of their country Baptist church spoke much of hell's dangers and little of anything else. The camp preacher spoke of hope, a purpose in the midst of pain, and God's love for all people. Not words that made her cringe and want to hide, but ones that stoked a desire to rise. She spoke them to the horses now to see how they tasted on her tongue. "Who knows but that you were born for such a time as this?"

Conrad emerged beside her, clapping with a lopsided grin on his face. "Spoken like a true patriot."

Her cheeks warmed. If only he knew. "The speech was for the horses, not you."

"It seems to have worked. They are peaceful."

True. Stillness radiated around them. "Are you here to fix the fence?"

"No. I'm hunting strays with you."

Fine. She would have preferred one of the few Americans in camp, but at least Conrad had been kind to her. And he was competent.

They chose horses to mount for the journey. Charles and Ralph joined them. The four of them headed off in search of the missing horses. They passed through Chili, Woodville, and Carthage with no luck. Finally, on their way to Quincy, she heard a noise.

She put out her hand. "Stop. Quiet."

The men stilled. Their raised brows and puckered foreheads spoke curiosity. And perhaps doubt. Or amusement. But there was no doubt in her heart about what she'd heard.

"They're this way." She led the group through the woods and into a small clearing where a dozen horses stood blinking back at them.

"Well, I'll be."

"How'd you do that?"

She shrugged.

One side of Conrad's mouth tipped. "Guess you're good at finding lost things." He winked.

His words tumbled through her. If only they were true, because she was the most lost thing of all.

~

November 26, 1861

Willow sat on a blanket next to Conrad on the frozen grass as they waited for the others to return from hunting deserters. They played at seeing who could make the biggest puff of smoke with their breath in the cold night air. Everyone else in the training camp had moved to Macon for winter quarters, but Camp Defiance remained until the horses could be sold. Oh, how she tired of the monotony of doing nothing but guarding horses.

At the sound of voices in the distance, Willow and Conrad clamored to their feet. "Is that them?" Conrad peered over Willow's head. "You think they're back?"

Willow craned her ear in the direction of the noise. "Sure sounds like Hubert."

Conrad slapped her back. "Come on."

The two of them barreled across the prairie until they came to the camp entrance. Sure enough, four of their men brought a shady-looking straggler with them. A deserter, for sure.

Hubert flashed a toothy grin. "We got him." He pointed a pistol at the man's back. "We'll keep him in the barn. Guard him good."

Willow and Conrad watched the men's retreating forms. "What will happen to him?"

"Once we send him to Macon, he'll likely get shot by a firing squad. That's what should happen to all deserters, anyway. I hope I don't have to be one of the ones to pull the trigger." He shuddered. "Killing a Confederate is one thing. Killin' one of my own is another, even if he is a scoundrel."

She swallowed. What if they called upon her to be part of the firing squad? Could she look straight at this solemn-faced man and shoot him point-blank? With all eyes watching, she'd have to or risk being branded a traitor and shot herself.

She sucked in a shaky breath. Best not to think of these things. Not tonight. She had the evening off from guarding both horses and the deserter, and she meant to make use of it.

Back in her corner of the barn, across the way from the deserter and his guards, she dimmed her lantern and searched under the straw until her fingers brushed against something hard. She brought it to the light. No. Not what she was looking for. This was the green journal she'd purchased in town on their way to Warsaw. She'd intended to write her adventures. So far, blank sheets stared back at her. What was there worth penning for posterity? She'd had no heroic exploits like warriors of old. The most valiant thing she'd done was bring back a few of Uncle Sam's stray horses.

No, she needed something with far more significance. Her fingers once again combed through the hay until they clasped another form. Ah, this was it. Her heroine called to her as she brought the book close. *Joan of Arc, the Maid of Orleans.* In her haste to leave, she hadn't thought to bring her copy along with her, and she missed it something fierce. She'd purchased this copy yesterday from a shop in town, saying it was for her sister, and promptly stashed it out of sight. But now, with the others distracted and on duty, she could devour the words of this saint who, like her, dressed as a man and fought bravely beside an army of men.

It did not matter that Willow's boots were worn clean through the toes, that she still hadn't an overcoat, that she'd yet to receive pay, or that her brother had abandoned her to this shabby horse camp while advancing in rank with the rest of the cavalry. Here, she could float away to another time, another place. A place of adventure instead of monotony. A place where she, too, might be a victor and not simply another name in a vast sea of bodies fighting for an unclear cause.

~

The next day she headed back to Camp Defiance after stopping in town to retrieve a letter. She waited until she was well on her way before she took out Milo's letter and read.

Dear Will,
I hope you are well there with the horses. Several of the boys have asked after you, inquiring of your

well-being. Sam and Dalton are especially eager for you to return so they can best you at cards and take your pocket money.

I regret to inform you, I've come down with measles, and I'm in the hospital for the time being. The doctor advised no medicine and said resting indoors would cure me. I pray to God he is right.

Macon has a wretched excuse for a hospital, and the men who come here fare worse after a week rather than better. There are twenty-five of us suffering here. The roof leaks, and one can nearly feel the diseases breeding in the moist atmosphere. The man in the cot next to me died this morning. The man next to him died yesterday of brain fever. I don't want you to fear I will be next. I have a strong constitution. I'm well enough to write to you, aren't I?

I only mean to advise you that when you rejoin the regiment, avoid the hospital if you can. You are better off fending for yourself, unless you have a bullet wound that needs tending. May that never be the case with you, little brother.

I hope that, in the pasture, you have found your parcel of peace and have forgiven me for sending you there. I've only ever wanted your good fortune.

I wish you the best.

Yours truly,

Milo

Her steps slowed as she bit the inside of her cheek. Forgive him? How could she hold a grudge against him when he was all she had in the world? Pa hardly knew she existed. Ma was wrapped in Pa's world. The only person who gave her a lick of attention lay in a hospital with a disease that had killed hundreds, maybe thousands of soldiers. Of course, she'd forgive him. If only her well-wishes could heal him.

As for finding peace in the pasture, she couldn't yet say. The solitude 'bout drove her mad, but it soothed the rough edges of her soul as well.

The minute she stepped back into camp, Hubert came out to greet her. "Will!" The man motioned toward the barn. "We need you on guard duty."

Willow hastened her pace. When she reached Hubert, he pressed a pistol into her hand. "The prisoner's father and brother visited about an hour ago. Something is shifty. We think the family means to break the deserter out. Perhaps tonight. We must send word to Macon to hasten his departure."

The weapon weighed heavy in her hand. "What do you need me to do?"

"Guard him good."

"I can do that."

"The rest of us will spread out and guard the property."

She glanced at the barn and opened her mouth to protest. Just her with this man? And only a cold pistol to keep the peace between them? But Hubert had gone.

No matter. Guarding a man wasn't much different than guarding horses. No way he would try anything when she had a pistol in hand. She wouldn't be forced to fire it. Not at this man who'd done nothing more than shirk from battle.

The prisoner slept for the first hour while she kept watch. When he stirred, she straightened from where she'd been leaning against the barn door.

"You got any food?" The man's voice rasped, clearly parched from thirst.

She cast a glance at the pot on the extinguished fire. "Beans. They're cold."

"Anything would be a mercy."

"Need a drink?"

"Whisky?" His mouth tipped in a smile.

She narrowed her eyes. "Water."

"Thank you."

She scooped beans onto a plate and poured water into a tin cup. She handed both to the prisoner, who took them in his trembling, bound hands.

"Much obliged. Haven't had a lick to eat since I got here."

Her stomach soured. "They didn't feed you?"

"'Fraid not." Water dribbled down his beard and onto his grimy hands.

She probably wasn't supposed to feed him either. But what was the use of starving the man? He was but a skeleton anyway. Too frail to pose much of a threat.

She took a step closer. "Why'd you do it? Why'd you run away?"

He shook his head. Dropped his gaze.

"I fought at the Battle of Belmont. Watched a Reb shoot my brother in the head. Stood there helpless as the life drained out of him." He brought clouded eyes to meet hers. She fought back the urge to shiver. "After that, I couldn't remember what I was fighting for. What's worth that?" He took another drink. "This army don't care 'bout you or 'bout me. Never did receive my pay. I'm one in a long line of nameless, faceless servants. Disposable. I thought to myself, my family cares if I live or die. They deserve to know 'bout Jeb. So, I set off to tell them. Now, they might lose another son."

She scuffed her boot in the hay. What could she say? No telling how she'd react if she watched Milo lose his life beside her in such a gruesome way. This deserter didn't deserve to die, but if she confessed as much, she'd be branded a traitor.

"Need more water?"

He lifted a sad smile and nodded toward his cup and plate. "Nah. This here was mighty kind of you."

Kind. The Bible said something about giving a cup of water to a person in need. If she remembered correctly, it also said something about visiting prisoners. It had been so long since she'd read from the Good Book. So long since she'd tried to win Pa over with piety. It hadn't worked. No matter how many of God's laws she followed, she was no closer to her father's heart than before. What would he say about her now, watering and guarding Uncle Sam's horses and showing mercy to a Union deserter? He'd likely be disgusted.

What would Ma say? Instinctively, her fingers found the lump at her neck. She pressed Ma's pendant against her skin, clearing her throat both to cover for her strange actions and to clear the building emotion. Ma would give him water, wouldn't she? Not only water but ale and a slice of plum pie. Perhaps Willow had some of Ma's feminine sensitivities in her after all.

But she needed to suppress them now. For the war.

Her shoulders drooped, and she backed away from the prisoner toward the barn door. If only she could hear the voice of angels—or of God Himself—like Joan of Arc had. Then she'd never feel uncertain or that she wasn't enough.

~

February 1, 1862

Willow scowled and stomped back into the barn. Of all the rotten luck. They'd finally gotten paid, after waiting for months, and Uncle Sam had doled out thirteen dollars a month instead of the eighteen dollars a month they'd been promised.

She kicked the barn door. "When are we going to move to Macon, anyway?"

They'd sent the prisoner on to Macon over a month ago, along with half of the men from camp. Only six of them remained now, waiting for orders to join the others in winter quarters.

Hubert harrumphed. "You're in a foul mood. What does it matter?"

110

She ran a hand through her hair. "I'm sick of being here. Sick of doing nothing." Sick of staring at empty journal pages. When would her adventure start? When would she finally have something heroic to pen? She could never advance in ranks as long as she was relegated to this horse camp.

"Would a letter from your brother cheer you?" He handed her an envelope.

She nearly tore into it. Milo had recovered from his ailment, despite the deplorable conditions in the hospital, and resumed regaling her with gossip of the men. She hungered for his tales.

> Dear Will,
>
> Men from your camp arrived in Macon talking of your keen ability to track down lost horses. They call you Needler and say you could find a needle in a haystack. They say you hear horses sometimes from a mile away and have a sense about you. They're fascinated. I didn't know of this rare talent of yours, and I'm as eager as the rest of the men to see it in action. I wonder if you'd be able to track guerrillas the same as you do horses. There's talk of little else around here but guerrilla hunting. Maybe you could be the one to bring down Quantrill and restore peace to the region. Greta says bushwhackers are terrorizing the countryside. Union troops must put an end to their intimidation. Only the guerrillas know the brush and are experts at staying hidden. I keep thinking that you know the brush too, as well as you know your own heartbeat. You've always been in tune to those things, far better than I ever was. I pray your orders to Macon will come quickly. I miss you, little brother.
>
> Yours truly,
> Milo

Willow reread the letter, slower this time, taking each word in. And what was this behind each word? Admiration? Respect? Love. Her heart warmed. Her father may never have wanted her, but her brother wanted her now. Saw her value. By the sounds of it, he *did* miss her, just as she missed him.

Could that be enough for her?

Chapter 9

Modern Day

The elders call me in for a meeting. I tamp down a niggling worry as I walk the long hallway to the boardroom. Mark will be there, and despite his earlier indiscretion of spilling my secret, he's been nothing but gentle and supportive. My feelings toward him are like ocean waves, crashing with affection, then retreating with suspicion. He may not be the safe place I've always trusted him to be, but he's all I've got. And he does love me. This much is obvious.

The hallway walls are lined with pictures of previous recipients of the Golden Servant Award. Each one shakes Cole's hand and smiles for the camera, holding a framed certificate. Their expressions glow with bashful appreciation. Francine McDaniel. Brenda Ignatius. Samuel Bullfrost. Margaret Rogunda. I brush their names with my finger. Good people. Admirable people. The longing to join them on these walls swells in my chest.

Mark has always said he's fine with me not bringing in income, but this apprehension never fully dissipates. I may be contributing to the church—his church—but I'm not contributing financially to our household, and we feel the pinch. The $2,000 in award money wouldn't be much in the scheme of things, but it would be something. Something I could do to alleviate the financial burden.

It's more than that, of course. So much more. Though I can't explain to anyone how having my picture on this wall seems like the holy grail of solid proof to me. Proof that I'm not my mother. That I will never be like her.

I must give more than I take. I must.

I have to finish the year strong. Despite everything, this has become my primary goal—summon the strength to make it through the rest of the year, including the Christmas gala. As soon as the new medicine from the doctor kicks in, I should be able to do this. I must. So many families depend on me.

As I walk into the room, their voices hush. All is not well. The elders not only cease conversation, each of them avoids eye contact.

Mark comes and pecks me on the cheek. "Hi, honey."

"Hey."

Cole feigns fascination with the single-paged agenda before him. The other elders are bent over, reading the Bible as if it's the first time they've ever laid eyes on the book.

I barely managed to drag myself here. I have no energy for these games. "What is it?"

Cole glances over the rim of his glasses but still doesn't meet my eye.

Mark hooks an arm around my shoulder and leads me to a chair. "Come sit."

My stomach sinks. This can't be good.

I sit next to Mark across from the other three men. All attention turns to me. Every muscle in my body tenses.

Cole smiles. "How was your doctor's appointment the other day?"

It's as if the room takes a collective breath. My shoulders relax for this nice little chat. "Great." I squirm slightly at the exaggeration. "I had a tilt table test."

"What's that?" Cole asks.

"They strap you to a table that tilts and hook you to monitors to see how your body responds."

He nods as if this is fascinating. "Like a carnival ride."

"Something like that." Only you feel like you're going to die because your heart gallops and pounds, then your head swims. You want it to stop, but you're strapped in, and there's no way out. More like a tilt torture test, but whatever.

"Anyway," I continue, "the specialist confirmed the diagnosis. He put me on a beta-blocker, which should help a lot." My voice sounds overbright to my ears. It's like a commercial for prescription drugs where they read the side effects in a speedy, cheerful voice. "It's salt tablets, electrolyte drinks, and compression socks for me." I grin as if I'm as happy about this news as my husband.

Cole mirrors my expression. "Wonderful news. We're so happy for you."

His words float before me like a balloon. Words for someone who recently got engaged. Had a baby. Got promoted. Not words for someone who was diagnosed with a chronic medical condition. One that would severely limit her for the rest of her life.

"Now, let's talk about why we asked you to come in today."

The balloon pops.

Tension rolls in like a cold front.

I move to the edge of the black, ergonomic office chair, hands braced on my knees. I'm on the precipice of something. Is this where I teeter off the edge of a world that I only assumed was round? I hold on to myself for a stability that my instincts tell me is fleeting.

Cole folds his hands in front of him, then looks up.

I blink.

"We're asking you to step down from your duties for the time being."

Dread claws at my chest. I choke out the only word barreling through my brain, "No."

Mark squeezes my hand.

Pressure.

Cole leans forward, face lined with regret. "It's only temporary. To give you time to rest and recover."

"Recover." The word tastes metallic. What has Mark told him? That all I need is water and sleep and I'll be as good as new? Sounds like the propaganda Delaney spouted when she visited weeks ago. Okay, she didn't know it wasn't true. She was hopeful. It's my fault for believing her.

It hits me then. *Mark.* I yank my hand from his as if it were on fire. I shouldn't say a thing. Can't air grievances publicly. I clamp my jaw tight, but "You knew?" slips from between my teeth.

His cheek twitches. He drops his gaze.

I bite my tongue to keep from saying more. To stop from asking why he didn't warn me, why he brought me before the firing squad to be publicly humiliated instead of telling me himself. Blood tinges my mouth.

"It's only temporary," Mark repeats Cole's pathetic reassurance.

The pity in the room is deep enough to drown in. I lift my chin as if that's going to keep me afloat. "I'm not sure what you've heard"—I shoot a pointed glance at my husband—"but my diagnosis is chronic." My throat swells around the ugly word. "That means it's not going away, so I've got to learn to live with it. I can't abandon my responsibilities." Conviction rises within me, and I stand. "Please don't fire me."

All four men speak at once, each spouting protests and denials, their voices indistinguishable. Mark sputters a small laugh that steals my attention.

"What did you say?" I ask.

The edges of his mouth twitch upward slightly. "You can't exactly get fired if you're not getting paid."

It's a dig at the men across the table from him who refused to put me on staff because it wasn't "in the budget," yet they chuckle as if he's told a grand joke.

My mouth parts. It's like a bad dream.

"What about the homeless outreach?" I fling an arm in the direction of a framed photo on the wall of last year's outreach. In it, I pose with a needy family in front of a donated blanket. Their smiles shine.

"Canceled."

"Canceled? You've got to be kidding me. You said you'd pray about it."

"We did. We felt the Lord's leading to cancel this year."

I scoff.

"It was unanimous, Amber." Cole's statement punches me in the stomach. *Unanimous.*

My husband voted against me.

If I look at him, I might say something that would get me kicked out of the church, so I direct my gaze at Cole. "You don't expect me to step down from nursing home visits, do you?"

He nods.

"The welcome desk? The nursery? The food outreach?"

Another nod.

"Okay, but the Christmas gala for foster and adoptive families is on, right?" Images from last year's gala flood my mind. Little girls with princess crowns watching in wide-eyed wonder as acrobats fly across the stage. Little boys in suits licking icing-covered fingers and giggling at the magician's tricks. Mothers' and fathers' faces lighting with pleasure as their children open a mountain of presents. "Right?" I ask again, urgency propelling me to splay my hands on the table and lean in.

Cole's jaw tightens. "No. Everything is off until further notice."

This knocks the wind out of me. I sit. My unfocused eyes take in little more than my brain. *What is happening?*

They cannot—they will not—take the Christmas gala away from me. They will have to pry it from the cold grasp of my dead body.

Cole rushes in as if he can rescue anything from this smoldering fire. "Of course, we'll put something in the bulletin asking if anyone else is willing to take over for the time being."

A deep laugh rolls from my belly and gushes out. If I could be any more humiliated, the snort that unleashes afterward does the trick, but I've no inhibitions left. Someone else taking over my role? Who would be so crazy? Tears form as my body convulses with laughter. Before I throw my head back, I catch the elders' nervous glances.

"Amber, are you okay?" Cole's question only makes me laugh harder.

I swipe at my eyes and shake my head. My laughter simmers, and yet the tears continue to flow. The room falls silent. I can't move my hands fast enough to dry the torrent streaming down my cheeks. I hiccup through my tears. Chairs squeak as the men shift in them. Outside, a bird sings, oblivious to my misery. Mark holds his hand out in invitation. I don't take it. Instead, I clench my fists until my knuckles turn white, giving up the futile effort of drying my face.

Unanimous.

They prayed about it.

Unanimous.

God voted against me too.

I catapult to my feet. Too fast. Much too fast. When the room sways, I step behind my chair, clutch its back for support, and fight to keep the dizziness from showing. The light-headedness passes, but the anger remains.

I shove the chair forward. It bangs against the table. The men startle and stare.

"Good luck trying to run this place without me." I snatch my purse and storm out.

~

The Sunday bulletin announces the cancellation of the Blankets for the Homeless outreach this year. Underneath that announcement is one asking for a volunteer to coordinate a pared down Christmas gift project for foster and adoptive families—a shadow of the outreach I founded. The one I will still pull off one way or another, with or without their help. I crumple the bulletin before depositing it in the trash.

Discreetly, of course. I'm still the pastor's wife.

I smile at everyone and greet them warmly. Shake hands. File into the sanctuary to sit in the front row with my two well-behaved children, waving to Mark who's deep in discussion with a parishioner. His apology after the fiasco with the elders rang cheap, but I told him I forgave him. I'm trying not to be a liar, but the hurt hasn't dissipated. When music floats past and the worship pastor asks everyone to stand, I do. Slowly. My vision blurs. My knees wobble. Bad idea. I sit. God can hear me from the pew.

Jordan sits too and enfolds her arms around herself.

"Stand up," I whisper.

"You're sitting."

"Mommy needs to sit. You can stand."

"I don't want to."

I lace my voice with authority. "Jordan."

She rolls her eyes but stands. Hopefully, no one saw that sassy display.

Mark finally joins us, pecking the top of my head with a kiss and wrapping both children in a side hug before belting out the lyrics in his rich baritone.

His sermon today will be on why God allows suffering. He did that thing where he ran through it with me last night and asked my opinion. He must think himself sneaky with this mind trick, as though he's not preaching solely to me, not truly seeking my advice on whether point one should be point three or if he should use catchier phrasing.

After worship, I get to hear it all a second time. How I should count these hardships all joy. I leave for the restroom and linger at the sink. The soap dispensers are half empty, so I refill them, as well as restock the paper towels. At least they didn't take away my church keys. I head back to the sanctuary but stop to check the coffee bar area first. It could use more cups and sugar packets, which I find in the supply closet. Now there's nothing more for me to do since the welcome desk is technically one of the official duties I've been fired from.

I'm shuffling back to the sanctuary when a woman steps toward me with purpose, arms extended wide. I freeze. She's coming to hug me. Do I know her? Wait, it's Jerry's mom. Ivy. She's practically a stranger, and my body stiffens as she wraps me in an embrace.

But then she says, "I'm so sorry for what you're going through," in my ear, and my defenses melt. My throat tingles. The bridge of my nose burns. And I hang on to this woman whom I don't know well but who has said exactly what I needed to hear. She hugs me tight, holding me together in the church where I've fallen apart. She doesn't say anything more. She doesn't need to.

"Thank you," I say when we finally let go. I swipe at my damp eyes.

"Anytime." Her eyes glisten as well.

When I return to the front row, Jordan is doodling in her notebook instead of taking notes on the sermon. Victor is slouching as if he's watching football on the couch instead of a sermon in church.

I still Jordan's pen with my hand and straighten Victor with a pointed look. I pull out my own notebook and pen.

Mark's voice booms with conviction. "God allows suffering to help us grow in understanding His grace. As it says in 2 Corinthians 12:9, 'My grace is sufficient for you, for my power is made perfect in weakness. Therefore, I will boast all the more gladly about my weaknesses, so that Christ's power may rest on me.'"

My thumb fiddles with the retractable pen lid, pushing it up and down, up and down. What to write? Something. Anything.

I can't walk away from my husband's sermon with a blank page. He'll ask me what I thought in the car. I need some semblance of a nugget of wisdom gleaned.

Mark says, "Everyone please stand as the worship team comes back."

I scribble *Grace in the midst of suffering* and slam my notebook closed. What does that even mean? Hopefully, Mark won't ask me to expound.

I stand. Sway. Sit.

No one will notice, right? Their eyes should be closed.

Mark's prayer barely registers. Suddenly, getting out of the sanctuary, to the car, and to home feels like too much. The magnitude of the amount of steps and time and energy this effort will cost sweeps over me. If only I could lie on the pew and nap first.

A chorus of *Amens* sound around me, followed by the rustle of movement. Deep breath. I can do this.

"Amber." It's obvious by the pinched way she draws my name out that it's Rhonda McMillion.

I brace myself before I turn. "Rhonda, hello."

The slight woman looks as if she stole the drapery clothing from the von Trapp children. The fabric of her green and white print dress looks as stiff as her neutral expression.

"I see there won't be any blankets for the homeless this year. I have to say I'm greatly disappointed."

I nod. "You and me both."

Her frown deepens. "It was a great service to our community."

"I know."

My mind wanders. We can place a pickup order at Theodore's Deli for lunch. Then I won't have to cook. I focus on my menu choices as Rhonda prattles on about her mounting frustration with the elders' decision. I can't focus on this conversation and not succumb to tears. So, I'll probably have a French dip. Perhaps slaw.

"I hate that you let us down." Rhonda's words stall my beverage selection.

"Me?"

"Well, yes. We've always depended on you to be our advocate in these things."

In my musing of deli meats, I missed the fact that a few of Rhonda's cronies have gathered around us, each one's expression is sour. This woman attracts complainers like a garbage can attracts flies. Where's Ivy? I search for her wavy black hair in the sea of people, eager for a reminder of the kindness that exists here. I don't find her, but a few feet away, a group of women laugh, their smiles bright. See? Rhonda and her friends are the exception here, not the rule. And even they must have a heart, right?

"I'm sorry, but I'm going through health issues right now, and the elders—"

"We've heard." Mrs. Lanyard crosses her arms. "A pity."

Only her frown doesn't convey pity. Not in the least.

I put my hands out. "Listen, I'm sure *the elders* will reconsider if one of you volunteers to take on the project." My heavy emphasis on the elders shifts the blame back to where it belongs. "It would be—"

"Can't," Rhonda spits out the word. "I'm far too busy."

Mrs. Lanyard shakes her head. "I would, but I have a full-time job."

The women all talk at once, their excuses melting together.

I smile. Nod. Back away. "I understand."

Where's Mark?

I find him across the sanctuary and catch his eye. I mouth, *Help,* and his lips twitch upward. He pats the man he's been talking to on the back and scurries in my direction, taking my arm. "Time to head out, sweetheart."

As we walk away, I hear someone whisper, "She's a bit melodramatic, isn't she? Do you think she's faking it?"

My steps slow as my ears stretch to hear the reply. "Probably."

My jaw drops. I stumble over Mark's shoe. His grip on my arm tightens. A couple of people gasp. My cheeks flame as I recover my balance.

"I'm alright. Not passing out. Just clumsy."

And, apparently, melodramatic.

"You okay?" Mark whispers in my ear.

"Let's get out of here. Fast."

He calls for Jordan and Victor, and we leave our perfect little church world behind.

~

I step into the coffee shop to find Delaney already sitting at a table. I check my watch. Only ten minutes late, but it's strange to have our roles reversed.

I rush over for a hug. "Sorry to keep you waiting."

"It's fine. I'm glad you could make it." *This time* hangs off the end of her sentence, unsaid, but there just the same.

"I know. Sorry to cancel the last couple of times. I wasn't feeling up to it."

She shrugs. "You don't have to explain."

But explanations and apologies bubble in my gut, belching out anyway, no matter how unwanted. "I feel horrible. I've been exhausted."

Her small smile wobbles. Silence weaves through the space between us. I shift from one foot to the other. What can I say to make this better?

Delaney sputters into the awkwardness. "I ordered you a blonde espresso and a scone."

"Thanks."

We sit. I put my phone on silent and slide it into my purse. She rolls her neck back and forth. Now what?

"How's the business going?" I ask.

Delaney's been building her photography business over the past year. She's moved from giving out freebie shoots to friends and family to growing a legit clientele.

She blows out a breath. "Fine. What's new with you?"

I strive to keep my voice light. "Hmm, let's see. The elders fired me, for one." Delaney's shocked expression makes me feel justified in my outrage. "Jordan got detention and a referral for counseling. Oh, and apparently, several people in the congregation think I'm making up the entire sickness because I'm *melodramatic*." I use air quotes and roll my eyes. It does little to diffuse the bitterness seeping through my tone. "So, yeah, trainwreck." I point at myself.

"You're not a trainwreck." She says this with such conviction that I wait for the rest of her motivational speech, but it doesn't come. Unnatural silence hangs in the air like a thick fog.

I blink as if I can peer through it to find more words. It has never been this way between us. When she still doesn't speak, I do the honors. "Okay, what gives?"

Her mouth twists. She shrugs. "I don't know. What's up with you? You've been different."

Different. I press my lips together. A young barista slides our order in front of us. We thank him, and he retreats.

Delany puts her hand on mine. "You've been pushing me away."

My mouth falls open as my defenses rise. "I have not."

Have I? Okay, I may have been slow at responding to her texts and calls. I wince. A few times I might not have even responded at all. But how do I answer the endless barrage of *How are you*? What's worse, how do I respond when she *doesn't* acknowledge this massive shift in my life?

"You want to pretend like nothing's changed, but everything has. My entire world has been tipped on its head. You invited me to a game night that started at seven. I'm in bed by eight, Delaney, if I get out of my pj's at all. You wanted to go walking in the park—"

"I thought the doctor said gentle exercise is good for you."

"I can't do it! I can't do any of this." I wave a hand in front of me to indicate life in general. It's too much.

She fidgets with her coffee cup. "I'm sorry. I want to be there for you. I just don't know what to do or say."

No one does. What do I need to hear? No clue. Nothing can make this better. Nothing can make this go away.

"Maybe go up for prayer on Sunday. Have you done that?" Hope trails her question.

I take a sip and let the warm liquid settle on my tongue before swallowing. "I haven't. Mark and the twins pray for me daily, but I haven't gone forward at church."

Seems like the pastor's prayers should be enough. There was a time when I thought *my* prayers were enough to move God. *Lord, I don't know what I believe about healing anymore. I know You can heal me, so why haven't You? You care about me, right?* How could a good Father see His child suffering like this and do nothing?

"It couldn't hurt to get extra prayer." She reaches over and squeezes my fingers.

I banish the doubts from my thoughts like cobwebs. I can't allow them to take hold. I'm Mark Prichard's wife. "True. Thank you." I use a napkin to pat my misty eyes. I focus on what I know to be solid and true. "You've always been there for me." Since that fateful Sunday night youth group meeting when we were the last two standing on our dodgeball team, we've always had each other's backs. "I know I can count on you."

Delaney's return smile doesn't reach her eyes.

~

Lily was opening the front door, keys in hand, when Mom's voice halted her.

"You off to class?" Mom rushed around the corner, untucking Oliver from his sling.

"Yep. World History." She took another step forward.

"Do you mind taking Olly? He ate twenty minutes ago. He'll be fine." She slid the sling off her shoulder, holding the infant in one arm. She'd perfected this juggling act over the past few months.

"I can't take him to class."

"Why not? Keep him in the sling, and he won't cause any trouble."

"Because it's *class*. I have to take notes. Pay attention. They don't let babies in there."

"I don't think that's a rule."

"Mom, no." She stared, stunned at the force of the word that had catapulted from her mouth. Did she tell her mother *no*? Had that ever been done before? Could it be?

Mom stared at her as if she, too, wondered if those two little letters had altered earth's axis. She pressed her lips together into a thin line. "Okay."

Air rushed into Lily's lungs. She'd gone against her mother's wishes, and it was okay. *Okay.* Boldness flooded her. In that case …

"I've been looking at transferring to a college in Michigan." The words tumbled out.

Mom's face paled. She still held Oliver in a one-armed grip. He fussed. Jamie headbutted her shin, and she didn't even flinch. She only stared at Lily with unbelief. "What?"

"Valley Creek Bible College in Kalamazoo." She infused confidence into her voice like this was the most logical choice in the world.

"Why?" Mom's voice broke on the word.

All Lily's reasons threatened to break with it. Her tight, hot throat couldn't croak out an answer.

"You want to go to church?" Mom asked, somber and still as Jamie rammed his head into her leg again.

An olive branch. A compromise. "Yes."

Oliver cried. Jana yelled something from the living room. Mom put her hand out to block another blow from Jamie. "I'll need you here next Sunday because Harvy has a sleep study scheduled, but afterward, why don't you start going to church?"

Their smiles met and mingled in the space above the chaos. In the space of shared understanding.

"I will."

Chapter 10

WE HAVE BEEN SCOUTING EVER SINCE. BUT HAVEN'T ACCOMPLISHED ANYTHING. ONLY BURNT AND DESTROYED A GREAT MANY HOUSES AND DESTROYED CONSIDERABLE PROPERTY ... AND I HAVE HEARD NOTHING TODAY BUT THE ... WOMEN BEGGING THE MEN NOT TO BURN THEIR HOUSES ... THIS IS A HARD WAY OF TAKING REVENGE, BUT IT IS THE ONLY WAY TO STOP SUCH PROCEEDINGS.

PRIVATE BENJAMIN GUFFEY
EIGHTEENTH MISSOURI VOLUNTEER INFANTRY

March 18, 1862
Macon, Missouri

Willow stroked Rustic's mane, thankful to finally be reunited with the men. Drilling had resumed, and those with horses got to drill upon them while those without had to drill on foot. Only about a third of the men had horses, and those who'd worked the horse camp got first choice. Hubert sat next to her upon Gallant. She quite enjoyed viewing Milo from upon her steed. *Sergeant* Forrester didn't seem high and mighty on the ground below her. It rankled her to no end that he'd advanced in ranks, yet again, while she'd been at Camp Defiance. She had catching up to do. But no matter. She'd do it.

The captain walked in front of their perfectly aligned row. "Men, as many of you as have horses will be starting on a scout tomorrow. Take your forty rounds of cartridges, your haversack, your canteen, and four days of provisions."

Excitement flowed through her. Her first scout! This was the adventure she'd been waiting for.

Guerrillas terrorized the countryside: shooting trains, burning railroad bridges, cutting telegraph wires, pillaging, and torching the houses of Union sympathizers to the ground. They had to find those guerrillas, or at least the people who supported them and sustained their activity in the area, and arrest them.

Fighting the Confederate army was one thing. It was quite another to fight an irregular army of people who fought close to home using the brush as cover and who followed no rules. Unpredictable and unprincipled, these dangerous men had to be stopped. Even if part of her was unsure about the role of states' rights in this whole mess of war, no one could live in peace where terror reigned. For the first time since Milo had rerouted them to Warsaw and the Union army, it was clear what she was fighting for.

Thirty-four soldiers from her company set out to headquarters where other scouts from other companies had gathered. After receiving orders, she set off with her squad for a house in the country where the owners were suspected of harboring guerrillas.

The closer they came to their destination, the more sober the men grew. The merriment that had accompanied them at camp dissipated with each noise emanating from the woods. At any moment, guerrillas could ambush them. At any second, a well-placed bullet could fly from the darkness and sink one of them to the ground. Each tree they passed harbored secrets.

Willow's senses stood on high alert. They trod on enemy ground, but this was not an enemy they could see. She would have to hear these fighters like she heard lost horses. Sense them with the hair on her arms. Her shoulders knotted with tension. No longer were they drilling and playing at bayonet matches. These were not words on the page of some book. Here she was, a soldier in the US Army. This was her chance to finally prove her mettle.

They approached the house, and Willow's throat burned at how it reminded her of home. The modest porch dipped a smidgen in the center. Rickety shutters needed fresh paint. It bespoke humility, but she didn't have to look far to see the marks of a hard-working family. The tidy yard. Remnants of a garden on the side reminded her of harvesting vegetables with Ma. The whinnying of a horse directed her attention toward a barn. It stood proudly by acres of farmland. This was a family much like her own in a countryside not far from home.

Pence dismounted and took off his hat. "Remember, we are to be civil and retrieve as much information as possible."

They followed Pence to the front door. Willow hung toward the back, half expecting Pa to throw the door open and holler about the racket. Could she do this? Interrogate? Intimidate? She squared her shoulders. She must.

The gray-headed man who cracked the door open peered at each of them with wary eyes. "How can I help you, gentlemen?" His voice lacked even a trace of welcome.

"We'd like to discuss some things with you. Over dinner, perhaps? My men are famished."

A creak of the floorboard betrayed his hesitation as he shifted his stance. No doubt weighing his options. If they were indeed secessionists—secesh—allowing Union soldiers in not only aided their enemy but made them prime targets for guerrilla retaliation. If they refused … well, the blackened homes and barns they'd passed on their way told the story.

A muscle in the man's jaw twitched. "Come in."

A female voice spilled out of the house. "Butch, who is it? Who's there?" A woman appeared in the doorway with dark hair, dark eyes, dark dress billowing like a storm cloud.

"Unionists?" She folded her arms across her chest. "Oh no. They are *not* welcome here."

Butch shot her a pointed look. "Goldie, I told these men to come inside."

"You what? I'll not have their filthy hands all over my things. Turn them away."

"If you please, ma'am—" Pence leaned forward in a polite bow.

"Do not address me, *sir*." The word snaked out in a hiss. She spun to face her husband. "I'll not abide this. If you let these men inside our home, I won't stay."

His brow furrowed. "Where will you go?"

"To my sister's. To a neighbor's. It doesn't matter." Her red face pinched tight. "I'd rather sleep in the swamp than cook a lick of food for the likes of those nasty, stinking, black Republicans." She stormed back inside.

The men looked at each other as banging reverberated from the interior of the house. Butch's mouth formed a tight line. He winced at each thunderous sound. Finally, another door slammed, and Goldie bustled through the backyard, making for the road and leaving the men a wide berth.

"Do you, uh"—Pence cast a sidelong glance toward the raging woman—"need to see to your wife?"

He pushed out a sigh, shoulders slumped. "She'll be fine. Her sister lives down the way." He gestured inside. "Come on in."

The soldiers shuffled past him through the door. Willow couldn't help but look him in the eye when her turn came. Resignation competed with rebellion in his gaze. If he could one-up them without suffering punishment for it, he likely would. She tilted her chin in a dare. Two could play that game.

"There's potato soup simmering on the stove." Butch shouldered past the line of men waiting in the hallway and led them into the kitchen. "Reckon I can dish y'all up some. We got bread and peaches. Not much else."

"That'll do nicely." Pence settled into a kitchen chair. Several men followed suit while the others hovered around, gazes ever shifting from the front door to the back. Willow's ears remained alert. No tellin' what bushwhackers were in the area ready to teach Unionists a lesson.

Butch took his time dolling small portions of soup to each man, handing them over with a frown and furrowed brow. "What brings you to my home, gentlemen?"

The men took small sips, miniscule bites, their hunger strangled by the tension in the room.

Pence took a sip of his soup before leaning forward and pinning the man with his gaze. "We've heard reports of guerrilla activity in the area. We need to know who's sustaining these irregulars. Where are they getting food? Clothing? Ammunition?"

Butch's eyebrow arched. "You suppose I know?"

"Don't you?"

"I stay out of the entire mess."

Pence stood and wandered to the pot of soup. He picked up the wooden spoon and stirred. "You're telling me your wife normally makes a pot of soup this large for merely the two of you?"

He shrugged. "Family stops by on occasion."

"Family?" Pence smirked. "An uncle or brother, perhaps? A guerrilla?"

Willow chewed a bite of bread. It made slow work of traveling down her throat.

Butch's Adam's apple bobbed. His voice came out hard. "Certainly not."

Pence turned on his heel. "Search the place."

Bowls clanked to the table in response as soldiers abandoned their meals to do his bidding. Willow followed Griffen upstairs but went left instead of right. A bedroom. She stripped the quilt from the bed, riffled through the chest and bureau. Nothing of consequence. She only found slippers under the bed.

She turned to leave the room when a flash of red from under the mattress caught her eye. She tugged at it to reveal a fold of fabric. She yanked it free and gasped. A Confederate flag. She bunched it in her fists and scrambled down the stairs to show her commander.

When Pence saw it, his eyes blazed with rage. Butch's widened in fear.

"Let's go, men," Pence called. "We've seen all we need to see here."

They filed out of the house and mounted their horses.

Butch ran after them. "I don't know where that came from. I swear."

They trotted a few paces before Pence gave the order. "Burn it."

Willow didn't light a torch. She didn't douse the house in flames. Plenty of other men were eager to beat her to the task. Still, her stomach sank as she watched Butch crumple in front of his home. She was the reason that family—that hardworking family much like her own—lost their home today. If not for her …

Shots rang out from the road. Willow flinched. Ducked. Frantically looked around.

"It's secesh. Go after them."

She was off, Rustic's hooves stirring dust. Her heart pounded. Her ears rang. A flash of blue disappeared into the brush. Blue? She shook her head to dislodge the confusion. Yes, they'd said guerrillas often wore stolen Union uniform coats to fuddle their enemies.

She pulled out her pistol, loaded, and cocked it. Hand only slightly trembling, she steered Rustic into the woods. No sign of the secesh anywhere. She stilled her horse, her body, her mind. There. The slightest rustle deep in and to her right. She followed the sound and found a horse with no rider. She stopped again and listened. A shallow intake of breath.

There he was, pressed behind an oak trunk. No weapon in hand. Had he run out of ammunition or lost it along the way?

She aimed her pistol. "You're whipped. Best come with me."

His face twisted, and anger blazed in his expression, but he didn't resist as she led him to the road where the rest of the regiment waited with two other prisoners.

"Great job, Forrester." She warmed under Pence's praise. "You're a mighty fine soldier."

"Thank you, sir."

"You must be aiming for promotion." He winked.

She attempted a smile. "I might be."

As they turned to head back to camp with three prisoners in tow, the odor of smoke lingered in her nostrils, and her pulse continued to race. She took deep breaths and told herself the danger had passed, but her body refused to believe her.

Her body told a different story.

~

May 20, 1862

Cyrus rode toward home; the slaves he'd hired out resting comfortably in the wagon bed. He wiped the sweat from his brow with his handkerchief. An hour 'til noon and already sweltering. What did that say 'bout the rest of the summer? He flicked the reins so old Buckeye would shimmy a mite faster. Even with the hired help, they'd have to hustle to get the ripe fruit harvested before it went to rot. With no children to help any longer, the burden fell heavy upon his shoulders.

Buckeye's ears perked at a sound in the distance. Cyrus strained to hear. Was that a woman's scream? He paused, and it came again. For certain, a female's cry for help. And it sounded like—no, it couldn't be—but was it Adelaide?

He tapped Buckeye's hindquarters to spur the horse to a gallop. They lurched forward for a stride, then lashed back with a snap. He spun around. The blasted wheel had gotten lodged in a tree root.

The woman's voice sounded louder now, fearful and incessant. Cyrus slid from his horse and broke into a run. He took the quickest route—through the ankle-deep creek, over the fallen oak, and through the bend of poplars—until he rounded his house from the back. Breath heaving and chest burning, he skidded to a halt at the blood-curdling sight.

Three Union soldiers stood on his front lawn around a sloppily constructed campfire. One held Adelaide from the back around the waist, dangling her mere inches above ground. She flailed and slapped at him, but he merely laughed. Another man bent near the fire with a shovel. What was he doing?

Cyrus sucked in a breath as realization dawned. The second man dug hot coals from the fire while the first man dangled Adelaide above them.

"Where do you keep your money, pretty lady?" The coal shoveler sneered.

"We don't have any. No one has any since this war ripped everything from us." She kicked and twisted.

"Care to try again?" The first man lowered her more, and her cry of pain rent the air around them.

Dirty, rotten scoundrels! Cyrus sprung into action. He rounded the house and crept through the back door, closing it quietly. He went straight for the gun he kept on the mantle, stepping over pots and broken plates, spilled flour and beans. Blast. The mantle stood bare. Them blasted Yanks must have stolen his rifle.

Watching for the creaky floorboard in the hall, he rushed for his bedroom. Surely, they hadn't found his pistol. He made quick work of unlatching the trunk at the foot of the bed and fumbling with the hidden compartment at the bottom. There.

The cold metal felt satisfying against the sizzling rage inside him. He loaded and cocked his weapon, then made his way outside where the Yankees continued their tirade.

"Liar. We know you're well-off. Give us what you're hiding, and no one gets hurt. Deny us and ..." The wretch put his hand on Adelaide's thigh.

She kicked, but he dodged.

Searing hot loathing billowed from within Cyrus, and he barreled out of the front door while releasing a rebel yell that rivaled any he had heard.

The Yanks startled and dropped Adelaide onto the coals, then fumbled for their guns.

She yowled in pain but limped off toward the line of trees.

Cyrus shot, grazing the shovel-man's arm. He shot again, barely missing the other Yank's foot. He ducked behind the rocker as bullets came flying. Glass shattered behind him. He aimed again and, this time, hit his mark. The man fell to the ground, grabbing his leg.

"Let's get out of here." The other Yank helped his buddy up, and they stumbled off, shooting behind them as they went.

When the sound of bullets faded, Cyrus ran to Adelaide, who sat with her back against a tree, studying her feet.

"Are you okay?" He dropped down and cradled her feet in his lap. Blisters were already starting to form. He was no good at doctorin'. What did they need? Bandages? Salve?

"You shouldn't have done that." The fight that had possessed her as she'd hit and kicked and squirmed seemed to have drained from her.

"Done what?"

"The rebel yell. So much for proclaiming neutrality."

He scoffed. "Lot of good it did us anyhow."

"We'll be branded as Rebels now." She sighed. "Word will spread."

"Addy," he said while stroking her cheek, "we're already terrorized as if we were. At least in joining the secesh, we'll be in good company and avoid retaliation from that side." His gaze swept the horizon. "I wanted to remain in the Union, but not like this. Not when Union men burn our neighbors' barns and fine our towns for suspected guerrilla activity. Not when they act like savages. In endeavorin' to root out the bushwhackers, they've destroyed our state. They killed our children." His hand clenched into a fist.

"You don't know that."

"Nah." He shifted his jaw. "I know it." When word reached him that Red Legs had chanced upon a company of young people from the area, shot them, threw them in a barn, and burned it, he'd known his children had been among them. They'd never been heard from again, and their bodies never recovered. How could Addy remain in denial? Everything had changed for him that morning. He'd tried to go on as normal, but regrets plagued him. Now, the shattered window mocked him. No use trying to avoid the fight. It was time to get right in the middle of it.

Her fingers found his and intertwined. "You came back just in time." A hint of a smile crested her face, weary yet beautiful.

"Buckeye and I heard you cryin' out from the road."

"Where is Buckeye? And them slaves you hired out?"

"Left them in the wagon when the wheel got stuck. I'll have to go fetch 'em."

Her smile faded. "Them Yanks went that direction. I doubt there will be much of anything to retrieve when you get there."

His shoulders stooped. Smart woman. Yanks and Jayhawkers alike saw it fit to steal slaves from Southerners. They wouldn't think twice about swiping a horse either. He had another horse—Dixie—but it'd be mighty hard to manage the farm without Buckeye too. Yet another reason why revenge seemed the sweetest option.

Adelaide eyed the direction the soldiers had disappeared. "They'll be back, you know."

He squeezed her hand. "We'll be ready."

~

June 1, 1862

Willow emerged from her Sibley tent into a dense fog. It covered the horizon with a dampness that soaked into her bones and sank her spirits. After marching twenty or more miles a day over dusty roads through Boonville and Independence, those who had the best horses were ordered to Lexington with some prisoners.

Lexington.

The city of the great battle last September. They'd talked to a handful of citizens last night who swore the Rebels hauled at least a thousand of their own soldiers' bodies down the river the last night of the battle. They claimed those bodies were mutilated and sank to the bottom, but also that surviving soldiers buried the dead in secret mass graves. All this to keep the true number killed in this battle a secret. The Confederates reported one hundred casualties, while the Union recorded 1,774. Willow shivered. Was it true? It could be true. Heaven knew humans were capable of such.

Milo stepped beside her and stretched. "Beautiful day, isn't it?"

She chortled. After she'd returned from her first scouting mission, she'd advocated for Milo to receive a horse. It was wrong for a higher-ranking officer to have confiscated Gallant just because he was a finer horse than most. She never wanted to go on a mission without Milo again. They were family, and they had each other's backs. The ever-pressing fear something awful was about to happen chased her. Milo's presence comforted her.

"Let's go walk around the fortifications."

She shrugged. As good of a way to pass the time as any.

They walked about in the misty morning, exploring breastworks and entrenchments, the boarding house and remnants of the college building. Damaged houses filled the city. Beautiful buildings marred by cannonball holes punctuated the landscape.

They meandered toward the entrenchments near where the home guards were stationed on the side toward the river.

"What's that?" Willow pointed to a peculiar-looking mound.

Milo squatted and examined the area. "I don't know."

He picked up a discarded shard of wood and began digging. The memory of him as a boy digging a trench in the soft earth behind their home caught her breath. Back then, they'd been inseparable and always covered in dirt.

The deep timbre of his grown-up voice shook her from the childhood memory. "Looks like someone is buried here."

"What?" She grimaced. "Leave it alone."

But he continued to dig. "I have to know whose side they were on. What army."

She wrapped her arms around herself and peeked at his progress. He'd dug down eighteen inches or so. A putrid smell arose, and she turned her head away.

When he cursed, she glanced back to see an arm and a hand that looked as if it belonged to a live person. She squeezed her eyes together. She couldn't watch any longer. "Milo, stop." But he didn't.

"There's got to be twenty-five or thirty people thrown in this hole. People and … a horse. Rebs. What do you know? The rumors must be true."

Bile rose in her stomach, but the tears pricking her eyes were a surprise. A tight, hot ball choked her throat. The world around her tilted, and she swayed.

"Willow? Are you okay?" Milo's arm supported her elbow. She leaned heavily against him.

"I'm fine," she said, but it came out as a slur. Her knees buckled.

"Whoa." Milo lowered her to a sitting position and kept his arm around her shoulders. "You're woozy. Take a minute to get your bearings."

She squinted. Bit the inside of her cheek. Willed herself to get it together. What was wrong with her? Soldiers did not get faint at the sight of death. Her voice trembled when she spoke. "I don't know wh-what happened."

"It's okay," he said, but his furrowed brow betrayed him. "Here, have a drink." He handed her his canteen.

She gulped cool liquid, then shook her head. "It's not okay."

"Sure it is."

"No. I'm no soldier acting like this." She wiped a hand over her clammy forehead.

"Nonsense. Don't you remember what Joan of Arc did the first time she saw battle?"

Her eyes stung again. She blinked rapidly. "She cried."

"She *wept*. Your courageous hero wept when she saw the destruction of war. Your compassion doesn't make you weak."

She chanced a glance over at the burial trench. Her heart stung at the sight of it. Then she looked around them. "No one saw, right?" And thankfully no one was in earshot to have heard him use her real name.

He chuckled. "Guess this fog is good for something." He bumped her shoulder. "You'll get used to it. Every soldier has a hard time the first time they see death. You won't react that way next time."

If only she could be sure.

~

June 30, 1862
Independence, Missouri

Since rejoining the regiment, Willow never received letters at mail call. She'd never written to Ma. What could she say? She might write after she accomplished something big— something noteworthy—but the only thing she'd accomplished was being responsible for burning a hardworking family's home and bringing in a guerrilla as a prisoner. Somehow that didn't seem worth bragging to her parents about.

Milo received letters from Greta regularly. She enjoyed watching his cheeks blush as he read them, then teasing him about it later. Today, though, as he read his letter, the corners of his mouth didn't lift. Instead, his face crumpled, and his shoulders shook.

She catapulted to her feet. "What's wrong?"

His watery gaze met hers, and her heart dropped. He was crying? Milo never cried.

After taking a shaky breath, he said, "Greta and her family fled for their lives."

She put a hand to her heart, then promptly dropped it. Too feminine. "Is she all right?"

He nodded. "Yes, but—" He waved the letter frantically. "Ma and Pa … Greta says she heard … she heard they were shot."

"Shot?" The word pummeled her. She doubled over. "Who?"

"I don't know. She doesn't know. Guerrillas and Unionists are both looting, killing, and burning homesteads left and right. She doesn't think there's anyone left in the area. Everyone's been burned out, like them, or killed."

Her stomach roiled. She stepped to her left and retched in the bushes. Her parents gone? Milo really was the only one she had in the world. No more worrying about trying to impress them. Earning Pa's affection was now officially impossible. That should free her, shouldn't it? He never cared about her. Why should she mourn his passing? But the ache of what would never be throbbed like the agony of a missing appendage. There was an empty hole where a father's love should be.

Chapter 11

ONE OF THE HARDEST THINGS ABOUT BEING ILL WITH A POORLY UNDERSTOOD DISEASE IS THAT MOST PEOPLE FIND WHAT YOU'RE GOING THROUGH INCOMPREHENSIBLE—IF THEY EVEN BELIEVE YOU ARE GOING THROUGH IT. IN YOUR LONELINESS ... YOU WANT TO BE UNDERSTOOD IN A WAY THAT YOU CAN'T BE.
FROM *THE INVISIBLE KINGDOM; REIMAGINING CHRONIC ILLNESS* BY MEGHAN O'ROURKE

Modern Day

I'm leaning heavily on the grocery cart, trying to decide between strawberry and blueberry yogurt, when Kelly Loren calls my name. I turn to see her pushing her cart in my direction. If only I could melt into the floor. I do not have the energy for this.

"Amber, so nice to see you!" Her magenta jumpsuit glares overbright under the fluorescent lights.

My mind trips over itself for something complimentary to say that wouldn't be a lie. My gaze lands on her cute purple flats. "Nice shoes."

She's nearly glowing. "Thanks. There's a sale going on at Nordstroms. You should check it out."

Nordstroms? Not likely. It'd have to be one steep sale.

She leans awkwardly close and inspects my necklace. "You're wearing that cardinal one again. I noticed it at the picnic but forgot to comment. It's gorgeous. Looks vintage."

I caress the pendant as if it were a mood ring. "My mother gave it to me when I was a girl. I don't know why—" I stop myself before blabbing to Kelly my mixed feelings about the jewelry. How it brings back bad memories and good ones jumbled so tightly in knots I'll likely never untangle them. How at times, I could fling it off a cliff for the pain it represents, and other times, I clutch it in a desperate white-knuckle grasp. My mother. Everything involving my mother is complicated.

When I say nothing more, Kelly gives me the once-over, and her smile dissipates. "Oh, Amber. I heard about your … illness. How are you holding up?"

What has she heard? I study her face. Does she think this is an act? "It's been difficult, but I'm hanging in there." A safe enough answer. Not at all melodramatic.

"Sometimes we have to wonder why the Good Lord allows these things in our lives." She places a hand across her heart.

I nod, grab the blueberry yogurt, and place it in the cart.

"It could be a test of your faith, to prove it purer than gold."

My head continues to bob as I push the cart forward toward the milk and eggs.

Kelly keeps pace with me. "I want you to know, I don't for one minute think it's all in your head."

I pause. All in my head?

My expression must register my confusion because she waves a hand in front of her face. "Ridiculous rumors. You know how people can be."

"All in my head?" Panic flips my stomach.

"They probably think that because mental illness runs in your family, but I know it isn't true."

I grasp her hand. "I have test results to prove it. I'm not … I'm not crazy."

"Oh, honey, you don't have to convince me." Her smile radiates warmth.

Melodramatic. Mentally ill. What else are people saying?

My gaze drops to our clutched hands and my white knuckles. I take a deep breath and release my grip. I force myself to continue moving down the aisle. It doesn't matter what other people think. God knows the truth. Okay, it *shouldn't* matter what other people think. Why do I care?

Lord, help me not to care.

Kelly keeps step with me. "You know, I listened to a phenomenal sermon on YouTube the other day on the Thirty-eighth Psalm. So enlightening. It really made me think."

I rack my brain. Psalm 38. Psalm 38. I might be a pastor's wife, but that doesn't mean I have the entire Bible memorized. "I'm afraid I've forgotten what that particular psalm is about."

"Oh, yes. It's the one that says something like, 'There is no health in my bones because of my sin.' The preacher talked about the importance of searching our hearts for hidden sin when we face sickness and trials. I can forward you the link."

I gape at her. The woman thinks I'm sick because I have hidden sin in my life? I barely manage to croak out a reply. "There's no need."

Her expression remains kind as she pats my arm. "Of course. I'm sure your husband has already explored this possibility with you." She moves her hand to cover her heart. "I just love Pastor Prichard. Such a godly leader."

I blink back at her. No reply surfaces. We stare at each other for an uncomfortable minute before I find words. "If you'll excuse me," I say while gesturing to my cart, "I have to finish shopping before school lets out."

"Of course." She leans in for an awkward pat-your-back hug. "See you Sunday."

Only, I don't have to wait until Sunday. She's in every aisle. Hovering. Peeking at me over cereal boxes. It's as if she's a detective out to decipher what Amber Prichard's hidden sin might be. She's looking for clues. I know it.

Now that it's too late, responses bubble to mind. All the things I could have said instead of allowing shame to freeze my tongue. *Yes, Mark is a godly man and a* compassionate *husband.* Cue a lifted brow. Or maybe *Mark's been so busy helping me he hasn't had time to judge me.* If only I had the courage for such snark. The one that burns hot like lava on my tongue is *Does your father have Alzheimer's because of hidden sin in his life?* Wouldn't that give the congregation something to gossip about? The preacher's wife went off on poor Kelly Loren in the grocery store. I swallow the fire. She didn't mean anything by it. She was only trying to help. She's my friend. Why does that make it hurt worse?

By the time I throw the last items in the cart, my hands are shaking. The store's fluorescent lights glare at me. Why is the store so crowded? So loud? My knees wobble.

Oh no. Not here. Not now.

The shelves tilt downward.

The last thing I see before I collapse in aisle three is Kelly Loren's purple flats.

~

The hospital visit this time is far less dramatic. Once given my diagnosis, they administer IV fluids and send me on my way. I remember the ambulance ride this time. Through every bump and jolt, the medical bill is the only thing on my mind.

On the drive home, Mark forbids me from taking any more shopping trips for the foreseeable future. That's not feasible, but I haven't the strength to argue. I lay my head on the window and start to drift off.

"I didn't tell the children. About your episode, I mean."

"Good." I yawn. It's better they don't know I fainted in the grocery store, but someone's bound to tell them. Kelly's daughter is in their Sunday school class. They'll find out. Again, it would take too much energy to speak these words. I let them die inside.

At home, I crawl into bed and sleep the rest of that day and all the next. I don't ask who's doing carpool duty or making dinner. I'm barely aware of Chipper lying at my feet.

By day three, I emerge from the weighted blanket of exhaustion and check my phone. There's a text from Delaney. *You were in the hospital and didn't tell me? Come on, now.*

How'd she find out? My finger hovers over my phone keys, and I scramble for an excuse. I should have told her, but when I got home, all I wanted to do was sleep. I've overused the exhaustion excuse, but it's all I've got. My brain hurts from trying to dig up anything else. Maybe I'll think of something later.

I put off replying and instead scroll through the online POTS support groups, then check my email. Jordan's teacher sent a message asking for volunteers for the fall party coming up. *Thank You, God, for this sense of normalcy.* I've lost all the ministries I care about, but I have this. The school can't fire me from being there for the twins.

A twinge of accusation circles the periphery of my thought. I asked God not to take away my ministry at church, and He didn't answer that prayer. He hasn't seemed to answer any of my prayers lately. Or even any prayers *for* me. What's going on?

"Where are You, Lord?" I whisper as I position my pillow and prop myself into a sitting position. "Why can't I feel You? Are You listening? Have You forgotten about me?"

I hear nothing in return, not that I expected to. I'm growing used to His silence now.

I send an email reply that I'll man the craft station, as always. I haven't received anything from Victor's teacher but go ahead and email her the same thing. I browse Pinterest for ideas. Both teachers reply they're thrilled to have me participate, and Jordan's asks if I'd like to coordinate the party. I reply, *Sure,* while plodding into the kitchen. See? I'm still a good mother.

"You're up." Mark looks from where he's reading his Bible at the kitchen table.

"Yep."

"Feeling better? Rested?" He comes to me, eyes bright with anticipation.

"Yes."

His body relaxes as he embraces me. "Good, because I've already made frozen pizza and fish sticks, so I've exhausted my culinary expertise."

I chuckle. "I'll put chicken in the instant pot for tonight."

He kisses the top of my head. His cologne surrounds me with comfort.

The microwave clock catches my attention. "Uh-oh. I need to get the twins."

His arms tighten around me. "No, you don't. Lisa Ganset is bringing them home. She got them yesterday too. I didn't want to leave you alone. Just in case."

I turn. Put my hands on his chest. "You didn't go to the office?"

"No. Wanted to make sure you were okay."

I frown. "I'm fine. What about all your pastoral duties?"

"You're most important." He looks into my eyes, and I know it's true. Next to God, I'm number one to him. Have been from the moment we said our vows. The bags under his eyes tell what that allegiance is costing him. But if this is true, how could he have thrown me under a bus? Why didn't he stand up for me with the elders? I ignore the twinge in my chest and push my reservations under what I want to believe.

"Honey, please. Don't neglect others on account of me. That will crush me. You know it will. If someone is hurting and going without the comfort of a pastor because of me …" I shudder. "I can't stand the thought of it."

He doesn't agree—why won't he agree?—only says, "I love you."

He moves to the cabinet, pulls down a tall glass, and fills it with water. He hands it to me with a smile.

A few minutes later, the twins barrel in. My heart leaps at the sound of their voices. I didn't realize how much I'd missed them. We thank Lisa Ganset profusely.

"Anytime," she says. "They're a delight."

Victor chatters about an epic basketball game in PE class and how he made the winning shot. I wrap him in a hug and tousle his hair.

"Congrats."

Jordan quiets when she sees me. I tuck hair behind her ears and hug her as well, but her shoulders stiffen at my touch. I try not to let her see how it bothers me.

"Guess what." I force cheer into my tone.

Jordan eyes me warily. "What?"

"I'm coordinating your class's fall party this year. I thought you could help me find fun ideas."

Her head drops. She steps back.

"What's wrong?" I try to catch her eye, but her gaze flitters around like a butterfly.

When she speaks, her voice is watery. Tumultuous. "Could you not. Please?"

"Not what?"

"Not do my party."

Now it's my turn to take a step back. "Why?"

She shakes her head as her eyes well with tears. Then she drops her backpack on the kitchen floor and runs off. The clomp of footsteps on the stairs tells me she's headed to her room. I stare at Mark. What just happened?

He sighs. "I'll talk to her."

He turns to leave, and Victor and I are left in the kitchen. He grabs a Gatorade from the fridge. "You can run my class party if you want." Then he's out the back door, soccer ball in tow, Chipper at his heels.

~

On Sunday, I gather my nerve and file into the prayer line at the end of service. I pick at my cuticles while I wait. Hopefully, no one notices how my hip leans against the wall for support. My mouth goes dry when I'm next in line and Kelly Loren's face pops into view. I cannot go to her for prayer. I will die. *Please, God.* I beg. *Don't let me get her. Anyone but her.*

There are three other prayer partners I could be paired with. Cole's wife, Pricilla, is the best option. Betty and Mary Sue are fine. I watch each one as they entreat heaven for the person in front of them. Who has the most clout with the Almighty? Until recently, I would have thought I'd make the A-list. Now? Who knows anymore?

My entire body relaxes when an elderly woman with a fist full of tissues shuffles away from Pricilla and she motions me forward.

Pricilla takes my hands in her own. Compassion melts off her onto me. "Oh, Amber. I'm so glad you came today. Would you rather sit?"

Before I can answer, she pulls over two chairs. Blessed woman. We sit.

"Is there anything specific you want me to pray for? Other than healing, of course?"

A sniffle helps me hold it together as I pour out my heart. "I feel like my body is against me. It's sabotaging my life. I have all these things I want to do—need to do—for the Lord, but I can't. My muscles ache. I'm exhausted. I can barely walk ten feet without needing to rest. Why is this happening? Haven't I been a faithful servant?"

Deep lines groove Pricilla's forehead as she nods. "Oh, sweetheart. You know what you need?"

Right about now, the answer is a nap. I've been awake for four hours, and I could sleep for three. Of course, she won't say that. She'll say something uber spiritual about resting in the Lord or waiting on Him. I nod so she'll get on with it and pray.

"You need more faith."

I freeze mid-nod. What did she say?

"The Bible says if we resist the devil, he will flee from us. Isn't that right? Well, girl, you'd better get resisting. Jesus tells us that we will be healed according to our faith." She pats me on the knee.

I stare at the spot she touched. It's cold. "So, you're saying this is happening because—"

She waves a hand in between us. "I don't know why it started, but I have a pretty good idea why it's continuing. You're allowing it, dear. Now, lift your head high, tell the devil to scram and get on with your life."

I twist my fingers in my lap. "You make it seem simple."

"Don't make it complicated." Her smile boasts confidence. "Now, let's pray."

We bow our heads. My mind reels. I lack faith? Is it true?

"Father, I ask You right now to forgive Amber for her lack of faith in You. Cover her sin and wash her clean …"

The rest of her prayer fades as I try to picture myself at Jesus's feet begging for forgiveness. It doesn't compute. What have I done wrong? As far as I'm concerned, my autonomic nervous system has wronged me.

She ends the prayer, then says, "Play worship music in the car. It will help bolster your faith." She grins like she's unleashed a great secret. I look at her in much the same way I viewed the doctor when he told me to simply drink more water to manage this condition. Worship music already flows throughout our home from morning until night, but maybe that's not enough. Perhaps God only heals people who play it in their car too. An extra hour a day could be the secret to ridding my life of this awful disease. Sorry, *syndrome*.

I walk away dazed.

Ivy steps in my path and places a hand on my arm, bending to meet my gaze. "Amber, are you okay?"

I offer a weak smile and nod, then sidestep her. I can't talk to anyone else right now. It's as if dirt coats my arms and legs. It's visible, isn't it? This grime that marks me as guilty. Sinful. Anyone who looks at me can tell that somehow, someway, this is my fault.

I go to text Delaney that I took her advice and it ended badly, but when a string of her messages I never replied to pops up, I hesitate. I'm not in the right frame of mind to communicate right now anyway. Sometime soon I'll set another coffee date to relay this nightmare.

I sigh and close out of the screen.

~

I bury myself under the plush down comforter for far longer than a Sunday nap allows. I should get up. The crisp autumn air begs me to enjoy apple cider on the porch swing as Mark kicks the ball around with Victor and Jordan gathers sticks for our next family bonfire. Last year around this time, we went apple picking. That picture perfect day is emblazoned in my memory. If only I could drag myself out of bed, we could go on another excursion. Laugh together. Make memories.

I groan and roll over, right into my cocoon. A memory of what? Mommy passing out in the orchard? Paramedics racing past tractors pulling gawking children on hayrides? That would be one for the scrapbook.

The medicine isn't working. Not like I'd hoped. They are not the magic beans that restore my previous glory. Is there no bouncing back from this? I look forward into a dark future, a tunnel of utter exhaustion. Helplessness presses at every corner inside of me, looking for a way out of this trapped existence. *Lord, help!*

I need to start planning the gala. There are a ton of logistics to finagle—venue, catering, gift baskets for each foster and adoptive family, sponsors—and time is running short. How on earth am I going to pull this off? And without church backing? Mark has no clue of my plans, and it has to stay that way, at least until this train is too far down the tracks for him to halt it. Good thing I can count on Delaney to run the photo booth. I bite my lip. I *can* count on her, right?

"I can do all things through Christ who strengthens me." I whisper this—my life verse—into the quiet room, but it fails to bolster me like before. Maybe because doubt clouds the edges. I used to believe this, but now it seems there are many things I can't do. Surely, He'll strengthen me for this monumental, righteous, generous task, though. Right? He cares about the foster care children even more than I do. He knows how much the yearly gala means to these families. He won't let them down.

Lord, please don't let them down. Don't let me down.

I look to the ceiling as if His reply will appear there. The verdict is out on whether He's heard this request and will answer.

Instrumental hymns play quietly in the background. Maybe He's not listening because it's not the right type of music or because I haven't said the right words. Perhaps He's forgotten about me altogether.

I press the heels of my palms onto my burning eyes. I know better. "God loves me. He loves me. He loves me." I whisper these words into the silence, but they bounce off the walls. If they're true, why do I feel so alone?

Pain sears my heart. I can't take it. Distraction. I need a distraction. I fumble for my phone and mindlessly scroll through social media. I heart the happy families and beaming selfies. Each press of my thumb leaves me emptier inside. Everyone else is okay, and I am not. I'm most definitely not okay.

I pass a picture, and my chest hitches. I page back to see Delaney's bleach-blonde hair and gleaming white teeth in a brilliant smile. One arm is draped around Rachel Fillibrand. The other around Holly Grant The caption reads *Celebrating a huge milestone for my business: a contract with B&K Studios! This calls for a night on the town with my two besties!*

I rub my eyes, then read the words again. Besties? Rachel and Holly? They're mutual friends of ours, but for nearly twenty years, Delaney and I have been inseparable. Rachel and Holly revolved on the outskirts. And now? Clearly, they've pushed me to the side. Left me behind. Delaney got a big contract and didn't tell me? No. It can't be true.

I search through my texts. I must have missed it. She wouldn't have neglected to inform me of something so major.

But the last text conversation between us—one where I actually replied—stares back at me, incriminating.

> Delaney: *Feel up to a coffee date this morning?*
> Me: *Too tired.*
> Delaney: *That's the point of coffee.*
> Me: *Sorry. Can't today.*

Reality slices through me like a sword.

She's given up on me.

I canceled one too many times, and now she's moved on. On to better friends who can keep their word and enjoy themselves. Friends who are probably full of faith and praise and positivity. People who aren't a jumbled mess.

I drop my phone and burrow into the pillow as if that could block out the raging voice of accusation.

She's not the only one who's given up on me.

God has too.

~

Lily ducked her head and pretended to scan the history text. As if medieval France was the most fascinating thing she'd ever considered. The tips of her ears were as hot as an oven. Matt Juper had caught her staring. How mortifying. She should throw herself at him while she was at it. *Ugh.*

The professor finished conversing with a student and stood to full height in front of the class. Lecture time. She laced her fingers together and gave them a good stretch before grabbing her pen and reading her notebook. All around her, laptop keys clicked, and screens glowed to life. Yep, she was a dinosaur using pen and paper in this digital age. She blamed it on Mom, on her old-school homeschool methods. Paper packets always. Limited screen time. No keyboarding training until ninth grade. Mom would argue she was better for it, and her college grades certainly weren't suffering. But this transition into the world of public education was awkward as all get-out.

History had never been her favorite subject at home, but this was the class she most looked forward to now. This and Children's Literature. Why? Because they were the two classes she attended on campus. Mom had advocated for only one on-campus class, but Lily had pushed for two. Well, "pushed" sounded aggressive. Her push had many pleases and thank yous attached.

The professor droned on, and Lily ventured another casual glance in Matt's direction. With his attention focused up front, she had a second to admire his perfect jawline and the way his brown hair fell softly against his brow. His fingers flew across his keyboard. Probably a hundred words per minute or more? He could be a typist.

Ridiculous. She fiddled with her pen. She knew next to nothing about Matt. All she had to go on were his good looks and the fact he wore Christian T-shirts from time to time. What did he want to do with his life? No clue. And she'd likely never know considering *How to talk to guys* didn't make it into her homeschool curriculum.

As if he could sense her staring, his gaze gravitated in her direction. Before she could look away, he made eye contact. The edges of his mouth tweaked up slightly as if he was trying to rein them in. It was just enough of a smile to expose an adorable dimple and send her stomach tumbling. Oh, goodness. Twice in one day. She had to transfer out of this class. She could not face him for the rest of the semester.

Concentrate. She needed to focus on class, not cute boys. The sooner she could graduate, the sooner she could move out and start her life. Her own separate life.

She didn't remember this class feeling so long. When the professor finally dismissed, she wasn't the only one who released an audible sigh of relief. Now, to keep her head down and duck out of class as inconspicuously as possible.

"Fascinating, isn't it? The dismantling of the Carolingian Empire?"

She winced at the sound of his voice, focusing intently on shoving her materials into her messenger bag. "Quite."

Quite? Was she British now? With nothing else to distract, she was forced to look up. Straight into his blue eyes.

"You seemed to be looking for someone to discuss the material with." He shrugged, clearly holding back a grin.

She froze, mouth parted. *Say something. Say something.* She stammered incoherent, almost words.

He bumped her arm with his. "I'm messing with you. I zone out too sometimes."

She let out a breathy chuckle. "Yeah."

He took a step toward the door. "Take care. See you Thursday."

He was leaving? Matt Juper had finally acknowledged her existence, had stopped to talk to her, and now he was walking away? No. She couldn't let this happen. Her mind scrambled for something to say, a way to keep the conversation going. He was nearly to the door when she blurted out, "You're a Christian."

He stopped. Turned. He took her in, his smile so slight it was nearly imperceptible, his eyes blazing with purpose. He adjusted his bag across his shoulder. "Yes, I am. You?"

She nodded. Too eager, perhaps. Not suave or sophisticated.

"Cool."

She ran her tongue over the inside of her cheek. Perhaps it was too forward to ask, but … "Do you go to church?"

His brows furrowed. Did he think her a Bible-thumper out to ensure everyone obeyed the rules about not neglecting fellowship?

"I ask because I'm looking for a church."

His smile broke free. "Yeah. I love my church. They've got a great young adult group." He pulled his phone from his back pocket. "What's your number? I'll text you the address and info."

Oh. My. Goodness. Matt Juper had asked for her phone number. Sure, it was for church reasons and not for a date or anything, but still. She rattled it off and tried to keep from floating out the door.

Chapter 12

TAKE UP ARMS AGAINST ME AND YOU ARE
FEDERALS. YOUR DOCTRINE IS AN ABSURDITY, AND I
WILL KILL YOU FOR BEING FOOLS. BEWARE, MEN,
BEFORE YOU MAKE THIS FEARFUL LEAP. I FEEL FOR
YOU. YOU ARE IN A CRUCIAL SITUATION. BUT
REMEMBER, THERE IS A SOUTHERN ARMY, HEADED
BY THE BEST MEN IN THE NATION. MANY OF THEIR
HOMES ARE IN MISSOURI, AND THEY WILL HAVE THE
STATE OR DIE IN THE ATTEMPT.

"BLOODY BILL" ANDERSON, JULY 7, 1864

July 20, 1862
Christian County, Missouri

Cyrus had scooped the last spoonful of beans from his plate when Riley's voice sounded from his lookout perch on the second story.

"Union men comin'. At least a dozen. Maybe more."

Cyrus downed his last bite and handed his plate to Susanna, the matron of the house. "Much obliged for the fine meal. Thank you kindly." His hand flew to his holster, then to his shirt pocket, ensuring his pistols were at the ready.

"Anytime. You got all the ammunition you needed? We have more under the floorboards."

"We have all we can carry for now. We'll be back for more when we see fit." He shook her hand, as firm with resolve as his own. The good Southern folk in these parts were as committed to the cause as any in Dixie. Missouri women were the bravest he had the privilege to meet.

The whinny of horses and clomp of boots came closer.

"That's our cue, boys." Cyrus dashed out the back door with the ten other bushwhackers. They headed for the woods and melted into the trees. A half mile in, they found their horses untouched. Untethering them, they maneuvered deeper into the bush, bellies full of warm food, pockets full of bullets.

What a night. Hopefully, Susanna could play innocent this time as well as she had the last. She'd signed an oath of allegiance to the United States government, and the large US flag that hung over the mantle served to convince most soldiers she was a law-abiding citizen and not a secesh aiding and abetting guerrillas. If they found out, they'd burn her house. A sliver of worry sliced between his shoulder blades. Feds had already torched Bobby's barn and crop after they'd visited last week. The scoundrels. But Susanna had a good head about her and a three-year-old daughter. They'd not sink low enough to deprive a woman and child of all they had left, would they?

"Where to, Cy?"

Funny how the men looked to him to lead when they split into factions. He was among the greenest of the bunch but was by far the oldest. They honored that even if most had more experience in the bush than he.

"We're meetin' up with the others at the train depot."

Riley hooted. "Another shoot-out!"

Cyrus frowned. He hadn't been there the last time the men had shot at a moving train. The papers stated they'd killed four passengers. Innocent passengers.

"I think we're going to tear up the track." Disrupting supply lines was essential to wreaking havoc on the North's warpath.

"That too." The boys laughed.

Boys. They really were young. Not much older than his own would be if Yankee traitors hadn't snatched them away. Maybe being a father figure to this brood was the Good Lord's way of giving him a second chance. Perhaps he could learn from his mistakes.

He pinched the bridge of his nose. Who was he kidding? The loyalty in this group ran as thin as water. That would only change with time and by proving himself not a coward. A few days prior, when one of their group suggested they surrender to Federal troops outside a house they quartered at, the men had shoved him outside and told the Federals to shoot the yellowbelly.

They'd turn on him just as quick if he showed a hint of fear.

"Hey, what's that?" Bear, as they called him for his impressive girth, pointed toward the road in the distance. "Looks like a supply train."

Sure did. "I count thirteen wagons. And only four bluecoats guarding the loot." He angled Dixie toward the plunder. "You boys thinkin' what I'm thinkin'?"

They didn't stop to answer but tunneled through the woods and burst onto the path with a holler. Guns blazing, two of their boys shot the first couple of bluecoats dead within a few seconds. The two Yanks farthest away took off on their horses. Cyrus pursued the one who barreled straight down the road. Riley took the one who veered into the woods. A minute later, a shot rang out. Hopefully, that meant the other bluecoat was dead.

The stitch in Cyrus's side testified to the fact that he wasn't a young buck any longer. He could muster bravado, however. "You might as well surrender. Your buddies are dead."

The man's shoulders lowered a fraction, and his hands lifted. "Don't shoot me." A tremor laced his voice.

"Give me your gun." He wasn't about to make any promises.

Cyrus kept his finger on the trigger of his pistol as the Fed slowly handed him his rifle. He slung it over his shoulder. "What other weapons you got?"

"A handgun."

"Relinquish it or die, soldier." Cyrus held his gun an inch away from the Fed's skull.

He gave Cyrus the gun, and when the man's clammy hand touched his, a twinge of pity pinged in his chest. Ridiculous. No room for that in this business. But their gazes interlocked as he took the bluecoat's horse by the reins and led him back to the rest of the guerrillas. This fella was young. Not much more than a kid. Too young to know what he'd gotten himself into, fighting for an invading army of abolitionists. Young people had lofty ideals that sounded good when they touted them to their chums but held no weight when immersed in the fire.

This was the fire.

He returned to find his band loading their saddlebags with hardtack, beans, and blessed coffee. "Look what I found boys."

His triumphant wave to his captive was met with raised brows and scowls.

"Why'd you bring him back alive?" Riley asked.

Cyrus shrugged. "He surrendered." And asked him not to shoot.

Riley crossed his arms over his chest and stepped close. He lowered his voice. "You've got a real chance to make something of yourself here, Cy. Don't mess it up by going soft. Shoot the devil and take his coat. What are we going to do with him?"

Cyrus scrubbed his beard. "I thought we'd trade him."

Riley shook his head. "No need. Arise and be a leader, Cy. Shoot 'im."

The men stared at him, temporarily at pause from their pillaging. Every eye questioned him. What was he going to do? Be a yellowbelly? Or rise in the ranks as a freedom-fighting guerrilla?

He trained his gun on the man. "Get off the horse."

The kid's legs shook as he did so. Cyrus pushed it out of his mind. Union soldiers had been terrorizing the countryside ever since the War of Northern Aggression started. Before that even, if you counted the Jayhawkers. Houses and farms destroyed. Livelihoods in ash.

His children murdered.

"Give me your coat."

The kid shook it off. Cyrus handed Riley his gun as he pulled the coat over his lean arms. Not a bad fit. Now he could blend in and avoid Federal fire, at least from a distance.

When he took his gun back, fear flashed in the kid's eyes. He knew Cyrus was about to kill him. He had to. That's why he started to run for the woods. Relief trickled down Cy's arm as he pulled the trigger and watched the kid crumple to the ground. At least he hadn't had to shoot him point-blank. At least he hadn't seen the kid's green eyes staring back at him as he snuffed out his life. And since the kid ran away, he had it coming, plain and simple.

There was nothing to feel guilty for.

"What else is in them wagons?" He sauntered over to fill his pockets.

~

August 11, 1862
Independence, Missouri

Willow searched for Quantrill in her dreams. The notorious guerrilla eluded her in her sleep just as he did in her waking hours. Still, she scoured each grove in the haze of night. There. A barn stood partly concealed by brush. Her ears perked at the sound of movement within. Footsteps soft and light, she approached.

"Will. Wake up." A familiar voice—Milo's—tried to break through the sleepy fog. A bugle sounded in the distance.

"Shh." She slung her arm over her eyes, pushing away the intrusion. "I almost got him."

His voice ground in her ear as he shoved her shoulder. "Up. Now. The enemy is coming."

Enemy coming. Enemy coming? Her eyes sprang open. "What?"

He grabbed his carbine and cartridge box, face somber. "To arms. This is the real thing."

She scrambled to her feet, mind reeling. To arms. What did that mean? What did she need to do again?

"Grab your revolver and fall into rank in front." He jerked his head toward the front of their tent. He handed her some ammunition.

Revolver in tow, she stepped outside where the rest of their company already stood in rank.

"The enemy's firing at Thomas's Company at the guard house. Charge them at the hospital." Lieutenant Vance led the way, shouting, "Come on, boys!"

They ran through corn stalks and jumped a fence. Willow's ears burned. Milo remained a few paces ahead, no matter how much she strove to match his pace. She gritted her teeth and doubled her efforts. Finally, she caught up to him. With a grunt, she passed him as they spilled into the hospital yard.

A spray of bullets exploded around them, almost as if they were jumping from the ground. She gasped.

"Keep going," Milo whispered beside her.

Yes, of course. Soldiers continued, even when the enemy opened fire. She steeled her resolve. They reached a middle fence that provided a scant bit of shelter.

Behind the far fence, a glimpse of the enemy appeared here and there in between the rain of bullets. Milo brought his gun to his shoulder and fired back. Right. Yes. That's what she needed to do. She loaded, cocked, and aimed her rifle with trembling hands.

Before she could fire, Lieutenant Vance fell by her side, wounded. "Boys, I am done." He limped toward the hospital tent.

Eyes wide, she refocused and pulled the trigger.

Balls fell all around them. Another comrade went down three feet from her. His groan sliced through her. My word. She was going to die. They all were. Her teeth chattered as her body shook.

"Retreat to the stone fence!"

She gulped in a relieved breath at the order and ran for the fence. Morning light tinged the sky now. Might it be a sign this wretched nightmare was coming to an end? She dropped to her belly and waited. Waited to live. Waited to die. Waited for it to be over.

The enemy remained at the hospital. She caught her breath. Blocked out distant screams. What made her think she could do this? She looked to Milo, jaw firm. It was as if he'd been made for this. She *could* do this. She had to. She wouldn't disgrace herself.

"They're coming through the corn. Southeast."

She turned in that direction, cocked her gun, and fired.

~

Though Willow had been a model soldier for the rest of the battle, the Confederates claimed the victory. When Union Captain Breckinridge raised a white flag, she—along with a handful of others—threatened to shoot him. They'd fight on and never surrender. She took her station in William McCoy's house with the rest of them, knocking out the windows and firing on the pickets and cavalry that came near. She didn't so much as flinch.

A spy reported that Colonel Buel of the Union had surrendered, so the soldiers that were holed up in McCoy's house left for Kansas City, following the river. Some men had lost shoes, others lost coats and hats. She had all three, though her boots were worn clear through so her big toe stuck out.

Milo walked beside her, shoulders slumped.

"How many men do you think we lost?" She squinted at him against the afternoon sun. A twinge of pain cramped her chest. She turned her head away to hide her wince. Why did her pulse continue to race this long after danger had passed?

"No tellin'."

"We put up a good fight."

"Not good enough."

A breeze tousled the ends of her hair under her kepi, and the ground seemed to shift underneath her. She stumbled into Milo.

"Are you okay?"

Her head pounded, and her mouth felt as dry as a desert. "Yeah."

"You sure? You look a little peaky."

"I probably should drink water." She brought her canteen to her lips and gulped the liquid. "That's better." But the path under her feet continued to move beneath her. She forced a smile. If she ignored it, it would go away eventually.

Too bad she couldn't loop her arm through Milo's. What would look natural as a sister would seem quite odd as a brother. Instead, she picked up a stick from beside the path to use as a walking stick. She twirled it every once in a while to make it look as if it were a plaything and to hide how heavily she leaned upon it.

Shouts sounded as they approached the city.

She released a breathy chuckle. "At least the citizens aren't treating us as retreating cowards." Her vision clouded, and her knees buckled beneath her. The last sound she heard was the crack of her walking stick as it split in two before she tumbled to the ground.

~

Once again, Milo's voice interrupted her search for Quantrill. This time, she'd been about to ambush the hospital tent he was surely using for cover.

"What's wrong with my brother?" he asked.

His brother? He didn't have a brother. When she pried an eye open, billowy white greeted her, along with the scent of antiseptic. A hospital tent? Her dreams must have merged with reality. She struggled to sit, but the doctor's hand gently pressed her back down. A bright light shone in her eyes, causing her head to pound.

"Will appears to have the fainting disease. It's the second case I've seen this week. Likely a case of irritable heart. A buddy of mine, Dr. DaCosta, is studying the phenomenon among soldiers. It presents with a rapid pulse, an irregular heartbeat, difficulty breathing, and often fatigue, sometimes to the point of collapse." The doctor pressed a stethoscope to her bound breast. "Have you had chest pain, Will?"

She nodded.

Milo scowled. "You didn't mention any of those symptoms."

She glared back at him, but her voice came out sleepy. "I'm not one to complain."

He rolled his eyes and focused his attention back on the doctor. "What's to be done?"

"Rest is the best medicine for irritable heart." He smiled at her. "A few days of bed rest and you'll be feeling much better. You'll need to reintroduce exercise gradually and watch what you put in your pack. Heavy packs slow recovery, as does restrictive clothing."

She bit the inside of her cheek. She had no choice but to bind her chest, and the pants issued to her would fall to the ground without a belt.

Milo's forehead dimpled with his deep frown. "What if this happens again?"

"It may," the doctor said, tilting his head in a thoughtful way, "in which case a period of longer rest may be advised. Some patients with irritable hearts need to rest as long as six months to recover properly."

She sputtered. "Six months?"

"Let's not concern ourselves with that for the time being. Rest a few days, then reenter your duties gradually. No heavy lifting. No stooping. No bending. At least for now."

Milo raised a brow. "You do realize he's a soldier, don't you, Doc?"

He chuckled. "I'll talk with your commanding officer. Perhaps there's a duty more well-suited." He shuffled away, leaving Milo and Willow alone in a room full of wounded and ill patients.

She twisted the sheet in her lap. "This is embarrassing."

He sat on the edge of her bed. "Why?"

"Not much like a brave soldier, am I?"

The corner of his mouth lifted. "You heard him. A lot of soldiers have this diagnosis. A lot of *men*. It doesn't reflect poorly on you."

Other men may have the same diagnosis, but Milo didn't. He could march and fight, stare death in the face and rally. All without pangs in his chest or without his knees giving way. Her eyes stung, but she refused to allow tears. She blinked hard to banish them.

"Hey, it's not all clouds and gloom." Milo playfully poked her arm and lowered his mouth to her ear. "The doc didn't undress you for the exam. Your secret's safe."

"True."

"How embarrassing would it be for him to find out you're a girl *and* flat chested."

She gathered her strength and slugged him in the stomach. His wince gave her the most satisfaction she'd had all day.

Chapter 13

ONE OF THE WORST PARTS OF CHRONIC ILLNESS IS
THAT YOU FEEL
LIKE YOUR BODY NO LONGER BELONGS TO YOU.

FROM *WHAT DOESN'T KILL YOU*
BY TESSA MILLER

Modern Day

Lily fiddled with her keys, the metal cool and heavy in her hand. She watched groups of people walk into the double doors of the church. Mostly families, but some groups of what looked to be friends. Everyone seemed like they belonged here. As if this was one giant family. The greeters didn't just politely shake the entrants' hands. They wrapped several people in an embrace. What would it be like to be welcomed like that? Wanted? Important to someone outside of her family?

As much as she longed for it, trepidation tripped in her chest. They belonged here. She did not. She was an outsider. She knew no one save Matt, and did that even count? What if her fumbling social skills failed her in there? Perhaps she would never belong. She could drive away right now, and no one would know the difference. Yeah, that would be best. She slid the key back into the ignition.

A knock on the passenger's side window made her jump. Matt stood, Starbucks cup in hand, navy knit hat tucked on his head in a way that pasted wisps of hair across his brow. Heaven help her.

"You came." Did his voice hold pleasure or was she misconstruing the situation?

She slid the key back out and unlocked her door. "Yep."

Guess she was doing this. She exited the vehicle as casually as possible. No big deal. Yet another tally in her long line of public outings.

"Most of the young adults sit in the back on the right. I'll show you."

She fell into step beside him as he wove through the parking lot to the entrance.

Right before they approached the front doors, he turned to her. "Watch out for Marty. He's a hugger."

The scent of peppermint and coffee lingered on his breath. If only she could keep him talking.

The doors swung open, and a burly man with a full white beard opened his arms and enveloped Matt. "Good morning. Great to see you."

Matt patted the man's back. "Good morning, Marty." When he extricated himself, he gestured to her. "This is my friend, Lily."

"Lily." His smile, along with his arms, stretched wide. She stood there awkwardly as he wrapped her in a hug. "Glad to meet you." He handed her a bulletin.

She chuckled.

"Don't scare her away now." Matt winked.

Lily's stomach flipped.

"Wouldn't dream of it." Marty laughed heartily, then turned to the next person entering.

She scrambled to follow Matt past a welcome desk and coffee bar and into the sanctuary. When he stopped at the back row, her arm brushed against his. Her knees wobbled. Seriously. She was being ridiculous. She needed to get herself together and act like a mature adult. She leaned her hip against a chair and focused intently as Matt introduced a group of people around their age.

Once again, he introduced her as his friend. Was she blushing? Hopefully, no one noticed.

She found a seat next to Matt and a girl named Bridgett, who struck up a conversation about gel manicures versus acrylic nails. Most of the girls had a strong opinion one way or the other. She stuck with a safe answer. "Tough to say." That sounded way better than *I've actually never had my nails done at a real salon. My mom did them once, and one time I let my little brother paint my toenails, but it ended up being a disaster that took an hour to clean up.*

A pesky little voice in the back of her head whispered that she didn't fit here. She told it to hush. She could fit here. She would. She'd do whatever it took to make a space for herself outside the four walls of her chaotic home.

Soft musical notes drifted into their conversation, a signal to wrap it up. As the chatter quieted, she glanced at her bulletin. The young adult group—called the Group, clever— met each Sunday night. Mom might not appreciate her being gone so much on Sundays, but she longed to go. She'd have to convince her mother it was best. Another announcement caught her eye. They were looking for someone to oversee a Christmas outreach. She smiled. For foster and adoptive families.

Her heart pricked at the thought. Helping families like hers. Yes. Yes, she could be the unselfish type of person who helped other people, served the less fortunate, looked after the interests of others. Just because she didn't take delight in serving her family didn't make her a bad sister or a bad *person.* She wasn't the scum of the earth. She just wasn't … Mom. She could prove that, couldn't she, by serving elsewhere? But— she checked the details again—they weren't looking for someone to *help* but someone to *lead* the thing. She'd only stepped through the doors for the first time. Who was she to think she could take on that role?

"Are you checking out the Christmas outreach?" Matt's voice near her ear sent tingles up her spine.

Oh gosh. He was reading the bulletin over her shoulder. So close.

"Yeah. It sounds like something I'd love to do, but I don't think I could lead it. I'm not even a member here."

He sat back, taking warmth and tantalizing aroma with him. If only she could lean back into his arms to recapture it. Her cheeks warmed as he studied her. "What if we did it together?"

A surge of anticipation bolted her upright. "What do you mean?"

He shrugged. "Think about it. Pray about it. You could take as much of the lead as you want, and I could help with whatever you need. Or however you'd like it to work."

Everyone around them stood, and she scrambled to her feet. "Oh, wow. Yeah, I'll pray about it." And she would, though she doubted *Thank You, God for letting this cute boy want to spend time with me* was the type of praying he meant.

Voices rose around her. She didn't know how to join in the unfamiliar song, so she listened. Pushed thoughts of Matt from her brain as she closed her eyes and took in the words. She was loved. Just as she was. Okay, but weren't Christians supposed to continually strive to be more like Jesus? That was what she needed to do. Be more like Him. More patient. More kind. More loving. She needed to work on that. If only she could be someone He could be proud of.

Matt's rich baritone glided around her. This is what she needed. To be in God's house. Around His people. Doing His work. This is how she could become Christlike.

And if eventually she became more to Matt than a friend, all the better.

~

Mark pops his head into the bedroom two weeks later when I'm on a phone call about the gala he doesn't know I'm still planning. Awkward. I try to keep my responses to the caterer as short and nondescript as possible while he eyes me curiously.

"Of course, Mrs. Prichard. We'd be happy to work with Ascend Community again this year."

I squirm.

"You're hosting this at the same venue as last year, correct?"

The Staybridge Center? Nope. They wouldn't budge on the pricing once they found out I wasn't calling on behalf of the church, and it's not feasible without the discount. I glance toward the door. Mark is still watching. "No."

"You're changing venues."

"Yes."

"Have you solidified your choice?"

"Not yet."

Mark takes another step into the room and stage-whispers, "Will you be long?"

I shake my head, hold up one finger, and smile.

When he nods and retreats, I breathe easier.

"How many people are you expecting?" the lady asks.

We continue to chat over logistics, and she offers to email me a quote to my church email address. The problem is, I don't have one. It's been "paused," just like my duties. My husband knows me too well.

"Please send it to my personal address." I rattle it off.

An awkward pause ensues. "May I ask why?"

I might as well come out with it. She'll find out eventually. "The gala isn't officially sponsored by Ascend Community this year. More like … unofficially." I cringe as I say this.

"Unofficially?"

"Yes."

"Mrs. Prichard, the prices I mentioned were for our church and noncorporate discounts. I'm afraid we'll have to charge you the normal rate if Ascend is not *officially* sponsoring the event."

I hold back a groan. Not again. No wonder I can't make headway in planning this thing. "I understand. Please email the quote."

Mark peeks back in, and I end the call.

"What was that about?"

I can't even think of a feasible lie, so I just shake my head and say, "Not important. Did you need something?"

He brightens. "I have a surprise for you." Chipper jumps from his cozy spot in the crook of my legs and runs in excited circles.

I yawn. Stretch. "What is it?"

"Come out and see."

It's obviously a ploy to get me out of the bed that I rarely leave. "Did the craft kits come?"

I used to plan elaborate crafts to do with the twins, as both adore art. While my traitorous body won't allow for such schemes any longer, I can still scour online sales, hit "Add to cart," and experience a small thrill as I anticipate watching the children unbox their new art kits. To think I've done this all with my thumbs. A set of watercolors should arrive at any time. I can't wait to spread the kitchen table with butcher paper and watch them paint this evening.

Mark doesn't answer, and curiosity propels me from the space I've inhabited nearly all day every day.

The nightstand is piled high with dishes. The rest of the house is likely equally as frightening. I can't worry about that, though. I run a hand through my tangled hair. How long has it been since my last bath? Not a good thing that I can't remember.

The bright sun hurts my eyes as I turn the corner and shuffle into the living room. My head throbs at the change in lighting. I shiver as my feet transition from warm carpet to cold hardwood. At least no dizziness assaults me at my first vertical attempt. That's something.

I stop in my tracks. There, in the middle of the living room floor sporting a bright red bow, is a rollator walker like a grandma would use.

Mark rubs it with tender care as if he was waxing a new Mercedes. "Surprise!"

"What's this?" Does my attempt to keep my face from screwing in disgust prove successful?

"It's a walker." He beams. "Now you can come back to church."

A hum starts in the back of my throat and pushes forward.

"I know you've been nervous to return. You're afraid of falling there and making a scene. Now you'll have support whenever you need it." He flips a small seat on the walker. "You can sit whenever you need to."

My tongue glides against the back of my teeth, clamped shut in an awkward smile. If only I could explain the constant support I need will not come in the form of a portable chair. And I've been avoiding church not because I'm afraid I'll fall but because I'm afraid I've already fallen.

I finally unclench my jaw. "How thoughtful."

Mark wraps me in a hug. He draws circles on my back with his thumb. "Everything's going to be okay. We're going to be okay."

"Okay." It comes out as a whisper, a wisp as thin as mist.

"Oh!" He pulls away and scurries to his briefcase that hangs from the coat tree. "I need you to sign something."

"What?"

"It's for a handicap placard. I called your doctor's office about it, and they're filling out their portion. You only need to sign the application."

My stomach cramps. "Great. It'll go perfectly with the old lady walker."

His smile dims slightly as he hands me the application and a pen. I sit on the couch and use the handy walker seat as a surface to sign the document.

"I think this will help. You won't have to walk as far."

"Yep." Except if I never leave the house again, we won't need it.

"Let's go to the zoo next weekend." The enthusiasm he injects into his voice sounds forced. Deep creases mar the edges of his eyes. This jolts me to reality, and all of a sudden, I see the piles of folded clothes on the coffee table and chairs. A signed permission slip lies on top of a fluffy blue towel next to a grocery list scrawled in Mark's chicken scratch. The scent of cumin drifts to my nose. Is he making chili? It has taken a toll on him to keep this place running without me. While I've been sulking under the covers, he's been manning up. How selfish of me to lay this burden solely on his shoulders.

Chipper barks at the back door.

"I'll let him out." Best not to make Mark do anything more. I take a step in that direction.

"Here." Mark slides the walker toward me. "Try it out."

"Sure." I push the contraption to the back door and slide it open. Chipper dashes out to chase a squirrel. A cool breeze swirls around me. Someone must be burning leaves in the neighborhood. A smile teases my lips as I close my eyes and inhale. It's too cool to go outside. Besides, I don't want any neighbors to see me with the monstrosity that is now my companion. But the air feels heavenly, and I don't want to retreat inside yet. I lean against the door frame and listen to leaves rustle as they chase each other across the yard.

When my eyes flitter open, I call Chipper to come inside. He doesn't respond. My gaze sweeps the yard, and there's no sign of him. Oh no. He got out again. I shouldn't have let down my guard.

"Mark," I call as I push the walker back into the living room, "Chipper ran off again."

In a flash, he springs from the couch and grabs the leash from the hook by the front door. "I'll find him."

There he goes. My hero. A sour taste fills my mouth. How long can he play both his part and mine before he breaks? God created me to be his helpmeet, not the other way around. Until recently, I've been exactly that. Now, everything is out of order. Everything's wrong.

Mark's phone belts out "How Great is Our God," his standard ringtone.

I rush to grab it from the couch cushion. I answer without looking at who's calling. "Hello?"

A beat of silence, and she asks, "Is this Pastor Prichard's phone?" Kelly Loren's voice drips as if she's been crying. Oh no. What's wrong? I lower onto the walker seat.

"Yes. This is Amber. Mark stepped out for a moment. Can I help you?" My fingers gravitate to the base of my throat.

A sob erupts from the other end of the phone. "Oh, Amber. He's gone."

"Your father." It's not a question. The knowing settles into me, thick like sediment. I picture Mr. Radley's face, drawn and pale as it looked the last time I visited. He'd called me Peggy and asked if I wanted to go out for a Coke. *Soon*, I'd told him. He hadn't left his bed in a week.

Flashes of the man he'd been even a month prior filtered past as well. We'd gone to the fellowship hall to play bingo once. The old coot gloated like a star when he'd won, even if his only prize was banana pudding. My throat burns as I remember.

"I'm so sorry."

"I can't … I don't …" She weeps.

My shoulders droop as tears flow down my cheeks. Our sniffles blend together.

"Mark can do the funeral, right? He won't be too busy for that, will he?"

"Too busy? Of course not." I dry my eyes with my sleeve.

"I asked him to come and pray over Dad when I could tell …" Her voice breaks. My stomach sinks as I anticipate her next words. "But he said he couldn't because he was taking care of you. That your health is struggling. Are you okay?"

My hands clench into fists. I could punch someone, but who? Mark? Myself? Mr. Radley breathed his last without the support of a pastor because I was pouting in bed. I pound my thighs, but it does little to ease the self-loathing.

I work to keep my voice steady. It's as if I'm walking a tightrope, struggling to maintain balance. "I'm fine. I'm so sorry Mark wasn't there for you when you needed him."

She speaks through hiccups. "It's … I'm glad you're okay."

"I'll have Mark call you back in a minute. And I'll be praying for you and the family." The last part comes out automatically as if I didn't choose the words. They're programmed into me. The preacher's wife. It's what I say. But I likely promised to be praying for Mr. Radley before, and I'm acutely aware I haven't offered a prayer on his behalf in months. I've been too wrapped in my own pain. My eyes sting yet again.

"Thanks, Amber."

"You're welcome."

I hang up and collapse against the couch cushion as if I've run a marathon. I could crawl back into bed and sleep another three days straight. Only I won't. I will force myself to push through so my husband can go back to being a pastor and not a homemaker. Mind over matter. Fake it 'til you make it. I can do this.

"Oh, Lord. Help."

The door swings open, and our grinning corgi dashes in as if he's come home from a parade. His tail is swinging nearly fast enough to propel him into the air.

"Chipper," I chide in a low tone with a frown.

He runs to me and licks my ankles.

"Naughty dog, running away. You have to stop."

He jumps in my lap and licks my face. I barely contain a laugh. I sit on my hands to keep myself from petting him.

Mark wipes his brow and hangs up the leash. "Man, he's fast."

"Stinker."

He plops next to me. "We've got to get an electric fence."

"I looked into them. They cost over a thousand dollars."

Mark winces. "We could take a special offering?"

I snort, then cover my face with my hands.

He pulls them away. "Stop. I love how you do that."

This gives me the perfect excuse to scrunch my face and make pig noises. We both dissolve in a fit of laughter. For thirty seconds, I am free. Free of sickness. Free of guilt. Free of a burden I don't know how to bear.

Chipper wiggles in between us. His tongue wags as he looks back and forth to see which one of us will give him attention. I cave and pet him.

My gaze falls on Mark's phone, and my conversation with Kelly comes crashing into my pocket of peace.

"Kelly Loren called. Her father passed away."

Mark's head dips.

"She said she asked you to come and pray over him before he died, but you said you were too busy."

He groans.

"I told you not to do that."

His head shoots up, and his expression steals my breath. I'd welcome anger. I could use a good fight right now. Instead, his eyes flash with hurt. The last thing I want to see. The thing I don't think I can bear anymore of.

He nearly whispers, but his words echo loud in my ears. "What do you expect me to do?"

I swallow. Leave the house to chaos? Challenge me to stop moping and get out of bed? No perfect answer materializes. "I don't know."

We both stare at our hands.

Now it's my phone's turn to break into the silence as "Way Maker" sounds forth from the bedroom.

"I'll get it." Mark rises and retrieves it for me. "Your mother," he says as he hands it over.

I take a deep breath before answering. "Hi, Mom."

"Oh, good. You're alive."

I roll my eyes. Mark smiles. "Yes, I'm alive."

"The woman with the tree name nearly died. She had the fainting disease too, you know."

"No, I don't know what you're talking about."

"I read about it in the green book."

Right. The green book. "Okay, Mom. Was that the reason you were calling? To see if I'd died?"

"Heavens, no. Tomorrow's Friday. It's been two weeks and six days since I had my hair done. You're picking me up at eight tomorrow, aren't you? We go to the pharmacy, then the grocery store, then back to unload the groceries, then the hair salon, and then the pet store."

I bite my lip. There's no way. Just listening to the list drained my energy. Maybe Mark could—no. He needs to get back to being a pastor. And I need to get my home in order.

"I can't."

"What do you mean you can't?"

"I haven't been feeling well. I don't have the energy to take you on all those errands tomorrow."

The silence fills with her rapid breath.

"What if you took a bus?" I cringe as I say this. It's ridiculous. My mother on a crowded, germy bus? She'd be the one fainting if that happened.

"Oh, dear. Oh, dear."

"There's got to be someone else who can take you. Mr. Hundle?"

Mark raises his brows at me and mouths, *Mr. Hundle?* Okay, okay, I know. The man may have taken Mom home after the recital but that doesn't mean the crabby old codger is jumping at the opportunity to cart women around town as an act of charity. Besides, he has a job.

"Oh, dear. Oh, dear." This, I hear clearly. What I can't quite make out is what she mutters afterward.

"What was that?" I press the phone closer to my ear.

"I didn't raise you to be selfish." Her words slap me.

My mouth hangs open. *Selfish.*

Mark questions me with his gaze.

Selfish.

I can't speak.

Selfish. The word's echo strikes me again and again.

That isn't fair. I want to stomp my feet and shout it. But I picture myself burrowed under the covers while Kelly Loren watches her father pass from this world to the next without a pastor to pray with her family, and the awful word burrows deep inside of me. My mom needs me. She *needs* me. There's no one else.

"Why don't you pick one thing from your list of errands to do tomorrow. What's most important?"

She huffs. "We always go—"

I dig my nails into my palms. "I know what we usually do, but I can't do all of that, Mom. Unless you want to watch the ambulance take me to the hospital again, I can't. Pick one thing."

"It's the fainting disease, isn't it?"

"Yes! The fainting disease like the tree lady from the green book. Now, which is it? Pharmacy, grocery store, hair stylist, or pet store? You do know the pharmacy and grocery store will both deliver."

"I don't like that. I want to ask the pharmacist questions. I want to pick out my own fruit."

My head hangs low before she finally mumbles, "Pet store."

I startle. I would have bet money she'd choose the salon. Now I want to take this pet store choice back. It's not a necessity. My mother does not *need* me to take her to see bunnies. This isn't worth the expenditure of my precious energy. I open my mouth to tell her so, but snap it shut. This is probably the easiest way to get off the selfish list. I'll comply.

"I'll pick you up at eleven tomorrow."

I hang up and find Mark's lips are pressed together in a thin line as he matches socks from a laundry basket.

"What?"

"What'd she choose?"

"Pet store."

"Do you think that's the best idea?"

"The salon might have been better." The edge of my mouth twitches with my sarcasm.

He shoots me a look that says he's not amused.

"She called me selfish." I cross my arms over my chest.

"She can call you whatever she wants. It doesn't make it true."

The problem is it might be true. The verdict is out.

I yawn. Stretch. Scratch the dog behind his ears. "You don't think I'm selfish, do you, Chipper?"

He grins at me as if I'm the most delightful person on earth.

"Well, I'd better rest for tomorrow." I stand, ready to shuffle back to bed.

Mark frowns. "The kids will be home any minute."

I squeeze my eyes shut, shutting off a flood of emotion. All those plans of watching my daughter paint wash away. "Tell them I'll watch a movie with them tomorrow night." I'm choosing my mother over my children this time, and it kills me that these are the choices I must make. If I don't conserve my energy, I won't make it tomorrow.

Next time they'll paint and I'll watch and we'll laugh. It will be almost like normal.

Almost.

Next time.

Chapter 14

August 17, 1862
Kansas City, Missouri

Willow stretched on the hospital cot, her toe tapping with nervous energy. How long would they keep her confined at the army hospital? She felt fine now. Completely normal. Ready to run and climb and fight. *Irritable heart.* Sounded about right. She was only growing more irritable by the moment the longer she stayed in this blasted bed.

Some of the men had ventured back to Independence. Who knew where Milo had gone? Being left behind stung something fierce. Over the past week, she'd learned to distinguish the putrid scent of vomit from the one of gnawing infection, and *that* wasn't a skill she ever longed to perfect.

Perhaps she could slip away when the nurse wasn't looking. Oh, to breathe fresh air! She hungered for it.

A commotion outside stole her attention. She craned her neck and pushed up on her elbows to try to view the source. The door opened, and several men were brought in on stretchers. Their groans filled the space around her. She shivered.

"What happened?" she asked no one in particular and everyone at once.

A medic shot her a glance before transferring a soldier to the cot beside her. "Battle at Lone Jack. Lost forty-three men. Three times that are wounded."

Her hand grazed her throat. Milo. Where was he?

As if she'd conjured his presence, he appeared through the entrance, pale-faced and tight-lipped. Her breath stalled as she willed him to meet her eye. A small moan—helpless and feminine—escaped as a splotch of crimson spread on his thigh.

He turned his head toward her. "Will."

She reached out her hand. "Milo." She catapulted upright and slung her legs over the bedside.

Across the room, the nurse's eyes widened. He put out his hand as if to stop her from a distance. "Sir, remain stationary."

"That's my brother."

"But, sir—"

"Is he okay?" She rushed to his side as they began to slide him onto a cot several spaces from hers. "Can't you place him near me?"

The medic paused, frowned, then gave a reluctant nod. Two others rearranged the cots as the nurse marched toward her tsk-tsking. "In bed."

She huffed but complied. As long as Milo was next to her, she could watch over him. "Is he okay?" she asked again.

"Took a bullet to the leg. Better off than many." Once they settled him down, they rushed back out.

"What happened?" She bit her lip. If he were well enough, he'd chastise her for it.

Instead, his face pinched as if he suppressed a cry of pain. Her heart leapt toward him.

"Quantrill," he eked out. "We had to retreat."

Heat rose in her chest. Blasted bushwhackers. Where did they get off causing such destruction? How dare they maim and kill such a decent lot of menfolk. These soldiers had integrity. Morals. Unlike those guerrillas. The selfish brutes had no sense of decency. They didn't abide by any law and followed their own whims with no care for who they harmed. Scoundrels, the lot of them. Lawless, dirty scoundrels. She'd be mighty proud to enact revenge on one of them with a well-placed bullet.

"I'll kill him." She spoke through gritted teeth, hands clenched at her sides.

Even with his strained expression, Milo managed to raise an eyebrow. "You'll kill Quantrill?"

The Bird. The notorious, infamous leader of the guerrilla bands. Yes. Yes, she'd kill him. Her eyes narrowed into slits as she nodded.

Did her brother laugh? Of course, he'd think her incapable. Oh well. She'd proved him wrong before.

Milo's words came out in between shallow breaths. "You kill Quantrill, and you'll be the most famous soldier in history."

What a perfect challenge.

~

August 18, 1862

Relief coursed through Cyrus as his home came into view on the dusky horizon. It was still standing, thank God. The blasted Federals had burned down the houses of Southern sympathizers all throughout the county, but his remained.

Hopefully, his wife was holding up well within those walls. When he'd left, Adelaide's father had come to stay with her to provide a measure of protection. He'd have to wait until the sun fully set to find out how they were faring.

He surveyed the woods around him. "Let's hitch the horses here."

The six men who accompanied him dismounted and tethered their horses to trees. Cyrus couldn't seem to pull his gaze from his homestead, from the farm he'd worked year after year, and the home where he and Adelaide had raised their children. He'd built that house timber by timber for his bride to be. When they'd married, he'd carried her across the threshold and into a new life of their own making. And they had made something honorable there. Through buckets of sweat and bullheaded determination, they'd hewn out a respectable life. Seething hot anger boiled inside him. How dare those Unionists rip this away from him?

When darkness finally fell, he slunk through the yard and pressed himself against the back wall, inclining his head toward the kitchen window. "Adelaide," he whispered.

He'd seen no sign of Union soldiers during his time watching from the woods, but he couldn't be too careful. The singsong of her humming away put his mind at ease. She sounded safe and well, happy even.

He rapped gently on the window and tried calling her name again a little louder.

The humming stopped, followed by a quick intake of breath. A few seconds later, the back door cracked open, and her beautiful blue eyes peeked out. He slipped along the wall toward her. Her eyes lit with delight as she motioned him inside.

The second the door closed, she was in his arms. "Oh, Cyrus. I'm so glad you're safe." Her tears dampened his shirt.

He kissed the top of her head, her face, her lips. He drank her in. The gratitude welling within him pushed down bitterness and regret. "Adelaide. Precious Adelaide." His hands ran up and down her arms. He had to assure himself she was all right, here, real.

"How long do you have?" Fear wrapped around her question.

If only he could squelch it. Tell her he had forever now, that all the threats had passed, and they could move on with their lives together. But war hung in the air, sultry and thick.

"An hour at the most. I can't put you in danger."

Tears coursed down her cheeks as she nodded, leading him to the sofa where they sat side by side. "What have you been up to?"

He frowned. "It's better you not know. Tell me what's happened here. Where's your father?"

"Resting, currently. He's been sleeping down here each night, rifle nearby, keeping watch." Her lip trembled.

"Have you had visitors?" If the bluecoats left her alone, it would be miraculous.

Her nod was hesitant. "Once or twice."

"Tell me straight, Addy. What did they say? Do?"

"They barged in here, demanding dinner and a song, and asked about your whereabouts."

He squeezed her hand, prompting her to continue.

"I told them I assumed you dead, as I hadn't heard a breath from you."

It registered then that she wore a black mourning dress. He patted her skirts. "Part of the ruse?"

"I hoped it a ruse." Her glistening eyes beamed at him. "My prayers for you haven't ceased. I am thankful they weren't in vain."

He brought her hand to his mouth and brushed his lips against her knuckles. She chuckled. "Oh, that beard. You look quite a bit more unruly since I last saw you."

He stroked it, smiling. "The boys and I have a pact not to shave until the war's end."

"Goodness. What a sight you'll be."

"The Feds let you be?" It was a wonder they didn't burn the house and turn her out.

Her smile faded. "They said they'd be back." She peeked out the curtain. "You're right. You can't stay long."

They stared at each other, and he committed each piece of her to memory. The two small laugh lines at the corners of her eyes, the wisp of gray hair at her temple, the freckle to the left of her chin.

"I have something for you." She stood and disappeared upstairs, returning a few minutes later with a blanket. No, something wrapped in a blanket. "I've had it hidden under the mattress for weeks now, waiting for you." She unfolded the blanket to reveal a beautifully embroidered shirt with red roses and white lilies intertwined, its large pockets perfect for holding extra ammunition. She patted it reverently. "All my love and prayers are stitched into this shirt."

His heart squeezed. "I'll wear it with pride."

She stroked his scruffy cheek. "And I'm proud of you, dear. For defending our homeland. For rising to the call."

"I wish there was no need." He leaned into her palm.

"But there is, and you're fulfilling your duty. Please, watch yourself. Stay safe and come back to me." Fiery determination had replaced her earlier weepiness. "Now, take flour and bacon with you. And dried corn for the horses." She rose and went to the kitchen.

He peeled off his Yankee coat and white shirt and pulled on the embroidered guerrilla shirt. Bringing the fabric to his nostrils, he inhaled. Goodness, it smelled like home. Like honeysuckle and yeasty bread and the love of his wife. The shirt wrapped him in everything good, surrounding him in innocence like a shield.

When he stood at the back door, provisions in hand, ready to depart, his throat burned. When would he see her again? "Fletcher has a score to settle that will take us far from this county. You're prepared? You know to go to Cousin Ebenezer's house if you're thrown out."

She nodded. "I know. Don't worry about me. Just stay safe."

He couldn't promise anything, so instead, he kissed her soundly, prayed for her safety, and slipped out the back door into the night.

~

August 20, 1862

While crickets and cicadas serenaded outside and snores whispered through the air within, Willow lay on her back, staring at the ceiling of the Kansas City hospital. Her first order of business was to prove she was well enough to return to her regiment. She worried her lip. What chance would she have of putting a bullet through Quantrill if she remained in Black Hawk's? They could send her on a scout or two, but she'd be just as likely to end up somewhere the Bird wasn't. Rumor had it the Missouri State Militia's main focus was to hunt guerrillas. Perhaps she could request a transfer.

"Psst."

She turned to find Milo blinking back at her. She couldn't help but smile. How many times had the two of them chatted late into the night while their parents slept? The night's lullaby emitted a lively energy when the siblings got into a whispered battle of wits.

"What are you doing up?" She tried for a scolding tone, but a chuckle broke through the end.

"Thinkin'" The way his hands were folded over his chest gave credence to his statement.

She studied him. "You've got more color."

"How can you tell? It's dark as pitch in here."

"I didn't mistake you for a ghost, did I?"

"Ha."

She turned on her side and relaxed into her pillow. His voice was no longer strained with pain. The medicine the doctor gave him must have helped. He'd recover, unlike many others. She pushed away the thought of how close she'd come to losing him. She couldn't bear it.

Milo propped himself up on his elbow, facing her with what seemed to be an earnest expression. Hard to discern in the darkness. "I need you to do something for me."

She leaned forward. Do something for him? She'd already pledged to enact revenge against the most notorious guerrilla in history. What else could he want from her? She'd do anything for him. "Yes."

"Yes? You haven't heard what it is yet."

"Yes. Anything you need. Anything you want."

She heard his smile more than saw it. "I want you to find me a plum."

"A what now?"

"A plum. I'm hankering for a plum."

She blinked. Was he jesting? Here she was, ready to do some great and noble feat, and he asked her for a piece of fruit? The gleam of his teeth proved he was smiling, but no laugh resounded. "You aren't serious."

"I am. You remember Mom's plum pies? I can't stop thinking about them, about how the house smelled as they baked. The sweetness on my tongue, the fullness of my belly. When the bullet struck, the image that flashed through my mind was Mama holding out a slice of her plum pie on a blue-flowered plate. A plum, Willow. A plum would be the closest thing to coming home."

Her throat swelled. Was it more from the mention of Ma or the use of her real name, which she hadn't heard in months? Perhaps both. All they'd shared together and left behind and lost swirled in her chest and threatened to come out in a sob.

"I will get you a plum." Heck, she'd get him ten plums. She only had to figure out how to sneak out of the hospital.

~

August 21, 1862

Willow preferred not to think of what she was doing as stealing. Rather, she borrowed the civilian clothes she found lying on a closet shelf. When she returned with Milo's plums, she'd return the clothes. She had her brother stuff her uniform under his mattress for safekeeping. Tiptoeing around the hospital ward in inky darkness proved to be the most fun she'd had since joining the army. When a nurse walked by, she slunk into the shadows. Milo staged a coughing fit that proved the perfect distraction. She escaped into the night without detection. Her senses buzzed with the exhilaration of adventure.

She was free! She only had to figure out where to find plums. Better head to town and ask around at first light.

The streets were quiet, and her thoughts wandered through the bumpy path that had brought her to this place in her life. She'd had a stable, hardworking family. A loving Ma. A brother who 'bout drove her crazy but whom she'd do anything for. Pa had been a tough man. Hard to please, without a doubt, but other girls had fathers who were consumed with the drink and who beat on the lot of them when they'd had too much of it. Pa hadn't been like that, at least.

No, she couldn't rightly say her family pushed her to this extreme. The reason she fought in disguise had far more to do with the burning inside of her than any outside force.

She'd always pointed at Pa and said no matter what she did, it was never enough. But now, she'd been without Pa for months, without his disapproving voice and condescending sneer. And still, if she could look into the gaping space in her chest called her heart, she'd label it with the words *not enough*. She never felt as if she had enough, did enough, was enough.

She bit the inside of her cheek as she passed rows of darkened houses. Surely, when she killed Quantrill, that would change. Or when she advanced in ranks. If they promoted her higher than her brother, would it quell the emptiness inside her? Maybe she didn't need to outdo Milo to achieve satisfaction. Perhaps she needed to please him instead.

Yes, that was it. When she brought him the plums and felt the warmth of his affection, she'd gain the peace she lacked.

Only uncertainty niggled. What if nothing she did ever alleviated this restlessness inside her? Was she destined to feel adrift all her life?

A cat moseyed across the path ahead of her, its form silhouetted in the lightening horizon. It stopped and arched its back in a stretch. Oh, to be so carefree.

Willow's ears perked at the sound of commotion coming from up ahead in the business district. She stilled and listened. The voices of many men. Officer instructions. A regiment? She hurried ahead.

When she came to the bakery, a man with an apron and a baker's hat stood in the doorway, looking out at the soldiers meandering past.

She came alongside him. "Do you know what's going on?"

"It's Colonel Burris. He just arrived from Leavenworth with about six hundred men. They're leaving for Independence soon."

She folded her arms across her chest. Did she appear to simply be an interested townsman? "What for?"

"Hunting Quantrill. Intelligence says he's out that way."

Willow's ears burned at the news. Her feet itched to run and join the men in their hunt. Perhaps she could tag along. She could act like a new recruit. She stepped in that direction.

The baker tossed a towel over his shoulder, sighed, and turned into his shop. "Wish they'd send someone else."

She paused. "What do you mean?"

"Burris." He scoffed as he tucked behind the counter and picked up a wad of dough. "He's got no control over his men. They're the most unprincipled lot of ignoramuses I ever did see. They terrorize everywhere they go, plundering from loyal men and Rebels alike. Shameful."

Her mouth parted. "From loyal men?"

He nodded, pounding his fist into the dough. "Just like Jayhawkers. They make no distinction."

She frowned. Surely, he was misinformed. It couldn't be that bad. And if they were hunting for Quantrill, they were pursuing a noble purpose. No harm in aligning herself with that, right?

A sweet fruity smell emanated from the bakery, mingling with the yeasty one. Oh yeah. Plums. She'd come here to find Milo plums. But how could that mission compare to bringing the most terrorizing killer of their time to justice? She could always grab her brother's plums afterward. He could wait.

She turned to bid the bakery man good day and found him staring intently at her.

"What?"

"Do you know how to bake? I could hire you on if you make a good cake and pie."

"Hire me?" She spit out a laugh. "No, sir. I'm a soldier." She looked at her civilian garb. "I'm signing up to be a soldier."

He narrowed his eyes. "They don't allow females in the army, little lady."

What? Her mouth fell open. Her hands flew to graze the ends of her hair. Had it grown too long since she'd joined. She assessed her clothing again. She'd been operating as a male for months without detection. She barely gave it a thought any longer. "What? How?"

"I watch too many women come in here each day to miss the signs."

She pulled the cap from her head and ran a hand through her hair. As soon as Milo was up to it, he needed to give her a trim. That had to be it.

The baker slid a plate across the counter. "Now, come here and have an apple cake before you run off and get yourself into mischief."

She stuffed the hat back on her head and crossed her arms. Her cheeks burned with offense, yet the tantalizing scent wafting from the apple cake was like a beckoning finger. If she turned this treat down now, her stomach would holler at her all day.

"Fine." She marched over and slid onto the high-backed stool.

With a straight face, he handed her a fork. "Enjoy. No charge."

Her frown mellowed a bit. Perhaps the fellow wasn't dastardly. Only slightly abrasive. It only took one bite of the cake to change her mind. He was an angel. A wonderful, heavenly man. "This is divine."

"You're welcome." Though his face had yet to lift into a smile, at least he didn't frown.

She stuffed another bite of cake in her mouth. "Do you know where I might get plums?" Crumbs splayed onto the counter and into her lap at her question.

"You eat like a boy."

She covered her mouth. Her mother would have been appalled. "Must have picked it up."

He shook his head. "There are some good ones in the countryside down a ways. Peaches are ripe too. I'll point you in the right direction when you leave."

"Thank you."

She'd get Milo's plums, return to the regiment, then request a transfer to the MSM. That had to be the right thing to do. If Burris's men found her out as easily as the baker had, they could have her thrown in prison. Her conscience stung.

Why did that bother her more than the rumor they acted without integrity? Didn't she mind being part of a group that pillaged from loyal men? Perhaps she'd become selfish through and through. Or maybe she always had been.

But when she returned with Milo's plums, she'd have put her brother above her own ambition, right? Even if the possibility of acclaim had pulled her heart in a different direction, he'd never know it.

Only she would.

~

It was late afternoon by the time Willow ducked behind the busy nurse and snuck to her cot. She tossed her gunny sack onto Milo's chest. His breathless grunt and shocked expression were nearly as humorous as the way the peaches and plums spilled every which way. She grinned. "Did you miss me?"

He leaned over the side of his cot to swipe a plum before it rolled too far to reach. "Your nurse sure did."

"There you are." Speaking of the tyrant. "Where did you run off to? The physician did not clear you to leave this floor." The young man's stern expression didn't become him. He looked nearly as old as her father when he scowled at her like that.

"I only needed fresh air."

The lines on his forehead deepened. "Do you have any idea what a ruckus you've caused?"

Her gaze fell to a stray peach an inch from the nurse's foot. If he took another step, he'd either squash it or end up sprawled on the floor. "I have an idea."

The man's face reddened, and a vein throbbed in his neck. His words came out clipped and sharp. "You are not to leave this hospital without a doctor's release. Is that clear?"

She leaned back against her pillow and folded her hands across her middle. "Perfectly."

With a huff, the nurse spun around and marched off.

Milo guffawed. "You've done it now."

"*I've* done it? As I recall, you're the one who begged me for plums." She checked to make sure the tyrant's back was turned, then retrieved the rest of the fallen fruit and tucked it back into the sack.

"And now I've gotten them, haven't I? And peaches too. I only had to listen to the nurse's tirade all day."

"Small price to pay." She settled back into bed and yawned. A nap would do nicely. She closed her eyes, but a thought occurred to her. She opened one eye. "You never answered my question."

"What question?"

"About whether you missed me or not."

"You're relentless."

"Answer the question, Milo." Both eyes open now, she turned to face him.

He squirmed. Uh-oh. That couldn't be good.

"It's not that I don't miss you when you're gone—today or at Camp Defiance. But I'm hoping with time apart from me, you'll find your way."

"My way?"

He sighed. "I keep hoping when you're by your lonesome, you'll find out who you are. Not who Pa said you are or who you are in relation to me. Not who you're pretending to be." He leaned close and dropped his voice. "Just you, Willow. And I'm hoping and praying that someday that'll be enough for you. That you'll find out that who you are is enough *for you* 'cause it doesn't matter if it's enough for anybody else. It's enough for God, isn't it?"

God? How would she know what was in the Almighty's mind? "I don't know? Is it? All we ever heard in church was God's wrath for sinners."

When she closed her eyes and tried to picture God's face, it was her father's scowl that came to mind.

"You heard the camp preacher, right?"

Something inside her stirred. "Yes." He'd said they all were God's children, dearly loved, and that their good heavenly Father had thoughts of peace for them. Good plans, the preacher had said. It sounded lovely. It sounded too good to be true.

"God's opinion should be all that matters."

"How would I know His opinion? You may find the Almighty close enough to whisper in your ear, but to me, He's as far away as the stars."

"Forgive me if this sounds harsh, but if there's distance between you and God, you're the one who put it there. You can be as close to Him as you want."

The bite of tears stung her eyes, and she wrenched her gaze away from him, turning to face the other direction. His words cut her. Why did he insist on withholding his affection from her and instead pushing her toward a God she couldn't see? One she didn't know.

She spoke over her shoulder. "Since you're so eager to get rid of me, you'll be pleased to know I'm requesting a transfer to the MSM. You won't have to put up with me any longer."

"That's not what I meant."

"I'll kill Quantrill and come home a hero. We'll see if that's enough for *you*."

He growled and mumbled something she couldn't decipher. She'd ask the doctor for a transfer as soon as he made his rounds. Since she hadn't run into any symptoms of irritable heart on her escape into town, he wasn't likely to deny her. The sooner she could get away from this whole dreadful place, the better.

Maybe Milo was right about one thing. She was better on her own.

Chapter 15

YOU KNOW THAT STAYING STUCK IN THIS NEVER-
ENDING NIGHTMARE COULD COST YOU EVERYTHING—
YOUR LIFE, YOUR SANITY, YOUR HAPPINESS, YOUR
DREAMS, YOUR FULFILLMENT, AND POSSIBLY YOUR
RELATIONSHIP, FAMILY, JOB, AND FINANCIAL
FREEDOM. MAYBE IT ALREADY HAS.

FROM *SICK OF BEING SICK*
BY DR. BRENDA WALDING

Modern Day

My outing with Mom proves successful, if one defines success as remaining upright for the entire duration of the excursion. Mom talks about the woman with the tree name so much I almost plug my fingers in my ears and hum, but other than that, there's little drama. Well, for anything remotely related to my mother.

While this bolsters Mark's confidence that I'll be able to tackle the zoo the next day, it has the opposite effect on me. I feel the same way I used to feel when I'd spent an entire day swimming. Every muscle in my body protests as if I've pushed it to its limit. My eyelids hang like heavy curtains, begging to shut out the light of day. If spending forty minutes viewing bunnies and fish from a temperature-controlled environment depleted me this severely, how could I possibly manage a grand jaunt into Springfield, followed by hours of walking amidst crowds?

I awake Saturday to rustling sounds. I haven't revealed my reservations to Mark yet. Thought I might feel better after a good night's sleep. I roll onto my back and find he's already dressed. He's sitting on the edge of the bed, tying his shoes.

His face lights up when our eyes meet. "Good morning! Thought it'd be best to get an early start. Made you coffee." He nods toward the nightstand where my favorite *Supermom* mug sits.

My heart warms. I should try. For him.

I sit, and instantly, hot pressure pulses at the base of my forehead. It spreads across my eyebrows. I wince.

Mark frowns. "What's wrong?"

"Headache." I wave a hand. "No big deal."

"I'll get you aspirin." He nearly sprints from the room.

As soon as he leaves, I test my strength by lifting my arms over my head. Oh. My. Word. They are lead. They're far too heavy to lug around a zoo. Amputation is the only reasonable alternative. I bite my lip to siffle a cry, and blood tinges my mouth. I must do this. There's no way I can let my family down. I'll push through.

The eyes that greet Mark when he returns are full of tears. I can't help it. This stupid body refuses to cooperate. It's sabotaging my life.

"Oh, honey. Do you have a fever?" Mark drops the aspirin in my palm and places a warm hand on my forehead. "No. You actually feel cool. Clammy."

I shiver. Lean into his body heat.

"Do you …?" He pauses as if he's afraid of the answer. "Do you think you'll be able to manage going with us to the zoo?"

"Of course." My answer rushes out before I'm able to put thought behind it. The tears on my face belie it.

"The medicine will help." I dry my face with the corner of the comforter. No use trying for a smile that will no doubt fail.

"If you're sure …"

The man is a fool to trust me. Why doesn't he argue? Can't he see I'm in no state to gallivant around? My lip trembles. He doesn't seem to notice.

"Want me to make you breakfast? A smoothie?"

"Sure."

"Great. Get dressed, and we can leave within the hour." He pats my knee and leaves the room.

After a shaky breath, I swing my legs over the side of my bed. My feet find solace in the soft carpeting. My toes curl, then relax. The floor is solid. It can hold me. It will not play games and move around. As much as I tell myself this, I don't trust the ground beneath me. Perhaps I never will again.

All holds steady as I stand and walk to the closet. The breeze rattles the windowpane, telling me jeans and a sweater are in order. My oversized teal one provides a cozy choice, or should I layer a T-shirt with the brown one in case the temperature climbs? As I contemplate this small choice, one of a million I'd normally make in one day, my head fogs. My legs wobble. I'm like a leaf blown in this direction and then that.

Mark's arms sweep under mine right before my knees buckle. "Whoa!"

I lean into his strength. He picks me up as if I'm a new bride he's carrying over the threshold. I blink as the softness of our bed envelops me.

"Guess you're not going anywhere." It's obvious he's fighting to keep disappointment from overtaking his voice.

"I'm sorry." My new mantra.

"It's fine." Only it's not. We both know this will never be fine. How can it be? "Rest."

"I don't have any spoons today," I mumble.

"Spoons?" Mark's forehead bunches in confusion.

I pinch the bridge of my nose. I'm not making any sense. "It's a whole thing in the POTS community." I've become privy to a new world via online support groups, complete with lingo and analogies using kitchenware. "Spoons represent the amount of energy a person has. You might have twenty or thirty spoons each day. I have maybe five, and I have to choose how to use them. Taking a shower uses a spoon. Brushing my hair, folding a few pairs of jeans, reading an email." I wave toward the closet. "Choosing an outfit. They all take spoons." I bury my face in my hands. "I don't have any spoons."

His frown deepens. "But you haven't done anything yet today. How come you don't have any to start with?"

"I used today's spoons yesterday."

He tucks a hair behind my ear. "How many spoons would it take for you to go to the zoo?"

I bite my lip. The truth? "More than I've had in months."

His shoulders droop. "I'm sorry. I didn't realize."

"I know. I love you." My face twists in pain that reaches far deeper than my uncooperative body.

"I love you, too." He bends to kiss the top of my head. A whiff of his cologne teases my senses, and I fist his flannel shirt, clinging to this man as if he's my last breath. Suddenly, I don't want to be left alone. *It's a scary feeling being left. Don't let it happen again.*

What if he gets sick of taking care of me? What if he decides he's had enough and walks out? The memory of the sound of the front door slamming as my father retreats from our lives echoes. Slam. Slam. Slam. I feel small. Helpless. Panic surges. I can't stand this. I'm going to jump out of my skin. Someone needs to make this stop, calm this storm inside of me.

I gulp in air, then choke on it. My coughs sputter. My face flames.

Mark wraps me in a hug. "Shh," he whispers in my ear. He draws gentle hearts on my back with one hand while stroking my hair with the other. "It's okay. God's got you."

I moan. God. He's the one I don't know what to do with. I can't turn my back on Him because He's all I have, but I'm not happy with Him right now. Raging emotions dare me to spit in His face, but my heart cries out for Him to hold me close.

It's like we were all part of this perfect Christian play. My lines were as familiar as my role as the pastor's wife. Then, suddenly, God went off script. I no longer know what to say or do, but Mark keeps spouting lines from the original script, even though they no longer make sense. "God's got you" made sense before everything fell apart. But now? Now, I bite back sharp words. *He's got me? Really, Mark? Because it seems like He's let me fall to the floor.*

These are not words that a preacher's wife would ever say, so I nod and ground myself in outside noises—a bird's song and the rumble of a motorcycle. My breathing slows. My head sinks low in the pillow. *Lord, I still love You. I just don't know how to trust You anymore.*

"That's it. Rest in Him, sweetheart." Another shallow line from the old script. My throat burns. One last kiss and Mark walks toward the door. "I'll text you when we're on our way home."

I'm half asleep when voices fade, and the front door closes.

A couple of hours later, I awake to the ding of a text notification. It's Mark. He sent a picture of the three of them in front of the brown bears. His message says *Wish you were here.*

My heart squeezes. Me too. My family is spending quality time without me. Scandalous. I should be in that picture. Who knows if the twins will even be interested in going to the zoo next year? Too soon they'll be too old to spend time with us at all. We'll only see them on car rides to and from events with their friends. This is precious time, and here I am, squandering it in bed. Again.

Chipper barks and whines. He must need to go out. I sigh as I free myself from tangled sheets and blankets. The walker stands right next to the bed. I didn't see Mark roll it in before he left, but gratitude fills me now. I make good use of it as I break free from my prison of a bedroom and to the back door.

Chipper turns in a circle, pleading at me with large eyes.

"I'm coming, boy."

Only I forgot slippers or shoes, and the porch must feel like ice to bare feet. A pair of Mark's flip-flops lie on the mat nearby. I slip into them and shuffle toward the whiny dog.

When I open the door, he shoots out. I follow much slower. Hopefully, no one sees me standing on the back porch with my walker. Frosty air nips at my toes. The wind whips a strand of hair into my mouth and another into my eyes. I swipe them away, shivering. Should have put on a coat. I struggle to remember what the children were wearing in the picture Mark sent. Are they warm enough? What did he pack for lunch?

Chipper finishes his business, and I call him to come inside. He ignores me, sniffing here and there around my rose bushes. His ears perk, and he dashes to the fence.

"Chipper," I warn. "Don't even think about it. Come here, boy."

Except he's thinking about it.

His head tilts to the side. He digs with his paw. His nose dips under the fence line.

"Chipper, no! No! Don't you dare. Come here!" I whistle or at least attempt to. Mark has always been the whistler in the family.

It's like the dog is deaf to my voice. The top half of his body is under the fence before I can make it to the edge of the porch. By the time I maneuver the walker down the two steps, he's gone.

"Chipper!"

I push the walker around the side yard and wrestle with the gate. His copper tail disappears from view. I speed up, zipping as fast as my legs will go. Mark's flip-flops slap against the ground. The walker squeaks with the erratic movement. My breath puffs out in clouds.

Where is he? Far down the road, a flash of white. I'm in the middle of the street now, clutching the walker. I try to jog, but the too-large flip-flops slip around on my feet and threaten to send me sprawling.

My lungs burn. Pain stitches my side. I stop to push a fist into my rib and gasp a breath. As soon as my legs stop moving, they turn to Jell-O. Whoa. No. I cannot pass out in the middle of the street. I manage to flip the seat and sit. Dropping my head between my knees, I struggle for equilibrium. And pray no one runs me over.

When I look up, I find I made it six houses down. The distance spans enormous now that adrenaline fails to propel me forward. How will I make it back home? I've always admired our quiet neighborhood. Mostly older people inhabit the homes around ours, which means not much traffic, surely no crazy drivers. As I sit on a walker in the middle of the street, I'm thankful for the latter, but the former gives me pause. How long will it be before anyone notices I'm here and helps me?

I wait, shivering, but no one comes. Mark's words echo in my mind.

God's got you.

Where is He now?

My feet are icicles. My fingers too. I can't even think about how Chipper is gone. If I let myself dwell on how the children will react when they find out, I'll dissolve right here in the street.

My limbs feel like magnets being pulled to the center of the earth. Down. My body wants to go down. I fix my gaze on our home and grit my teeth. I must make it there. Stooped over as if draped with weights, I plod forward, one miniature step at a time. Tears start prickling my eyes at first. By the time I make it into the front yard, icy rivers flow down my face.

Only ten, maybe fifteen more steps to go, but my feet refuse to move. My mind shouts at them. Pleads. But they remain rooted. The top of my body moves forward, however, rolling with the walker. My chin slams into the little black seat before pounding onto the prickly grass as the walker escapes from my grasp.

Once again, I am horizontal in a vertical world, only this time I am fully conscious. Each blade of grass announces its presence. My teeth chatter. They are the only part of my body that seems capable of movement. My arms refuse to budge. My legs will not maneuver. I'm stuck. My body has given up on me.

Just like God.

~

Lily stepped over a screaming Jana and dodged Jamie as he dashed in front of her path in pursuit of a bouncy ball.

"Where are you off to again?" Mom's haggard voice snuck up on her from behind. Shoot. She'd hoped to avoid that.

"I'm meeting with the church elders about overseeing an outreach." The elders and Matt, but no need to let Mom know a cute boy was involved.

Mom frowned and queasiness swirled in Lily's middle.

"What? I told you about this."

"I know." Mom sighed. "But you said it in passing. I didn't know you were serious." Oliver fussed. Mom bounced him on her hip.

"You thought I was joking? About volunteering." Lily raised her eyebrows.

"Not joking. I just didn't know you'd follow through."

"Well, I am." She had to shout to be heard over Jana's fit. Or maybe that wasn't the true reason she raised her voice.

"There's plenty to keep you busy right here." Mom tried for a smile. It didn't reach her eyes.

"Believe me. I know." She turned and rushed out the door, shutting it with more force than necessary. The noise. The stress. The chaos. It was getting to her. She pinched the bridge of her nose. She wasn't a bad person. She had a good heart. She was out to make the world a better place. Her way looked different than Mom's way was all.

Her way.

Her path.

Attending Ascend Community was like breathing fresh air after being confined to a stuffy room all her life. She hadn't known this much oxygen existed free for inhaling. Warm welcomes. A group of people her own age she could almost relate to. And after the meeting today, perhaps a purpose too.

Maybe she didn't need Michigan after all.

~

Hours pass before the crunch of tires on our driveway signals Mark's arrival. In the time I've waited for him to return, dozens of cars have driven by. None have slowed or stopped. No one seemed to notice the woman sprawled out in her front yard. Dried, crusty tear splotches mar my cheeks. I prayed for someone to come help me. My prayers once again went unanswered.

A gasp marks the moment my husband notices me. "Oh my God," he says. Is he taking the Lord's name in vain, or is it a prayer? A part of me hopes the former, if only so that someone else might be as blasphemous as my own traitorous thoughts.

His strong arm slides underneath my head, and welcome warmth seeps into me. "Oh my God." His soft lips brush my cheeks. "Your cheeks are like ice. Oh, Lord, what have I done?"

So, he's praying. He's never seemed to doubt the kindness and faithfulness of God.

He grunts softly as he sweeps me into his arms and carries me inside.

"What's wrong with Mom?" Victor's voice sounds from behind us. My heart pangs at the concern in it.

"She must have fainted outside."

I crane my neck. If only I could glimpse my son. The sight of him would do me good. And Jordan. Where is she? I hear not a sound from her and can't manage to bring either into my line of sight.

"Why was she outside?"

"I don't know." Mark kicks a pile of clothes off the couch and gently lays me down. A soft blanket drapes over me. He tells Victor to make me hot tea.

I close my eyes and begin to drift off as I thaw. Then I remember, and my eyes shoot open. I force a swallow down my parched throat. "Chipper," I croak.

Victor hands me the tea, and Mark supports the back of my head as I raise myself enough to take a sip. "What's that?" he asks.

"Chipper ran away."

"Chipper ran away?" There it is. Jordan's voice. It whines and whimpers. Not about her mother's safety but about the dog.

I nod. "I tried to go after him, but … couldn't."

Mark slumps onto the cushion at my feet and drops his head into his hands. Jordan's purple jacket flashes by as she runs toward her room. Victor backs away from me as if I've slapped him.

"I'm so sorry."

Victor retreats through the kitchen. The back door slams.

I drift off to sleep, and when I wake, Mark is still sitting at my feet.

"I should have never left you alone." Mark's voice breaks. I've broken him.

"It's not your fault." I reach for his hand and find only air. He's not looking at me. The floor consumes his attention.

"I'm not leaving you by yourself again."

"Honey, don't do that."

His tenuous gaze finds mine. "What?"

"So many people depend on you."

His jaw firms. "You're the most important."

"I appreciate that, but I *need* you to continue being the amazing pastor you've always been." I try again to take his hand. This time he grabs hold. "I'll take it easy. Some things around here might have to slide. It's fine. Kingdom work has to be your priority. As long as you're doing good in the world, what I'm going through doesn't have all the power. If you give it up because of me, this sickness has won, and everything is without purpose."

"Okay."

My stomach churns.

What have I convinced him to agree to?

~

Two days later, I am lying in bed when the doorbell rings. Mark is at a church meeting. The twins recently got back from school and are playing in the backyard. A salesman? I wait to see if whoever it is will go away.

Another ring rouses me from bed, but what follows propels me faster than I've moved in weeks. A bark! Chipper? I push my walker to the front door, stopping for only a second to straighten my rumpled T-shirt before throwing open the door.

Chipper charges through, dashing straight for the kitchen. He must be headed for his food and water bowls. A leash dangles behind him. I clap my hands together. "Chipper!"

A woman shifts her weight on my front porch. Her face is pinched in a sour expression, and she reminds me of the

Wicked Witch of the West. "Your dog was doing his business on my front lawn. Number two."

I scrunch my nose. "Sorry about that. Thanks for bringing him home. The children were worried sick."

"He's a handsome one. If I had a dog like that, I'd take care to keep a better eye on him."

My cheeks warm. What can I say? I run a hand through tangled hair.

She points toward the kitchen. "He ran off with my leash."

"Oh." I wave in that direction. "By all means."

She steps forward, her gait and expression draped in suspicion. She leads the way into the kitchen. I hear her hitch of breath before I see what she must.

The room is a disaster. Dirty dishes are piled on both the kitchen table and counters. A puddle of milk graces a chair and the floor. Mark must have swept spilled Cheerios into a pile and left it there without depositing it into the trash. Perhaps because the trash is so full the lid won't close. A fly buzzes around the can. A pan of uneaten, burnt scrambled eggs adorns the space by the sink.

Nervous laughter bubbles out of me. "Oh my."

Chipper's whine brings our attention to his panting tongue near two empty bowls. The woman scoffs. "He doesn't have food or water."

"I'll get him some." I wheel over and fill his water bowl at the sink. "I haven't been feeling well. My husband isn't the best housekeeper. He tries, but …"

She harrumphs as she unhooks her leash from Chipper's collar. She crosses her arms and watches as I fill his food bowl like I'm an unruly schoolgirl and she's the principal. I scramble for how to get into her good graces.

"Thanks again for bringing him back. It's been two days. We were afraid the worst had happened."

Her frown deepens. "You're lucky it didn't."

"I know."

The back door bursts open and the twins rush in. Victor kicks a soccer ball across the kitchen floor. It barely misses the Wicked Witch and instead ricochets off the oven, then the chair, finally landing in Chipper's water bowl with a splash. Splotches of dirt and grass now mark each place the ball touched.

Jordan gapes. Victor covers his mouth and laughs. His cheek is streaked with grime and dust coats his hair.

The Wicked Witch's eyes narrow in a glare.

My voice croaks as I say, "You know you're supposed to keep the ball outside."

He retrieves the wet ball and tosses it out the door. "Sorry."

"Chipper's back!" Jordan's jubilation breaks through their contrition.

The dog barks and dashes out the open door.

"Go watch him!" My panicked cry borders on hysteria. My shoulders creep around my ears.

The Wicked Witch clenches the leash with a white-knuckle grip. "It looks like your dog isn't the only one you need to take better care of." With that, she huffs out, slamming the door behind her.

The next day, I'm lying in bed, staring at the ceiling and replaying yesterday's events. The trash truck rolled by moments ago, squeaking and clanging. It took with it all evidence of the previous day's humiliation. I spent hours cleaning after the Wicked Witch left. Now the kitchen sparkles, but the memories remain. The disdain in her face haunts me.

Mark apologized profusely for the incident, but it wasn't his fault. I'm the homemaker, the one who has forgone working outside the home to take care of the household. I'm the one who should have ensured all was in proper order.

The ring of the doorbell jolts me, and it feels like déjà vu. I catapult from bed. Chipper. Where's Chipper? As I still, the pitter-patter of his feet relaxes me.

Perhaps the woman has come to apologize for her atrocious behavior. I snort. Not likely. What if she's come to have another round of shaming the slovenly wretch of a dog owner? My steps slow, but I continue toward the front door, stopping to peek in the mirror before answering. Presentable, at least. Better than yesterday. Still in sweats. No makeup. But I brushed my hair and cleaned my face this morning.

When I swing open the door, a woman in a business suit greets me with the smallest of smiles. The clipboard she carries obscures her name badge. I relax. Another salesperson I can politely tell to be on her way.

"Good morning, are you Mrs. Prichard?" The woman's short, curly hair looks stiff as if sprayed into place. In fact, all of her looks that way. Her clothes. Her face.

Wariness creeps into my tone. "Yes."

"I'm Belinda Ramond with the Children's Division. May I come in?"

I freeze. "Children's Division?"

"Child Protective Services." She flashes her badge.

Thankful for my walker now, I lean heavily upon it. The ground has shifted.

"May I come in?"

I shake my head. I feel the blood draining from my face. No. No. She looks nothing like the petite blonde who carted me away from my home, suitcase in tow, when my mother was admitted to the mental hospital, but she's one of *them*. The ones who snatch people's children away. I take a step back. Put my hand on the doorknob. She cannot come in.

A glint of sympathy flashes across her features. "Things generally go much better if you cooperate."

I bite my lip. Better? What does better look like in this situation? I know what worse looks like. Worse must look like my children staring at me with wide, tear-filled eyes from the back of this woman's car as she smuggles them to a stranger's house while I watch helplessly from the front porch. Worse rivals every worst-case scenario I've conjured thus far. I can't endure it. With a trembling hand, I open the door wider and nod.

"Thank you." She steps inside. Chipper greets her with a wagging tail. Her gaze roams the tidy surroundings. My muscles ache from the effort of folding laundry and scrubbing counters. "I realize it must be difficult to see a Children's Division worker on your front stoop."

I nod again.

"We received a call—"

"My kitchen is clean." This fact blurts from me like a sneeze. I rush to qualify it. "I know who called. This neighbor came yesterday, and it was messy, but only because I wasn't feeling well. Everyone has off days, right? It's clean now. Do you want to see?"

A hint of a smile precludes her answer. "I'll take a look."

I lead her into the immaculate kitchen. She jots something on her clipboard.

"The children were dirty yesterday. Well, my son was. But he's a boy, right? Boys play outside and get dirty. It doesn't mean we're ..." I can't even finish the thought. Can't say the word *neglectful*.

"I've already seen and spoken with your children at their school, Mrs. Prichard."

I blink. "You've what?"

"Whenever there's a call, we must investigate. That requires interviewing the children. I visited Jordan and Victor this morning and spoke with them at their school."

Heat creeps up my neck. The CPS worker went to their school? The principal, secretary, school counselor, and teacher all must know someone called child services on me. I could melt into the floor.

My voice wobbles. "Please don't take my children away from me."

Her eyes radiate kindness. Not so stiff anymore. "The last thing we want to do is take children away from their parents." She pulls her clipboard out again. "Now, can you give me the names of a couple of references I can contact regarding your ability to care for your children?"

"References?"

"We usually prefer one family member and perhaps a neighbor."

References. My mind fumbles. *References.* A neighbor who would say something good about us. Who wouldn't be annoyed that our dog runs away all the time or that our son constantly kicks balls into their yard or that we let our grass grow an inch too high before finding time to mow.

"Kelly Loren." Where did that come from? She's not a neighbor, and who knows what she'll say about us. My husband ditched her father during his last moments. She thinks I'm sick because of hidden sin. Can I take it back? Oh sure. *Never mind. Don't talk to her.* That sounds like something a perfect parent with nothing to hide would say.

"What's her address and phone number?"

I look both up on my phone and relay the info, praying Kelly remembers all the good things she loved about Mark and me before we turned into a hot mess.

"Good. And a relative?"

Uh-oh. A relative. "I don't have close family, except for my mother, but you don't want to talk to her." My palms sweat.

Ms. Ramond's eyebrows shoot up.

"She has mental health issues." She is the reason I was placed in foster care at eight years old. Will she be the reason my twins are placed there at eleven? *Oh, Lord, no. Please, no.*

"We'll keep that in mind. What's her address and phone number?"

I rattle them off and chew on my nail as she transcribes the information. She's going to call my mom? Or visit. Oh no. Nothing good can come out of that. My mom might tell the woman our house is germ infested. Or that I'm selfish.

"Thank you. Do you need any resources? Information on parenting or governmental assistance?" Her question scrapes two inches from my height.

I shake my head. I could tell her that we're good. That despite living off a pastor's salary, we've managed to enroll our daughter in dance and our son in soccer. I could tell her I'm up for the Golden Servant Award this year. I could tell her I've taught parenting classes at our church or that I've organized dozens and dozens of outreaches. We are the assisters, not the assisted. We are the ones generously giving toward those less fortunate. We are not needy. *I* am not needy.

All these things burn on my tongue, but instead I study the tile floor.

"Okay. We'll keep my notes from today's visit with you and the children in your record. Once I speak to your references, I'll add those notes as well. If you need anything from us, please let us know." She hands me a card and angles toward the front door.

"That's it?"

"As long as your references pan out, this will go in the file." She pats her clipboard.

In the file. On record. I now have a record.

"Okay." I walk her to the door. Our parting is awkward. What do I say? Thank you for coming? Thank you for not taking my children away? "Have a nice day."

"You too."

I'm closing the door when it hits me that I could have given her Delaney as a reference. Why didn't I think of that? As awkward as things have been between us, surely Delaney wouldn't say anything negative about my parenting. Should I yell for the CPS lady to wait? But she's already slipping inside her car, and I've made a big enough fool of myself already. No need to add the fact that I forgot I had a best friend. Plus, it's possible Delaney would mention that my fatigue gets in the way of everyday tasks. Best to take my chances with Kelly.

I close the door behind me and lean against it, sliding to a seated position. Blocking out any further intrusion. After a few moments of staring numbly ahead, hot tears bubble to the surface and spill down my cheeks. My shoulders heave with my sobs as it all rushes back.

The knock on the door. The petite blonde lady with her badge. Ms. Alvira, the old lady from next door who babysat me after school, explaining that my mother was sick. *Sick.* What an awful, terrible, all-encompassing word. She didn't tell me it was Mom's mind that was sick, not her body, but I understood.

"They took her to a hospital to get better. While she's there, you're going to go live with a nice family across town."

The blonde waited while Ms. Alvira helped me pack a suitcase with a dozen outfits, a doll, and toiletries. At the last minute, I tucked Mom's necklace in the side pocket. I'd never liked the pendant. It looked like something an old woman would wear, not a little girl. It had a red cardinal on it, and I liked pink, not red. It was just like Mom to give me a birthday present that didn't make sense. My friends got toys and candy. I got a travel first-aid kit and an ugly old necklace.

I wore that pendant every day for the next five months and eighteen days until I returned home. Every night I grasped it and prayed for God to make Mom better, to make her *normal* like the other moms, and to bring her home.

As I grew close to my foster siblings—Tim and Kelsey, Sadey and Pat—I learned that there were worse things than a crazy mother and an absent father. That's where my fearful, broken heart first learned to break for someone else.

And perhaps it's where I learned to look outward and focus on others to avoid facing the pain of my own heart.

Chipper scrambles into my lap and licks my face.

"This is all your fault, you know." I swipe at my wet cheeks, then scratch behind his ears. "If you wouldn't have run away …"

He attacks my face with his tongue. I can't help but laugh. I have to blame somebody, but it can't be him. He's too sweet. My husband has been too, despite his earlier betrayal. Blaming myself only makes everything worse. Guilt and shame confine me to sulking in bed and look at where that got me.

Do I blame God or the devil or Adam and Eve in the garden? Who can I pile this suffocating load onto? There are darts in my hand. I need a board and a bullseye.

A good Christian woman wouldn't think like this.

A good Christian woman wouldn't have CPS called on her.

Obviously, I'm not a good Christian woman.

I don't know who I am anymore.

Chapter 16

REVOLUTION, EVEN WHEN SUCCESSFUL, IS A
TERRIBLE MEANS OF REDRESS. NOTHING CAN
JUSTIFY IT, EXCEPT THE STERNEST AND MOST
URGENT NECESSITY ... THE WORK OF REVOLUTION
CANNOT BE DONE PEACEABLY AND AMICABLY,
UNDER WHATEVER INGENIOUS NAME INTRODUCED,
AND THEY WHO UNFURL ITS BANNER ARE OPENLY
DECLARING WAR ...

FROM A DISCOURSE FOR THE TIMES
BY REV. W. G. ELIOT, DD, AUGUST 18, 1861

September 18, 1862
Sedalia, Missouri

If Willow was going to kill Quantrill, there was no better place to do it than as part of the Missouri State Militia Cavalry. Her request for a transfer was met without resistance, thanks to the doctor's ready endorsement. Guerrilla hunting would keep her off a standard battlefield, where most cases of irritable heart seemed to erupt. That period of dreadful rest must have done her good. She felt as spry as a spring chicken now.

Rumor had it, her new unit's uniforms would differ slightly from the one she'd been wearing for months, so on the road from Kansas City to Sedalia, she sold her old coat and shirt to a member of the Enrolled Missouri Militia for $1.50.

Order No. 19 called for every able-bodied man between eighteen and forty-five to join the EMM, if not already in service, and to bring whatever arms and horse he had at home. As most of these men weren't outfitted, they happily purchased whatever veteran soldiers disposed of.

Finally, she'd arrived at her MSM unit at the same time as a handful of what appeared to be new recruits. They exuded an excitement too raw for them to have already spent time in mundane military life or bloody battles. She approached heaps of trousers, coats, and shirts. A man with three inverted *V* stripes on his coat—a sergeant—tossed her an item from each pile.

She held up the pants and whistled. Two of her could fit inside one leg.

"I'll swap ya." A large, muscular man next to her raised what looked to be a far better fit.

"Deal." She handed him the enormous trousers and took the slim ones, holding them to her waist. "Much obliged."

"Likewise." Despite the man's scruffy beard, his voice came out smooth and gentle. He held out a hand. "Dedrick Summerhill." Of course. Another German. She couldn't seem to get away from them. Then again, the men she'd served with thus far had been decent soldiers and comrades.

She offered a firm shake. "Will Forrester. You from around here?"

"Down the road. You?"

"Near Ozark. Transferred from the Black Hawk Cavalry." She scrutinized the shirt and coat. They'd do.

"I brought my own horse. I'll get paid forty cents extra per day for the risk of his use."

She managed a smile for the naive man. He assumed Uncle Sam would pay him when and as much as promised.

Dedrick stuffed supplies into his haversack. "You want to stick together? We could button our shelter halves together to make a tent on the march."

"Sure." She eyed his heavy sack. It would prove brutal for the horse on a long march. "Want to know a trick?"

His brows raised in invitation.

"Take two gunny sacks and tie them together like this." She lifted her own to demonstrate. "Then sling them over the horse's saddle. It'll distribute the weight far better, and your horse will be happier."

"Thank you. That's a mighty fine tip." He emptied the contents of his bag onto the grass. "Heard we're getting Austrian Lorenz muskets. Can't wait to get my hands on one of them."

She scoffed.

"What's that for?" He lumbered to a pile and exchanged his haversack for gunny sacks. "They're reliable weapons."

"Perhaps, but they're no good for cavalry service and certainly not in the brush. Think about it, they're so long and heavy, they're liable to get caught in the undergrowth while we're chasing a guerrilla. We could lose our weapon or fall off the horse ourselves trying to carry and fire that thing while mounted."

"What would you suggest?"

"Guerrillas use revolvers. That's what we need. It's what I have."

"I had a Remington at home."

"You should have brought it."

"Left it so my mother would have protection. No tellin' how the secesh will retaliate when they find out I've gone off to fight."

A chill sliced through her. Had someone found out she and Milo were fighting for the Union? Was the attack on Pa and Ma retaliation? But no one could possibly know. She couldn't be responsible for their deaths. The whole countryside was burning.

"Now, we're supposed to turn the brim up on the left side? And attach the plume here?" Dedrick fumbled with his wide-brimmed Hardee hat and feather.

She stifled a laugh. He looked ridiculous. She stuffed her old slouch hat on her head. "I'll stick with this." She wasn't about to go parading like a chicken unless forced to do so.

"Have you been in battle? Or were you scouting mainly?"

"A bit of both and a lot of horse duty. I became rather well known for my ability to find lost horses, though, so I'm fairly confident I'll succeed on my next mission."

"Which is?"

"I'm going to kill Quantrill."

A slow smile curled up his face. "Are you now? You must be a mighty fine guerrilla hunter."

She puffed out her chest and spoke what simply had to be true. "I am."

"Then I'll follow you."

Satisfaction warmed her.

Finally.

~

October 1, 1862

Rumor had it, thirty bushwhackers were hiding out in the cave around the next bend in Hickory County, Missouri. Tricky business deciding how to proceed. Willow's company could sneak up on the Rebels far easier without the horses' snorts and nickers giving them away, but if the guerrillas fled—*when* they fled—the cavalry had no chance of keeping up without horses.

Newly fallen leaves crunched beneath them no matter how lightly they attempted to tread. Autumn in Missouri. There was nothing like it, no air as crisp and vibrant, no colors as beautiful. It'd always been her favorite time to tromp about the woods, executing one adventure or another. But no work of the imagination could have prepared her for hunting murderous, merciless thugs.

An idea struck her. She sniffed the air, and a smile slowly spread. Yes, of course. Why hadn't she thought of it earlier? She sidled up to her sergeant. "If I may, sir."

"Speak freely, Forrester." Whether she'd earned the commander's respect from her brave conduct thus far or whether Dedrick had boasted her merits, she couldn't decipher, nor did she care. Being treated as if she had something worthy to contribute soothed like a balm over still-festering wounds.

She sat straighter in the saddle. "I reckon there's a creek bed not a quarter mile from here, and if I'm not mistaken, the water level will be low enough for the sound of our approach to get lost in the mud if we take that route."

He dipped his chin in respect. "And how do you know this? We've come across no creek."

"I can smell it in the air, sir. The places water has touched have a distinct scent of moisture, even if it's been licked up for a spell."

The faintest hint of a smile edged the sergeant's lips. "Lead the way, Forrester. Or should I say Forrest-nose?"

She attempted a smile in return for his jest but couldn't force one past the weight of trust he'd placed in her. If her hunch proved wrong, their detour could provide time for the guerrillas to slip away before her company arrived. But if she was correct, how long would it be before her coat displayed bars?

Lord in heaven, let me be right. This prayer came as natural as her breath, surprising since she hadn't uttered more than a few words to the Almighty since leaving home. There, if Pa's ire didn't drive her to seek God's favor, her mother's nightly reminders of "Say your prayers" would. But those words had fallen from her lips, memorized and rote, and as ingrained in her as Pa's beliefs regarding states' rights, filthy

Germans, and dreaded abolitionists. Without her parents hovering over her shoulder, telling her what to believe, she found the world far more gray than black and white.

So, was this prayer, forged out of desperation to avoid humiliation, the first sincere one she'd ever prayed? The thought struck her with a pinprick of awareness, and her eyes immediately searched for something to mark this occasion. She should commemorate this moment in her memory, the moment of her first true interaction with the Almighty. But each tree looked the same as the last, each gnarled root similar to the one before. Then, out of the corner of her eye, came a flash of red. A cardinal. It swooped low, nearly drawing an imaginary line in front of her for her to cross, and landed on a mossy stump.

She sucked in a breath. Was this a sign? Her hand flew to the spot her necklace inhabited underneath everything she was pretending to be. This cardinal stayed with her always. If it were a real being, it'd be the only one besides Milo who knew her secret, who knew her true identity. With her always. Knowing her fully. Almost like … God?

And now when she prayed, a bright red bird spoke clearer to her than if a voice had boomed from the sky. God had heard her. He'd listened to this pretender in a forest full of mystery and danger and … Did that mean He'd answer? Suddenly, the answer didn't matter much anymore. Not nearly as much as the realization that she'd been heard. After a lifetime of being passed over, the most important being in existence took note of *her*.

"By George, Forrester's right," the man behind her said.

She startled from her thoughts to see a creek bed ahead to the right. A smile trembled on her lips. God heard *and* answered? It was almost too much.

As the men rode their horses down the muddy bank and into water so shallow it barely covered Rustic's hooves, gratitude spilled from her heart. *Thank You, Lord. You see me. You hear me.*

Her eyes misted, and she shut them tightly to quell that tide. She certainly couldn't cry, but her heart could beat a rhythm of praise.

Mud squelched softly beneath them. She pictured it coating the horses' feet as they snaked toward the cave. Sarge gave the signal. They followed him up the embankment, through a line of trees, and onto a dirt path. Willow's stomach tumbled as the cavern came into view. Her hand clasped the cool metal of her musket as they neared.

She waited for the signal.

Ready.

Set.

Fire.

A barrage of bullets flew into the cave, followed seconds later by a return in kind. Dust billowed around her as the bullets splayed. A horse whinnied and dropped to the ground underneath Johnny, tumbling the man to the ground.

Men dashed out of the cave, pistols in both hands, firing manically. Though their blue coats claimed they were Union soldiers, their long beards and hair, as well as the embroidered shirts underneath the blue coats, showed them to be the guerrillas her company sought.

The soldier to the left of her cried out and fell from his horse. She chanced a glance, breathed a sigh of relief it wasn't Dedrick, then pushed down the roil of guilt that came with her thought. She snapped her attention back to the bushwhackers who were retreating into the woods behind the cave.

She honed in on the one with the longest beard—likely the leader—and gave chase. The man ducked and dodged behind tree trunks, firing at her all the while. Ears and eyes as alert as a rabbit, she followed. She wouldn't lose him.

She was gaining on him, her horse giving her the advantage.

She fired again, and the man grunted in return. If that didn't hit him, it came mighty close. A little closer and she'd have him.

Rustic made a sound of pain, and his steps faltered. He lifted his front hoof as if something was caught in it. He'd injured it somehow. "Shh, baby. I'll be right back. I've got to catch this bad man, then I'll help."

She slid off the giant, snatched her revolver, and ran. They came to a small clearing, and the guerrilla dashed across, turning twice to fire in her direction. She ducked his bullets easily and sprinted after him. Closer. Closer still. She almost had him.

Heart pounding, breath heaving, she bounded back into the woods. The trees around her swayed to the left as her limbs shook. Oh no. Not here. Not now. Not when she was this close.

Pain seared her temples. She gritted her teeth and forced another step, then another, but her body was turning into molasses. Every movement slowed. Her chest flamed, and her legs wouldn't obey her internal command to run. Instead, they gave way, and she plummeted to the ground. Her chin crashed against a rock before her face slid into dirt and fallen leaves. A twig poked her eye, and grime coated her teeth.

The sound of gunshots and shouts faded into the background as if she were drifting on a boat at sea. The edges of her vision darkened. Then, with a bang, the outside world came rushing in with startling clarity.

A horse's nostrils stood above her. She squinted to see the sergeant as the rider.

"What happened, Forrester? You nearly had him."

"I …" What could she say? She couldn't tell him she'd fainted, not if she wanted to continue in his service. Not if she wanted to kill Quantrill. And she couldn't claim a wound without proof. "I tripped."

"You tripped?" The disgust in his voice draped her like a shroud. So much for winning the man's respect.

She managed to nod, though pain sliced through her head at the movement.

"Dust yourself off and go tend to the wounded. At least Martin managed to capture one of them." He shook his head, disappointment radiating from him. "All of that and only one prisoner."

The words *I'm sorry* hung from her lips, but she couldn't seem to push them out. Not with the taste of dirt and crushed leaves in her mouth. But as he rode off, she did manage to lift her head and slowly rise from the dust. She brushed herself off.

A swipe to her chin with the back of her hand revealed blood and more pain. So, she was wounded, but not by the enemy. Her own body had done this to her. Her infuriating irritable heart.

She hobbled back toward where she'd left Rustic, legs tingling, body stiff. She felt as if she'd been run over by a wagon, but at least her body obeyed her when she told it to move.

Rustic stood where she'd left him, clearly favoring his right hoof.

"I'm back, baby. Sorry to leave you like that." She bent low and searched the pad of his foot, finding the culprit easily. A thorn. She pulled it free. "There you go."

She stroked his mane. She couldn't tell him it wouldn't hurt anymore, but she comforted him the best she knew how.

Red danced in the branches in front of her. Another cardinal? Sure, it wasn't uncommon to see the bright birds in Missouri, but twice in such a short span of time was unusual. What if God was still communicating with her? Her chin, knees, and back ached. Her pride too. Frustration brewed within her at the feeling of her own body being out of control. But what if God still saw? Still heard? Even now. She didn't have to see or touch her pendant to feel the weight of it against her skin. Was God like that? Always present with her?

A certainty settled within her chest. She wasn't alone. She could walk forward now, fearing no one.

~

October 6, 1862

Cyrus buttoned his blue coat to hide the guerrilla shirt underneath as they neared the town of Greenville, likely infested with Federal sympathizers. The streets were oddly quiet on this Sunday afternoon, but that failed to bring comfort. None of the seven men hailed from this area, and they'd yet to discover which families were friends and which were enemies. A precarious place to be, as his taut muscles testified.

Ahead, a man in civilian dress rounded the corner, headed straight toward them. As he neared, his face lit, and he offered a friendly wave.

Cyrus smiled back at him. "There's our informant, boys. You smile pretty. I'll do the talking."

The man rushed forward. "Gee, am I glad to see Union presence in these parts. The name's Flint McGee."

Cyrus dismounted and shook his hand. "Fibber Grately."

The men stifled laughter. McGee apparently missed the irony as his bright smile never wavered.

"Say, are there Rebels in the area?" Cyrus stroked his long beard while eying McGee's trimmed one.

"Oh, yes. There's a company of them not five miles from here." He rubbed his hands together and leaned forward in a conspiratorial way. "Actually, I spent two days among them. I went there pretending a desire to enlist and learned of their plans. I can tell you a great deal."

Cyrus reared back, feigning being impressed. "You're a spy?"

McGee's eyes twinkled. "Yes, and a right good one at that. They never suspected a thing."

"You learned of their plans, then snuck away?" The scoundrel.

He nodded. "I've been waiting to come across Union men to tell of them. You are a godsend."

"Indeed." White hot indignation clawed at his throat. Words of how worthless this scum was begged to be released. He pushed them down. Forced another smile, however tight. "Do you happen to know the Southern sympathizers in the area?"

McGee reached into his breast pocket. "Yes, sir. Got a list right here." He handed it over. Though barely legible with such atrocious handwriting, they'd likely be able to decipher it and figure out which homes were safe to visit for a good meal while in the area.

"Thank you." He tucked the list into his jacket.

"You're welcome, but I do think you should join your forces before making a move. The Rebels here are quite numerous. You don't plan to attack apart from your regiment, do you?"

Cyrus forced a chuckle. "Of course not. We're on our way to Greenville to rejoin our regiment now. Perhaps you can travel with us a ways and tell us what you know?"

The scamp heartily agreed and mounted Cyrus's horse with him.

Thankfully, Cyrus no longer had to keep a straight face as the spy sat behind him. He rolled his eyes and mocked away as the man prattled on, feeding them information about their people in the area. When they were five miles outside of town, he could take it no longer. He halted the horse.

"What's that? What's the matter?" McGee's voice took on a nervous edge.

"I heard something."

"A Rebel?"

"Perhaps."

Following Cyrus's lead, the men dismounted, tethered their horses to trees, and took a few steps into the woods. McGee followed with stumbling steps.

"You hear that?" Cyrus whispered.

"What? A Rebel? A guerrilla?" McGee's knees nearly knocked together.

"No. A scumbag traitor." Cyrus swung his revolver toward the spy and, with one shot, took him out.

The men hooted with laughter. "Good one, Cy."

Cyrus dug through the man's pockets, found a few dollars, and claimed them as his own. Blood from the bullet wound smeared on his hand. He wiped it onto his pants as he walked back to Dixie, refusing the twinge of remorse that attempted to wedge its way in. The scallywag had it coming. He practically begged for that bullet as pompous as he was. No way could they have let him live and jeopardize the Southern cause.

Riley wiped his brow with his sleeve before mounting his horse. "You boys hungry? That town had a nice general store."

Cyrus added his voice to the general assent. They stripped off their blue coats and stuffed them into their haversacks before returning to town. They'd come through once as Union men, but now they returned as guerrillas. They tread loudly. Best to strike fear in the heart of every citizen disloyal to the Southern cause.

They stormed into the general store, guns at the ready.

"May I help you?" the elderly man behind the counter asked, then his eyes widened in recognition, tufts of white hair standing on end.

"We're here to take what we please." Cyrus opened his sack wide and tossed in contents from each shelf. Flour, apples, a blanket, matches, dried cabbage, and, most important, whisky.

The grocer stared pale-faced and tight-lipped with only a flair of indignation igniting his tired eyes. Of course, he'd make no move to stop them. Union soldiers were stationed too far away to come to his aid, and no one wanted to face the wrath of a bushwhacker. Being pillaged was the least of their worries.

Why shouldn't good Southern men take whatever they needed? The Federal government had taken everything from them. Their homes, their livelihoods, and the lives of their friends and family. These men were minding their own business when greedy Union fingers snatched everything away, leaving them with no choice but to retaliate. And the newspapers portrayed the guerrillas as the outlaws—the bad guys—in this scenario? Not one of these men had picked up a gun until a Fed forced their hand.

Cyrus met the grocer's stare, fire for fire. "Charge it to Uncle Sam." Then they rode off, hooting and hollering to strike fear in every person they passed.

Chapter 17

SOMETIMES WHEN YOU ARE SICK, LONELY FOLLOWS
YOU NO MATTER WHERE YOU GO AND NO MATTER
WHO YOU ARE WITH.

FROM *SICK OF BEING SICK*
BY DR. BRENDA WALDING

Modern Day

The next time the doorbell rings, my pulse catapults. They've contacted Kelly, and she told them about my hidden sin. They contacted my mom, and she told them about my selfishness. Children's Division is here to rip my children away from me. I'm frozen in place on the couch, my heartbeat thundering in my ears.

Clean. My house needs to be clean. I haven't swept in two days. Or is it three? I haven't mopped since the day the Wicked Witch left in a huff. I wiped down the counters, didn't I? Perhaps that was last night, not this morning. Hopefully, she'll see I'm trying. It's not an utter disaster, but it isn't as sparkling clean as on her first visit. How clean does a house need to be in order not to have your children taken away?

The bell sounds again, and I brace myself for a fight. If that's what it takes, I'll bring it. They can't do this to me. They can't rush in and tear my life apart because of dirty dishes. My hands clench on the walker. My shoulders stiffen as I crack open the door.

On the front porch, it's not Belinda Ramond from Children's Division nor the Wicked Witch from Hades. It's a beautiful young blonde from … well, perhaps from a fashion magazine. A bucket of cleaning supplies hangs from one arm. She's wearing slim-fit jeans and a button-up plaid shirt. The synapses in my brain work to rewire everything I previously believed about plaid. This isn't my grandpa's plaid. The blue in the pattern draws out her bright eyes. She's stunning.

I open the door wider. "Can I help you?"

"Amber." Her eyes light up even more with her warm smile. She speaks my name as if we're best friends who haven't seen each other in years. "Glad to finally meet you."

I tilt my head, mesmerized.

"Oh, sorry." Her hand flutters to cross her heart. "Did Mark not tell you I'd be stopping by?"

"No, I'm afraid he didn't mention it." I return her contagious smile. She must be from church, though I'm positive I've never seen her before.

She laughs, light and free. "Isn't that just like him? I'm Lily. I've heard so much about you."

I open my mouth but find no words. I can't exactly tell her my husband has never mentioned her existence. Instead, I continue to smile and nod.

"Sorry to surprise you like this. I'm new to Ascend Community but plugged right in. Mark's been great. Made me feel right at home. He shared with me some of your health struggles, and well," she says as she lifts the bucket between us, "I'm here to clean your house."

A cough sputters out of me. I cover it with my elbow, hold up one finger, and cough again.

Lily's brows dip. "Are you okay?"

I nod and clear my throat.

"Let's get you water." She angles herself to step through the doorway into my home.

"That's not necessary," I croak out.

"Are you sure? You sound like you could use a cool drink."

I push words past the thorns in my mouth. "I mean, it's not necessary for you to clean my house."

"Oh." She waves a hand in front of her. "Mark warned me you'd probably say that. He told me not to take no for an answer."

He's ambushed me. Again. He set something up without my knowledge and conveniently had someone else break the news to me. My face flames. And *Mark*? How does this new girl get off calling my husband by his first name when nearly all the congregation calls him Pastor Prichard? I take the woman's measure, from her silky hair that crests over her shoulders in soft waves to her stylish suede boots. Perfection personified. She cannot set foot in my house. I wedge myself in the doorway, blocking her entrance.

She has the nerve to laugh. She pulls a phone from her back pocket, presses one button, and holds it to her ear.

"What are you doing? Who are you calling?"

She winks. "Mark said to call him if you wouldn't let me in."

My skin crawls. One button. She has my husband on speed dial?

She's standing close enough to me that I hear everything. The phone only rings once, and Mark picks up.

"Lily! Is she giving you trouble?" His voice lilts as if it's a joy to hear from this woman I knew nothing about five minutes ago.

"Currently blocking my entrance."

"Let me talk to her."

Lily hands me the phone.

I take it like it might be infected. "Yes?"

"Honey, let Lily inside. She's there to clean the house for you. Relax and allow her to do that, please. For me."

I cross an arm across my whirling stomach. "You could have warned me."

"If I did that, you wouldn't have answered the door."

I bite my lip. He has a point. I drop my voice. "I'm managing." I don't want to have this conversation on my front porch on Pretty Girl's phone, but I can't seem to back away.

"You're doing the best you can, and I appreciate it, but now it's time to let someone help you."

The best I can.

The best I can is not enough.

His pastor's voice oozes full force. "Lily volunteered. She's amazing. You'll love her."

This doesn't comfort me, but I am trapped between the man I chose to marry and a woman I didn't choose at all. They press at me from both sides.

"Fine." I hang up, hand Lily her phone, and retreat into my living room.

Lily follows. "What a charming place! I love how you have it decorated." It's as if she throws sunshine confetti everywhere she goes. I fight the temptation to roll my eyes. I never did switch out my summer watermelon decorations for the autumn ones, so the room pops with red accents under the piles of laundry. Annoying, but changing it out is not a top priority.

She meanders to our family portrait that hangs above the fireplace. "Aw. Jordy looks adorbs with twin braids. And Vic in a suit." She turns to me with both hands on her heart. "How long ago was this taken?"

I blink. She knows my children? Well enough to use nicknames? And adorbs? How young is this girl anyway? "Uh … three years ago, I think. We had new ones taken on Labor Day, but I haven't ordered prints yet."

"I'm sure they turned out stellar. The twins are remarkable."

The portrait slants. The ground shifts.

"Goodness, Amber." Lily is at my side. Her arm hooks around me as she guides me to the couch. "You sit and rest. I'll get you that glass of water."

I try not to lean on her, but the floor pulls at me. She settles me onto the cushion. A twinge of satisfaction rolls through me when a strand of her hair snags on my watch. She tries to hide the flinch, but it sneaks through. Not perfect after all.

She rushes off and returns a minute later with a tall glass of water. I guzzle it, and she's off again to grab another. After downing half of the second glass, I lean back against the couch cushion, and my eyes drift closed.

"That's it. You rest. I'll work."

I'm too tired to argue.

Before I fade into oblivion, Lily's voice drifts to my ears from the kitchen. "Oh, and Mark wanted me to tell you I took over the blanket drive. Well, me and someone else. He knew you'd be thrilled it's no longer canceled. And I'll be doing the Christmas outreach as well. You don't have to worry. I've got it covered."

Covered? What she has covered is only one Christmas present per foster or adopted child. A meager offering compared to the usual fare. "It's supposed to be a gala," I murmur before leaving reality for a world of incohesive dreams.

I awake to Jordan and Victor bursting through the door. Victor slings his backpack on the couch I inhabit. It crashes onto my feet. He doesn't seem to notice. "Is Lily here? That's her car, isn't it?"

"Lily?" Jordan calls, dropping her backpack on the floor with a thud.

Lily appears from the kitchen with a dish towel in her hands. "Jordy! Vic!" She opens her arms wide.

The twins rush into them.

I gawk. Who is this woman, and what kind of magic did she use to get both children to run into an embrace?

"What are you doing here?" Jordan beams at her.

"Cleaning."

"Oh, good," Victor says. "It needs it."

His words sting, but not as much as the expression on Jordan's face as she looks at Lily. Like the woman has righted her world. I need to interject. To remind them I'm still here. That I'm their mother.

I clear my throat.

"Oh, hi, Mom." Victor acknowledges me with a slight wave. "Lily's here."

"I know."

Lily tousles Victor's hair. "Now come into the kitchen and have some of the homemade cookies I brought."

"Yum."

The three bound off, and I'm left contemplating my place. Should I follow them to the kitchen?

Lily peeks her head around the corner. "Do you want a cookie, Amber? Chocolate chip."

I shake my head. They're probably poisoned with sunshine and positivity.

Bits of their conversation make their way to me. Jordan's telling Lily about a new girl at school who loves dance. Someone is getting made fun of at school. The new girl? Surely not Jordan. I strain to hear more, but it's no use. I ready myself to stand. I need to go in there, to hear more. Only Jordan snaps closed as tight as a clam when I try to get her to talk. If I insert myself into their conversation, will it stall? I blink rapidly to dispel the threat of tears. I hate that Jordan no longer confides in me—that for some reason I am no longer her safe place—but it's good she has someone to talk to. I won't ruin that for her.

My phone blares from the side table. Mom.

"I found the green book," she says.

My palm grazes my forehead. "Huh?"

"The green book. That tells about the woman—"

"With the tree name who had the fainting disease. The one that had to eat a banana."

"Don't be ridiculous. *Her* doctor didn't tell *her* to eat a banana. *My* doctor told *me* to eat a banana. You never listen."

"Okay, Mom." Laughter filters in from the other room. It pokes me like thistles. I squirm.

"Do you want it?"

"The book?"

"Yes. Do you want the green book? I already sanitized it with Lysol."

I press my lips together and count the cost of paying my mother a visit. Walking to the car. Walking from the car into the wide double doors, down the hallway to the elevator. Taking the elevator to the seventh floor. Down four more doors. Can I do it?

Jordan's voice rings out, sweet and innocent. "Can I have another cookie, Lily? They're delish. I've never had one this good before."

Suck-up.

"Yeah, I want it. I'll be there in twenty minutes." I'll bring my walker. It'll be fine. I have to get out of here.

I push my walker to the front door and hook my purse to the handle. I call over my shoulder, "I'm running to my mom's. Be back in a few."

Lily is in the hallway before the front door shuts. "You're what?"

I ignore the question and plod on. It's a bit tricky to fold the contraption and shove it in the backseat, so I'm forced to overhear her call to Mark from the front porch. "Hey, Mark, is she allowed to drive?"

I scoff. Allowed to drive. As if I'm a teenager. Or someone with a history of drinking. As if this pretty church girl is my babysitter, and she has to call my daddy with a question. Allowed to drive.

I get my companion safely into the backseat and duck into the driver's seat before I hear any more of the conversation. My phone sings from my purse. At a stoplight, I turn it on silent.

I barely make it out of the subdivision before reservations threaten to overtake me, but I push them down. I forgot my trusty water bottle. A run through a drive-thru is in order. I could go for a Monster energy drink, but in order to grab one of those, I'd have to exit my vehicle, something that would expend much needed energy. I settle for a Powerade and sweet tea. Once I force the dyed electrolytes down my throat, I treat myself with caffeinated sugar. That should be enough to propel me through those halls and to my mother's door without collapsing along the way.

My steps are quick as I enter the retirement community. Whether I'm running toward that green book or away from the pretty church girl is anybody's guess. Maybe I'm trying to outrun POTS.

I'm out of breath by the time I reach my mother's door, but I'm upright. Triumph has little time to settle over me before her voice douses it.

"Oh, hello. You don't look well. Not well at all. You're not sick, are you?" She studies me with narrowed eyes.

"I don't have a virus, if that's what you're asking."

"No virus. That's good."

"Yep. All I have is the fainting disease."

"Wipe your feet." She steps back to allow my entrance and thrusts a container of disinfectant wipes in my direction. "Use these on your walker."

No use arguing. I do as I'm told and wipe the legs and seat before proceeding further into the immaculate space. Not a speck of dust to be seen on either bookshelf or entertainment center. Her end tables shine as if recently polished. The carpet sports orderly vacuum lines. The scent of bleach lingers in the air.

I came from this. I should be able to do better with my own home. Rosalin McNeil's daughter should not have Child Protective Services called on her due to a dirty house. What would Mom think? I dip my head to hide warm cheeks.

"Sit. Sit."

I move to sit in the faded blue recliner Mom's had since I was a child.

"Not there." Her voice jumps at me. I startle. "That's an unlucky spot. You don't want to sit in an unlucky spot. Not when you already have the fainting disease."

I freeze. "Where do you want me to sit?"

"On the couch. Center cushion."

I maneuver the walker as close as I can to the middle of the couch, but the coffee table creates a barrier I can't squish past. I end up hobbling without assistance the rest of the way. I sit on the edge of the cushion lest my imperfection tarnish the vinyl.

"Here." Mom shuffles over and, to my surprise, thrusts a faded hunter-green journal in my direction.

"A green book." I caress it with a gentle finger. The spine is loosely threaded together. Bottoms of yellowed pages peek out at odd angles. "How old is this thing?"

Mom sits next to me and folds her hands in her lap. "She wrote it during the war."

"Which war?" But as I open the cover, I find the answer.
Willow Forrester
1861

My breath hitches. The woman with the tree name. Willow Forrester. "This is from the Civil War." I turn the brittle page and take in the elegant script. Some letters are faded beyond recognition. Many are difficult to decipher. "How do you have this? It should be in a museum somewhere."

"Oh no. No. No. No. Keep it in the family. You must promise to keep it in the family."

"Okay. Okay."

"She was a brave soldier."

"A soldier? No, Mom. Women didn't fight in the army back then."

"She did." Her serious expression tells me she believes this to be true, as ridiculous as it is.

I pat her hand. "I don't think so, Mom."

Her voice rises. "She fought as a man. Will Forrester. She fought in the war."

The conviction in her voice sends chills up my arms. She's sure of this. Is she right? She was right about the green book. What if this woman had POTS? Could she have pretended to be a man and fought in the Civil War? Maybe Willow knows something I don't. She might have the secret to thriving in the midst of this illness.

Tenderly, I close it and pet the cover before sliding it in my purse. I'm ready to go now, ready to rush home and devour this journal from the comfort of my bed.

Mom mashes her lips together. Her hands inch toward the journal. It's as if she's magnetically drawn to the thing. As if at any moment she might snatch it back.

"I'll take good care of it."

"I don't know." Her fingers finagle their way into my purse, grazing the frayed spine. "This was a mistake. Give it back. I want it back."

Oh no. No way. No how. I will tackle my mother to the floor before I give up the right to read this journal. Okay, I can't assault my mom. But … "What if I read it here? I'll come here and sit on the center cushion of your couch and read a little at a time." The idea spills from me before the logistics catch up. How will I manage to get out of the house and here multiple times? Will Mark put me on lockdown after the stunt I pulled today?

I'll figure it out.

Willow Forrester pulls me. I must know more about her. I'll do whatever it takes.

"Okay."

My shoulders relax. A smile inches up. "I'll start now."

Mom nods. "I'll make us tea."

She's just risen when her phone rings.

"Hello? Yes, she's here. Hold on a second."

I groan. Mark. And I've only reopened the cover.

I work to keep my voice bright and unbothered. "Hi, honey."

"Why aren't you answering your phone?" His voice doesn't sound very pastoral now.

"Oh, it must be on silent." Not a lie. Not at all.

He nearly growls. "I've been worried sick about you."

I squirm. "I'm fine. My mom called, and I decided to pay her a visit. A few months ago, you wouldn't have blinked an eye."

"A few months ago, you'd never been rushed to the hospital."

I have no rebuttal, so I stare at the journal in my lap.

"Lily and I are coming to get you. She'll drive your car back, and you can ride with me."

My throat feels like I swallowed a fly. A cough sputters. *Lily and I?* I pound my chest.

"Are you okay?"

I can't choke out words past this cough.

"We're on our way."

We. Our. No.

I try to say, "That's not necessary," but the hacking strangles my words. He hangs up.

My mom places a cool glass in my hand. "Drink."

The liquid cools my throat and must flush the fly to my stomach because it's unsettled now.

"Mark sounds mad. He's mad, isn't he?" Mom asks.

I drop my head into my hands. "You're not helping, Mother."

She once again sits next to me. She rocks back and forth, rubbing her hands on her legs. "Your father was mad. He left me."

"Dad didn't leave because he was mad. He left because you were—"

The word freezes on my tongue. *Sick.* This is the narrative I've spouted over and over throughout the years. My mother is mentally ill. She's sick. Dad left because he couldn't handle it. Dad left because Mom was sick.

Mom doesn't ask me to finish the sentence, which is good because I can't. I can't vocalize the words that could very well be my mirror.

~

Lily turned up the dial and sent worship music blaring throughout Amber's car. She kept Mark's maroon Toyota in sight. What an amazing family. When she and Matt had met with the elders about the Christmas outreach, they'd offhandedly mentioned having to cancel the blanket outreach. A couple of nosey questions as to why, and they'd unloaded the whole sad story. Amber. Once a shining star of a volunteer. Now riddled with a chronic illness. Unable to assist the church in any way. Mark was stretched. Their family, stressed.

"Keep them in your prayers," Cole had said.

Prayers, sure. But she'd squirmed in her seat at the bistro. Her gaze studied the three elders before her. They seemed like good men, but what was being done to lighten the load? "What else can I do for the Prichards? Practically, I mean."

They'd stuttered and stumbled over answers. Pricilla had organized a meal train when Amber was first in the hospital, but now? They had no clue. Ask Mark on Sunday, they suggested.

Turns out, Mark had several thoughts on the matter, though it took many pledges of sincerity to weasel them out of him.

"Maybe you could take the twins to practices when I'm unable."

"Sure."

"I'd like them to get to know you first. What would you think about taking them to lunch? I have a meeting directly after church."

Typically developing children? Ones she could carry on a normal conversation with. "I can do that."

He shoved his hands into his pockets, and his gaze slid to the carpet. "I hate to ask but ..." His hand grasped the back of his neck. "It would also be helpful if someone could clean the house. Amber tries her best, but—"

Lily put out a hand. "Say no more."

"Really?"

"I'd be happy to."

But as happy as Lily had been to spend time with children who didn't drain her energy and as delighted as she'd been to feel like she was positively contributing to society, Amber put off a different vibe entirely.

Amber didn't want anything to do with her.

Lily pressed her lips together. It was fine. Normal. The poor woman had gone through so much lately. Lily needed to win her over. She could do that.

"Sorry, car, you can't come over. I'm following that couple." Did everyone talk to other vehicles who tried to merge? Probably not. At least she used polite words.

As long as she was already certifiably crazy, she might as well keep talking. "They're an amazing couple. A picture-perfect family. Everything I want for myself someday." Well, minus the sickness that had overtaken Amber as of late.

She was a magnet, drawn to the family in front of her, repelled by her stressful, chaotic family of origin. She couldn't stop it if she tried.

She didn't try.

~

I force a polite smile when Lily returns the next afternoon with four freezer meals and one piping hot pan of lasagna. She wheels the feast inside using a rolling utility cart like a professional. The muscles at the base of my neck tense.

"Were you up all night cooking?" I lean my hip against the kitchen counter and watch her unload pans onto the kitchen table. Good luck finding room in the freezer for all of that.

She brushes a perfectly curled strand of hair behind her shoulder. "No. My family helped. I have six siblings. They all pitched in."

So, I'm a community-building pity project. "Nice."

When she opens the freezer, my jaw drops. It's spotless, and what was a jumbled mess of half-empty boxes and bags strewn about is now neatly stacked and organized. She did this yesterday? How did she find the time to organize my freezer and scrub every inch of my kitchen until it gleamed? She slides the freezer meals in with no problem and turns to me.

"Mark has to stay late for that budget meeting, so here's the plan. We'll have an early dinner, I'll drop Vic off at soccer practice at five thirty, take Jordy to dance from six until seven, pick Vic up, then come back here and supervise bath and bedtime. After they're down, I plan to tackle cleaning the upstairs bathroom since I didn't get to it yesterday."

I stare at her. My mouth moves, but no words come out.

"I'm happy to help."

Sure, she is. Happy to take over my role. In my home. With my children.

"You're planning on giving them dinner at what? Four thirty? That's really early. We normally grab something on the way home from practice."

She winces. "Call me old-fashioned, but fast food is not what we want to be feeding the kids, right? Nothing beats a home-cooked meal."

I shudder at her use of *we*. As if there's a *we* here.

"You were homeschooled, weren't you?"

She beams. "Yeah. My mom homeschooled all seven of us." She chuckles. "Well, six of us. Olly is only a baby."

Oh my goodness, she stepped straight out of a Christian homesteaders magazine and into my kitchen. She's the perfect Christian woman I've always tried to be. My hand gravitates to my tight throat.

"Look, I appreciate everything you're trying to do here." I focus on her cross stud earring and avoid meeting her eyes in case she has the gift of discernment and can tell I'm lying. "But it seems a bit excessive. We can manage."

Her chin dimples with her frown. "Mark asked me to help out. He had to reschedule several meetings when he stayed home with you, so he's playing catch up right now. He wants you to rest." She takes a step toward me and puts a hand on my shoulder. It's warm, steady, and confident. Like her. Something inside me shrinks. "I know it's hard to accept help, but God made the body of Christ to need each other."

The body of Christ. I huff. What part of the body am I now? It seems like Lily is the heart and I'm the little toenail.

The little toenail who has yet to make much headway in terms of the gala. I got one quote from a banquet hall and another from the community center. Both made me cringe. I'm waiting for the local grocery store to call me back about a donation. I'm on the PTA with the manager, and I'm hopeful. Curiosity overrides my desire to avoid further conversation with Miss Perfect.

"So, tell me about the Christmas outreach." I twirl a strand of hair around my finger, attempting to appear nonchalant. Does it look as unnatural as it feels?

Her eyes brighten. "Oh, I'm so excited! We're going to gather requests from foster and adoptive families and write what the children want for Christmas on the back of paper ornaments. Members of the congregation can choose an ornament and shop for that child. The group will hand deliver the presents to the children the week before Christmas."

I scramble for something polite to say. "Oh, how ..." Unoriginal. Anticlimactic. Disappointing. "Nice."

"What's wrong?" She squints at me as if trying to see past my words to the true meaning.

"Nothing. It's just that ..." I shouldn't say anything. "We used to do a gala. It was the biggest event of the year. A chance for these children from such hard backgrounds to feel like princes and princesses for an evening. They were pampered with good food, quality entertainment, and many presents, not just one."

Lily's eyes mist. Her smile wobbles. "That's beautiful."

"For many of these children, Christmas harbors bad memories. Or at least it's a hard time of the year, being away from their birth families. They deserve something magical, don't you think? One spectacular, memorable night where they feel safe and loved and celebrated."

A few tears dampen her cheeks now as she nods. "Yes, they do deserve that." She looks at the ceiling and blinks rapidly before her gaze finds mine again. "I wish I could give them such an evening."

I press my lips together. I bet she does. But while she might be the one to take over my role at the church, she won't take over my gala. There's no way she could put the heart behind it that I can. She hasn't been where I've been. Hasn't seen what I've seen.

"The elders said no to a gala," I say, jaw tight.

That will certainly stop her from trying, but it won't stop me.

At least now I know she hasn't stolen the corporate sponsorship I need to make this a success. Determination rises within me like a tidal wave. I'm going to do this. For kids like Kelsey and Tim, and for the little girl huddled next to the bedroom window, clutching her mom's cardinal pendant, praying for a miracle.

Lily may have taken over my life, but she can't have this.

~

That night I toss and turn. Lily's perky smile haunts my thoughts. My stomach is full of her lasagna. I hate how delicious it tasted and how, even now, the spices dance on my tongue. I roll back over onto my right side. My restlessness jostles Mark awake.

"Honey, what's wrong?"

I groan. "Can't sleep."

He wrestles with the sheet and blanket until he finds my hand. He squeezes it. "What's on your mind?"

I bite my lip. If I say what I'm thinking, I'll sound petty.

As if sensing my inner struggle, he says, "Come on. Tell me."

"How old is Lily?"

"I'm not sure. Why?"

"She's pretty, isn't she?" My voice sounds small.

"Again, why?"

"She's like the perfect Christian."

He rolls onto his side, propping his head on his hand. "You know there's no such thing. Where is this coming from?"

"Sometimes I listen to classic rock in the car. Not worship music. Guns and Roses. Led Zeppelin. Jimi Hendrix. Only I'm so embarrassed, I turn the volume down so no one at stoplights will be able to tell."

The bed vibrates with his suppressed laughter.

I swat at him. "Stop. I'd bet Lily only listens to Christian music."

"Why are you comparing yourself with her?" A slice of moonlight illuminates his upper lip.

"Can you honestly say you're not?"

"Yes."

"You've never once thought about how she's better at my role as your wife and the twins' mom in every way."

A gentle hand strokes my cheek. "You have nothing to worry about. I promise." Soft lips brush against my hairline. My temple. My mouth. I meet his kiss with hunger. A hunger to be needed. Wanted. Indispensable.

He nuzzles my neck.

"I have another confession."

"Yes?" His response is muffled against my cheek.

"I told you I've been drinking the full one hundred ounces of water a day my doctor prescribed, but at least half the time, I'm pouring Monster energy drinks into my water bottle."

His laugh resounds. "What am I going to do with you?"

"Kiss me again."

He does. His kisses trample the weeds of worry that sprouted when Lily walked into our lives.

Too bad weeds are hard to kill.

Chapter 18

October 9, 1862
Cedar County, Missouri

Willow forced a smile and pushed aside the men's unkind words about her fall to the ground for her horse to trample instead of allowing them to lodge in her *irritable* heart.

"Watch that tree root, Will. Wouldn't want you to trip."

Laughter rippled through the woods at that remark.

"Yeah, the ground can jump out of nowhere and bite ya."

They would not let it go. They were worse than Milo with their teasing and pestering. At least it was all in fun. No one seemed to hold it against her that she'd lost the chance to capture or kill the leader of a guerrilla band. None of their voices held animosity or condemnation, thank goodness. She rolled her shoulders backward and thanked the Lord for small mercies.

Exhaustion clung to her muscles, and her head ached, but she pushed both from her mind. Where was Milo now? What was he doing? She hadn't received a letter from him in a couple of weeks, and that one had held little information. Her brother reported he was healing well and should be strong enough for active duty soon. Had he rejoined the fight by now?

They emerged from the woods and onto a gravel road. Even as lighthearted banter pinged through the air, tension hung thick. They were out there somewhere. Bushwhackers. She peered through curtains of golden leaves. She'd bet money they hadn't run far. They could be anywhere.

"Will, Will, took a spill. Couldn't make it up the hill." This from Rufus, who likely took to reciting a nursery rhyme because he was barely old enough for his Ma to stop reading such to him.

"Clever," she quipped, but she couldn't keep the corners of her mouth from turning upward. It was good to have something to laugh about, even if it was at her expense.

"Well, what do we have here, boys?" Sergeant asked, trotting to some cut telegraph wire. An eerie feeling swelled within her. The ends of the jagged wire trailed into the brush.

Something wasn't right here. *Lord, what's going on?* Her fingertips tingled, and her earlobes burned. A plan came to her. Clearly, it was wisdom from above—finding the horses and the creek—not her own intuition that saved the day. She was coming to see how very weak she was apart from His strength.

Robert ran his fingers over the wire. "Should we repair this first or go after the scoundrels? They did a poor job of clearing their tracks."

"Neither." She put out a hand as if to reel the excited men in from the precipice of danger. "It's a trap."

"What are you talking about, Forrester?" Robert raised a brow at her.

Rufus snorted. "He's white-livered at the thought of tripping in front of another guerrilla."

"No." Her voice came out clear and firm despite her insides quivering like blowing leaves. "No bushwhacker is so dumb as to not cover his tracks. You know that. They want us to follow them into the brush so they can ambush us. Or they want to attack while we're out here repairing the wire. These men might be ruthless and bloodthirsty, but they're not careless. They're calculating. You stay here or take a step into their territory, and you'll be playing right by their playbook."

Sergeant crossed his arms over his chest and peered at her from under bushy brows. "What do you propose, Forrester?"

"I have a plan." She met each man's gaze with her own determined one. "Do you trust me?" So much to ask, for them to trust the one who fumbled last time, the one who'd lost the chance to capture a notable guerrilla leader. She didn't remind them how she'd found the creek or that she'd found lost horses time and time before. She didn't build a defense for herself. Let the Lord defend her if she needed defending.

Sergeant's eyes flickered with something. Respect, maybe? "What's your plan?"

"We turn and head back to town."

Rufus's head tilt showed his skepticism. "And leave the bushwhackers be?"

She left his question hanging unanswered as she led the way down the road, gravel crunching underneath Rustic's hooves. There were only a few seconds of hesitation before other hooves beat in time behind her. Gratitude caught her breath. They trusted her. This group of men trusted *her*, a woman, to have a wise strategy. If they knew they were putting their faith in a woman, they'd likely not give her a lick of attention, but it was enough to know they prized her ideas. Her head wasn't full of cotton after all.

When they neared the general store, she slowed and brought her horse next to Rufus's. "You got the names of those Southern sympathizers?"

He patted his breast pocket. "Sure do. Right here."

"We need to find four or five of them and compel them to go and fix that wire."

Sergeant's eyes lit. "The guerrillas won't attack their own."

"No, sir."

Rufus grinned. "But that'll draw them out of the brush. Do you mean to lie in wait and then attack?"

She nodded. "We wait at the ready on the other side of the road. When they see it's their buddies repairing the wire, they'll let their guard down. Then we'll pounce."

"Brilliant." Robert chuckled. "Let's find our bait."

They rode through town, questioning the men at the bar, the barbershop, the butcher shop, and the bakery. They ended up escorting six men to the road with the command to repair the wire or have the town face a hefty fine.

They watched the men disappear and waited until all footsteps faded before trailing them through the woods, silent as still air. Hidden behind thick trunks, they watched as the men chatted and took their time lazily stringing the wire back together.

Every muscle in Willow's body stood taut and attentive as the townsmen's jovial banter drifted past her. A rustle of leaves made her heart leap, but it was only a squirrel. A snap of a twig caused her pulse to catapult, but it was merely a vole. Then footsteps—or was that her heart beating in her ears? No, most definitely footsteps.

A call of greeting, and they emerged from the woods like wasps whose nest had been disturbed. They swarmed the road, clasping their friends' hands and patting their backs. Their smiles were bright, beards long, requests plenty.

"You got any ammunition?"

"Bread?"

"Whisky?"

The townsmen dug into their pockets and bags, dishing out whatever they had to give.

Sergeant gave the signal, a single nod.

The cry of "Hurrah" they gave with their charge was far less intimidating than the rebel yell, yet it did the job of startling the enemy so that the MSM had a few seconds of advantage. It was enough to take a few shots. Enough to take one guerrilla down, shoot one in the arm, and shoot another's horse. All before bullets began splaying in their direction. And before they retreated into the brush.

Willow glanced at the guerrilla who lay dying on the side of the road, courtesy of her bullet. He was the same man she'd narrowly missed killing the other day. Part of her wanted to whoop at the victory, but she couldn't when she looked into his pained face. She'd taken the life of a man. How could she rejoice in that? She'd done her job, and done it well, but she couldn't dance a jig.

She took off her hat and held it against her chest. "Be with him, Father, and bring him into eternal peace."

Okay, enough of that. She had to track down the rest of them. She took off through the brush, gun at the ready. Rustic whinnied. "Stay steady beneath me, baby. Even if I falter, stay steady." Kind of like the Lord. She was forever stumbling and faltering, but He remained steady and true. No matter how much she wavered, He never did. He was steady ground underneath her feet.

As she raced over tree roots and under branches of dangling colorful leaves, her pulse rose, and her head filled with clouds. She clamped onto Rustic's bridle, clinging to his steadiness. Her knuckles turned white. Or were those white spots in her vision? She skidded to a halt and leaned her head against his neck, rising and falling with his breath. No longer concerned with where the guerrillas were or how she could catch them, she focused on slowing her breathing and forcing the ground to still underneath her. Her hand grappled for her canteen, and she gulped in a cool drink of water.

Her vision cleared, and her head unclouded. She glanced around. Where was she? And where were her men? A swatch of blue to her left caught her attention. A Union coat. Someone was hiding behind a tree. Without a horse. She'd been in plain sight of the man. If it were one of her own, he would have identified himself. It must be a guerrilla in a Union coat. But why hadn't he shot her? Probably out of ammunition.

Gun drawn, she steered Rustic close to his hiding place. One step. Two steps. Three.

He burst out and ran, making for another tree trunk a couple of feet away.

She fired.

He fell headfirst into a pile of leaves.

As she slipped off her horse and approached the man, his exit wound glared at her. She'd shot him clean through. Her chest burned. She'd killed two men today. Two men with families. They each had a ma who would mourn their passing with wet handkerchiefs and bittersweet stories. Did they leave wives behind? Children? Would tots cry for their fathers tonight?

She couldn't dwell on it. She'd done what she had to do. Orders were to kill all guerrillas on sight. They'd do as much to any of them, anyone loyal to the Union. They'd wreaked destruction throughout the state, ruthlessly killing one person after another. It had to stop, and someone had to stop it.

She always knew she'd be a good soldier.

Only she hadn't considered what that entailed. Or how it'd feel.

Her actions today might be enough to earn her a promotion. She should be delighted, but her spirits sagged, along with her exhausted limbs. She was fooling herself to think rising in ranks would satisfy her. Milo was right. She needed to know she was enough, just her. Rising in ranks would prove Will Forrester was worthy of acclaim, but what about Willow? She remained hidden. Or did she remain at all? Had she gotten swallowed up in the ruse?

She led Rustic away from the dying man, choosing to walk a ways instead of ride. The crunch of fallen leaves under her boots connected her to the woods again, the way she had been when she was a young girl exploring its wonders.

A cool breeze waved the branches overhead, clearing a path for brilliant sunlight. Something glinted from beneath the bed of orange and yellow ground. Something silver? She bent to brush off dirt, acorns, and foliage. Her breath caught. It was a silver spoon. Delicate.

How did it get here? She scanned the area for signs of a house nearby, but it was an isolated area. She ran a finger across the etched roses on the handle. Her chest burned, and her eyes stung. How long had it been since she'd touched something so feminine? She'd been living as a man in a man's world, playing a part she should have fit into naturally. She'd played it well, but she couldn't deny that she'd left a piece of herself behind when she donned male attire. She may have always loved to hunt and fish, run and climb, but she was a woman. No one but Milo knew her as such anymore. Milo and … God?

Had the Lord led her to this dainty silver spoon in the middle of the brush to show her He knew her and—her throat tightened—loved her, just as she was?

I keep hoping when you're by your lonesome, you'll find out who you are. Not who Pa said you are or who you are in relation to me. Not who you're pretending to be. Just you, Willow. And I'm hoping and praying that someday that'll be enough for you. That you'll find out who you are is enough for you 'cause it doesn't matter if it's enough for anybody else. It's enough for God, isn't it?

Nothing Milo had said that day made sense to her then, but perhaps she was beginning to understand.

He saw her.

He knew her.

He loved her.

This spoon was the proof her heart needed. Though it could have been dropped by a thief or a family in flight, the Lord had placed it in the sun's path and brought her gaze to it for one reason: to show His love for her.

She turned it in her hand, marveling, then gasped. Something was etched on the back. She rubbed away more grime with her thumb until the inscription *Isaiah 40:29* was visible. What did that verse say? Hungry for answers, she dug into her pack and grabbed the Bible that Milo had given her. It took her a few moments to find Isaiah, but when she discovered the verse, awe filled her.

He giveth power to the faint; and to them that have no might he increaseth strength.

Tingles inched down her spine. It was almost as if the Almighty hovered over her, breathing on her neck. She could have no doubt this spoon was a gift from God to her. To the one who fainted in the day of battle. The one whose weakness was a target for men's teasing. God was promising to give her power. Strength. Grace. She felt all of it flowing through her now from His presence, thick in the autumn air.

She had to write this down. Who cared if the others were looking for her? This was the adventure she'd been longing for all along.

~

October 12, 1862

Cyrus thanked little Mrs. Martin for the hearty breakfast of eggs, bacon, and blackberry pie. Though a wiry woman with gray hair as thin as a morning mist, she shook hands as firmly as any man.

"You come back anytime now, you hear?" She patted his cheek as if he were her son.

"We'd love to." And wasn't that the truth. Everywhere they went, they encountered warm welcomes and homemade meals, but Mrs. Martin's feast beat all the fare in Cass County. The only thing better would be Adelaide's cooking. His heart panged at the thought of her. How was his sweet wife? Safe, he prayed to God. *And Lord let her not be starving.* "We'd best be going now."

"Yes. Yes. Godspeed." She shook hands with the rest of the men before they slipped out her back door.

Thankfully, she'd reported no Federals in the area. They could breathe easier. And they were nearly to the home of the man who'd murdered Fletcher's brother. Once Fletch killed that man, they could head back toward home.

The morning air felt crisp and cool against his face. He'd grown used to traveling at night and sleeping in the woods during the day, so much so that he yawned now even though he'd gotten more sleep in the past twenty-four hours than he'd gotten in a month. He stretched and shook his limbs awake. They could travel without fear here, and they would.

The sooner Fletch did his deed, the sooner Cyrus could hold his wife again. He spurred Dixie to a steady clip, the image of Adelaide's gentle face emblazoned in his mind. She was all he had left in the world.

His throat tightened. If he could figure out who killed his children, he'd draw a bead on them and take them out. They stole his chance to make things right with his children before it was too late. But he had no names, only that they were Red Legs and not from the area. How fortunate Fletch was to have a singular target for his revenge. But no. All his rage and regret had nowhere to go. Nothing to do but fling it at the entire Federal army.

They crossed the gravel road, the birdsong that normally marked a lullaby now prodding them forward. Leaves cascaded to the ground all around them, the array of colors fluttering with the breeze. Birds flitted from branch to branch, while squirrels clambered up trunks and jumped. How strange to notice these sights when normally they moved in a cloak of darkness so thick they could barely see the man and horse in front of them.

Suddenly, a splay of bullets interrupted the peaceful morning. Shooting from the brush. An ambush. Cyrus whipped his gaze around to find dozens of Bluecoats firing from the woods on the opposite side of the road.

Pulling out their revolvers, the guerrillas took off into the trees on their horses. They chose the roughest paths they could find, dodging to one side, then the other. At a fallen timber, Cyrus stopped and shot. Once, twice. The Federal soldier went down with a cry. He continued deeper into the woods, bullets whizzing past. At a steep bank, he stopped again and fired behind him. One shot took another pursuer down. He pressed Dixie to hasten, and when he came to a high rock, he again stopped and turned. This time he took out four Feds. No one else trailed him. He rode a little farther to make sure, then slowed. He needed to regroup with his men.

He pulled off his hat to wipe his sweaty brow and froze. There was a bullet hole straight through the thing, a mere inch from his skull. He checked his person, and a sickening feeling oozed over him as he found another bullet hole through his sleeve.

He stopped to catch his breath. He'd come a hair away from dying today. If he'd been an inch to his right or left, he'd be horribly wounded, if not a goner. A bullet to the chest or head wasn't good news. If he had died, what then?

He'd go on to meet his maker, surely. He'd served the Good Lord all his life. Said his prayers. Read the psalms. If he passed on to glory, would he see his children again? His chest ached with desire for it. To see those two faces that had always been precious to him. His wife and children had been his world. Did they know that? His stomach soured. They might not have known. He'd never told them. He wasn't raised to voice emotion. It wasn't what a man did.

His children may have died without knowing he loved them. Without knowing he was proud of them. But Addy knew, didn't she? Surely, she did. He stuck his finger into the hole in his hat and felt around the edges. He couldn't die without being sure she knew. He had to get back to her, to say those words. *I love you.*

He wouldn't be able to live with himself if he didn't.

But what if he was too late?

Chapter 19

UNTIL I BECAME CHRONICALLY ILL, I HAD NO IDEA
THAT THE PEOPLE I KNEW WHO HAD ONGOING
HEALTH STRUGGLES WERE GRIEVING. NOW I KNOW
THAT THERE'S A LOT TO MOURN ...

FROM *HOW TO LIVE WELL WITH CHRONIC PAIN AND
ILLNESS*
BY TONI BERNHARD

Modern Day

I no longer have a good excuse for not attending church, but no one seems to realize this as Lily arrives early on Sunday morning to help Mark with the children. Everyone assumes I won't go, and I'm not about to correct them, though I do consider it when the twins inform me that they'll be singing onstage with the middle school class. Instead, I persuade them to practice for me in the living room. Though it's not the same without the accompaniment, perhaps it's better since I don't have to siphon their voices from those of their peers.

Their maturing voices touch me in a tender place, and I tear up. Victor rolls his eyes, but his erect posture shows me he's proud of himself. When they finish, I hoot and holler. I even give a valiant but pathetic attempt at whistling, which causes everyone to laugh. If only I could bottle the sound emanating from Jordan. It's been a long time since I've heard her so carefree.

My spirits are bolstered from this time with my children. Perhaps I can brave a morning at church to hear them sing again. But Lily sweeps in, French braiding Jordan's hair and asking Victor to wash his face. Neither child complains, and life continues on. There's a host of things that could go wrong if I were to attempt attending church today, and any one of them could ruin the morning for my family. Staying home is a safer choice. Better for everyone.

I take my steaming travel mug of hot coffee and wheel toward the back door to enjoy quiet time on the porch.

"Hold on, honey." Mark pulls a bulletin from the briefcase by the front door. "Thought you'd want to see this. It'll make you feel more connected."

"Thanks." I take it and shuffle along. I shut the door before Chipper can sneak outside. I'm not having a repeat of the last fiasco. He went outside a few minutes ago. He'll have to wait until the family gets home to go out again.

The weather is unseasonably warm for October, and I'm toasty in my sweater and slacks. The tree above smiles like a child who has lost several teeth as the sun shines through the holes the fallen leaves have left. In the distance, someone's running a leaf blower. A basketball bounces. A bird chirps. I sip the warm caffeine, close my eyes, and absorb this moment of peace.

Sounds burst forth. The front door opening. The twins chattering. Car doors banging closed. Engines revving. Two engines, right? Surely Lily isn't riding to church *with* Mark. That would be entirely inappropriate. I concentrate and confirm two engines. My shoulders relax. *See, Amber. It isn't that bad. Lily is a nice girl who wants to help. A bit overeager, perhaps, but not a threat.*

Lord, will You help me like her? I know You like her— love her. Give me Your heart for her, because my heart is swollen with hurt.

I open the bulletin in my lap. What's Mark's sermon about today? Strange not to know. Even before we married, he rehearsed his sermons for me. A wistful smile dances on my lips as I remember how I set out on a mission to catch his eye way back when he was in seminary. I could think of nothing better, nothing more secure, than marrying a pastor, and Mark's entire demeanor radiated stable kindness. We bonded through long afternoons of him practicing sermons, asking my opinions, and altering order and wording according to my feedback. He found my input valuable then.

The past few weeks, he hasn't voiced a word. Are my opinions no longer helpful now that I'm in this hard place? The thought stings, but then again, I have no desire to be preached at like the last time he ran a sermon by me. I know I should count these trials as all joy, but I don't.

Sermon Topic: Endurance.

Wonderful. Now he's preaching about how he has to put up with me.

My gaze skims the announcements. Yep. It's official. Lily has taken over both the blanket drive and the Christmas outreach. Good for her.

I come to the next section, and my blood turns to ice.

Golden Servant Award Nominees:
Pricilla Gradett
Kelly Loren
Amber Prichard
Lily Ware

I blink. Lily? How did she weasel her way onto the nominee list? She's attended Ascend Community for what, two and a half weeks? She hasn't even served, has she? Only promised to. Who knows if she'll follow through?

Pricilla and Kelly, of course. Their names are natural for the list since Pricilla oversees the yearly blood drive and Kelly is over the prayer team. The time commitment for both is minimal, yet I get it. But Lily? She has no right to share this space with me. She's already invaded my home. How dare she invade this coveted spot on the nominee list?

The word *coveted* glows white hot in my mind, glaring at me incriminatingly. *Thou shalt not covet.* I squirm. But it's only an expression. I'm not truly coveting anything or anyone, right? I may want to win the Golden Servant Award, but I've served the Lord with all my heart and with pure motives.

My now tasteless coffee no longer holds any appeal. Nor does the day that had seemed picture-perfect moments before. My bed calls to me, tempting me to surrender. Lie down. Give up. But no, I have to snap out of this. Will myself better. I have a gala to prepare for. I must find the strength to fight.

The strength to *fight*.

The green book flashes in my mind. Suddenly, I thirst for it like a nomad wandering in the desert thirsts for water. I must read it. I whip my phone out and text Mom. She attends early service in the chapel at the retirement home, so she should be back in her room by now, but she's taking forever to reply.

Okay, it's been two minutes, but it feels like forever.

Chipper scratches at the back door. I stand and give him the stink eye. "You are not coming out here."

He grins at me like I said he could have a whole chicken for lunch.

"No." I shake my head.

I could swear he nods yes.

Somehow, I need to get inside without allowing him to escape outside, but how? With my walker, it's not like I can squeeze through a tight space.

"Lord, a little help here."

A flash of red in my peripheral snags my attention. A cardinal soars by and lands on the porch railing not three feet from me. He cocks his head and stares at me. I stare back. It's like he's trying to tell me something. My hand trails to my pendant as we blink at each other.

Someone must come down the sidewalk out front because Chipper dashes away toward the front windows, barking wildly. With the dog distracted, I am free to enter the back door. It's almost as if the cardinal nods before fluttering away. My heart thuds as I open the door.

God answered my prayer.

"You're still listening?" I whisper.

I haven't stopped talking. This entire time, I've cried out to Him, sometimes whining and complaining, sometimes yelling. I've asked many questions, but I haven't heard answers. I've felt entirely alone. But maybe … I'm not.

Perhaps I never have been.

Could God have sent the cardinal to let me know He's with me? That He's always been with me? Perhaps I'm being ridiculous, but my heart burns with the possibility.

My phone dings.

Come on over. I'll make tea.

I'm repocketing my phone when another text comes.

Bring hand sanitizer.

~

Lily leaned in for Marty's hug, herded the twins past a throng of people loitering in the lobby, and steered them toward the front row of the sanctuary. A lady with a glower stopped Mark not two feet after he entered the door. Lily glanced over her shoulder. No sign of him. "You two will be fine here until your dad comes, right?"

Vic's raised brows made her regret her question. Of course, they would. They weren't toddlers.

But Jordan patted the seat next to her. "Can't you sit by us?"

Lily bit her lip. It was one thing to help Mark get the children ready and out the door in time for church. Quite another to sit in the front row as if she belonged there. It wasn't like she was their nanny. She stood on her tiptoes to see past a woman's topknot. She couldn't tell if Matt was there, but he would be. And she wanted to make sure she got a seat next to him.

"You'll be fine. If you need anything, I'll be right back there." She pointed to the unofficial young adult section.

"Yeah. Okay." Jordan fiddled with the end of her braid, lips in a pout. The girl had better not take her hair down. Lily had spent a good twenty-minutes French braiding it that morning.

"Tell you what. I'll go save my seat and come back to hang out until your dad comes."

Jordan's lower lip retreated a fraction.

A spark of delight lit inside her when she circumvented topknot lady and Matt's handsome profile came into view. She hastened her steps.

"Hey." She grinned like a fool and placed her bulletin on the chair to his right. "Just saving my seat. Gotta hang with the Prichard kids for a few minutes."

"Sucking up?"

"Hardly."

"Heard you've been helping out a lot around here lately."

She shrugged. "It's no big deal."

He chuckled. "It might be a big deal."

"What do you mean?"

"Nothing." He stretched, revealing muscular biceps. "Don't worry about it."

"Mkay. Well, I'll see you in a few."

What on earth was that about? Uneasiness gnawed at her. She gave her head a slight shake to dislodge the odd conversation from her mind. She caught Jordan peeking over the front row for her. Sweet that the girl had managed to bond with her in such a short amount of time. Better to focus on that. Boys were strange anyway.

At the third row back, a woman stepped into the aisle, blocking her progression.

"Are you Lily?" The woman's short, dark bob swayed as she stepped backward to take Lily in.

"Yes?" Again, Lily's answer sounded like a question. Like she wasn't sure who she was. But that much might be true.

"Sorry if I startled you. I'm Pricilla, Cole's wife. My husband told me about you and your generous heart to help the church."

"Oh. Thanks." Thanks? Why had she said that?

"I could hug you. Do you mind?" Without waiting for a response, Pricilla wrapped her arms around Lily and squeezed. "You are a godsend."

Lily's stilted pat to the woman's back was awkward. She pulled away, face warm.

"Cole mentioned your parents don't attend here. Are they believers?"

Lily blinked back at her. What a candid question. She ran her tongue over her teeth, gathering her bearings. How to reply? "Y-yes. They are but … my siblings have special needs, and a … difficult time attending church."

Pricilla's expression fell, as if this news pained her. "Your family has tried to attend church before?"

"Several times."

"And the churches weren't able to accommodate your siblings' needs?"

"No."

Pricilla put a hand on her heart and shook her head. "I hate to hear that. I would love to pick your brain sometime, see what ideas you have about how we can do better. Would you be up for that?"

Lily watched as Mark shuffled into the front row. Jordan turned and pouted. It was remarkably easy to disappoint children. She refocused her attention on Pricilla. "I don't know if I'm qualified."

"Nonsense. Who better?"

Praise band members took to the stage. Guitar and keyboard music filtered through the air.

"I'll think about it."

Pricilla smiled as if Lily had agreed to launch an entire special needs ministry. "You do that."

Lily spun around and found her seat next to Matt, half listening to the tail end of his discussion with Clark and Aaron about basketball. She picked up her bulletin and skimmed, her mind twirling around her conversation with Pricilla. Until she saw her name on the list.

Wait, what?

Her hand tightened around Matt's arm. "What's this?"

"Told you it might be a big deal."

"What's the Golden Servant Award?"

"Only the biggest honor this church can bestow upon a fair maiden."

She cocked an eyebrow.

"Sorry. Too much Shakespeare in English Lit." He leaned closer. His piney, masculine scent teased her senses. "Every year a committee gets together and chooses someone who they feel has contributed the most to the church and community. An anonymous donor gives a two-thousand-dollar check to each Golden Servant Award winner. There's a banquet. It's a big thing."

Wow! What an honor. And two thousand dollars? What would she do with that amount of money? But wait. They thought *she* was in the running for contributing the most? "I'm confused. Why am I on here?"

"Um, let's see. You waltzed into our church and started serving up a storm."

"With you! Where's your name?"

He shrugged. "They know I wouldn't have jumped in if not for you." His deep gaze penetrated hers, and for a second, she forgot where she was.

Then she snapped herself out of it. "That doesn't make any sense. If I'm on here, you should be too."

"Nah. I'm just your arm candy."

Heat crept up her cheeks. If only. Oh gosh, she had to focus. "Are you telling me I'm competing with Amber Prichard for this award?"

"Pretty much."

Oh no. This could not be happening. "Who's on the committee?"

A frown shadowed his features. "Are you okay? You look pale."

She grabbed his wrist. "The committee. Who's on it?"

"It's supposed to be anonymous."

Her shoulders slumped.

"But everyone pretty much knows Sally's on it. And Rhonda. Why?"

"Point them out to me, will you?"

He did so as they stood with the congregation. Okay. Good. Now she knew who to beg to take her off the list.

"Seriously, are you okay?"

"I will be." Once she got them to withdraw her name.

"It's something to be proud of, Lily."

Proud of. Right. Everyone should throw her a party for dodging her duties at home in favor of something she found far less demanding. She was a picture of unselfishness. She rolled her eyes.

If she won this award, it would mean Amber lost. Nausea sloshed in her insides. Amber lose to *her*? She could never accept that. The guilt would eat away at her.

Her mind rolled through scenes of her snapping at Harvy, grumbling about helping Davy, refusing to help with Oliver, and pretending she didn't hear Jana's fit. A Golden Servant? Give her a break. She didn't deserve to be in the same room as the other nominees.

She had to fix this.

~

I settle on my mother's middle couch cushion and pry open the green book, eager to read. I pour over pages and pages of the tree woman's story before Mom interrupts.

"You'll have tea, won't you? I always have chamomile tea on Sundays."

"Sure, Mom," I mumble, engrossed in the journal.

Cups and saucers clank as she sets a gaudy faux golden tray onto the coffee table. She adds a scoop of sugar to both cups and hands me one with a silver spoon inside it. I absentmindedly stir while reading a few more lines, then take a sip of the scalding liquid. Wincing, I set the cup down. I'm repositioning myself on the cushion when the spoon's handle catches my eye. It boasts an ornate flowered pattern. Roses? I pull it from the cup, suck off the liquid, and study it.

No. It can't be. My mother would not be plunking an antique spoon into our afternoon tea as if she'd purchased it from Costco. It must be a replica.

"This looks like Willow's spoon." I cringe as I say it. Because my mother might be *that* crazy. I hesitate to turn it over. When I finally gather the courage, the inscription of *Isaiah 40:29* stares back at me. "This is Willow's spoon." Mom actually served tea using a centuries-old spoon.

My heart ignites.

I'm holding Willow's spoon.

"Don't worry about the germs. I soaked it in Listerine." Mom takes a sip of her tea.

I blink back at her. "You what?"

"Over a hundred years of germs." She shudders. "I had to kill them. I soaked the spoon in Listerine. It's sanitized."

"Mom!" She jumps at my overloud voice. "Do you understand how special this is?" I hold it delicately like a treasure. "This spoon changed Willow's life."

Her brow furrows. "The spoon did that?"

"Well, not the spoon, exactly. God did it through the spoon." I pinch the bridge of my nose. How can I explain what I barely understand myself? "The spoon showed Willow that God saw her and loved her just as she was. She didn't have to pretend with Him." My voice chokes up. "She didn't have to prove anything to Him."

I trace the inscription. Why does a silly spoon prick my heart? I page back until I find Milo's words to Willow.

> I keep hoping when you're by your lonesome, you'll find out who you are. Not who Pa said you are or who you are in relation to me. Not who you're pretending to be. Just you, Willow. And I'm hoping and praying that someday that'll be enough for you. That you'll find out who you are is enough *for you* 'cause it doesn't matter if it's enough for anybody else. It's enough for God, isn't it?

Not who you're pretending to be.
Who have I been pretending to be?
The perfect Christian. A flawless model of faith and selflessness.
Who am I really?
The small spoon feels weighty in my grasp.
I have a gnawing ache and precious few answers. I don't know this Amber who remains after everything else has been burned with fire. I don't know if she's enough for me or God or anyone.
But I want her to be. Oh, how I want her to be.
Wait, if this is truly Willow's spoon, then is my pendant …? No, it can't be. It must be a replica. My mom would not have entrusted antique jewelry to an eight-year-old. Then again, she soaked an antique spoon in Listerine. What if …?

"Mom, where did you get this cardinal necklace you gave me when I was a little girl?" I splay my fingers around the pendant. I'm afraid to touch it now. For years, I've treated it like a common thing, as if it were a gaudy trinket from a department store. Grimy fingers have smudged it. I picture my eight-year-old self wiping my face drenched with snot and tears before clutching it. I've showered with it on, for goodness' sake. Have I been wearing a treasure all this time?

"It stays in the family. Must stay in the family." Mom perches nervously on the edge of her seat as if I've threatened to sell it at a garage sale.

Oh my goodness. It *is* Willow's. It feels heavier now. Weightier. My eyes mist at the thought of a spiritual heritage I didn't know I had before now. I've been carrying it with me ever since I was young.

"It must stay in the family," Mom says again, her voice laced with panic.

I put my hand on her knee. "It will. I'll keep it in the family." Someday, I'll give it to Jordan, only when I do, I'll tell her the story that goes with it. How long ago this woman with a tree name saw a cardinal and went from knowing about God to knowing Him intimately. I'll add my story too, how in the darkest season of my life, the Lord used a cardinal to show me I wasn't alone.

It isn't finished—this testimony being forged by fire. But the pendant burns hot like an ember on my chest, the spoon glistens in the light, and the green book beckons me to read further. Even as my heart is raw and aching, a whispered promise of healing to come breaks through.

~

When we deplete the meals Lily made, she brings more. My smile is stiff as she slides them into the freezer. "You're a wonder woman."

She chuckles. "Hardly." She closes the freezer and folds the paper bag into a neat square. "Don't look so impressed. I didn't make those. Someone gave them to us when we got Olly, and half my siblings can't eat them because of food sensitivities. Thought I'd pass them along."

"Okay, fine. But I'm not retracting my wonder woman assessment." I tuck a stray strand of hair behind my ear. "Everything was falling apart. Now it's not."

She rolls her eyes. "Not here."

Now there's a curious statement. I debate asking her what she means, but she changes the subject. "You're sure you're okay with me coordinating Victor's school party?"

I shrug. "Sure." What does it matter anymore? I tell myself this is a good thing. The children are happy, and that's what matters most. They enjoy chattering with Lily as she shuttles them back and forth to practices several nights a week. And Mark is back to focusing on the congregation instead of his needy wife. That's what I wanted. That's what needed to happen. It's for the best.

And as long as I've unloaded the rest of my responsibilities onto this woman, why not the most taxing of all? "Would you want to take my mother on a few errands each Friday?"

"Of course." Her countenance radiates with purpose. "I'd be happy to."

I snicker. She has no idea what she's agreed to. Is it horrible to hope Mom will be on her worst behavior for Little Miss Perfect? Of course, it is. I need to repent for the thought crossing my mind. Only I don't feel sorry.

A thought occurs to me. "Do you work?" Why hadn't I thought about it before? She's always here. Always available. She's like an angel. Almost not real.

We move to the couch to sample mugs of the apple cider her mother made using apples from a nearby farm. It's spiced perfectly. Do I resent that or not? Since Lily didn't brew the concoction, I guess it's okay to enjoy it without reservation. The twins will be home from school soon. Though Lily offered to start picking them up, Lisa Ganset said she's happy to do it.

"I'm in college." She studies her mug.

"Oh. Wow." I knew she was young, but college-aged?

An unfamiliar rosy tint graces her cheeks. "I take some morning and night classes in person, but most courses are online. I have a lot of flexibility in my schedule. Friday mornings are no problem."

I take a drink before answering. "That's great."

She sets her mug on the coffee table and fidgets with her hands. "You're right. I should get a job."

"I didn't mean—"

"No. It's true. I'm too old to be living at my parents' and to be dragging college out for as long as I have. I need to grow up. Start a career."

I lick my lips. What to say. This is the kind of situation my husband faces on a regular basis. He always has wise words on the tip of his tongue. All I have on my tongue is the taste of cider.

"Why?" The question falls out of me. It's the word that's churned inside ever since I passed out at the carnival. The word that fills the hollow spaces of my heart like a shout in an echo chamber. I open my mouth to qualify it, only I don't care which *why* she answers. It doesn't matter if she explains why she doesn't want a job or why she lives with her parents or why she's still in college. The point is she's afraid. This woman I deemed flawless is held captive by fear, and I want to know *why*.

She shrugs. Closes her eyes. Presses her pinky fingers to the corners of her eyelids for a full thirty seconds. What in the world? Her mouth is set in a grim line, but her body remains calm. Not a ripple in her serene waters. Yet, it's as if she's pulling herself together.

Her nostrils flare with a deep breath, and her eyes spring open. Once again, her smile is bright, as if it had never faltered. Fascinating. Something lies beneath that polished exterior.

Since she's apparently not going to answer my last question, I try for another. "What will you do with the money? If you win the Golden Servant Award." Though I work to keep my voice even, it trembles ever so slightly at the word *win*. My hand also shakes, causing the cider to ripple in my mug.

"I won't win." Her tone brokers no argument. She's resolute. Certain. Still, I press.

"What if you do?"

"I won't."

I sigh. "Okay. If someone were to hand you two thousand dollars for another reason, what would you do with it?"

She answers with nearly as much certainty this time as she did the last. "Go on vacation."

Vacation? What does this young, vibrant girl need a vacation *from*? Instead, I ask, "Where to?"

"Anywhere. Antarctica, for all I care."

My mouth parts. I scramble for something to say.

Her eyes widen as if she's revealed too much and wants to take it back. She tosses back her head and laughs. "A vacation to Antarctica. Wouldn't that be something? Now, I've heard Alaskan cruises are amazing. You ever been?"

I shake my head.

"Me neither. Never been much of anywhere. Well, we did go to Disneyland when I was seven. That was fun. And the beach the summer before. I don't remember much. Being chased by seagulls? The waves frightened me. I don't even remember what beach that was. I'll have to ask Mom …" She trails off as if chasing the memory.

The whimsical look on her face speaks of carefree days.

"What about you? When you win, what will you do with the money?"

"*If* I win."

"*When.* I'm sure of it."

"I'm not. But the money would go toward an electric fence to keep Chipper safe."

Her hands fly to cross her heart. "See, you'd even use the money for an unselfish reason. Unlike me."

Unselfish? Maybe. Maybe not. It's not like I offered to donate it to orphans in a third-world country.

She sits forward, and her eyes brighten. "So, I talked to the elders, and guess what?"

I have no guesses. No clues as to what that group could throw at me next. "What?"

"They've agreed to let me do the gala!" She claps.

My stomach plummets. No. Not my gala. The last thing I have. She can't take this from me too. My voice comes out in a squeak. "Really?"

Her face dims. "What's wrong?"

"Nothing."

She tilts her head, scrutinizing.

I squirm. Okay, fine. "I've been planning the gala myself. Apart from Ascend's oversight. Or at least, I've been trying to. It's harder than I anticipated."

Her mouth parts. "I had no idea. The elders didn't say anything."

"They don't know."

"Mark didn't tell them?"

I wince. "Mark doesn't know."

Her mouth forms a wordless *Oh.* She's quiet for a moment. Should I be preparing myself for a fight? Only she looks contemplative, not angry. "This must be really important to you."

I nod, not trusting myself to speak. My throat is suddenly thick with emotion.

"What if …?" She nibbles on a fingernail. "What if I ask the elders if they'd be okay with you helping out? We could do it together. I'm sure you'd make more headway with the church backing you up."

Together? With Lily? This option is as tasteless as unseasoned soup, but she's right. The caterer refuses to give me the same discount he's given Ascend six years in a row. The bank, hardware store, and boutique all declined to contribute this year despite the fact they've made regular donations since the event began. No one seems to want to work with me after they find out I'm no longer calling on behalf of the church. I've tried leaving out that tidbit of information, but it always wiggles its way to the surface.

This could be my way back. Back to doing what I've always loved, even if at a slower pace. If I help Lily with this, the elders will see I'm still capable. They'll let me resume my duties. All will return to normal.

"Yes. Please ask them." Hopefully, they'll listen to her better than they listened to me.

"I will." Her eyes shine with solidarity. If only I could despise it, but it's my lifeline right now. "Oh, I almost forgot." She jumps up, excuses herself to the kitchen, and returns a moment later with a pamphlet. "Mark asked me to look into something for you. You may not like it." She scrunches her nose.

Tension creeps into my shoulders. "What is it?"

She hands me the brochure. The cover shows a white-haired lady smiling at a nurse who is taking her blood pressure. *Home Health Services*, it proclaims. I roll my eyes.

Lily sits beside me. "A nurse would come to the house once a week for a short visit and to check your vitals. If you want, they also have in-home physical therapy, which Mark said your doctor recommended to gain stamina and strength. The goal is to be able to exercise several times a week, right?"

I cross my arms. "Yes, but on a recumbent bike or rowing machine." How dreadfully boring compared to my old aerobics classes.

"But you can't do that yet, right?"

I chuckle. "Not a chance." Folding a few towels leaves me sore and exhausted. How can anyone expect me to exercise?

"Then PT could help." She takes my hand. I stare at our joined fingers. I didn't want this. Didn't want her. But she could be right. The doctor said exercise is the best thing for me. The stronger I am, the better my heart can pump blood throughout my body. If there's any chance to return to my former role, this is likely it. Do PT. Gain strength. Get back to my life and release this woman to move on with hers.

I squeeze her hand. "Okay. I'll do it."

"You will?" Her eyes widen. She'd been preparing for a fight, no doubt.

"Yes."

"Great! I'll see if I can call and set it up. I don't know if they'll allow me to, but I'll try."

Car doors slam, footsteps pound, and the door thuds open. Victor's voice rolls through the entryway. "Joey Doyle is not the fastest boy in sixth grade. Who told you that?"

Jordan drops her backpack by the front door and plants a hand on her hip. "That's what Iris said, and her uncle coaches cross country."

"Well, she's wrong. Patrick Mills is way faster."

As if suddenly noticing their surroundings, they both turn and face the couch.

Buoyed by the possibility of regaining stamina, I join in their banter. "Neither Joey nor Patrick have anything on me."

Victor scoffs, the edges of his eyes crinkling in his effort not to smile. "Right, Mom."

"No, seriously. Lily's hiring me a bodybuilder. I'm going to be the strongest member of the PTO and far faster than any sixth-grade boy." I wink at Lily.

Her shoulders shake with suppressed laughter.

Jordan rolls her eyes. "A bodybuilder?"

I shrug. "A physical therapist, a bodybuilder. It's all the same. Point is, I'll challenge Joey Doyle and Patrick Mills to a race."

"With your walker?" Victor's head tilt looks eerily similar to his father's.

"Well, you're going to push me, of course. I'll sit. You push." I saunter to my walker, flip the seat down, and sit with a dramatic flair. "Let's practice."

"Clear a path!" Lily shouts like a referee. She scoots a chair and rug out of the way.

The twins pick their backpacks off the floor and deposit them on the couch.

Victor grabs the walker handles.

Lily holds her hand out like a flag. "On your mark, get set … go!"

I squeal, and Victor propels me forward, through the living room, over the bumpy threshold to the kitchen, and to the back door. Chipper barks and thrashes his tail at the commotion.

"A new world record in walker racing!" Lily cheers.

We're all laughing now. Even Chipper seems to laugh as he chases his tail in circles.

When Victor settles, he pushes me back into the living room. As I resettle on the sofa, he calls out, "Got anymore cookies?"

Lily pops her head into the room. "Not today, but I have homemade apple cider and banana muffins."

Muffins? There are muffins? I sit up straighter.

She must notice because she says, "I totally forgot earlier. I'll bring you one."

I relax. "Thanks. Can I have more cider too?"

Guilt coats me as soon as I ask. Who am I? Royalty who has a servant to wait on me hand and foot? Ridiculous. I should get it myself … only how does one navigate a walker with a mug of hot cider?

Lily doesn't hesitate. "Of course."

But it's Jordan who brings the cider. I shake off the shame and focus on my daughter. "Jordan." I pat the space beside me, still warm from where Lily sat. "Come sit by me."

She hesitates and casts a longing glance toward the kitchen. "I was gonna grab a snack."

"And you can. In a minute. I'm only asking for a sliver of your time." My lip trembles with my request. Her life has been made of slivers of time. Some I've caught and treasured. Some have drifted through my fingers. This is one I'm desperate to hold on to. "Tell me about your day."

Her sigh is more visible than audible. I try not to deflate along with it. Her steps drag on her way to join me.

I pat the couch again as if she needs help finding her way to me. Maybe she does.

She plops down and brings her knees to her chest, hugging herself in a defensive ball. She's an armadillo, and I'm a predator somehow. How did we get here?

"What was the most interesting thing that happened today?"

She shrugs. I wait.

When Lily sweeps into the room with two muffins, I swipe Jordan's from in front of her nose. "Answer my question, and I'll let you have the muffin."

She huffs. "So unfair."

I stare at her, unflinching. I won't be the one to cave here. We have to break this stalemate.

"Greta Mechano got a detention for sassing the teacher. Is that interesting enough for you?" Her head tilt punctuates the attitude in her question.

My tongue glides on the back of my teeth. Should I address the sass in *her* tone? But her answer is the ideal segue to deeper conversation. Better let it slide.

"Speaking of detention, you never told me how yours went." I hold the muffin out of her reach.

"You said I had to answer your *question* to get a muffin. Singular, not plural."

"I'm glad to know you're still a star grammar student." I take a bite of my muffin. "Yum, this is good." Crumbs splay to my lap with my pronouncement.

"Mom!"

"How was it?" I inch the muffin toward her.

"It sucked."

"Zero stars, would not recommend?" I pick up muffin bits and pinch them into my mouth.

"Definitely not."

I hand over the treat. "So, why'd you refuse to do the assignment?"

She peels back the cupcake wrapper with thoughtful precision. "It was our personal narrative assignment. We picked topics at the beginning of the year. Before … everything happened with you. I couldn't do it, Mom."

I study my sweet pixie who's always felt so deeply. She nibbles the edge of her muffin as if not wanting to hurt its feelings.

"What was the topic?"

Her mouth twists. "Mr. Mires."

My chest constricts. "Mr. Mires?"

"Yeah. When he …" She looks to the ceiling and blinks several times. "When he fell and died in front of us."

In front of *us*? My mouth parts. I close my eyes and replay the horrid scene. I could never forget the image of the man collapsing at my feet. How his eyes rolled back right before his body went down. How I stood in shock for a second before it hit me that I needed to pull the emergency cord. It was only a second, and the paramedics reassured me it would have made no difference, but I'd berated myself for not moving faster. The crack of his head as it made impact. His pale cheeks squished against the linoleum. I'd sworn I'd never forget these things, no matter how much I wanted to. But the thing I *had* forgotten was that Jordan was with me that day.

Once a month, her school released early on Thursdays, and she accompanied me on nursing home visits. How could I have forgotten my daughter had watched a man die? I shudder. "I'm so sorry."

I reach for her hand as Lily reached for mine not long ago. Jordan's hand is bigger than I remember. She's far too close to being all grown-up, and yet on this precipice of in between, there's turbulence I haven't recognized.

"I saw you faint at the dance recital," she whispers.

Tears prick my eyes as I wait for her to continue.

"I was watching from backstage. I had pointed out my family to a friend when I saw you go down." Her voice cracks. "It was just like Mr. Mires."

I wrap my big, little girl in a tight hug and kiss the top of her head.

"I keep thinking I should learn to live without you because I never know if … when you fall … if you're going to get back up."

My tears dampen Jordan's hair. Her tears wet my sleeve. It's unbelievable that this child has carried such weight around and I've known nothing of it. "Have you talked to your counselor about this?"

She nods. That's something, at least.

"That's good, but I want you to be able to talk to me too."

She pulls back and swipes at her cheeks. "I don't want to put any more stress on you."

A cough sputters out. "Jordan, that's not your concern."

"But—"

"No buts. I don't want you to worry about that for a minute."

Her lip trembles. She says, "Okay."

Have I convinced her? Will she now share her heart with me? Doubtful. Fear continues to fill her eyes. Fear that she will break me.

Or perhaps I'm looking into a mirror.

Chapter 20

IN READING BOTH YOUR PAPERS I SEE YOU URGE THE
POLICY OF THE CITIZENS TAKING UP ARMS TO
DEFEND THEIR PERSONS AND PROPERTY. YOU ARE
ONLY ASKING THEM TO SIGN THEIR DEATH
WARRANTS. DO YOU NOT KNOW, SIRS, THAT YOU
HAVE SOME OF MISSOURI'S PROUDEST, BEST, AND
NOBLEST SONS TO COPE WITH?

"BLOODY BILL" ANDERSON, JULY 7, 1864

October 16, 1862
Jackson County, Missouri

Bone weary and soul heavy, Willow followed Sergeant away from another burning house and onto the dirt path winding toward the main road. Her throat thickened at the thought of the woman and child they'd left weeping by an oak tree as everything they knew crumbled to the ground. She didn't know the woman, but she might as well have. The way the lady's auburn curls hung around her heart-shaped face was hauntingly similar to Willow's old neighbor, Mrs. Wessex. The Wessex family had loaned the Forresters their mule two harvests ago.

When would this carnage end? Their mandate to starve the guerrillas out of the area by assuring they had nowhere to run for provisions was likely necessary. But the ones issuing orders didn't have to look into the empty eyes of those with shattered spirits.

Some soldiers rode with their heads held high, the supposed victory their destruction brought bolstering them to face yet another day. She couldn't manage such bravado. Not when she could nearly taste Mrs. Wessex's pie on her tongue. Memories were tricky things, weaving the scent of apples in with the smell of fallen leaves.

"We'll travel another ten miles tonight and make the last twenty tomorrow, God willing." Sergeant's voice sounded tired, yet strong and assured. "Rumor is, Quantrill's band is hiding out there."

Just what she needed, a chance to face the Bird himself. The sizzle coursing through her veins at the thought made her sit a bit straighter. Everything she'd been through would be worth it. Every action justified. But then her fingers found the cool metal of her silver spoon, hidden in her pocket. Did she need fame when she had *this*—solid proof of a God who loved her?

They hadn't made it the full ten miles when Sergeant motioned for them to leave the main road and find a place to settle for the night.

Though chilly air nipped at them, no one lit a fire. Doing so could make their presence known to their enemies and invite an ambush. Instead, after a meal of cold beans and hardtack, they settled for the night with only their blankets to warm them.

Willow awoke before dawn the next morning. Gentle snores surrounded her. Robert and Sam kept watch, eyes drooping with exhaustion. Robert acknowledged her with a nod before pulling his gaze back toward the road.

She needed to use the necessary, so she crept off deeper into the woods, walking lightly so as not to wake the others. Faint light from the beginning sunrise illuminated her way. She took a deep breath of the fresh morning air, something inside her springing to life at the reminiscence of a childhood birthed in woods such as these. Whether she'd hunted squirrels or imaginary dragons, trees and moss and earth surrounded her.

An owl hooted as a blue jay took flight. The night and the day mingling together. Crickets' song tangled together with the whispers of butterflies. What a sacred space, this place between dreaming and waking.

Rustling sounds came from somewhere beyond. Her ears perked. She stilled. An animal? Larger than a squirrel, for sure. Her hand clamped around the revolver in her belt. A fox or wolf? The rustling stopped, and in its place, came a soft whistle of a sound. Almost like a snore.

Goosebumps rose on her arms. There was a person deep within this brush. Her stomach cramped. The only people who would be here besides the guerrilla hunters were the guerrillas themselves. Quantrill? What if Sergeant had been wrong about the Bird's whereabouts. He only had rumors to go by, and rumors could prove false. The Bird could be here, now, sleeping peacefully. Unaware of a bullet that could end his atrocities. Her bullet.

She aimed her revolver in front of her and chose her path carefully. Stepping on tree roots and stones to avoid detection, she slunk closer to the noise. When a figure came into view, she sucked in a breath.

There he lay, nestled next to a huge tree trunk. An embroidered shirt peeked from under a blue Union jacket. A wide-brimmed hat hid his face, though his long, scraggly beard moved slightly with each exhale. This couldn't be Quantrill. He'd never be sleeping alone. Still, it was clearly a guerrilla, and she was a guerrilla hunter.

She cocked her gun. One shot was all it would take. They'd been commanded to shoot all bushwhackers on sight, and here was one directly in her path. She'd already killed two of them, but this seemed different. The others had been running from her. This one lay peacefully. But she had her orders. She only had to pull the trigger. Her hand trembled.

The figure startled and catapulted upright, his hat fluttering to the ground. Wide blue eyes bored into hers. Familiar eyes on a familiar face. "Willow?"

Recognition punched the air from her so that her voice came out as a strangled croak. "Father?"

The gun fell from her shaking hands.

Orange, yellow, and red leaves spun around her as her knees buckled, and she toppled to the ground.

~

She awoke to a piercing sliver of light. She blinked open her eyes. Where was she? A wooden ceiling stood above her, and something solid cradled the back of her head.

"Willow?"

She startled at the sound of her father's voice, much more tender than she'd ever heard it before. She craned her neck backward and met his soft gaze. Her head was lying in his lap. What on earth? She scrambled to sit upright, the movement making her head swim.

"Father? What are you doing here? I thought you were dead." She huddled, knees to chest, near the door of—where was she?—some sort of shed.

"I thought *you* were dead." His gravelly voice filled with emotion. "You and your brother."

She shook her head. "You're one of them?"

Had Ma sewn the white lilies covering his shirt? Had she stitched the red rose on his pocket? Willow's stomach roiled.

"You joined the Union army?" What was that in his voice? Not disgust, but betrayal.

She couldn't stop staring at this man who had filled her every memory with his looming presence. He'd thinned out, and his unkempt appearance was unlike the man she'd grown up with. "Milo and I joined the Black Hawk Cavalry. Then I transferred to the Missouri State Militia." She swallowed the hard knot in her throat. "Why'd you think we'd been killed?"

"Red Legs shot and killed a group of young people, several of your school chums among them. Threw them in a barn and burned it. Everyone thought you two were among them, and since we couldn't find you afterward … Your Ma held out hope. She contacted troops in Lexington to see if Milo'd arrived, they said he hadn't." His glistening eyes looked beyond her. "What else was I to think? You disappeared without a trace."

Guilt gnawed. She'd never considered what he might think. What he might do.

"You joined the bushwhackers? What about your touts of remaining neutral?"

His jaw firmed. "There can be no neutrality in this war. Not in Missouri." He dusted off his hands on his trousers. Had he killed with those hands? "They left me no choice but to choose a side."

"And kill for that side." She bit the inside of her lip. If only he'd tell her it wasn't true, that he hadn't participated in heinous slaughter.

"Haven't you killed for your side?"

She scoffed. "That's different."

"Because it was done on a battlefield and not in the brush?"

She had killed in the brush, but only because his side had started it. "Because it was in civilized war! It's not like I've scalped anyone."

"Some of your soldiers have. They started the practice."

"And you've celebrated it." She spat out the words. Had he hung any scalps from a pole? Bile rose in her throat. She should ask, but she couldn't push the question out. Better not to know.

"I did what I had to do to protect our home. Our family."

Her gaze scoured him. "And I did what I had to do to fight for our country." Sure, that wasn't why she left home or why she joined up, but somewhere along the line, she began to believe in the cause. In the rightness of preserving the Union, banishing irregulars, and securing freedom for all. Her gaze dropped to the bulge in his breast pocket—no doubt a revolver, if not two—then to the rifle at his side. "You could have killed me."

He smirked. "You were about to kill me."

She shuddered. What if she hadn't hesitated? What if she'd shot first and found out it was her father later? She reached across the space between them, offering her hand. "Truce?"

He eyed her offering, her dirty, calloused fingers. "I can't give it up. The bushwhacking. These men are like family now, and I'll not abandon them."

"What about Ma?"

"I have her full support."

She let her hand fall to her side and squared her shoulders. "I'll not give it up either. Fighting for the Union. Where does that leave us?"

A glint of something fresh in his eyes—something like respect—caused her chest to expand. Though the line of his mouth remained grim, the edges of his eyes crinkled as if he wanted to smile. "It leaves us on opposite sides of the war."

"So be it."

~

He and his daughter had spent at least an hour catching up before Cyrus stood. "If they find you here, they'll kill you, and I won't be able to stop them." God forbid.

"Where are we?" Willow asked. It was as if the outside world had faded away while father and daughter talked.

"The McCaffreys' garden shed, about half a mile from where you found me."

"The McCaffreys are secesh?" Dust drifted in the beam of sunshine cascading through the high window.

"Oh no. You'll not be getting intelligence out of me. I'm not breathing a word about the families in the area. Won't have you torching their houses on my account." He cracked open the door and scanned the horizon. All clear.

"Fair enough."

"Wait an hour after I leave before you sneak out and find your men."

She stumbled to her feet. "This is it, then?"

"This is it." He shifted his weight. What should he do with his hands? They hung limply at his sides. He'd never been a hugger. Leave that to the women. He scrubbed at his beard and crossed his arms about his chest. That wasn't right either. Not when they were saying goodbye. Perhaps a handshake? He stuck out his hand.

The side of her mouth tipped upward as she grasped it. She had a firm shake. Impressive. Everything about her was impressive, actually.

Words lodged in his brain, his throat. "Be … I … Take care."

He wiped his brow, nodded at her befuddled expression, and let himself out the door. A web of unspoken words tangled behind him. He felt them clinging to his boots. He clamored to free himself of them, of everything that had happened these last few hours. He should focus on the truth that his children were alive and well.

Milo. Willow. Neither had died at the hands of Red Legs. Both were Unionists, in fact, but best not to dwell on *that* tasteless fact. They lived. They breathed with beating hearts and wills as strong as ever before. He couldn't help but chuckle. Like father, like children. He hadn't raised docile, complicit whippersnappers who fell into line and did everything they were told. His children thought for themselves and followed their convictions. Bravo. Looked like he'd done something right after all.

He dabbed at his misty eyes. Now *that* was something his men best never see. Cy choked with emotion? Preposterous. But the Almighty had returned his children to him from the grave. That second chance? Perhaps he'd get it. Raising a girl had been a conundrum, and much more the feisty girl God had granted him.

He'd been raised with firm boundaries—men had their place and women theirs—but Willow blurred those lines. His job was to teach the girl her place so that she'd find her way in the world and marry well. It was his responsibility to ensure his little girl was taken care of. And what man doted on a woman who shot and skinned squirrels instead of tending to the house?

He remembered penning these questions into his journal, which had since gone missing.

> *I prayed earnestly for another boy, and instead, I got Willow. Why'd the Good Lord give me a girl? Why'd He give me this girl? I don't want to do wrong by her. Tough love is likely what she needs to help her find her way. It was good enough for me, and truthfully, I don't know any other way. I only hope she finds happiness.*

When he thought he'd lost her, regret fell upon him like an avalanche. Perhaps tough love wasn't what she'd needed. He should have been kinder, softer, gentler with her. He shouldn't have run his home like the king of the roost, pecking down at her. Perhaps in trying to secure her future, he'd trampled her spirit.

But look at her now! Far from crumpled in the dust, she'd risen with fortitude and resolve. True, these weren't qualities that would likely garner her a husband, but they were ones she'd need to survive in the uncertain future of their country. She was going to do fine.

Now, to find his men and figure out why Fletch hadn't been standing watch like he was supposed to. Good thing, though, or his buddy might have shot his daughter. What would he have done? Of course, she wouldn't go down without a fight. No telling who'd win in that match. Still, the mystery remained of where his men had gone and why they'd left him sleeping in the woods without a guard.

He combed through the brush for a bit without finding a trace of them before giving up. He asked around at secesh homes to see if they'd seen his buddies. They hadn't, but Mrs. Milling offered him a slice of rhubarb pie. How could his friends abandon him? So much for loyalty.

It was near nightfall with no sign of his fellas when it occurred to him: he hadn't told his daughter he loved her. Not that morning. Perhaps not ever. After his brush with death, he'd vowed to voice his affection for his wife. How could he not do the same for his children? His only daughter stood feet away from him, and he only managed to shake her hand. What was wrong with him?

He had to find her. To let her know he cared. More than cared. That he *loved* her. That he was proud of the strong woman she'd become, of the strong person she'd always been. She was brilliant, courageous, and passionate. If only he could brag on his little girl being in the army! But it was illegal, and spilling his pride here and yonder could get her kicked out, or worse. He'd have to keep that locked inside, but he could tell her.

And he must.

Chapter 21

MY BODY FELT LIKE A VOW THAT HAD BEEN IRREVOCABLY BROKEN.

FROM *THE INVISIBLE KINGDOM; REIMAGINING CHRONIC ILLNESS*

BY MEGHAN O'ROURKE

Modern Day

Mark doesn't meet my eye when he hands me the bulletin on his way out the door for church. Something's off, obviously, but I can't question him in front of Lily and the twins. I'll find out soon enough.

Lily hugs me before shooing the children out the door. "I have a lunch meeting with the elders after church. I'll let you know what they say."

I inhale a shaky breath. So much rides on their verdict. What will I do if they say no? Stubbornly insist on planning my own gala while Lily plans one for the church? How will I ever get any sponsors if I have to compete against Ascend's event? But if I let go and allow Lily to plan a gala by herself, the task will swallow her whole. And where will that leave me?

Here on the sidelines, taking, taking, taking everything. And giving nothing back. Just like my mother.

I cannot be that person.

When the purr of their car engines fades in the distance, I settle onto the couch to peruse the bulletin. An insert flutters into my lap. Odd. They rarely do inserts.

Warily, I read.

> After much deliberation and prayer, we have decided to cancel the Golden Servant Award and the ceremony going forward. While we desire to honor those among us who serve our church community, we believe this award fosters an unhealthy spirit of competition and does not reflect the humble heart of our Savior. The donor of the award money has agreed to allow us to transition these funds to the Christmas gala for foster and adoptive families. Thank you for your understanding.
>
> We would like to thank all of our volunteers.

Below the announcement, there are a list of names. Alphabetical. My name is included, along with every other volunteer in the church. All of them equal. No one receives more honor for greater time invested, more energy, more heart. There I am, listed next to Randall Meriwether who prepares coffee once a month.

No award.

No ceremony.

No accolades.

No picture on the wall.

My heart pings in my hollow chest. The second hand from the wall clock ticks. There is nothing. Nothing to prove myself worthy. Nothing to prove myself more. Nothing to prove I'm not a needy, clingy, trainwreck like my mother.

Oh no. I *am* just like my mother, aren't I? Unable to do a thing for myself. Dependent on the neighbors and a college student to function as a mother and homemaker. Not making a difference in the world at all. Pathetic.

Unless … I'm able to help with the gala.

Yes. All is not lost.
I clutch the pendant in my hand.
There is hope.

~

When Mark returns with the twins, he continues to avoid eye contact. It's almost humorous, the way he dodges my gaze. When we sit to a lunch of chicken salad sandwiches, I wave the bulletin under his nose.

"Nice of you to warn me."

He mumbles, "Sorry," and spoons potato salad onto his plate. "The list of nominees was never supposed to be published in the bulletin. Sally's been helping out in the office since …"

He lets his sentence dangle, and I fill in the rest: since they fired me. Bulletins used to be one of my duties.

"Anyway, she found the list on my desk and assumed it needed to go in. She didn't know we'd hit pause on the whole thing." He pinches the bridge of his nose. "She meant well, but it caused unnecessary drama."

Did it now? I didn't breathe a word of my frustration, which means he's referring to someone else. My curiosity's piqued, but I can't exactly dig for dirt. Mark abhors gossip. So, I ask a different question. "When did you decide to cancel the award?"

His cheek twitches. "Last week. We fasted and prayed for a week, then made the decision at our Wednesday meeting."

He fasted for a week? I hadn't noticed. Shows how much attention I'd been paying to the household. I point my fork at him. "I'm noticing a pattern here. You used to keep me abreast of everything that was happening with the church. Now, you intentionally leave me out of the loop." I wouldn't normally have this conversation in front of the twins, but I'm afraid if I don't speak now, he'll dodge any further efforts.

He wipes his face with a napkin and finally meets my gaze. "It'd be easier to talk about these things if you didn't get so defensive."

My mouth falls open. Defensive? He called me defensive? "I am not—"

He shoots me a pointed look. Okay, getting defensive about being called defensive isn't the best strategy. I suck in my bottom lip.

I try again. "It's hard not to get defensive when I feel like I'm being attacked."

A hint of a sad smile breaks through his bleak expression. "I understand. But I'm not attacking you. I wish you could see I'm on your side. I've always been on your side." He takes my hand with his soft, warm one and fiddles with my wedding ring. "And I'm not going anywhere."

His assurance seeps under doors I've barred closed and over walls I've built. Is it true? *It's a scary feeling being left. Don't let it happen again.* I swallow.

I'm not going anywhere.

Even now? Even when I'm a helpless shell of the woman I once was? Even when I have no shot of ever receiving a Golden Servant Award? Even though he can't show me off as "perfect Christian wife eye candy" on his arm? What if I'm needy? Clingy? Crazy? Will he stay?

I squeeze his hand. "Promise?"

"I already did when I said, 'I do.'" He winks. "But yes, I promise." He kisses my ring finger.

I find a smile.

An hour later, Lily bustles through the door. "Amber! I have great news."

Anticipation straightens my spine from its languid position on the couch. "Yes?"

She sits next to me and takes my hands in hers. "The gala is on. Full-fledged on."

"Yes?" I already knew that.

"And they've agreed you can play an advisory role, provided you don't lift a finger."

"An advisory role?" That's good, right? It sounds prestigious.

"Yes." She beams. "Provided you don't lift a finger."

I picture myself lugging heavy AV equipment onstage and guffaw. "Thank goodness! I can't even lift a brush."

She pulls out a legal pad and pen. "Mind if we start brainstorming now? Can we come up with a to-do list?"

I sit forward, more energy coursing through me than I've felt all month. "For sure."

Her pen flies across the page. "We need to choose the venue, secure the caterer, find corporate sponsors ... What else?"

"I normally find a photographer and entertainers. And, of course, we need a wish list from each family attending and volunteers to put together the gift baskets."

A near-tangible current of anticipation charges the atmosphere between us. It's the most connected I've ever felt to this woman, and I'm caught by such surprise I snort a laugh, which makes her laugh. For a few minutes, we dissolve into giggles like a couple of teenagers.

When I catch a steady breath that doesn't rumble into further laughter, I turn her legal pad around to view the listed items. "Okay, tonight I'll get started on items one, three, and five. You can take two, four, and six." I pull out my phone to make notes.

Lily's nervous chuckle sounds nothing like her carefree giggles from moments before. "Um, Amber?"

I glance up. Why does she look like she might toss her cookies?

"You're not supposed to lift a finger, remember?"

"I'm not," I say slowly, as if she's the one who's confused instead of me. "I'm merely sending a few emails."

She shakes her head.

"Are you serious? I can't send emails?"

She winces as she answers. "No."

"Make phone calls?"

"No."

My shoulders slump. Advisory role, huh? Sounds like the elders are letting me do a whole lot of nothing.

"I'm so sorry, Amber, but they were adamant. Advise only. But it'll be great." Her perky smile reemerges. "You tell me exactly what to do, and I'll do it. You have the expertise. I have the energy. Together, we'll be a power team."

I try for a smile but likely don't succeed. Surely, she could figure it out on her own. I feel superfluous. Like an appendage. Making connections was my superpower. Speaking so passionately about the cause that others could feel the conviction and were compelled to do something about it. I can't advise on that. It's part of my DNA.

My disappointment radiates from me and bounces off her positivity.

"Don't worry. It's going to be great!" she says again.

But will it?

~

A knock on the door at nine in the morning on Wednesday fails to send me into a panic. I'm expecting the nurse's visit. I've prepared for the sound and for Chipper's subsequent barks. Besides, if I happen to be wrong and this is a Child Protective Services worker again, she'll find no incriminating evidence here. Lily's seen to that. She's the superhero that swept in and saved my children from being carted off to foster care. I should be dripping with gratitude.

The woman who stands on my front porch is most definitely not from CPS. The Sesame Street scrubs and blue Cookie Monster Crocs coax a small smile from my lips. Her bright red headband matches her lipstick. She smiles. "Hi, I'm Sasha with Missouri Home Health."

"I'm Amber. Come in." I hold the door open.

Chipper's tail whaps against my walker as he tries to get a better view of our guest. He whines and presses forward until he can sniff her pant legs.

"What an adorable dog." She bends forward in the doorway and scratches behind his ears.

He tilts his head and grins, eating up the attention.

"He's cute, for sure. A handful, but cute."

Chipper releases a playful growl, then walks in a circle and sits, looking with wide-eyed anticipation for more petting action.

"Okay, Chipper, that's enough. She's here to do a job, not to pet you."

Sasha chuckles and moves into the house, but Chipper backs onto the porch.

"Chipper, come on in." I click my tongue and tilt my head toward the living room.

He sniffs something on the wind.

"Chipper." I change my tone to all business. "Don't think about it."

He takes a tentative step toward the street.

I lunge toward him.

He sprints off.

"Shoot!"

"Oh no." Sasha's mouth parts as she watches him go. "I'd go after him, but I had knee surgery last month."

My shoulders slump. Now that there's no Golden Servant Award money, will we ever be able to afford an electric fence? How will I keep this dog alive?

I can feel Sasha studying me. "Will he come back?"

"Sometimes a neighbor brings him back, but it's really not safe, and my kids will be so concerned. Give me a minute while I try to track him down."

She follows me back out the door and watches as I scoot my walker down the sidewalk in the direction Chipper went. Then, I catch a flash of his auburn tail.

"Chipper," I call.

It would be helpful if he could call back as if playing Marco Polo, but I receive no response. Are the neighbors home? Would it be entirely inappropriate to nose around their bushes?

But there. I think that's his tail two houses ahead. I rush up the sidewalk.

He's not sticking to public pathways. He's cutting through people's lawns, dodging through fences, racing behind obstacles. Every couple of houses, I catch a glimpse of him, but I can't get close enough to coax him to me. Before I know it, we're no longer on my lazy street. We're four streets over, nearing a busy intersection. How did I walk this far? Fierce determination tunnels my vision now. I've come this far. I cannot go back without my dog.

"Lord, help!"

Street noises intensify. Car engines idling. The roll of tires. An occasional honk. Stereo beats. Danger. Chipper is nearing a danger zone.

I must get him before a car runs him over.

There he is. His back paws graze the sidewalk, but his front paws veer into the road. His nose lifts toward the aroma of barbecue emanating from the restaurant across the street.

"Chipper!" I jog toward him, legs pumping.

He sees me. Darts from me into traffic.

This stupid walker is holding me back. I push it to the side so I can run faster. He dashes right in front of an oncoming car. "Chipper!" I shout. "No!"

Brakes squeal.

My knees buckle.

I fall forward into the yawning road. Black cement greets me with a smack. A tire careens toward my head. I scream. My arms fly to cover my face. It veers away at the last minute. I gasp in a breath.

I startle as a bike wheel collides with my arm. Pain shoots through me. A grunt, and weight falls onto my torso, knocking the air from me. I can't breathe. My vision clouds. Then fades.

~

The sound of heart rate monitors pulls me from grogginess. What is happening? As soon as I pry open my left eye, I regret leaving the land of unconsciousness. Pain stabs my temples. Every muscle in my body is stiff. It will probably hurt to move. Better not to find out for sure. Wait, can I move? Something's preventing me from turning my neck.

"Hello," I say, but it's as if my throat is full of gravel. I'm in a hospital. That much is clear, but why? And who's here with me?

"Honey?" Mark hovers above me. He's blurry, and his voice sounds like he's talking through a paper towel tube, but it's him. I blink a few times, and his image sharpens. He doesn't touch me. Why doesn't he touch me? "You've been in an accident. Do you remember? You were hit by a bike."

An accident. I close my eyes to concentrate. Everything is fuzzy. Like dialing into a radio station and being a few numbers off, there's static. So much static.

"You have a concussion," Mark continues, but I can't process new words when I haven't grasped the last ones. "And a broken arm. You have a lot of lacerations. Cuts. But you're going to be fine. If you had been two feet to the left, it would have been a car that ran you over instead of a bike."

I try to make my mouth form words. They come out painfully slow and with intense effort. The *r*, in particular, is difficult to form. "Car accident?"

His brow furrows. Is he processing what I asked or how? Is he wondering if I will talk this way forever? Will I?

"No. You weren't in a car. You were walking. Do you remember walking in the middle of Fifth Street? The home health nurse called me first, then when I was driving home, I got a call from the hospital."

Walking in the middle of 5th Street? A loud dinging sound assaults my ears. Each ring of a bell sends painful reverberations through my skull. I wince.

"Looks like your IV bag is finished. Let me page a nurse to start you on another one."

He disappears, and I shiver at the coolness his absence brings. I have no sense of my place in this space. I can only see the white ceiling above me. What hospital am I in? What ward? I strain to remember something, anything, of how I got here.

A flash of auburn. Chipper's tail. It comes back to me in a painful rush. Chasing after that stupid dog. Ditching the walker. Falling without it. Did Chipper dodge the car as well, or was his fate worse than mine?

Oh my goodness, I almost died. My husband was nearly left without a wife, my children without a mother. I would have missed their transition to adolescence, driver's tests, high school graduations, college, marriage …

But I would also have woken in paradise without any pain, without a body that wars against me every minute of every day. Two feet away and I could finally have been at peace.

Lord, why did You keep me here? What is the point of having this life that I can't participate in? I'm a mere spectator while the world spins around me. Why didn't You take me home? I'm so tired. I want to be with You. Just let me be with You.

Mark would be fine. The children would be fine. They had Lily.

Someone bustles into the room and fiddles with something beside me. The IV machine? The annoying beeping stops.

"There you go," a friendly voice says.

"Thanks." Mark returns to his place in my line of sight.

Again, speaking requires much effort, but the word comes out clear, although slow. "Chipper."

"Oh, honey. It's okay. Chipper is fine. He's at home with Lily. The children and the dog are safe with Lily."

This only makes me cry harder.

Mark should be at home with the family instead of at the hospital with this insane shell of a woman who chases dogs into oncoming traffic. After over a decade of telling my children to look both ways before they cross the street, I bolted into a busy intersection like a lunatic. I'm my mother. I've metamorphosed into her. It makes sense for Mark to move on from me to someone more fit for the role of a pastor's helpmeet. There's nothing left of me for him any longer. He can leave me. He *should* leave me. As long as he doesn't walk out on the kids.

"Go home." The speed at which I speak this makes me sound much like ET. The comparison twinges. I remember the four of us piled onto the sofa when the twins were eight or nine watching the movie, fingers buttery from fistfuls of popcorn. They scoffed at the special effects that seemed enthralling when I was a child, but something about the bike flying across the sky made us sit up straighter.

Deep lines groove his forehead, interrogating me.

"The children need you," I plead.

A quick breath puffs from his nostrils as he seems to consider this. "You need me."

Familiar words swish around in my mouth: *I don't need you. I don't need anyone.* I've never said them out loud, but they've shouted in my head every day for the past twenty years. There are needy people and independent people, and I'm the latter, thank you very much. I'm the person you call in a pinch, not the person calling someone else, begging them to bail me out. I'm the indispensable one, and I can stand on my own two feet.

But clearly, I've been knocked off my feet.

I'm lying here, and I can't even see my husband unless he moves into my line of sight. I can't say those words. They're not true. What I can and do say are words that reverberate in my chest as I think of Jordan's solemn eyes when she told me she should figure out how to get along without me in case I didn't get back up. I strain to mold these words with my mouth, thrusting behind them the conviction that burns in my veins. "They need you more."

He frowns. His gaze wavers. "Okay," he finally says before retreating from my view.

~

If I would have planned this better, I'd have made sure I packed a pair of earbuds in my pocket when I left the house. The thought makes me chuckle. Bad idea. Pain rolls over me from all sides. I recoil. That hurts too.

As it stands, I didn't even bring my phone when I ventured out to go after Chipper, whatever day that was. Yesterday? Last week? Who knows? Day and night are the same here. The medicine they give me for pain makes me drowsy. Everything melts together. I'm left with a puddle of regret.

Mark might have brought my phone. I wouldn't know. I can't turn my head to view the side table. I wouldn't be able to answer it if it rang, which it hasn't. Is it not there or does nobody care? I haven't seen Mark since I banished him. Hopefully, he's providing the children with the stable presence I can't be for them right now. I might never be able to be that for them again.

I wait for a visitor. Though I'm sure the next familiar face I see will be Mark, I yearn for Delaney. Does she have any idea what's happened? Mark informed her last time I was in the hospital. Did he do so again? Would she care if she knew?

I can't imagine she wouldn't. After all the secrets shared, the late-night chats, the tears, the triumphs, how could she not be moved by the thought of her friend in the hospital? She threw a "Clay Sucks" party when Clay Washborn broke up with me junior year, complete with dart boards adorned with his face. She held my hand as I panted through labor and gently dabbed my forehead with a wet washrag. Where is she now? Why must I face this yawning chasm of helplessness alone?

I can talk more clearly now. With every visit from a nurse or doctor, the words flow easier. My body aches, but my mind is like a machine that took a while to pick up steam. Now it's chugging along near to normal.

I'm sleeping a lot. When nurses come, I wish them away. I hate being poked and prodded. When they leave, though, the loneliness of the empty room seems unbearable. When someone not sporting scrubs finally enters my room, I bite my tongue to ensure I'm awake and not hallucinating.

"Amber? Is that you?" It's my mom's voice, and it's muffled. Am I awake? There's no way my mother would brave a hospital. It can't be.

But the hiss of hand sanitizer dispenses, and she hunches close. The furrowed brow does belong to Mom. Two masks cover her face, a paper one and a cloth one.

"Mom?"

"Oh, good. I found the right place. They said Amber Prichard, Room 333, but that didn't sound right. Three is a lucky number, and you're not a lucky person. Not with the fainting disease. They put you in the wrong room."

"Yeah. They should move me to 666."

Her eyes widen, and she rocks forward. "Oh no. No, no, no."

Bad joke. "It's okay, Mom. They don't have a sixth floor." I have no idea if this is true, and apparently, she doesn't either.

"Good. That's a bad number. The devil's number. Good thing they don't have that room."

"How'd you get here?"

"Cab."

I laugh. She's joking, right? Mark must be in the hall. He brought her, and she likely complained the entire way. There's no way she braved riding in a stranger's car to come to the hospital.

"Stuffy cab. Driver's name was Mitch. He had yellow teeth, but he sprays for lice."

"He sprays for lice?" Oh my goodness, she's telling the truth.

She nods. "I asked if he sprayed for lice. He said he did. I wouldn't get in until he said he did."

I hold back a smile, picturing the taxi driver's face when she asked for these credentials. "Good, Mom."

"And he knows CPR."

"You had the safest cab in the Midwest."

Her enormous purse hangs from her shoulder. Something green peeks out of it. I suck in a breath. "Is that Willow's journal?"

Her gaze follows mine and lingers.

"The green book?" I ask again.

She hefts the bag in front of her torso and sets it on top of my legs. I wince at the weight on scrapes and bruises, but I'm not about to ask her to move it. She lifts the journal free. "You didn't get to finish it."

This precious treasure left the haven of her apartment? This woman is full of surprises today.

"I also brought this." She thrusts something small made of cool metal into my hand. When I bring it into my line of vision, my eyes mist.

"Willow's spoon." I breathe the words in awe as I trace a finger over the delicate flowered handle.

"Mark said you keep falling because you don't have enough spoons. Would this one help?"

I bite my lip to rein in a watery laugh. I can only imagine Mark trying to explain the spoon analogy to my mother. "Yes. It would help." I turn it in my hand and find Isaiah 40:29 engraved on the back, fascinated with how Willow did the same more than a century before. "He giveth power to the faint; and to them that have no might he increaseth strength."

For months I've declared that I haven't had enough spoons. I've focused on the things that have taken my spoons away. Yet here is this spoon, clearly given to me by God. It has traveled over a hundred and sixty years to make its way to my palm and its message shouts *grace*. I have grace for today, and that grace—His grace—is sufficient.

"It's yours, then. Keeping it in the family. She has more to say about the spoon. You have to read more." Her bunched brows speak her seriousness.

"I can't read very well right now." The lunch menu gave me trouble earlier today. The words kept jumbling together, causing my head to ache.

"I'll read to you."

Weight lifts from my legs. Mom disappears from view. A chair scrapes across the floor. Pain scours my temples at the sound, and I clamp my jaw shut. Soon, though, it's finished, and Mom huffs slightly as she sits. Pages rustle, and her gravelly voice transports me to another time and place.

Chapter 22

OUR COUNTRY IS DESOLATE, INDEED ALMOST ENTIRELY A WILDERNESS, ROBBERY IS AN EVERYDAY AFFAIR SO LONG AS THERE WAS ANYTHING TO TAKE. OUR FARMS ARE ALL BURNED UP, FENCES GONE, CROPS DESTROYED. NO ONE ESCAPES THE RAVAGES OF ONE PARTY OR THE OTHER; WE WILL REMAIN WHERE WE ARE THIS WINTER BUT THIS SPRING WE SHALL BE OBLIGED TO LEAVE. WHERE I SHALL GO, OR WHAT DO; I DO NOT KNOW ...

LIZZIE E. BRANNOCK TO REV. EDWIN H. WHITE
CHAPEL HILL, JANUARY 13, 1864

October 25, 1862

Orders had taken Willow and her company north toward St. Louis for a duration. Though no one had a clear idea why and though each step took her farther from her mission to kill Quantrill, she breathed easier the closer she came to the city. St. Louis was firmly Union-controlled territory, and while there were Southern sympathizers sprinkled throughout the population there, no one could argue they were headed to far less dangerous ground.

They only had to get to Benton Barracks and they'd be among friends, without fear of a guerrilla jumping out from behind a tree trunk and shooting them dead. And they were indeed growing closer, as evidenced by the number of US flags flying from buildings and housetops.

Safe. When had she last felt completely safe?

You're safe with Me.

She sat straighter in the saddle. Was that—could it be—the Almighty speaking straight to her heart? She'd only recently gotten used to talking to Him beyond the memorized prayers of her youth. The knowledge that He heard her uncoiled the hard knot inside her. But that *He* would also speak to *her*? It was nearly too much.

Her eyes misted, and she blinked several times to clear them.

Safe with Him.

Clearly, the safety He spoke of wasn't protection from anything that might go wrong in this life. She'd seen too many people die in this war to fancy herself immune. Her aching muscles testified that her battle with irritable heart still raged.

But … safe with Him. She took a deep breath, crisp fall air filling her lungs, and conceded it was true. As long as He was with her, no matter what happened, she was safe. With Him.

A red bird flitted from branch to branch above them. The cardinal reminded her of how God had met her in the Hickory County brush, even on one of her weakest days. Her hand instinctively went to the spoon nestled in her pocket. Isaiah 40:29.

> *He giveth power to the faint; and to them that*
> *have no might he increaseth strength.*

What was the Scripture Ma always used to recite? *His strength is perfected in my weakness.* Well, thanks to Willow's irritable heart, God had many opportunities to show Himself strong in her life.

The birdsong wrapped around her like a warm blanket. It was true, wasn't it? She couldn't get any lower than falling on her face in the dust. And yet, even when she was at her lowest, He had never left her. Instead of hollering at her to buck up, He stooped, extended His hand, and lifted her, infusing her with life. Each time. Over and over again. How different this Savior was from how her own father had been. How different from everyone she'd ever known.

She tilted her head backward and soaked up the setting sun filtering through the trees. No need to try and be anything other than who she truly was, anything *more* than who she was. Not with Him. She had no reason to strive and nothing to prove. Unfathomable. No matter how this War between the States ended, she could move on and live completely free. Free on the inside, where it mattered most.

In front of her, Sergeant slowed. "Let's break for supper."

They'd come across a large clearing, and in the last county, they'd procured bacon and a few chickens to roast. Her mouth watered at the thought.

An hour later, they sat around a roaring fire and savored the feast as darkness rose around them. The men bantered back and forth. Willow didn't participate much, content to listen in, chuckle, and breathe in the air of camaraderie.

A whisper behind her interrupted the serenity of the moment. What was that? It sounded as if someone had called out a name. They quieted, and she sat so still she could sense gooseflesh rising on her arms.

It came again. Wait. Was that … *her* name?

Her gaze searched the perimeter.

"Willow!"

She gasped in a breath. Father? She catapulted to her feet. Swayed. Breathed deep. Steadied.

Out of a grove of trees, her father sneaked near the perimeter of the clearing. His face brightened when he laid eyes on her.

She had to get to him before the others spotted him. She made her way toward the wooded area as if to go relieve herself, but she hadn't made it but a few steps when his gaze wandered beyond her, and his expression fell. He threw up his hands.

She looked over her shoulder to find every man in her company with guns raised.

"Willow," he cried again.

Robert spit. "A guerrilla." The cock of his revolver sliced terror through her.

"Don't shoot." Her plea came out with feminine edges. No one seemed to notice.

"Why's he talking about trees?" The disdain in Rufus's voice rankled her.

Robert's eyes narrowed. "A distraction tactic, no doubt. He's probably got a team of men in those woods ready to ambush us."

"No! Don't shoot. It's my father." If only she could swipe the gun from his hand. But she had a better chance of talking reason into him.

"Your father's a guerrilla? What are you? A spy?" A small shift of movement behind her showed two of the men had refocused their aim away from her father and onto her.

"No!"

"It's orders. Shoot any guerrilla on sight. I knew you couldn't be trusted."

The revolver's blast melted with her scream.

Her father's body flopped backward and thudded to the ground. She ran to him, skidding to her knees beside his convulsing form.

"Father?" She shook his shoulders, needing his steady gaze to prove to her there was life in him yet. His eyes rolled backward. "Father!" Her hands searched, looking for the bullet wound. There. On his abdomen. She wrestled him out of the blue Union coat he wore and ripped a strip off. She pressed it to his wound to staunch the bleeding.

"Willow," he rasped out, and she found his blue eyes focused on her.

"Father. I'm so sorry."

"Came to"—a wheezing inhale—"tell you that I love you."

She blinked at the sky as emotion rolled through her. She hid it under a layer of irritation. "That's hardly worth dying for."

"Love is … the only thing … worth dying for." His eyes fluttered closed.

Oh, she should slap him. How dare he give up so easily. Determination bubbled in her chest. She took his hand and squeezed. "Well, if it's worth dying for, then it's worth living for all the more. Now, be a man and buck up." Might as well give him a dose of his own. She'd heard him say as much to Milo a multitude of times.

Was that a chuckle or a cough? Either way, it proved life remained in his lungs.

"You're strong. Like your Ma." The smallest semblance of a smile played on his lips.

"I'm strong like you. Don't prove me wrong."

Behind them, her company was dousing the campfire. All jesting ceased, and they went about their work of packing up camp somber and straight-faced. When she met Robert's gaze, he had the audacity to look hurt, as if she'd betrayed him and not the other way around. She needed to claim her horse before they took it as spy contraband or something ridiculous.

"Stay here," she told her father, then she rolled her eyes at herself. As if he was going anywhere. She walked cautiously toward Rustic. Technically, they could take her prisoner for aiding and abetting the enemy. Or perhaps they truly did suspect her of being a spy. Sergeant approached her as she untethered the animal.

She spoke first and with a tone that brokered no argument. "I'm taking him home." Wow. That was far out of line from how she should address a superior. She added, "Sir."

"You expect me to look the other way?" His raised brow sought to intimidate. She wouldn't let it.

"Yes, sir." She swallowed. "I promise, I'm no spy. Until a few days ago, I thought my parents were dead. Then I found out my father was fighting with the guerrillas. I don't agree with his ideals nor his tactics, but he's family, and I'll not walk away and let him die in this clearing. I've done my duty as a soldier. Now let me do my duty as a—" She'd almost said *daughter*. Best not add that indiscretion to the growing list. "Child."

"If anyone asks, we'll have to say you deserted. You know the penalty for such?"

Her stomach clenched as she imagined standing before a firing squad. "Yes, sir." She'd pray no one would ask.

He stuck out his hand. "It's been a pleasure fighting with you, Forrester."

She shook it, gratitude rising like a creek overflowing its banks. "You as well."

Now, she—a deserter of the Union army—needed only to get her ailing guerrilla father to their home hundreds of miles away without being captured or shot.

Chapter 23

WHEN ILLNESS FORCED ME TO SPEND MY DAYS IN THE
BEDROOM INSTEAD OF THE CLASSROOM ... I CLUNG TO
THAT IDENTITY AS IF IT WERE A LIFE RAFT,
REPEATING TO MYSELF OVER AND OVER IN A PANIC,
"IF I'M NOT A LAW PROFESSOR, WHO AM I?"

FROM *HOW TO LIVE WELL WITH CHRONIC PAIN AND
ILLNESS*

BY TONI BERNHARD

Modern Day

Lily tapped on Oliver's door, careful not to disturb the baby who slept in Mom's arms as she rocked in the rocking chair.

"Come in," Mom whispered.

Lily sat on the floor and ran her hand across the plush beige carpeting. A beam of moonlight shone through the window and cast a soft glow on Mom's exhausted face. Eyes closed, her hand continued to pat Olly's back.

Lily smiled at her mother. Forever dedicated, even half-asleep. "He looks out of it."

"That's what I thought last time. As soon as I stopped rocking, he started screaming again."

"You need rest."

"I don't mind." Mom yawned. "What time is it?"

"Twelve thirty. I finally got Jana to sleep."

"Lord, please no more nightmares." Mom's prayer ended with another yawn. "What's on your mind, firefly?"

"Two things, actually. You know Amber? From the family at church that I've been helping?"

Mom nodded, eyes still closed.

"She was in an accident. She's at the hospital."

Mom's eyes fluttered open, concern evident in them, even in the dark. "Is she okay?"

"Her husband says she's banged up but will be okay. Only he said she hasn't had any visitors. Seems odd that someone who did so much for the church wouldn't be flooded with flowers and balloons and people wishing her well." She drew a cross on the carpet with her finger. What did it mean to be the church? "I plan on visiting tomorrow."

"I'd love to visit as well. If you could watch the children while I do so."

"Really?"

Mom nodded sleepily. "I don't know if you remember, but I used to do hospital visits all the time. When we went to our old church." Her voice turned wistful. "It's one of the things I miss."

Oh yeah. How could she have forgotten? She'd even tagged along a time or two. "Of course. That would be great. I mean, I'll ask her, but I think it would be great."

"What was the other thing?"

"I met with a lady from church today about the possibility of Ascend incorporating a special needs children's ministry into their existing program."

Mom gazed intently at Lily. Serious and unsmiling. "And?"

"And I suggested training buddies for one-on-one assistance as a first step. Adding a sensory room as a second step."

"Those sound like good suggestions."

"Yes, but—"

"They want you to head this up?" Mom tilted her head in a knowing way.

"Yes! I'm completely unqualified."

"How so?"

"Mom, I'm not you. I'm not good at this."

"You're far better than you give yourself credit for."

Lily rolled her eyes.

"If you're hoping I'll say I'll do it, sorry. I'm not going to take this torch from you."

Lily blew out a breath and lay on her back on the floor. "I *was* hoping that."

"But I'll help."

Her eyes snapped to her mother's. Was a twinkle there? "You will?"

"Sure. And if we can get this up and running, I'll even start going to church with you."

Lily grinned. "That would be perfect." The patting on Oliver's back slowed. Mom must be falling asleep. "Mom, go to bed. If Olly wakes, I'll take care of him."

"You sure?" Mom's words slurred in a sleep-deprived way.

"Positive."

She rose and placed Oliver into his crib and then stumbled out of the room without another word. Lily grabbed the pillow from the rocking chair and a blanket from the shelf in the corner and snuggled in, listening to Oliver's rhythmic breathing.

Imagine that. She'd had a normal conversation with her mother. Wonders never ceased. Maybe she was right where she needed to be, after all.

~

An upbeat voice crests into the hospital room. "Hello."

My ears perk at the familiar sound. I'm drawn to it like the sun breaking through the clouds after rain. But it's as if my subconscious has betrayed me. This is another prayer God hasn't answered. I'm still waiting for supernatural adoration for this woman to kick in.

"I come bearing gifts." Lily leans over my hospital bed, smiling brightly. Two Get Well balloons fly above her head. One displays a pink daisy, one a yellow smiley face. "The twins picked them out themselves."

A smile breaks through.

"And they made you these." She hands me a small Tupperware container. "When I say they made them, I mean it. I had nothing to do with it, and I can't vouch for them. I didn't have time to taste one before leaving. They're straight from the oven."

"I'll love them." Of course, I will. They are Lilyless. The best kind.

Her shiny blonde hair swings above me like a pendulum. When she tucks it behind her ear, I'm struck by the kindness in her eyes. She's concerned about me. It's obvious. She's not looking to knock me out of the picture and take over my family. My stomach recoils. How did such a thought cross my mind?

She scoots a slender hip onto my hospital bed, making herself at home right where I can see her. When she takes my hand, her touch is as soft as a flower petal. The kindness she offers is like an ocean wave. It stings on open cuts yet cools and soothes at the same time. I've no intention of drawing nearer to her, and yet she pulls at me, and I stumble forward on wet sand.

"I'm glad you're all right." Emotion laces her voice. She cares. Why does she care?

"My mom wants to come visit later. I hope that's okay."

Her mom? I feel my forehead scrunch. "Why?"

"She's heard so much about you. I talk about you all the time. Plus, forever ago she used to be a part of the ministry at our old church that visited people in the hospital. I think she misses it. Along with conversations with adults. Please say she can come."

If this woman is another version of Lily, it's the last thing I want, but I can't say so. "Okay."

"Great. You're my hero, you know?" Her gaze grazes the ceiling before falling over me like a mist.

What? "Me?"

She squeezes my hand. "Yes, you. You would not believe the wonderful things people at Ascend have to say about you. You visit the elderly on a weekly basis, organize food baskets for the less fortunate, volunteer in several areas throughout the church on Sundays." She speaks in present tense, as if I still perform these tasks. Why? "You oversee the carnival, the blanket drive, the toy drive, and the diaper drive in the spring. All on top of caring for your own mother and children." Her awestruck expression and words are out of place. I'd shake my head if I could.

I manage to croak words out. "Not anymore."

She leans closer. "You're on a little break is all. You'll recover and be back at it, filling the world with goodness yet again."

I bite my lip. Maybe it's true. Maybe not.

"The point is you do all these things out of the goodness of your heart. That's why you're my hero."

Her words swirl inside me like a twister picking up fallen leaves. They threaten to lift me off the ground and throw me somewhere else entirely. Threaten to overhaul all I thought I knew.

Because they aren't true.

The goodness of my heart is hollow. Empty. Wanting.

Here, in forced stillness, I'm unable to distract myself with busyness. I can't look around for things to do. I can only look down or up. Perhaps that's why the truth now gapes obvious. It's not that I don't care about foster children. I do. But if I'm honest, there's a deeper motive buried underneath the surface. It reeks of festering wounds I've tried to ignore for far too long. I've spent countless hours serving to make myself indispensable. I need to be needed. Wanted. Unleavable.

I've coveted the Golden Servant Award because no one abandons a golden servant.

I married a pastor because pastors don't believe in divorce.

Everything I've done is to secure my place as the one who will not get left behind.

I picture my mother sliding her wedding ring up and down her finger incessantly. She won't take it off, won't move on, won't give up, but everyone's given up on her. Pathetic. I won't be pathetic.

The goodness of my heart? I let out a humorless chuckle. My ribs ache with it. "I shouldn't be your hero. I'm afraid."

"Aren't we all?"

What? This beautiful, vibrant, take-no-prisoners girl is afraid? But yes, I caught a glimpse of her fear once when she talked about graduation and her future career.

She laughs. "Don't look so shocked. Can I tell you a secret?" She pries open the Tupperware lid and takes out a cookie. "There's a guy at church I'm kind of crushing on, but I'm pretty sure I'm not good enough for him." She nibbles a bite, then nods. "This is actually pretty good. Want one?"

A guy at church? I blink. Do I want one? I have whiplash from the change of topics. The baked cookie scent reorients me. "Yes."

She hands me a cookie before continuing, "Matt Juper. You know him? Super cute, dark brown hair with a goatee."

I grin. "Yeah." I taught Matt's Sunday school class years ago. His hand flew up the minute I asked a question every time. A perfect match for Pretty Church Girl. A way better match than my husband. "Why do you think—"

"That I'm not good enough for him? C'mon. He's the whole package. Handsome. Loves Jesus. A hard worker."

"And you're not the whole package?"

She shrugs.

"Don't sell yourself short."

She takes another polite bite of the cookie and brushes her hands together as she chews. After she swallows, she says, "Someday maybe I'll be as amazing as you."

Her words dip and swirl like the autumn wind. The assumptions I've clung to are fallen leaves, now tossed this way and that.

Whoa. Suddenly, my eyes are opened. Lily sits before me not as my competition but as a young girl wrought with her own insecurities. She's hungry for approval, for acceptance. I see it in her eyes. Rough edges of my heart crumble, exposing tenderness underneath.

Lily looks to her right. "What's this?" She leans over and re-emerges with the green book in her hand.

"She left it." This is unthinkable and perhaps the greatest act of sacrificial love my mother has shown.

"Who?" Lily touches the cover gently, as if she knows what great treasure waits inside.

"My mom." I suck in a breath. "Wait, is there a spoon? Do you see a spoon?"

I may sound crazy, but who cares?

"Oh, yeah. A little silver one?"

Delight courses through me. "Yes!" I explain about the spoon and the journal while she leans in with enraptured attention.

"Wow. This is so exciting! Can I read to you?"

My mother's admonition to keep the journal in the family replays in my head. As I take in Lily's eager expression, warmth fills my heart. She is family. She's my sister. Christ has knit us together.

"Please do." Because where Mom left off can't be the ending. There must be more. God is the author of redemption. If it's not good, it's not the end.

As Lily carefully turns to the marked page, I repeat that to myself.

If it's not good, it's not the end.

~

The neck brace comes off the next day, and when Mark visits, he leaves a brand-new journal and sparkly colored pens. Being known this well wraps me in comfort like a fleece blanket. The doctor stressed minimizing time spent on my phone or any electronic devices. I have no brain space for podcasts at the moment, so light instrumental music lilts through my earbuds as I await my promised next visitor.

Lily's mother is exactly how I pictured her: an older, less hip version of her daughter. Her sun-kissed, wavy blonde hair crests above her shoulder. She sports glasses and mom jeans, but she radiates the same positivity as Lily.

"Hello!" She steps into the room with a bouquet of pink roses in hand and stretches the word out like a parade. "I'm Rayanne, Lily's mom."

Of course. Like a ray of sunshine. I smile and pull out my earbuds. "Nice to meet you." Crazy how I mean it.

"Thank you for allowing me to visit." She places the flowers on the side table and sits in the chair Mark recently vacated. "Lily raves about you. Says you're one of the kindest, most inspirational people she's ever met."

Warmth fills my cheeks. "That's generous of her."

Rayanne's smile is knowing. "From what she's told me, you're normally quite a busy bee. These health problems probably have thrown you for a loop, eh?"

My smile falters. "You could say that."

"So, tell me about yourself. Who is Amber Prichard? In your own words, not those of your fan club."

I snort at the ludicrousness of a fan club, then sober. How to answer her question? I fumble. "Well … I'm a wife to … the pastor, so naturally, I do a lot at the church. Or did. Do. Did. Um, the Labor Day carnival. I organized that, and I normally head up the blanket and Christmas outreaches, as well as nursing home visits and weekly food basket distribution—"

She puts out a hand to interrupt. Her eyes are kind, but a challenge lies inside them. "I've heard of all you do, Amber. It's admirable. But this isn't a job interview, sweetheart. I asked who you are. You are not what you do."

"Yes, of course. I know." Everyone knows that. Why had I gone on about my accomplishments like an idiot? The tips of my ears flame. I try again. "I'm a mom to two wonderful preteens." My chest expands at the mention of them. "They're amazing. Victor is in soccer. Jordan dances. I go to all the games and recitals. I coordinate who brings snacks what week for the parents. I'm in the PTO and normally organize their school parties."

Rayanne clicks her tongue. Her face is scrunched as if she's holding back a laugh.

"I'm doing it again, aren't I?" I cover my face with my hands. "I keep spouting off what I do."

She chuckles. "It's a hard habit to break."

My hands fall to my lap. They twist at the thin hospital sheet. My gaze transfixes on their movement. "Honestly, since all this happened, I haven't a clue who I am." Dread shoots up like a rocket. Did I admit that out loud? "I-I mean …" A Bible verse. I need to pull out a Bible verse. Um, 1 Peter 2:9 comes to mind. "I know I am a chosen people, a royal priesthood, a holy nation, God's special possession so that I may declare the praises of Him who called me out of darkness into His wonderful light."

"Spoken like a true pastor's wife."

"The first part or the second?" I venture a glance up and find no judgment in her gaze.

"Both." She pats my arm, featherlight. "I'm sure you know many verses about who you are in Christ, and I'm so thankful for His Word. But I'm even more thankful that this friendship with Jesus is about more than only memorizing verses. Good friends have good conversations, right? They both talk and listen. In our friendship with Christ, we can share what's on our mind, and we can also hear what's on His."

I'm not convinced I want to hear what's on His mind. What if He's as disappointed in me as I am in myself? "I've been mad at Him lately." I cringe. I've revealed too much to this woman, this stranger.

Her smile doesn't waver. "Understandable. I've been mad at Him more times than I can count."

"You have?"

"Why, sure. Has Lily talked about our family?"

"She said she has six amazing siblings who help her cook and a supermom who's homeschooled them all."

Rayanne laughs so hard the bed shakes. "Well, it's not a lie." She wipes the corners of her eyes with her pinky finger. "It's not the whole picture either."

What hasn't Lily told me?

"The reason your Christmas gala means so much to Lily is because *we* are a foster and adoptive family. Lily has five adopted siblings with special needs, and they each deal with trauma from their pasts. Oliver, the baby, is our first official foster. We're not sure whether we'll end up adopting him eventually or not."

"Wh-what?" I sputter. "Lily's never breathed a word of this."

All this time, I thought I had the corner on heart for this outreach. How could I have been so wrong? Lily and I have had something in common this entire time—a knowledge of the system and a compassion for those in it.

"Our home life is … challenging. Every time we've adopted, we've done so because I've felt a clear leading from the Lord, and yet it's been hard. Believe me, I've aired my grievances with Him about that. If He led us to do something and it's His purpose for our lives, why is it so hard? That's what I've asked Him time and time again. Why?"

"It's the question I keep asking as well," I admit.

"It's universal, I guess. But it's the wrong question. Or at least, it's not a question He seems to answer often. Except that doesn't mean He's not willing to talk to us. It took me a while to learn that He has much to say. We just have to ask different questions."

"Like what?"

"Instead of *why*, try asking *what* and *who*. What's one word to describe me? Who have You made me to be?"

I quirk an eyebrow. "He answers those questions for you?"

"Every day." She beams. "Every morning before my feet hit the floor, I ask the Lord for a word to describe who I am to Him. Then I listen. When I hear His still, small voice whisper to my heart, I receive that word and write it in my journal."

"You hear a new word from Him every day?"

"Psalm 139 says the thoughts God has toward us can't be numbered, right? He has so many thoughts about who He created you to be, so many words to tell you about your identity. The only one who can tell you who you are is the person who created you. I figure, best to go straight to the source."

Straight to the source. Like Willow did. *If there's distance between you and God, you're the one who put it there.*

Instead of offense, relief fills me. "He's only a breath away."

~

After she leaves, my journal beckons. I crack it open to the first page.

In purple, I scrawl *Who am I?* Temptation clambers to pen the right answers. Child of God. Wife. Mother. If this was a test and the elders were looking over my shoulder, what would make them nod in approval?

I am not what I do. I know this, and yet my fingers itch to list my accomplishments. As to why I'm worth something. Only right now, I can continue none of those things, so am I now worth nothing?

The answer has to be no.

I am not what I do.

There's no way to earn God's affection.

I've learned this through a hundred sermons, Bible studies, books, and podcasts, but the knowledge has never sunk deeper than my head.

I flip the page and write, in blue this time, *Lord, who am I to You?*

I close my eyes and wait. If God has words for Rayanne and for Willow, He must have words for me too. He doesn't play favorites. If only I could tune out the medical cart rolling past my room, the chatter of voices next door, and the beeping down the hall. But God is everywhere, and I can meet with Him no matter where I am. *Lord, meet me here.*

Exquisite.

The word comes to me like a hot spark. I suck in a breath. Is this word from Him? Is it what He thinks of me? Surely not. It sounds an awful lot like pride. I picture a cocky rooster strutting around crowing, "I'm exquisite. I'm exquisite." And yet …

Warmth spreads through my chest. What if it is the Lord? What if He values me like this? I nibble my lip and glide my pen across the page. It feels a bit like plunging into icy water. Terrifying. Thrilling. Invigorating.

Unparalleled.

This time, confidence this word is from Him blooms within me. Confidence and … joy. I wish I had a dictionary to look up these words and find the deeper meaning, but I believe He's saying He doesn't compare me to anyone else. He's not watching from the judgment seat as I race against Lily or Kelly Loren or anyone else. He's not scrutinizing my weak areas next to other women's strengths.

There's no one like you, Amber.

My shoulders relax. My jaw loosens. Tension drifts away.

I am loved. Here in my brokenness. Here in the hurt and the not quite and the not yet. I've fallen short of who I've wished I could be, who I thought I should be, in a thousand ways, yet none of that matters here with Him. I am fully and completely loved just as I am, without ever having to change. Exquisite, unparalleled me.

Gratitude hitches my voice with emotion as I whisper, "Thank You, Jesus, for loving me just like this."

Chapter 24

TO ALL WHO WERE REBELS, TRAITORS, SYMPATHIZERS AND THEIR FRIENDS DURING THE WAR:

WE, THE L. & U. A. A. OF THE STATE OF MISSOURI IN GRAND COUNCIL ASSEMBLED, MAKE THE FOLLOWING PROPOSITIONS:

WHEREAS, YOU MADLY PLUNGED THE COUNTRY INTO A FRATRICIDAL WAR OF UNPARALLELED SEVERITY, WITHOUT CAUSE OR PROVOCATION, TO PERPETUATE A SYSTEM OF HUMAN BONDAGE MORE DIABOLICAL AND REVOLTING THAN ANYTHING THE WORLD EVER SAW BEFORE ...

THEREFORE, THIS CIRCULAR IS PUBLISHED TO NOTIFY YOU ... THAT WE DESIRE THE PEACE, PROSPERITY AND HAPPINESS OF THE WHOLE COUNTRY, THE NORTH, THE SOUTH, THE EAST, THE WEST, AND THIS DESIRE HAS LED US TO BEAR UP UNDER WRONGS AND INJUSTICE THAT NO OTHER SET OF MEN EVER WOULD HAVE BORNE; THAT WE SHALL HEREAFTER HOLD EVERY ONE OF YOU ACCOUNTABLE FOR THE MURDERS AND ATROCITIES THAT ANY OF YOUR PARTY MAY COMMIT; IF UNION MEN CANNOT LIVE IN PEACE AND QUIET WHERE YOU ARE IN THE MAJORITY, YOU CANNOT ENJOY PEACE AND QUIET HERE.

GRAND COUNCIL OF L. & U. A. A. OF THE STATE OF MISSOURI

April 18, 1863

Gibson County, Tennessee

Cyrus waved off Adelaide's attempt to wipe porridge from the end of his newly trimmed beard. "Enough, woman. I can do it myself." He patted his chin with a napkin.

"I'm only trying to take care of you, Cy." She smiled a honey-sweet smile, and his irritation dimmed.

"I know. That's all you've been doing for months, taking care of me. But I'm recovering nicely, and there's no need to coddle me. I'm no invalid."

She clasped her hands in front of her slim waist. "I know, dear. Can't help myself, I guess. I spent so long worrying about you, and now that you're here. You can't expect me to stop straight away."

Oh, the woman was adorable, even if she couldn't stop meddling. "Come here and give me a kiss."

Her cheeks reddened. "Gladly." She sat on the edge of the bed and leaned over to meet his puckered mouth. His Addy. Sweetness and light. What would he do without her?

"Why don't you work on the garden?"

Their new homestead in Tennessee was far smaller than their previous one in Missouri, but it was something. And it was safe. No Unionists or Jayhawkers burning houses here. No guerrilla bands running wild through the countryside either. The country remained at war, but here it was as simple as North versus South.

"I will." She patted his arm. "After your morning walk."

The doctor advised copious amounts of rest, but also one walk a day in the fresh air. His favorite part of each day.

"Willow said she wanted to take me today." He leaned forward to peek out the window. "Where is that girl?"

"She'll be along soon. She ran to the post office."

As if on cue, his girl burst through the door. "A letter from Milo!"

She waved a paper around wildly, face alight. Her hair had grown out soft around her shoulders, and with the purple frock she wore now, he struggled to believe she'd ever been taken for a man, so beautifully delicate were her features.

Addy stood with her hands clasped by her mouth. "What does he say?"

"He's doing well. They're almost ready to leave winter quarters. Here." Willow thrust the letter in her mother's direction. "I devoured every word on the way here. Your turn." She bounced on her toes. The eager anticipation that had characterized her as a young child hadn't dimmed. "I can't believe it got through." She pressed her hands to smiling cheeks.

Yes, it was a wonder, indeed. It was illegal for Northerners to communicate with Southern sympathizers through letters. One could be arrested for sending a letter to secesh, and everyone knew his guerrilla history.

A knock sounded at the door, and Addy bustled to answer it.

A male voice greeted them. "I'm looking for Will Forrester."

Cy's stomach constricted. His gaze snapped to Willow in time to see the color drain from her features. Had the Union Army tracked her down to try her for desertion after all? He clenched his fists. He'd fight to his death before he saw his daughter shot in front of a firing squad.

Addy looked to him, eyes wide.

Willow's brow furrowed, and she moved toward the door. "Dedrick?" She stood next to Addy with her hand on her hip. "What's this about?"

The man's mouth fell open, then moved as if attempting to talk, though no words came out.

Cyrus pushed to his feet and joined his girls.

Willow cast him a glance before rolling her eyes at the man. "Yes, it's me. Will. Yes, I'm a woman."

Thank God she was finally comfortable with who the Good Lord created her to be. A feisty female.

Dedrick licked his lips. "By George, Pence was right. He said there was something different about you. Just couldn't put his finger on it."

Willow brushed her skirt with a flourish. "Surprise!"

That earned a twitch of a smile from the young German.

"Now, why are you here? You plan to drag me before a firing squad?"

He blanched. "Firing squad? Will, no!"

Cyrus's shoulders relaxed in relief. Her life wasn't in danger. Now that they'd gotten that out of the way ... "Her name is Willow."

He shook his head as if to lodge this new information into place. "Pence sent me to track you down, and boy, did I have a tough time of it. He wants to enlist your services. As a spy."

"A spy?" Willow and Cyrus asked at the same time.

Dedrick nodded. "You had a way about you. An intuition." He swiped his hat from his head and ran a hand through his hair. "Perhaps it's feminine intuition. At any rate, we need it."

Her lips twisted. "But what will he say to this?" She twirled a strand of hair around her finger.

"I imagine it won't matter. There are plenty of female spies, and your talents are appreciated, no matter what garb you wear or what name you go by."

Her bright eyes shone with excitement. "Can I talk it over with my folks and let you know tomorrow?"

"Yes, of course." Dedrick settled the hat back upon his head and nodded to each of them. "I'll call upon you this time tomorrow for your answer."

She bid him farewell, closed the door, and leaned upon it. Pressing her palms to rosy cheeks, she looked back and forth between Addy and him. "What do you think?"

He frowned. "We just got you back." Back from war. Back from the dead.

"Oh, Pa." She rushed over and wrapped him in a hug.

Addy's lined expression showed the concern he felt. "What about your condition?"

Willow sighed. "These past few months of rest have been good for me, I'm sure."

He snorted. Rest? It's not like the girl was lounging in bed. Sure, her activity levels here didn't match what the army doled out, but *rest* was not the term he'd use.

She continued, "I also know I have limitations because of my body right now. However, that doesn't mean I can't do anything. It means I must do things differently. Slower, perhaps. I need to make adjustments, but I don't have to stop living life because my body decided to go off the rails. I can do this." She gave his shoulder another squeeze.

He nearly growled. "I'd prefer you stay out of it." Stay safe at home. Not to mention her services as a spy would work against a cause he still believed in.

"I know you would." Her straightened stance showed her newfound confidence. "I also know you admire courage and resolve."

He couldn't help but smile. "I do."

"Then it's settled. I'll set off for a new adventure tomorrow." She nearly glowed.

He managed to push words past the tight knot at the base of his throat. "As long as you stay safe."

"Always."

~

Cyrus and Adelaide stood side by side on their front porch, watching Willow trot off on Rustic. At least this time, he knew where she was going and why.

At least this time, *she* knew where she was going and why.

Her story of how Milo tricked her by going to Warsaw instead of Lexington had him in stitches. Probably wasn't funny at the time, but the way those two had always pranked each other, it served her right.

Now, she was leaving to voluntarily join the same cause as the brother she'd always loved as much as she'd competed against. It didn't seem like this time she was out to outdo him or best him out of a title. Perhaps she knew how much she was loved, just the way she was.

Wait. He'd done it again. He'd allowed her to go—to leave and head into danger—without making his feelings toward her plain. With a growl, he grabbed his cane and took off down the road at a fevered clip.

Addy's voice rang out behind him. "Cy? What on earth?"

"Willow!"

She turned. Stopped. Tilted her head and brow at him in question.

He caught up to her, then leaned heavily on his cane, catching his breath. "Have I ever told you I'm proud of you?"

Her smile broke forth. She shook her head. "You didn't have to."

"I do. I need to. I'm proud of you, Willow Girl. So proud of the feisty woman you've become."

"I know." Her face shone. "I love you, Father."

Warmth spread through him. *Love.* Yes, love was worth living for.

Chapter 25

THIS SEASON OF BROKENNESS WAS ONE OF THE MOST
DIFFICULT I EVER FACED, AND IT BROUGHT ME TO THE
END OF MYSELF ... SOMETHING FOR WHICH I AM
ETERNALLY GRATEFUL.

FROM *CHRONICALLY FABULOUS*
BY MARISA ZEPPIERI

Modern Day

When I come home from the hospital, it's to a brightly colored homemade banner and balloons. Lily must have sketched out the bubble letters spelling *Welcome Home*, but the twins surely colored them in. A cake awaits me as well. The three inches of sloppy blue frosting tell me the children had a hand in this surprise too.

Though Lily no doubt helped set up every detail, she's left me to enjoy my family without her. I will have to thank her when I see her next. My appreciation will be genuine.

I sit at the kitchen table. My family surrounds me.

Jordan bounces on her toes as she thrusts a construction-paper card at me. When I open it, homemade coupons fall into my lap. Each proclaim she will do an extra chore around the house. She emanates pride at her ingenuity.

Not to be outdone, Victor hands me a long box crudely wrapped in snowflake wrapping paper.

"It's all I could find," he says, cheeks pink.

I thank him and rip the paper off. A picture of an elderly man stares back at me. He's holding a grabber tool and smiling like he's won the lottery.

"It's one of those robot grabber arms." Victor moves in to extract it from the box. "That way, you don't have to bend down. Since bending makes you dizzy."

Mark steps closer and tousles Victor's hair. "He spent his entire allowance on that."

My heart warms. "How thoughtful."

How could I ever have thought I wasn't wanted or appreciated here? How could I ever have wished myself dead?

"I got you something too." Mark's lips twitch like he's holding back a smile. He hands me a small, thin square wrapped in the same Christmas snowflake wrapping paper. A CD? Likely a new worship compilation or teaching series. Our older car doesn't have Bluetooth capabilities. I'm probably one of the few people who still uses and gets excited over CDs. I bite my lip in anticipation as I tear open the surprise.

A squeal leaps from my throat. "U2? Are you serious?"

I don't own—have never owned—any music from a non-Christian band. Is it okay?

Mark winks at me.

Victor quirks a brow. "Is this old people music?"

"Yes." I laugh.

"Whatever." He balls the wrapping paper and shoots a basket into the trash can.

"Nice shot." Mark high-fives him. "Ready for cake?"

After all I've been through, I am most definitely ready for cake.

~

A month later, I prepare to return to church. There's no telling what I'll face when I walk through those doors, but I'm coming armed. Armed with words from the mouth of God about my identity. It turns out *exquisite* and *unparalleled* were only the beginning. My Father has quite a high opinion of me. It seems He doesn't create worthless things. *Radiant. Stunning. Wondrous. Captivating. Humorous. Faithful.* These are all words He has clothed me with. I wear them now like beautiful adornments. I wear them now like the breastplate of righteousness and those shoes of peace. I walk forward covered in His words.

My past defensiveness glares at me now, so obvious. How I've tried to prop myself up. Make myself bigger and better in order to shine above all others and prove my worth. How futile. When I'm with Him, I have nothing to prove.

The early December air whips around us as we exit the car and make our way toward the church entrance. I tuck my scarf tighter under my chin and stretch my fingers before taking hold of the walker. Two steps toward the door, and my stomach flutters with nerves. *Stunning. Wondrous. Captivating.* I picture the Lord walking with me, right next to me. Peace floods me again.

Rayanne and Lily stand at the door, drawing me toward them. Mark has only placed a hand on the door handle when Rayanne flings it open and Lily's arms envelope me. The morning chill nips around us, but I am safe and warm.

"I am glad you came!" She rocks us side to side, her enthusiasm buoyant and anchoring at the same time.

As soon as she lets go, her mother swoops in for a turn. The fragrance of an essential oil blend drapes around us as she kisses my hair. "Welcome home."

"I didn't know you started coming to Ascend," I whisper in Rayanne's ear.

"Lily has started a special needs children's ministry. Roped her friends into volunteering. I finally feel like I can attend church without being a burden."

Wow. That girl has a remarkable way with people. Does she have any idea what a gift she is to the people around her? This is revolutionary for our church and community. How many other people are out there who stopped attending service because their children had needs that the church wasn't equipped to meet?

In typical fashion, a man stops Mark two steps inside the door. Jordan and Victor rush off to talk with friends. But the two women walk on either side of me as I make my way toward our familiar place up front. I cast a quizzical glance behind me to the foyer. "Aren't you greeters this morning?"

Rayanne chuckles. "No. We were just your welcoming committee."

Oh, I see it now. Marty is waiting in the wings. I can't help but grin. *Cherished.* I am cherished by the Lord and by these friends.

Kelly and Pricilla stop by to say hello. Everything about their greetings seems genuine and kind. Kelly may have once insinuated my illness was due to hidden sin and Pricilla may have once blamed it on a lack of faith, but now they are not watching for me to mess up, waiting to point out my faults. They want my good. My heart twinges as I realize this. They've always desired my good.

"Amber! It's great to see you." Ivy half jogs, half dances to me and wraps me in a rocking hug that lasts a full three minutes. "I've missed you."

"I've missed you too." I didn't realize it until this moment, but it's true.

As for the women who may think me dramatic, who may think I've feigned symptoms for attention, this is not my problem. Something in them caused them to believe the worst about me. Not something in me. They must have a hurt that Jesus needs to heal. And He will, as surely as He is even now healing the deep hurts in my own heart. He's working on us all, meeting each one exactly where we are at and walking us into freedom. If He is so patient with me in my journey, can I not be patient with these women in theirs?

We file in to find our seats together.

~

Lily straightened the strap of her sapphire chiffon dress and checked her teeth in the mirror for traces of lipstick. All clear. She exited the restroom into the glow of twinkle lights and the hum of excitement in the Goetz Banquet Hall.

Little girls in sparkly princess dresses and boys in pressed suits filed in beside their equally dapper foster or adoptive parents. Awe filled their faces as they took in the starched white tablecloths and flickering fake candles surrounded by holly. The festive touch reminded them Christmas was merely a week away. They were royalty in a Christmas fairy tale tonight. Lily pressed her hands to her smiling cheeks. Amber was a genius. These precious families would have a remarkable memory to treasure forever.

The cadence of familiar voices met her ears, and she rushed to greet her family, immensely thankful Dad had the night off and could come. He held Jamie's hand and pointed to the electric train that encircled the stage.

"Wow, Mom. Brave move." Lily gestured to her mother's white dress, then to Olly on her hip.

"Oh, I know." Mom tilted her head to the side to dodge Olly's grab for one of her hoop earrings. "I've already dabbed at more than one spit-up stain. But it's all I had."

Lily gave her mom a side hug and kissed the baby on his fuzzy head. "Well, you're stunning." She bent down to compliment her siblings on their fancy attire before leading them to their assigned table. "If it gets to be too much and they need a break, there's a sensory room out the door and to your left." She pointed.

Mom's face brightened. "Truly?"

Lily nodded. "We lugged several materials here from the new sensory room at church."

"This is amazing, firefly." Mom's gaze roamed the room.

"Just wait." Lily did a silent cheer before backing away … straight into Matt.

"Whoa, there." He put his hands on her arms to steady her.

She spun around and lost her breath at his nearness. Man, he cleaned up nice. And smelled so good.

His gaze drank her in. "Wow. You're breathtaking."

Her mouth parted. Did he just say that? Now it was her in the Christmas fairy tale. "Th-thank you. Y-you too." Obviously. Because she couldn't breathe.

"We did plan to have dancing at this thing, didn't we?" The mischievous glint in his eyes caused her knees to wobble.

"Yes."

"Save me one, will you?"

She bit her lip on her smile. "I don't know. My dance card is pretty full with handsome gentlemen." She gestured to her brothers behind her. "I'll try to fit you in."

The edges of his eyes crinkled. "I appreciate the effort." He pulled a piece of paper from the inside of his suit jacket. "Now, according to this schedule my boss gave me," he said as he shot her a pointed look, "it's time for me to dress up like a Disney character and mingle with the crowd."

"Shh," she said with a laugh. "Don't ruin the magic."

He put a finger to his lips. "Sorry. I'll leave you for a while. I hear Buzz Lightyear will make an appearance in a bit, though." He winked.

Once he sauntered away, she made a beeline for Amber, who sat at a table, looking magnificent in a hunter-green wrap dress. Mark chatted with a couple a few tables over.

Lily leaned in to hug her friend. "This is magical."

Amber's gaze swept the room, a satisfied smile on her lips. "It is, isn't it? What a great idea to put the basket of fidgets at each table."

"Between those and the coloring books, most children seem content so far."

"It's hard to balance a fun night for children and a relaxing evening for parents. Most events kids find enjoyable are chaotic and stressful for moms and dads. Thanks for helping to brainstorm a way to do both."

Lily waved her off. "You already had a good thing going. I only added a few ideas."

"A few game-changing ideas."

Disney characters infiltrated, milling about and taking pictures with children at each table. Not long after, the waitstaff served dinner. Cornish hen, roasted asparagus, and potatoes for the adults and chicken nuggets, fries, and apple slices for the children. A glance at Matt's table showed he was indulging in the kid's fare. Lily chuckled.

After dinner, dancers took the stage, followed by two skits performed by the local actors guild. Laughter filled the space, warming Lily's heart.

And now? Now it was time.

Lily smoothed her dress, stood, and made her way to the stage. Taking the microphone, she looked out at the crowd of people before her. Smiling children. Peaceful adults. Her mother wore a near blissful expression, a far cry from the haggard look that normally draped her features during public outings. Her heart swelled with gratitude that she could take part in something so meaningful.

Her voice came out thick with emotion. "Thank you for coming. On behalf of the committee that made this gala possible, I want to express our gratitude for the big and small ways you love the children in your care every day. Your job may seem thankless at times, but it's vital. You're making a difference one child at a time, one day at a time. It's this kind of love that will change the world." She cleared her throat and prayed for God to help her through this next part without breaking down.

"Speaking of world-changers, I would like to take a few minutes to honor someone. This person has worked tirelessly organizing dozens upon dozens of outreaches, blessing our community time and time again. She's been the one to come early, stay late, and put others' needs above her own. She has served well.

"But this isn't the only reason, or even the main reason, I want to honor this person. You see, it's one thing to serve strangers. It's another thing entirely to serve your family. It's difficult to give yourself to the people closest to you day after day. It's thankless. People on the outside don't see your faults clearly. They see a filtered picture of you. But your family, those closest to you, they see it all. They see the worst in you, and they can bring out the worst in you. This person has served her family well throughout the years. Even throughout great trials, she endeavored to serve her family as best she could. Even when the best way she could serve was to take care of herself and rest, she did it for them.

"She has been an inspiration to me to never give up and to never stop loving." Cole stepped from the side of the stage and handed her a large bouquet of roses. Tucked in between the blooms, hidden from public view, were a dozen metal spoons. "Tonight, I'd like to honor the founder of this gala, Amber Prichard."

The room erupted in applause. From the front to the back, people popped to their feet. Amber swiped at wet cheeks. Mark helped her stand and grab hold of her walker. Slowly, she made her way up the ramp and to center stage.

Amber's arms wrapped around Lily. "Thank you. For everything."

Lily sniffed. "Right back at ya."

The weight lifted as she slid the bouquet into Amber's hand. The room quieted. People took their seats. Lily stepped back from the microphone to let Amber have her turn, but Cole placed a hand on her shoulder before she could begin.

"Please allow me to say a few words as well."

Amber's mouth parted.

"Lily said it perfectly, and I won't belabor the point. Suffice it to say, we've watched Amber serve faithfully year after year. She's not only poured out her heart for others but also done so with joy. We at Ascend love you, Amber, and we're one hundred percent behind you."

Applause broke out again, along with cheers and a few hearty *Amens*.

"Thank you." She wiped stray tears with the back of her hand. "Wow. I wasn't expecting this. I'm honored and blessed. I have been through a trial lately. I know many of you go through various trials on a daily basis. I don't know about you, but for me, it has exposed all kinds of gunk in my heart. But God's been working on me and teaching me to rely on who He says I am. That's the only thing that matters. And it turns out, He thinks good things about me." She chuckled, and the audience joined in. "Who knew? So, I'm learning to receive His love for me daily. And I encourage all of you to receive His love for you too. It's the only thing that can sustain us when times get hard. His love truly is enough."

As Amber backed up from the microphone and walked off the stage, applause and cheers swallowed the room and flooded Lily with warmth. She took the mic but waited until the buzz died down before speaking.

"Now, let the fun continue! Some of you asked why we had assigned seating." She leaned forward conspiratorially. "Want to find out?" She brought her voice to a mock whisper. "Check under your table."

A flurry of activity was followed by squeals of delight as children found baskets overflowing with presents chosen specifically for them. Lily found Amber's gaze, and they shared a moment of triumph at pulling off their surprise. Thankfully, the fidget/coloring book combo kept children from crawling under tables earlier in the evening, safeguarding their secret.

Dessert soon followed, then dancing. Members from the Group passed out glow sticks to the children as the lights dimmed and the disco ball switched on. Lily danced with each of her brothers, Olly included, while she eyed Matt from across the room. A plethora of little girls in tutus monopolized his attention. He threw her a sheepish smile.

Amber sat alone with Mark, observing. Lily linked arms with Harvy and marched up to her, out of breath. "Come join in on the fun."

Her smile dimmed. "You know I can't."

"Sure you can." She turned to Mark. "Can we borrow your wife?"

"By all means."

Lily patted Amber's walker seat. "Hop on. I'll push. Harvy will try not to step on your toes or your wheels, right Harvy?"

Her brother grinned.

Amber burst into laughter. "You're not serious."

Lily patted the seat again.

"Okay." Amber scooted onto the seat, still chuckling. "Here I go."

Lily wheeled her friend to the dance floor, instructed Harvy on how to hold Amber's hands, then pushed to the beat. By the end of the song, the three of them were doubled over, laughing so hard they couldn't breathe.

Amber waved her hand in front of her face. "I can't remember the last time I had this much fun."

Neither could she. "Glad to be of assistance."

"Thank you for the spoons." Amber squeezed Lily's hand as they arrived back at the table.

"Anytime. I've got your back."

A tap on her shoulder sent her spinning around. There Matt stood, tie slightly askew, shirt a bit rumpled, but every bit as handsome as ever. "Hurry up and dance with me before I get accosted by another preschooler."

The faux panic in his eyes caused more laughter to bubble up. Her sides ached. She took his hand and schooled her expression. "We can't have that."

He bowed. "Come, milady. Let's see what adventures await us yonder."

What adventures, indeed.

~

Christmas lights line the stage. Majestic evergreen trees decorated with ribbons and bows stand proudly on either side of the auditorium. I push my walker down the center aisle, taking in the festive atmosphere. More than another recital, this is a second chance. A redo. A time for the Lord to restore what the enemy has stolen. This is the season of new beginnings, of redemption, and I breathe it in now with the scentof pine and peppermint.

Mom arrived via cab forty minutes ago. A Christmas miracle, if there ever was one. She's saved us seats in the first row on the right—the same row we sat in at the last recital. The same place I walked from when my life went into a downward spiral. Ironic. Or providential. Or perhaps neither, considering my mother is a creature of habit.

My walker won't fit down the row, so I leave it at the end of the aisle and squeeze my way through. I haven't yet sat when I spy Lily and Rayanne bustling in. I wave my arm high to ensure they find us. Lily's eyes light up when her gaze meets mine. They walk around the other direction to avoid having to scoot past Mom, Mark, and Victor.

When Rayanne unbuttons her coat, there's a baby nestled in a carrier against her chest. She angles herself so I can view his sweet, scrunched face.

"Hi again, Oliver." I kiss my finger and touch his nose. "Precious."

"When he's not screaming," Lily says.

At the same time, Rayanne says, "Even when he's screaming."

Both women laugh. I do too.

"Hey, Lily." Victor leans forward to get her attention. "You said you know about constellations, right?"

She nods.

"I have this science project due after winter break. I was hoping you could help me with it."

"Sure, buddy."

Lily and I switch seats so she and Victor can converse without speaking over me. This gives me a better view of the cute baby and a chance to chat with Rayanne, which I do until the lights dim.

I don't realize I'm nervous until the first chords of music play. The familiarity of *that day* dries my throat and turns my heart rate up a notch. Lily must sense this because she takes my hand and squeezes.

Unlike last time, I don't have to wait until after intermission to see my girl perform. She glides onto the stage in her sparkling tutu during the first number. She's magic. My breath catches at the sight of her. Such beauty and talent, and she's *mine*. She's my daughter. I couldn't be prouder. Arabesques and pirouettes. Perfect posture and poise. I'm smitten with this angel on stage. So much so that I forget to be nervous. Forget everything I've been through to get to this moment.

The number concludes and applause erupts. This is only the beginning, not the time for a standing ovation, but I can't help myself. I scramble to my feet to clap for my baby girl. As I'm in front, people take my lead. Around me, chairs squeak as others stand.

Too fast. I stood too fast.

The room tilts. I sway.

Faster than I can blink, the women on either side of me take my arms, holding me steady, holding me upright. Their strength supports me.

I take a breath. My knees firm. My vision clears.

We cheer together.

Here I am at my daughter's recital. Standing. Cheering. Leaning. Loving.

Believing.

Epilogue

Two Years Later

"Great picnic." I add the bag of chips I brought to the ensemble to the picnic tables at the community park.

Lily grins at me and flashes her American flag temporary tattoo on her forearm. "Victor did a great job, yeah?"

I give a thumbs-up. "Stellar idea, having the teens man that station."

She steps closer to where I stand by the food tables. "I know this isn't as fancy as you're used to."

I wave her off. "Nonsense. It's way less stressful."

"That's what I figured. You up for a game of volleyball?"

"Depends. Are you and Matt on the same team again? And is that power team the opposite of the team you plan to put me on?"

Her hands settle on her hips. The diamond on her engagement ring glitters in the sunlight. "I thought you got over the whole 'If I can't win, I won't play' thing."

I scrunch my nose. "Still don't like being slaughtered by Olympic-level talent."

"Olympic level? Wow. Must be the homeschool co-op PE class I joined freshman year." She forms a muscle with her slim arm.

"I was talking about Matt." I smirk.

Her laugh bubbles forth. "Fine. I'll put him on your team. Happy?"

"Very."

Harvy and Davy dash around the table, nearly knocking a basket of rolls to the ground. I catch them before they topple.

"Hey, boys." Mark jogs up beside me, hair damp with perspiration, football tucked under one arm. "I was about to toss the ball around over there." He points to an open field. "Want to join me?"

The boys' faces light up. "Sure!"

"Yeah!"

The guys run off together.

I put my hand on my heart. "Sweet."

Lily's gaze follows them. "They like being included."

"Doesn't everybody?"

I take in this lively scene. Groups of young people sit in lawn chairs and on benches chatting. Guys throw a frisbee back and forth. Some high school girls smother Oliver with attention as he toddles on the dirt path. Kelly and Sally seem deep in conversation by the barbecue pit. Kelly keeps waving smoke away from her face as Cole and Sam flip burgers. If she'd only step a foot to her left, she'd avoid the problem, but she must be too engrossed to consider this. Pricilla and Rayanne throw their heads back in laughter.

Then there are the guys who just finished a basketball game. Lily's fiancé crushed that too. They take turns teasing each other and talking about who is going to beat who in the upcoming volleyball match.

"A volleyball match? I'm in."

I turn toward the voice, and my arms fly open to embrace my friend. I don't stop to weigh whether I'm ready to forgive her. I don't contemplate making her apologize. I don't feel the burn of abandonment before my arms enclose her.

"Delaney!" I squeeze for all I'm worth.

Her fingers dab the corners of her eyes. "I heard there was a carnival—"

"Picnic," Lily and I say at the same time, then laugh.

"I know I don't go to this church but—"

I speak close to her ear. "You know you're always welcome."

The apology I didn't wait for comes. "I'm sorry."

"I forgive you." And I do. It's an easy thing now, though it's taken time to get here. While once this betrayal squeezed and splintered my heart, Jesus's love has since coated these cracks in my heart. They don't hurt anymore. I don't have to fake it 'til I make it. He's made it. He's made my heart whole.

Delaney, Lily, and I sit at a picnic table and munch on chips and salsa, postponing the game until after we catch up. I can't wait to tell my therapist about this new development. After hearing updates from Delaney, Lily insists I spill Willow's story and show off the spoon. I keep it nestled in my purse in a protective case, with me always. I never know when I'll need a reminder of how God loves me just the way I am. He adores the Amber He created.

"So, she ended up becoming a spy for the Union?" Delaney asks.

"Yes. Both Willow and her brother, Milo, lived through the war. And get this: They both married Germans. Milo married his sweetheart, Greta, and Willow married a man she fought with in the MSM—Dedrick."

"You've got German in your family line, huh?" Delaney crunches a chip.

I run my fingers over the spoon one last time before I put it away, then I finger my pendant. "I have so much more in my family line than mental illness."

"Here, here." Delaney clinks her plastic cup against mine and Lily's.

Lily stands and brushes crumbs off her shorts. "Up for that volleyball game now?"

I turn my head to the sun and smile. Gratitude wells up within me for this church family, for these friends who have walked with me through a great trial. Most didn't do it perfectly. I wouldn't even say they did it well. But they're still here.

What a wild thing to be human. To be so flawed. To have broken bodies and wounded hearts. To act out of pain instead of God's perfect love. To be full of questions instead of answers.

Somehow, someway, God healed me. He didn't do it in an instant, with a single prayer. He didn't do it with one revelation. He did it over time, as I walked hand in hand with Him. He did it by having me press into a community I wanted to run from. He did it bit by bit. He healed my body. He healed my heart.

He's healing me still.

In that dark season when I wondered where He was, all I had to do was fall back and find Him.

Author's Note

Writing this story was a journey of the heart. Nine years ago, chronic illness accosted my body. After nearly a year of visiting multiple doctors and going through various tests, doctors diagnosed me with a form of dysautonomia called POTS (postural orthostatic tachycardia syndrome). For many years, I was very sick. At times, I was bedridden. During a portion of this time, I passed out three to four times per week. I used a rollator walker or a wheelchair to get around, if I got around.

Some of Amber's story closely mirrors my story. Some things people said to Amber were said to me. Some things she experienced, I experienced. I drew heavily from my own journey in writing this novel. With that being said, it's not an autobiography. Amber is not me. We have different histories, different families, different wounds, and different passions. This is a work of fiction.

Everyone with POTS has a different journey, and someone with this diagnosis may experience different symptoms, treatments, or reactions. Each experience is valid. I hope that if you deal with a chronic illness of any kind, you feel seen from reading this book, even if your experiences differ.

As far as Willow's story goes, I wanted to weave in the historical aspect of irritable heart/Da Costa's syndrome. When I was first diagnosed with POTS, I learned that some thought this syndrome dated back to the Civil War. There is considerable debate on what Da Costa's syndrome was. The diagnosis is no longer used and has been replaced with these more specific diagnoses of PTSD, chronic fatigue syndrome, mitral valve prolapse syndrome, and dysautonomia. Fainting was not nearly as common as extreme fatigue and chest pain in those with Da Costa's syndrome.

I hope you enjoyed reading about my home state during Civil War times. If you'd like to learn more, I recommend the books *Bushwhackers: Guerrilla Warfare, Manhood, and the Household in Civil War Missouri* by Joseph M. Beilein, Jr.; *Guerrilla Hunters in Civil War Missouri* and *Guerrillas in Civil War Missouri* by James W. Erwin; and *Missouri's War: The Civil War in Documents* by Silvana R. Siddali.

The Lord healed my body from chronic illness. He didn't do it quickly, like I wanted Him to. He took His time, and while I waited on Him, He did an even greater work in me: He healed wounded places in my heart. This process of receiving healing from the Lord occurred for me much like it did for Amber, by receiving His words of truth over me. And I'm still receiving them daily. It's a never-ending process of becoming more whole, more full of joy, and more like Him.

I pray you'll hear from His heart as well and receive the words of love He is speaking over you.

For His glory,

Sarah Hanks

Other Books by Sarah Hanks

Mercy Will Follow Me (Mercy Series Book 1)

Mercy's Song (Mercy Series Book 2)

Mercy's Legacy (Mercy Series Book 3)

Awakened to Life

A Battle Worth Fighting (Sister in Arms Collection Book 1)

Scan to connect with Sarah Hanks.

www.ingramcontent.com/pod-product-compliance
Lightning Source LLC
Chambersburg PA
CBHW030114310726
48970CB00004B/1275